D0820690

DISORIENTED

A Novel

Acknowledgements

The author would very much like to thank the following people for their contributions to this story:

Mom and Dad for reading, encouraging and helping to edit it . . . it hurt, but it was a good kind of hurt.

My kids for their contributions and keeping the fires of my imagination constantly stoked.

My wife for not throwing me out while I kept her awake with my tippity tapping on the keyboard deep into the night.

Cornerstone Publishing. I had always wondered what it would be like to work closely with a publisher and editor, what a learning experience! Thanks Richard for believing in this project, and showing me how to get it done!

DISORIENTED

A Novel

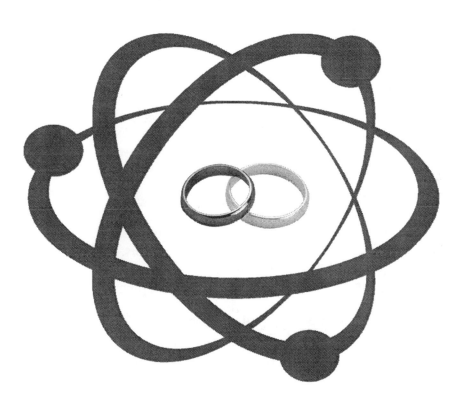

MICHAEL RITCHEY

Cornerstone Publishing & Distribution, Inc.
Salt Lake City & Phoenix

© 1999 Cornerstone Publishing & Distribution, Inc.

All Rights Reserved

Printed in the United States of America
03 02 01 00 99   10 9 8 7 6 5 4 3 2 1

International Standard Book Number   1-929281-03-X

Cover design by Adam R. Hopkins

Preface

This novel is a story of love and adventure; my efforts were directed to that end anyway. I wanted to make love the greatest character trait visible in the book, and have a fun, adventurous (and even scary) time with it. I wanted my main characters to be good and likable people. You know the kind... honest, true, chaste, and not given to worldly vices, even though the world around them is crawling with dark and evil souls. Do these kind of people actually exist you ask? Of course they do! The world would have us believe they don't, or if they do, that they are somehow strange or weird. But in the Church we have come to believe it is not only possible to possess those qualities, it is expected of us! How peculiar! I hope you see a little bit of *yourself* in them.

Oh yes, there is some imaginative speculation about the spirit world in this story. Please don't get too caught up with that! I haven't been there since . . .well, before I was born! So it was kind of hard for me to remember. I hope you understand. This is a work of fiction, so just have fun with it. *But*, there are some underlying truths woven into the fabric of this story to give us something to ponder; the gospel, missionary work, and love . . . the kind that lasts forever.

Enjoy!

Forty miles off the coast of Mexico, in a sea as still as death, the fishing boat *La Luna* drifts. The nets draped over her sides are empty and lifeless. Her once full storage bins are a vague memory; not one fish has graced their parched walls in over a week. On deck, Luis Rivera, his mind baked half-mad by the relentless glare of the sun's torturous rays, squints up at the sky, unable to move or blink.

"Where are the fishes?" he whispers to himself.

High above him in the air a black dot circles, drawing closer with each passing hour. Fear and apprehension overwhelm him. He knows it is Death, and Luis Rivera is its next customer.

Too far gone to worry about the dread that seethes within him, slipping in and out of consciousness, Luis dreams of his wife and family. There is peace in these dreams, as there was in Rosa's love. He would come home from the sea, and she would greet him with her smile. He would jingle his money purse and she would run the length of the yard to jump into his waiting arms, and they would fall to the ground, laughing.

But Luis Rivera is not laughing now. The black dot circling above him is getting closer, and his fear is mounting.

"This world has gone loco," he mumbles, his lips swollen and sticking together. "What has happened? The sea has betrayed me! And what of Rosa?"

Again he dreams. This time he watches his first child being born, a daughter. Rosa smiles and says, "Is it possible that life could be so wonderful?" He beams and his lips echo the same words to her. He takes her hand, and whispers gently, "I will always take care of you and our children. The sea has been good to us."

He wipes the sweat from his brow. The images fade, and in their place, searing light pours into his eyes. He is being cooked alive. How did he fall to the deck? Visions of empty nets fade in and out. Ten days of empty nets, ten days! Luis Rivera never had an empty net in all his life!

Something terrible has gone wrong. He can't think what it is, but for the last six months he has smelled the breath of fear at sea. Frantically he worked the nets till his hands bled, till his muscles cramped him to a stop.

"For Rosa and the children, please; just one haul!" But the sea gave up little, then nothing.

Suddenly, the feelings of fear and betrayal are gone, sapped from him as his body weakens under the sun. "So this is how the fish feel when Rosa cooks them," he mumbles. He pictures himself as a large fish baking on the grill in the back yard of their Agua Sublima home. He wonders when someone will come and flip him over, maybe spread a little sauce on him for flavoring. Life is full of irony, he thinks, and tries to smile.

"What is wrong with me?" he rasps defiantly. "I will not die here like somebody's meal!"

Raising his dying body on one elbow, he looks over the gunwale at the sea. A hundred feet off the starboard bow, sticking out of the glassy surface, is an object that looks to Luis like a bizarre TV antenna. There is no wind, not even a breeze, yet the boat drifts steadily toward this object. Confused, he drops back to the deck.

"Now I know I am mad!"

Death never entered his mind when he left the port in Agua Sublima, but he thinks about it now. That, and the dark thing in the sky coming closer and closer. An eerie calm sweeps over him as feelings of euphoria envelop his body. His thoughts are confused, dreamlike; he can't seem to focus. Ah, but the euphoria. Yes, how peaceful it is; how wonderful is life . . . and death. His gaze fixes on the heavens. The black dot above him fills the sky now, circling closer, closer.

Suddenly it dives. Luis tries to scream, but all that passes his parched lips is a gasp. A loud bang hits the deck three feet to his left. He looks. It is a seagull.

He sighs. It is the hungry gull that has been following the boat for hours, hoping for a scrap of food. Circling the boat till it could fly no more, it fell from the sky, dead before it hit the deck.

A puzzled look fleets across his face; then it contorts with nausea. A few more moments and Death has taken Luis Rivera and the gull to a better place.

Forty miles off the coast of Mexico, in a sea as still as death, the fishing boat *La Luna* drifts, a floating casket for two.

Chapter 1
RESTLESS

The plane ride to Dallas wasn't starting out well. Tara sat nervously in her window seat just over the left wing. The flight was going to be rough. Huge billowing thunderclouds were ushering yet another monsoon storm into the Valley of the Sun. As Sky Harbor airport disappeared behind them, black demon clouds lurked in the miles ahead. Lightning streaked across her window as the plane shuddered and bumped, clawing its way upward. Involuntarily, Tara's grip tightened on the armrests.

"Good afternoon, and welcome aboard flight 383 to Dallas. This is your captain speaking. As you already know we are experiencing a bit of rough weather this afternoon. We'll be above the storm in about five minutes, then it'll be smooth sailing all the way to Dallas. Please keep your seat belts fastened until then. We hope you enjoy your flight, and thank you for flying America West."

Tara tried to relax. She usually enjoyed the summer storms. Their cleansing freshness invigorated her and brought new life to the desert, and she thrilled at their unleashed power. But today there was something else out there in addition to the storm. Ominous and foreboding, it seemed bent on forcing the very light from her soul. Instead of life, it made the storm wreak of death and darkness.

It wasn't just a physical darkness, either. What Tara felt was something that smothered whatever joy it could find in her heart, leaving nothing behind but a black void. It threatened her personally, as though she stood in the presence of evil. She didn't know the source of this darkness, but she knew it was real. She had seen it!

Looking around at the other passengers helped to calm her a little. They all seemed to be engaged in pleasant conversation. How could they? Certainly they had to know something wasn't right. Could it be that she alone felt the dark forces at work, a growing premonition that something wicked lurked just out of sight . . . waiting?

Waiting for what? she probed. To kill? To destroy? Destroy what? The feeling had been eating at her for months now, but she had only a few clues. The answer loomed just out of reach, driving her crazy at times like this when all she could do was think.

She bowed her head and tried to close out the world around her. "Come on Tara, get a grip," she whispered. "Let's just get to Dallas. Maybe the answers will be there."

"Excuse me, but are you all right?" A woman placed her hand gently on Tara's arm. "You seem a little worried. Really, these storms look a lot worse than they are."

"What?" Tara turned her gaze from the window. It was the woman in the seat next to her on the crowded flight. She looked to be in her mid-forties, attractive, beautiful skin and nicely dressed. Tara noticed a copy of *Phoenix Magazine* on her lap, the page open to an illustration of one of the plush homes in Scottsdale.

"Oh, I'm sorry. Is it that obvious?"

"Well, you look scared to death! We'll be fine, really. It's just a little storm. Is this your first time flying?"

"Uh, yes," Tara lied awkwardly.

"Well, you just take a few deep breaths and lay your head back." The woman turned her attention to one of the passing flight attendants. "Miss, could we have a pillow over here?"

Tara studied her closely. The woman had an air of calm serenity, and her smile was warm as the desert sun. Tara liked her immediately.

From her early childhood, Tara had been able to sense things about people. As she got older, she had developed the gift into a fine art. She could usually see through them, into their hearts, where nothing is hidden. Unfortunately, she was often disappointed. Far too many were false and selfish. This woman was neither. In fact, she was the opposite, and having her in the next seat soothed Tara's nerves.

The woman extended her hand, touching Tara's and patting it gently. "My name is Norma Welker."

"Well, I'm pleased to meet you, Norma Welker. I'm Tara Johnson, and I must say I'm glad you're here. I've been feeling a little nervous lately, but just seeing your smile has helped me tremendously." She took Norma's hand and gave it a squeeze.

The flight attendant brought the pillow, handing it to the woman who in turn handed it to Tara.

"Try putting your head back and closing your eyes. Imagine you're taking a nice drive in a car. It worked for me on my first few flights. If you'd like to talk, I'm right here. But for now, just try resting that anxiety right out of your body."

"Thanks." Tara leaned back, smiling.

Turning her head toward the window, she watched flashes of lightning illuminate the otherwise dark and swollen clouds. The scene made her think of an unholy cauliflower garden. Suddenly the feeling of blackness flooded her again. She tightened her grip on the armrest and felt her fears return.

Something was wrong out there, something terrible, something evil. Whatever it was, it had to be stopped. If not . . .

She closed her eyes, trying to shut out the alternatives. Her mind felt like it was on overload. She needed to clear it, but as hard as she tried, she couldn't. She closed her eyes tighter.

Only fifteen minutes had passed since the plane lifted off from Phoenix, but it had already fought its way above the storm and was sailing smoothly toward Dallas. The gentle hum of the engines helped to calm her, but staring out the window, she found no rest.

The events that had haunted her for over a month raced through her mind against the backdrop of the receding storm. They felt like insane visions of a world out of control, and they all started in the desert east of Mesa, where she had been working in the Superstition Wilderness Area, alone.

A post-graduate student in biology at ASU, she resolved early in her studies to be the best field biologist the university ever produced. She had an inquisitive mind and loved the isolation of her desert studies. The hours she spent there by herself were always precious. Not only was she able to advance her studies, she could get away, out of the dreadful city that seemed to magnify society's flaws.

Of course, her little junkets were only temporary escapes. Each day, when she finished, it was back to the city, fighting traffic and the hustle and bustle of college life, with all its challenges. But now, along with all of society's ills, the world seemed to be falling apart as well . . . literally.

Of course, everyone knew something was wrong. These were strange times. The last three years had seen the extinction of several mammal species around the world. Most recently, zoologists were mourning the loss of no less a species than the African elephant! The Indian tiger had gone a year earlier. When the most common of all birds, the sparrow, began to disappear, U.S. authorities finally started to notice. By then, however, almost a third of all flowering plants on every continent had disappeared. The world's scientific community was in shock. Global warming, of course, and pollution were taking the blame, but Tara knew otherwise.

Two years ago, severe degradation of the world's topsoil had begun. In less developed countries, this meant death. And when it came, it wasn't just a few people here or there, but hundreds, even thousands of unwilling souls who slipped into slow and painful starvation as their world disintegrated around them.

What a difference these years had made for Tara as well. Two years ago she was the happiest of people. She radiated optimism and joy at the start of her post-graduate studies. She danced, dated and went on family vacations. She even attended their local church occasionally, though only to please her father. Now that was all over. Tragedy, both personal and global, had turned her world upside down.

Of course, it had been years since she rejected religion as an explanation for the universe. Since her junior high school science class, evolution, though something of a stretch, had been more rational to her than the god she learned of in Sunday School, a god who was somehow three separate persons in one single "Being." Not that she totally rejected the idea of God. Really, she felt more like He had rejected her.

Her first sign of God's rejection was the death of her best friend Anne, killed in a horrible automobile accident when they were seniors in high school. The fog was heavy and the driver of the semi didn't see her car. In the space of seconds, young, vital Anne and the lifetime of beauty that lay ahead of her were reduced to a twisted mass of flesh and metal.

Tara cried for weeks after Anne's funeral. Even now, on the plane, a tear escaped, rolling silently down her cheek. Of course, the thought of Anne triggered an even deeper scar, one she found even more difficult to handle, the final indication that God had abandoned her.

As a sophomore at ASU she had begun to date Devin. Just when things looked promising between the two of them . . . it happened. Devin was at a convenience store when two young kids with guns opened fire. All he wanted was a cold drink. Instead, he never knew what hit him . . . and the kids were never found.

The funerals of her friends had only confirmed her feelings. They left her dark and lonely. Though Anne and Devin were of different faiths, neither service convinced Tara that God cared about them, or the fact that their lives, their existence as loving, free and independent men and women, had just been snuffed out. The messages had left her feeling . . . lost, incomplete. At that point she decided to forget about God for a while. Maybe she would see his love someday, but she didn't expect it any more. Instead, she had her studies, her research.

There were many theories about the recent global tragedies, ranging from environmental pollution to depletion of the ozone layer, but no one really had any hard facts. There had been a flurry of information gathering and guesswork, but no conclusions.

Then Tara was selected as part of a micro-ecology group from the university. Her particular area of focus centered on the relationship between certain ant species and the dwindling desert topsoil and vegetation. It was all part of a project funded by the Federal government. Tara's findings, along with those of many similar groups across the nation, would be turned over to a select group of scientists and other leaders from the U.S. Bureau of Land Management, the Environmental Protection Agency and a Senate sub-committee.

The findings were being presented at the Macro-Ecological Symposium of World Events in Dallas, where she was headed now. Each of the micro-groups was to give their individual suggestions for a course of action. The scientists and leaders would then take the information to Washington and lobby Congress for help.

It all seemed easy enough to Tara; and it was, after all, a great opportunity to prove her merit. Putting her shoulder to the proverbial wheel, she plowed into her work in the desert. And everything was going well until *it* happened . . . right before her eyes.

She turned once again toward the front of the airplane, hoping the sight of other people would help her relax. But even Norma Welker's pleasant smile didn't help. Her thoughts insisted on replaying the mental images that led up to that final insane moment in the desert.

The sun was high as she slipped off her pack, and dropped it under the shady arms of a *palo verde* tree. She wiped the sweat from her forehead. It was eleven o'clock in the morning, and already 107 degrees.

"Yeah, but it's a dry heat!" she muttered to herself, mimicking the local weatherman. It always amazed her how that line comforted the local residents. To Tara, 107 degrees was 107 degrees, no matter how you sliced it, and wet or dry 107 was hot!

She took out a pad and pen, and jotted down the time and date. Suddenly, she became aware of a presence. Whirling around, she expected to see someone, but no one was there. A dark chill washed over her, lingered an incredibly long three or four seconds, and passed.

"What the . . . Come on Tara, get hold of yourself!" She tried to reassure herself as a menacing emptiness filled her soul, but it didn't work. Again she spun around, heart racing, eyes and ears alert, and scanned her surroundings for anything out of place. There was nothing, nothing unusual at all. The only sound came from some locusts buzzing away in a clump of mesquite about fifty yards away.

"Hmm, that's odd," she whispered. Perplexed and still looking, she tried to repress the feeling that someone, or something, was watching.

From that day forward, the same eerie feelings became a routine during her studies in the desert. She fought through them to complete her work, but they always unnerved her. When she told her brother Jeff about them, he laughed, called her a typical girl and accused her of having a wild imagination. But the feelings didn't go away; they only intensified, making Tara feel all the more foolish. She vowed to keep her fears hidden from her family and her colleagues at the university.

As the oldest of four children, she had always shared everything with her family. She tried to picture them now sitting in the family room of their home talking. Sometimes they would all play games, or just talk for hours about life, the world or whatever subject came up.

Tara recalled her ten-year-old brother, Joey, asking, "How can you spend so much time in the desert by yourself, Tara?"

"Easy," the answer came. "After spending crazy nights like this with all you nuts, I need time to get away just to remember who I am." She hoped the humor hid her real feelings.

"You're just kidding, right?"

"Of course she is, son," replied Dad, "she just likes hanging around desert animals because they look so much like her family!"

They had all laughed then. If only she could laugh now.

The plane continued its gentle ride toward Dallas as Tara tried again to relax, this time by looking around the crowded cabin. She focused for a moment on a baby crying toward the rear of the plane, but it didn't help. Her body was rigid with the fear she felt all around.

Norma glanced up from her magazine again and smiled. Tara forced a smile in return and the woman turned back to her magazine—some article on *Lifestyles of Famous Arizonans*.

Looking out the window again, Tara's thoughts pulled her back to the desert. She had been studying a colony of desert ants. On this day, as always, she stood ready to record her ongoing observations, notebook and pen in hand. The ants were said to be one of the main culprits in a process that turned semi-arid desert into virtual wasteland, where nothing at all would grow. They did this, it was thought, by stripping seeds in huge quantities from plants during times of drought, and storing them in vast chambers far below ground. This robbed the plants of the opportunity to perpetuate themselves.

Theoretically, when the rains returned, the seed population would be greatly reduced, and over a period of two to three years, huge areas once thriving in plant and animal life were being turned into nothing but dust and sand. In many countries, ants were being exterminated in an effort to stop the process. Tara hoped to exonerate the ants through her research and stop the exterminations.

This particular colony was only one of ten she studied, but it was her favorite, a very robust and thriving member of the desert community. She had been studying it off and on for almost thirteen months now, tracing the ants' marches through the desert in search of food, and recording everything from foraging distances to types and amounts of food brought back.

She found that over the course of any particular foraging trip, the ants were taking only what they needed, leaving more than enough to perpetuate the plants. Something else was causing the desertification, but what?

On this particular day, Tara had finished her report, complete with its conclusion exonerating the ants, but she was reluctant to abandon them and return to her world. She really did enjoy herself in the Superstition Wilderness and actually had fun with her studies, despite the dreadful feelings she had been experiencing lately.

She had developed her own series of brightly colored paints to mark the ants, helping her to follow their course through the desert. This had proved invaluable. She spent hours at a time staring down at them, and the markings enabled her to look up, log her journal entries, stretch her muscles, then look down again and pick out her tracer ants. Although her work was done, she wanted to use her paint on one more ant before she wrapped up her study.

She had become so accustomed to these little desert dwellers that she was able to tell some of them apart, even without the paint. Some had distinguishing marks or physical traits, despite the fact that they were all fairly large and all the same color. She gave names to some of the more familiar ones.

One in particular she called Old One-Eye. While most of the ants were black and shiny, Old One-Eye was a dull charcoal. One of his eyes was apparently blind. At least, she assumed it was. It was a foggy off-white color. He didn't work like the others, but spent most of his time wandering back and forth between the colony and a large boulder some thirty yards away. Tara had followed him on several occasions to see where he was going, but she had always given up and returned to the colony, assuming by his direction that he was headed for the boulder. Today she was determined to seek him out.

Sometimes it took her several days to locate a particular ant, due to the sheer size of the colony, but today she was lucky. She stumbled across him right away. He was exiting the mound and heading in his usual direction toward the boulder just as she turned to look for him. This was the one direction the other ants never went, and Tara wanted to find out why he alone made the trip.

"Maybe he's got a girlfriend!" she laughed to herself. "I can see it now; Old One-Eye spurns colony for harlot!" She knelt to the ground and put her face close to the ant. "Better watch it bud; I think the others are on to you!" She laughed harder as she thought of how silly she was being. "Sorry, but it's hard to be serious when you hang around the desert all day talking to one-eyed ants!"

For a moment she was embarrassed, but a quick look around assured her that she was alone. It was just her, the ants and the desert. She smiled and put a dab of hunter's orange paint on Old One-Eye's thorax, then sat back to give him a head start.

She had erected a canopy under a *palo verde* tree as a kind of base camp. There she sat down and looked around, taking simple joy in her surroundings. She wondered how it was, that so much ecological chaos had come into the world. It had all happened so fast! She tried to count the species of plants and animals that had become extinct in the past two to three years. Even the fish were vanishing, though some thought they had gone to the lower depths of the ocean to find cooler waters.

She remembered reading that sea levels had been dropping steadily for the past eighteen months. "Nothing to worry about," the article said, "just something to keep our eyes on." She wondered how her studies in the desert could be significant, given the magnitude of the problem, then reassured herself that every piece of the puzzle was important.

The desert was indeed beautiful, she thought, but it was hot! Still, the sights and smells invigorated her. The backdrop of the Superstition Mountains made Tara feel as if she were part of a huge mural, perhaps a landscape painting hanging in some cosmic gallery.

"Guess I'd better catch up to Old One-Eye" she muttered aloud. Picking herself up, she headed for the boulder.

Thirty feet before reaching it, she caught up to the old ant. He had slowly meandered his way toward the huge rock, and was easy to spot with his newly painted back. Tara followed him for another fifteen feet when suddenly the oppressive chill she had experienced earlier overwhelmed her. She spun around quickly, hoping this time to confront its source. But there was nothing, nothing but fear like a heavy blanket over her soul. She wasn't sure what it was, but again she was certain someone or something was watching.

Carefully, she scanned the surrounding area. No sounds, nothing in sight, but the feeling of oppression remained overpowering as she turned again toward the boulder. She took one more step toward it and the fear increased. Whirling around, she sprinted for her pack, which was propped against the *palo verde*.

Many months of desert hiking had given Tara a body of pure energy, and she sped like the wind. When she reached the *palo verde's* branches, she dropped to the ground and fumbled in the pack for the gun her father had given her.

"Never know when some weirdo might show up," he told her when he gave it to her. She never thought she'd need it, but right now she was acting on pure instinct. Jerking it out, she whirled toward the boulder. There was no one there.

Only then did she notice that she was no longer afraid. In fact, all her feelings of uneasiness and fright were gone. Nothing had changed except her physical location, but she felt perfectly safe! She still felt the rush of adrenaline and could have crushed rocks with her bare hands, but she no longer felt any danger. Maybe it was the gun, she thought.

"What on earth?" she muttered out loud.

"Excuse me?" the woman next to her responded, snapping Tara back to the present.

"Oh, I'm sorry Norma. I was thinking out loud. I do that quite often these days." Tara forced another smile and rolled her eyes.

"Well, you ought to see me. Everyone at the store calls me Ms. Yakety Yak. I'm just glad to know I'm not alone!" She laughed, and Tara couldn't help but laugh too. "So you just keep on talking. Things work out better when you don't bottle them up. Trust me, when my husband left me, all I did was talk to myself. But it worked wonders."

"Thanks for the tip, but I'm sorry to hear about your husband."

"Oh, that's okay. He's the loser. He ran off with the pretty real estate woman who sold us our first house. After a month, she dumped him. We were only married for a year, but the marriage was a bad decision for both of us. I should have seen through him. My mistake. Live and learn, right?"

"He must have been a blind loser to have left *you* for another woman. You're so beautiful!"

"Oh, thank you," she said, blushing, "but you should have seen the real estate woman!"

Tilting her head to the left, Norma gazed intently at Tara. "I have this lovely brunette doll at my shop in Scottsdale with these gorgeous, large brown eyes. I swear you look like the model for that doll."

"I've never modeled for anything, but I'm flattered. Thank you."

"Do you have a husband, or a boyfriend?"

"No, not me. I've kind of given up on love."

"Oh Tara, never give up on love. I haven't, even though it's been . . . well, I won't say how long it's been. Anyway, I'll bet it's right around the corner for you. That's how it usually happens. Just when you give up! So keep your eyes open. Okay?"

Tara laughed. "We'll see. But whatever happens, thanks for the encouragement."

"Oh, no problem." She patted Tara's hand once more.

The man to Norma's left chose that moment to ask her about the magazine she was reading. Tara smiled. She couldn't blame the guy for hitting on Norma, though he looked much her junior. As Norma turned to answer him, Tara turned back to the window, and again her thoughts returned to the desert.

She recalled being terrified, running from the boulder, pulling the gun out of the pack, and then feeling calm. It was disturbingly odd, something she did not want to relive. The boulder and Old One-Eye would have to keep their secrets, she had decided. Heading back for the Jeep, she wondered if, perhaps, she had been in the sun too long.

The Jeep was parked about a half mile away, and even though she had no ammunition in the gun, she thought that the fact she was holding it in her hand would give her at least the appearance of a good defense. With some trepidation, however, she began the walk back. The route led along a trail with a rather steep bank, on the other side of which lay a dry riverbed. Halfway across, she noticed something lying in the middle of the wash. As she approached, she realized it was a dead coyote. But it hadn't been there that morning.

"Oh you poor thing, you can't be dead; there are so few of you left!" She sat down in the sand ten feet from the dead animal.

The coyote was once a thriving, noble member of the desert. Now it too faced extinction. Tara never could handle death well. Most of the time, when she was forced to face it, she cried. This was no exception.

She thought of her little brother's question about the time she spent alone in the desert. When he asked why, she had been unable to tell him the truth. How could she tell him that life is a beast; that it can chew you up and spit you out with no regard; that she could no longer bear the thought of getting close to anyone. Then there was the most important reason of all: in the desert, no one could see her cry.

Six miles above the earth and half way to Dallas, Tara again wiped tears from her eyes, and continued to think of the desert. The day after her encounter with the dead coyote, she came back to satisfy her curiosity about the odd and terrifying boulder. Reaching into her pack, she pulled out the gun, a .38 automatic, and released the clip to check the load. She wouldn't be without ammunition this time. Snapping it back into place, she tucked it into the waistband of her khaki shorts.

The man at the gun shop in Apache Junction never said a word when she bought the ammo. That was a relief. She was nervous, but felt better knowing she had a loaded weapon. Of course, she had no idea what or who she was up against, if anything at all. But after yesterday she was determined to find out.

In a fleeting thought, she wondered why she hadn't asked someone to come out with her. Perhaps she was refusing to admit there was a danger. No, she knew she was taking a risk, but somehow she didn't care. Why? It was uncomfortable to think about it, so she decided to take it up later. Instead, she forced the train of thought from her mind, and concentrated on the job at hand.

She took the path leading to the dry riverbed. She knew it well. After all, she had made it! Over the course of the past thirteen months, it had gone from a rabbit trail to a narrow hiking trail, blocked only by the occasional tumbleweed. The path ran over a low rise, then along a small dry wash for about a hundred yards. To the west of the path and just along its edge, was a grove of mesquite trees. In the spring their blossoms attracted all kinds of attention from what remained of the desert wildlife. Honey bees and hummingbirds flocked to them in ever-dwindling droves. The smell was exhilarating, especially after a rainfall. Sometimes Tara would stop there to plan her day, catch up on homework or just rest in the shade of their branches. The rest of the way was littered with sagebrush two to three feet high, and an occasional cactus.

Suddenly, Tara felt her heart racing all the way up her throat. She swallowed hard, trying to choke back anxiety, a fear laced with something else, something she couldn't quite identify. At that point, she almost turned and fled, never to come back. But holding herself in check, she struggled to continue, one foot in front of the other, until her fears were subdued. The experience renewed her resolve to repress the strange feelings she was having until she could get some answers. Answers she had to have!

These were strange times, she decided, calling for action that produced results, and Tara was bound by an unwritten law: *To be a true scientist, thou shalt not allow anything to keep you from the truth. Therefore, go and do . . . and learn!*

In this particular doing, however, a subconscious battle raged within her. Since the death of her two friends, she had felt her own mortality as never before; not that she wanted to die or was frustrated with her own weaknesses. She had things in life she wanted to accomplish, places to go, answers to uncover. But she realized now that the Beast of life held no regard for things beautiful, and she wondered if her time was ever meant to be. Perhaps the Beast would take her too.

This had become a daily battle for her, though she was not without dreams and ambitions. She had given up on love, and it seemed to her that God was allowing the Beast to win. Still, she clung to the hope that maybe, through her studies, she could help life conquer death, light banish darkness or, as she most liked to think of it, beauty conquer the Beast. But it wasn't a dream in which she had great hope.

The late morning sun was rising just over her right shoulder as she continued along the trail. She watched her shadow bob up and down on the path as she walked. It would soon shrink to nothing, when the sun loomed straight overhead in a painfully bright blue sky.

Ahead of her now was a small rise. The muscles in her long legs glistened in the morning sun as she rushed up the incline. Stepping up and over the edge, she moved down the back side, through the loose rocks, coming finally to the riverbed.

She looked to the right then the left, wiping the sweat from her eyes. Her heart began to pound, and she felt a wave of adrenaline course through her body. Turning to the left, she hesitated just long enough to feel for the security of the pistol in her waistband, then drew a deep breath and continued her march.

The sound of the sand crunching underfoot was the only thing she could hear now. It was good that she had spent the money she got for Christmas on a good pair of hiking boots. It was hard to walk in sand, but her Sierra Diamondbacks were the best. Ultra-light and exceptionally tough, the boots allowed her to cut across the desert terrain with the greatest of ease.

Turning a bend in the riverbed, she was startled from her thoughts by the sight of the coyote. Only, it wasn't a coyote any more, at least not as it was the day before. What she was looking at now was only a skeleton.

How could that be? she wondered. If scavengers had worked on it, they would have scattered it from there to Tucson. She approached with caution. The skeleton appeared to be intact.

When she got within ten feet of it, just like the day before, she felt herself flooded with feelings of dread and foreboding. Stopping in her tracks, she pulled the gun from her waistband and nervously glanced around. Slowly she inched forward, her heart racing wildly. Goosebumps climbed her back, as she felt an anxious chill. Something was wrong, but what? It was nothing she could see. Still she continued to inch ahead.

Suddenly the feelings changed. A strangely pleasant feeling swept over her, almost euphoric. Distrustful of this new sensation that tingled through her, she continued her slow advance. As quickly as it had come the pleasurable sensation left. The feelings that replaced it pressed in with such force she had to run. She had to . . . but she willed herself to stay. Then she started backing up, slowly. One, two, three steps she took, her eyes riveted on the skeleton.

Suddenly the strange, oppressive feelings disappeared. All she felt was the morning sun at her back and a slight breeze from the south. She looked around. There was nothing. She looked back at the skeleton. She felt no fear, anxiety or pleasure, just calm. Perplexed, she crouched in the sand of the riverbed.

Several minutes passed. Determined to find the explanation for this strange phenomenon, she stood and moved toward the bones again. Ten feet from the skeleton, a solid wall of raw emotion hammered her. Another step and she was wrapped in euphoric bliss. Her thoughts were unfocused and dreamlike. If there was a heaven, she imagined it felt like this. She moved a little further forward and suddenly she was filled with fear and darkness so intense she felt ill. Again she forced her body to retreat slowly to a safe distance.

She spent the next several minutes circling the skeleton, approaching it from different sides, all with the same result: ten feet from the skeleton there was a wall of fear and darkness, a step further, euphoria, then gut wrenching terror. Beyond ten feet, there was nothing but the desert, peace and safety.

She had no idea what it meant, but one thing was certain; she was not going to get any closer to the coyote! Images of demonically possessed skeletons chasing her through the desert did not sit well with her. Someone, something, maybe the skeleton itself, did not want her any closer and she was going to give it all the room it claimed.

She thought back to her experience of the day before. Could this be the same strange, invisible wall she encountered at Old One-Eye's boulder? She set out immediately to find the answer. There had to be some connection.

At the anthill, everything was quite normal. Ants were scurrying back and forth at the entrance, some bearing food to store below, others rushing back out into the desert to forage. Looking beyond the anthill toward the boulder, she stepped carefully over the ants and through her small, secluded camp under the *palo verde*. The boulder was just over a small rise that was covered by a cluster of desert willows in full purple bloom. Their beauty seemed to radiate peace and calm. Right now, that was conspicuously out of place.

Passing through the willows and out into the open, she stopped to stare at the large boulder roughly thirty feet away. About six feet high and eight feet wide, it was the largest of many rocks strewn over the desert floor near the towering formations of the Superstition Wilderness. This monster of a boulder must have rolled from a loftier perch high above to settle there. It looked like the "Mother of all Rocks," and the smaller ones surrounding her looked like her toddlers. Together they were a family out for a picnic in the desert, Tara thought. She felt almost as though she were intruding on them.

With a great deal of uneasiness, she edged forward, half-expecting Mamma Rock to pick up some of her kids and throw them at her. Five feet, then another five feet. Each time, she stopped to test her feelings. There was nothing. She raised her hand and looked at the gun in it. Somehow it gave her the strength to continue.

She was now fifteen feet from Mamma boulder. One more step and she hit the invisible wall; another and she felt a repeat of the euphoric high. Her head swam. Her entire body tingled from head to toe in a wave of physical pleasure. Then, just as suddenly, she was confused and frightened. The next step forward gave her such feelings of fear she could hardly keep from running. But, clenching every muscle in her body, she took another determined step forward. This time she was overcome by a wrenching need to vomit.

Something was happening to her body, something totally out of control. She could stand it no more. She turned and ran back headlong toward the desert willows. There she fell into their shade to recover.

After a few breaths, she realized that she had regained her normal array of senses and was none the worse for wear. Sitting up, she drew her knees under her chin, and thought about the situation.

"Is anyone there?" she called out.

No response. She picked up a rock and threw it at the boulder, thinking perhaps an animal, possibly a mountain lion, might be in back.

Nothing. How strange. Yesterday she had been within ten feet of the boulder before she felt anything, today fifteen. What was going on? Was this force, this influence, growing? If so, what in the name of . . .

She heard a grunting noise coming from her left and froze. Something was moving in her direction. As quietly as she could, she turned her head. Just a stone's throw away was one of Arizona's wild desert pigs, a javelina, working its way through the brush. It was headed for the boulder. Apparently it hadn't seen her. The javelina's eyesight wasn't too good, but its sense of smell was remarkable. Luckily for Tara, she was downwind. The javelina ambled on its way, ignoring her.

Twenty feet from the rock, the javelina stopped as if unsure whether to proceed. Tara wondered if it were feeling the same sensations she had felt. The pig lowered its head and moved forward cautiously, sniffing right and left.

Ten feet from the boulder, it stopped, dropping to its knees. Rising awkwardly, it staggered forward a few more feet, squealed, shook its head a few times, then started to pitch back and forth.

A full minute passed, as the javelina struggled with its equilibrium, managing again to move forward another foot or two. Then it stopped and began to weave in a tight circle. Suddenly it let out a blood-curdling screech, shook its head violently and dropped on its side, convulsing wildly. In less than a minute and a half, the javelina was dead. Tara sat staring at it, dumbfounded.

It was at this point reality crumbled away and the insanity she felt even now in the sky outside their airplane introduced itself for the first time. Goosebumps started a slow climb up her back as she recalled the event. There in the bright sunlight of the desert's noonday, while she stared intently at the body of the javelina not thirty feet away, it disintegrated and disappeared into the Arizona sky.

Chapter 2
I'LL MAKE YOU PAY!

It was 9:15 p.m., and Ryan McKay was working late. He sat at the computer in his lab at Molecular Dynamics, overlooking the Denver skyline from the foothills of Golden, Colorado, and waded through a pile of daily journal entries. Not long after he was hired by Mol-Dyn six months ago, late nights at the lab had become a regular practice. He was single and new to the area, however, so there were few distractions. No one cared where he was but him.

Besides, nights were less of a hassle. The last of the employees left at five and no one else ever stayed much past that; they were in too much of a rush to beat the traffic home. Most nights, the only people left in the building were Ryan and the security personnel.

Putting in the hours never bothered him. He always worked hard to insure that his experiments were backed up with good records. The new software package, programmed for him by Rusty Philips from ModTech across the street, was making this part of his work much easier. But the icing on the cake was the fact that he loved his work.

He assumed that was the reason for his success. Only twenty-seven years old and he was already regarded as one of particle physics' brightest newcomers. Six months ago, Mol-Dyn was more than excited to offer him a six figure salary, his own lab and two assistants to entice him there. All that, and he was only one year out of grad school!

Actually, Ryan was a little perplexed by all the hoopla over him. Sure he was good, confident, had some wonderful theories to work on, but there were plenty of good physicists out there. Certainly there were men who had more years of real lab time under their belts than he. Even to be thought of at the same salary level as those men was humbling.

In reality, he knew it all boiled down to the project he was working on. He knew where he stood. He was just another little nothing to be used by corporate America, squeezed of his creativity and discarded like this morning's orange peels. In the process, however, he figured he would enjoy the orange juice like everyone else.

Finishing up his journal entries, he backed out of the system and turned off the computer, leaving the disc in the slot. The disk was new, hardly anything on it yet. He wouldn't need to back it up until later. Standing up, he stretched his six foot three frame and yawned.

Another Friday night, working alone at the lab, he thought. Something is definitely wrong with this picture.

"Man, I need a stiff soft drink!" he muttered. Walking out into the hall, he headed toward the lounge. It was one of those newly furnished corporate snack areas that look like the inside of a new refrigerator with uncomfortable chairs and sterile tables. He opened the fridge and pulled out a cold soda. Snapping it open, he plopped down in one of the hard-backed white Formica chairs, put his feet up on a table, and drank in a large gulp of the highly carbonated beverage, then waited for the belch.

"This is the life!" he muttered facetiously. "Alone, just me, my cheap pop and my project. Yep, everything I need is right here." He looked at his lone reflection in the mirror across the room and thought for a moment. "Yeah, right! Who am I kidding anyway?"

Though Ryan loved his work, he didn't particularly love his life. Particle physics was inspiring, but something just as important was missing, and he knew exactly what it was. After his two-year LDS mission, he had returned home thinking that the Spirit would quickly lead him to a beautiful Mormon girl and a temple marriage. But he was mistaken. Sucked up by the local college machine, he had been turned into a scientist without a single interesting prospect in sight.

His testimony was a constant in his life that kept him from losing hope, but it was getting more and more difficult. Every night was the same. Finished with the day's experiments, he would sit and pour everything into the computer, then look at the results. True, it was a give and take relationship, but the computer wasn't as soft as a woman, and a CPU couldn't share his life.

Sure he was excited about his work, but he wanted to share it with someone—someone very wonderful! There just wasn't anyone like that at Mol-Dyn. Denver was a great place, but it was still new to him!

Sunday was his only day off and though he was active in the local single's ward, he didn't have time to attend their weekly activities.

Even if he could take the time, there was no one there that interested him. He'd never been married, so he had little in common with the divorcees, and the other women were all pretty young and immature for his tastes. Things just weren't working out on the social side of his life. With an hour every morning at the gym, then twelve hours at the office, it wasn't much of a life! Life, in fact, was passing him by at a pace that seemed to increase daily.

He tried to recall the last time he was out on a date. Ah yes, he recalled. It had been months ago, four to be exact, while vacationing in Idaho. He met Jocelyn hiking north of Blackfoot, and invited her out for dinner . . . and that was that. He dropped her off at her house and raced to catch his flight back to Denver. He was into his second skimpy bag of peanuts, thirty thousand feet in the air, when it hit him that he had forgotten to ask for her phone number!

"What a jerk!" he said out loud.

He was starting to worry about something that had never really concerned him before. Would he ever get married? If it was ever going to happen, it would have to start with a date . . . *and* a phone number!

He imagined himself an old man, feeble, hunched over, desperately chasing equally old and feeble women around the shuffleboard court at the old folks' home. Not a pretty sight! He shuddered involuntarily.

Gulping what was left of the soda, he shot the can across the room into the wastebasket. A split second before the can hit the trash, however, he heard a loud crack. A dark, cold feeling sent a wave of adrenaline through his body at the sound. Cocking his head, he listened for what could only have been seconds, but felt like forever. The sound seemed to have come from his lab.

Rising, he headed for the hall. Since he was used to being alone, except for the security people, odd noises didn't usually bother him. There were countless experiments in varying degrees of completion and in all kinds of containers throughout the building. They had a propensity to pop or react due to time and temperature, or sometimes just because they felt like it. Labs were labs . . . but this sound was different.

Before he reached the door, Ryan felt a chill. His long-sleeved, knee-length lab coat was suddenly inadequate as he stuffed his hands into his pockets for warmth. Pushing the door open, he stopped immediately, physically struck by a wave of nausea.

From the floor directly in front of him, Rusty Phillips stared up at him; his eyes glazed and helplessly fixed on Ryan. The smell of gunpowder was still in the air, and a pool of blood was slowly widening around Rusty's prone body.

Without a thought, Ryan lunged for him. "Don't move buddy; I'll call for help!" Finding a weak pulse, he sprang up and grabbed for the phone on his desk.

"Ryan," Rusty whispered.

"Nine-one-one operator?" Ryan was saying into the phone. "Yes, we have an emergency! Send the police and an ambulance to Mol-Dyn on Southshore Drive. Now! A man's been shot!"

"Ryan," Rusty whispered again.

Ryan cradled the phone and knelt by his only friend in the entire city. Leaning over, he put his ear to Rusty's lips.

"I'm . . . so sorry, I . . . "

"Quiet now, Rusty; an ambulance is on its way."

"Get your back-ups," Rusty struggled, "my office. You'll need them."

His hand went limp in Ryan's, as he exhaled softly without taking another breath. Ryan stared into his eyes, fixed and blank now.

Before he had time to react, he heard a noise in the hall. Relieved that security was finally there, he jumped up and headed for the door. But as he approached, he could see through the glass a man dressed in black, his face covered and . . . Yes, he could see when the man moved that there was a gun in his hand!

Without thinking, Ryan ducked behind a counter. His heart was racing wildly! He tried to listen for the man's entrance, but all he could hear was his heart. Surely the man with the gun would hear it too.

By now the killer knew he had made a mistake. Moments before, he entered stealthily through an unlatched window in Lab 3. He knew Ryan McKay would be in Lab 2 across the hall, and sure enough, a man in a white lab coat was there sitting at the computer. He entered quickly and snapped off a shot, hitting the man in the back. The victim pitched forward, hit the computer monitor and fell back, toppling the chair. As he hit the ground, the contents of his coat pocket scattered across the floor, his nametag sliding to a stop a few feet in front of the killer.

With cold indifference, he looked at the tag. It told him he had just killed some computer geek from ModTech, across the street. He felt his anger flare. He never made mistakes! Stepping to the computer, he discharged the A drive disk, stuffed it into his pocket, raised his gun and fired a shot into the main frame. It exploded with a loud crack.

Stepping back over "Rusty," he watched the man's labored breathing with idle curiosity. He knew the geek would die soon, and he would love nothing better than to sit and watch. But time was short. Though his gun was equipped with a silencer, the bullet that smashed into the computer had made more noise than he needed right now. What he really wanted was Ryan McKay. He couldn't risk another shot, with the possibility of more noise alerting his intended victim. So, instead of finishing this man, he wheeled and strode out of the lab.

The restroom! That's where the mark must be. Turning right, the killer raced down the hall in the direction of the signs. Silently he entered. With raised gun, he checked each stall. Nobody was home.

So this was how it was going to be. He was going to have to work for this one. He hated to work. His gun was supposed to do the work, not him. His gun had made him hundreds of thousands of dollars. So, when he had to work to find someone, he made sure they paid. Death would be painful, he thought. Of course, if the man let himself be found right away, he might still kill him quickly.

The killer began to sweat, and that made him even angrier. Oh when I find this one, he thought, I'll make him pay . . . fifty dollars every day! A bullet in the lung, one in the kidney, a couple in the kneecaps. Oh, he'll pay all right; he'll pay!

In the dark recesses of his mind, a memory flared. Suddenly, he was a child again.

"Don't make me have to find you, boy!" his mother yelled. "If I have to find you, I'll beat you so bad! Now come on back here! I'll make you pay . . . you little twerp! I'll make you pay . . . fifty dollars every day, for the rest of your miserable life!"

The boy hid in the woods. He hid a long time, until he was so hungry he could hide no more. When he finally sneaked back into the house late that evening, his mother was waiting. Whomp! She got him right on the side of the head with a cake pan!

"If I woulda' come lookin' for you, broke a sweat for you, I'da beat you for a week!" she yelled. "I'da made you pay, little mister; yesiree, fifty dollars every day. Now, git to your room or I'll tie you to a leash!"

So the boy learned hate, boiling hatred. It had been boiling for years, seething like . . . lava! Yes, lava, angry lava, ready to burst forth upon the world! The kind of lava he felt seething up right now.

The man in black shook off the haunting nightmares of his childhood, and turned again to his task. Heading for the lounge, he passed Lab 2 and checked briefly to see that "Rusty" still lay on the floor, unmoved in his blood.

Then, like lava, he flowed toward the lounge, boiling with hatred, yearning to kill. Lava, lava with bullets!

Ryan watched the killer stop and peer through the door at Rusty. He couldn't control the beating of his heart. He was sure the man would hear him. But he didn't. Instead, he went on down the hall toward the lounge. Ryan was motionless, unable to breathe. He knew that now was his chance, the moment the killer entered the lounge.

"Please Father, help me out of this one," he whispered quietly.

Then quietly but quickly, his heart still racing, he slipped around the door, out into the hall and through the side exit. As soon as he opened it, the alarms went wild and he ran for all he was worth, driven by a powerful instinct for survival. Down the outside length of the building he flew, knowing that the killer would be right behind him.

Just as he rounded the corner, he heard the killer burst through the exit. As he ran, Ryan fumbled in his pocket for his keys. Rounding the corner, he came to the west entrance, and jammed a key into the lock. Throwing open the entry, he dove back, away from the building to the sidewalk and the bushes separating Mol-Dyn from its expansive lawn. He lay there motionless, almost impaled on the branches, trying to keep his breathing under control and his heart from giving him away!

He heard the killer run to the open entry and stop. Peering through the bushes, he saw the man look around, then reenter the building. Seizing the opportunity, Ryan jumped up and ran across the immense lawn to the street. Crossing Southshore Drive, he headed up the steps to ModTech and through a crowd that had just gotten off shift.

"Rusty's been shot!" he yelled. "Get inside! The shooter's there!"

As he entered with the excited mob, a chubby-faced security guard grabbed his arm.

"Hold on there young man! What are you talking about?"

Most of the group had backed through the doorway into the foyer, mumbling and pointing as looks of fear flashed across their faces.

Before Ryan could answer the guard, a loud explosion shattered the night air, and a plume of dark smoke billowed from the Mol-Dyn building, as tongues of fire flicked from its roof. An ambulance pulled up to the front entrance, apparently in response to the 911 call he had made from his lab. Fire and police sirens could be heard in the background, bearing down on the scene.

As Ryan stared out the glass door of ModTech, he heard a car speeding away from the scene as two police cars pulled into the drive that separated the two buildings. It had to be the killer, Ryan thought. He's getting away!

While everyone's eyes were fixed on the growing flames, Ryan slipped past the guard and made his way to Rusty's office. It was small and cluttered, while at the same time curiously neat. "A place for everything and everything in its place" were Rusty's watchwords.

Where to begin, he muttered; there were so many *things*! He crossed the room in four steps and pulled open the file cabinet. To his surprise it was unlocked. No doubt Rusty thought he'd be right back.

"Okay, where is it? Desktop, Diplomas, Disks, Dis . . . got it!" He grabbed the file folder and reached inside where he found two floppy disks. Dropping them into his lab coat pocket, he slid the drawer shut.

Before leaving the room, he paused. Stepping back to the file cabinet, he used his coat to wipe any prints from the drawer handle. He did the same with the doorknob as he closed the door behind him. Reentering the foyer, he found everyone still focused on events across the street. Some were leaving for a closer look. Ryan followed as inconspicuously as possible.

Once outside, he could see the Mol-Dyn building exploding and collapsing on itself. The night sky was a brilliant orange. Even from the front steps of ModTech, he could feel the heat. Lowering himself slowly onto the first step, he felt the sensation of shock start to build within him. Lights were flashing everywhere now, even in his mind.

Memories long repressed began to surface, visions of firemen trying desperately to save his family while he looked on helplessly in horror.

He was eight years old then, car wreckage was everywhere and somebody was screaming, "They're all dead!" while he looked on from a ditch twenty yards away.

When the car rolled over the first time, he had been thrown clear. But the car kept rolling and rolling, over and over, Mommy, Daddy, his baby sister, they were all gone. Then a woman screamed, "Look, look! A little boy!" as she pointed at Ryan, dazed, bloodstained, covered with dirt, and wavering unsteadily on his feet near the ditch.

"Excuse me, sir?" A man in a shirt and tie shook Ryan out of his trance. "Are you all right?"

"What?"

Ryan felt shaky. He rubbed his face to clear his mind. The man displayed a badge, then tucked it into his belt.

"I'm Detective Murphy. I understand you may know something about what happened here tonight."

Murphy was thin, Ryan observed, maybe five foot seven and in his early thirties. He spoke with a faintly Southern accent, and his eyes spoke wisdom beyond his apparent age.

"Yeah, I'm the one who called," he responded. "I'm Ryan McKay." He extended his hand to Murphy. The detective's grip was firm and confident.

"All right, Mr. McKay; why don't we step inside out of the noise and have a talk?"

He motioned Ryan toward the ModTech lobby. They walked inside, followed by another man who also looked like a detective. All three headed for the conference room to the right of the foyer. They could see the mayhem across the street through the room's floor-to-ceiling smoked-glass windows, but the sounds of the night were shut out.

"This is a little better. Sit down please, Mr. McKay. By the way, this is Detective Mullins, my partner."

Ryan glanced at Mullins, then back at Murphy. "Did you find the killer?" he asked.

"What makes you think there was a killer, Mr. McKay?"

"I *saw* him! After I saw Rusty on the floor, murdered! Rusty was shot in the back, right in my lab! I watched him die! I don't *think* there was a killer, I *know* there was a killer!"

"No need to raise your voice, Mr. McKay. We're on your side. Why don't we start from the beginning? Take your time, and tell me everything and anything that would help us find this man." He sat down in a chair opposite Ryan, and took out a note pad and pen.

Ryan recalled the events of the night, beginning when he left the lounge. He explained how he found Rusty, his run from the killer and ended with his run across the street to ModTech. Of course, he was careful to leave out the part about what Rusty said and his going into Rusty's office to retrieve his disks. He didn't know if the police might take them as evidence, and he wasn't willing to find that out just yet. They were *his* after all, and the project was at a sensitive stage.

"Okay Mr. McKay . . ."

"Ryan, please. Call me Ryan."

"All right, Ryan; just a few more questions."

"Excuse me, Lieutenant." A uniformed officer entered the room.

"Yeah what is it?" Murphy responded, patiently.

"We found the security officers." The man appeared nervous, as if he were new to the job. "One was in the closet off the front lobby. The other was in one of the restrooms. Bullet to the head in both cases. We were able to get to them before the fire reached the front."

Murphy spun his chair around to face the man. "What about the back, in the laboratories? Were you able to get back there?"

"No way," he replied. "It's a raging inferno. Most of the back half of the building has already collapsed. That's where the explosions were. The fire department won't have it under control for at least another hour." He glanced out the window, then back toward Murphy. "And that car that was speeding away when you arrived; Evans and Hopkins ran into it up on 48th. Shots were fired hitting their cruiser in the grill. They gave pursuit, but lost it in that maze down by the new theaters. They've headed back to the station so Ballistics can dig out the slugs. We'll compare them with whatever we get from the security guards."

"Did they get a make on the car?" Murphy asked.

"A red Camero, '93 or '94, with this plate number." He handed Murphy a slip of paper.

"Good report officer, thanks."

The policeman nodded and smiled then walked out into the lobby. When he was gone, Detective Murphy returned his attention to Ryan.

"How long have you been with Mol-Dyn?"

"A little over six months."

"Does this Rusty work with you?"

"No, he works here at ModTech."

Murphy turned to his partner, who was staring intently through the window at the scene across the street. "Have I.D. go over Mr. Philip's office before they leave."

Without a word, Mullins stepped out through the front door.

"So what was Rusty doing in your office this time of night?"

"I don't know. I mean, he's been helping me with my computer software. He worked up a program for me to organize my notes. I can only assume he dropped over to talk about it. He knows I work late. I am a little surprised, though."

"Why's that?"

"Because he never works late."

"So, you didn't know he was coming over?"

"Of course not. I can't believe this! Of all the nights for him to come over!"

Ryan wiped the sweat from his forehead with the palm of his hand. He was still feeling the effects of his close encounter with death. His heart beat fast, his skin was cold and clammy and he felt a light-headed.

"Do you have any idea who this killer might be?" Murphy asked, staring at Ryan with invasive eyes.

Ryan felt like the man was trying to bore a hole into his head to look for truth, or maybe lies. "I have no idea. I just can't believe it!" He shook his head and slumped forward wearily. Shutting his eyes, he tried to lock out the horror of the night.

"All right, Ryan, bear with me here for a minute longer. Let's assume Rusty was an innocent bystander, for the moment anyway. He was in the wrong place at the wrong time. A man gets into Mol-Dyn, whacks both security guards—with a silencer no doubt, or you would've heard him. He then comes into your lab, kills Rusty, and chases you, trying to do the same. Right so far?"

"Yeah, I think so."

"All right, where were you when Rusty was shot?"

"I was in the lounge. I was only in there for a few minutes drinking a soda. That's when I heard the sound I told you about." He paused as a thought occurred to him. "Rusty was supposed to bring over some disks this afternoon. He must have been running late, and decided to drop them off on the way home."

"Okay, so does this other guy come to rob the place? Doesn't sound like it. He's is obviously a professional. If it were industrial espionage, or he wanted some information, he'd wait until everyone was out of the place. You know; sneak in, get what he wants, sneak out."

"Yeah, makes sense."

"But, after you went to the lounge, Rusty walks into your lab. Minutes, or seconds later, he's shot. Obviously, this guy came to kill. So why would he want to kill you, Ryan?"

Ryan stared at the detective. "What makes you think he was trying to kill *me*?"

"Oh, I don't know; it was your lab, he shoots a guy in the back who's in your lab. Why didn't he just get out after that? Why did he chase you around the building?" Murphy paused, but Ryan said nothing. "Are you sure you didn't recognize him? You're tall, good looking . . . any jealous husbands out there I should know about?"

"Huh?"

"Would anyone want to kill you? Think about it, man."

"Look, I hardly know a soul here in Denver. I don't socialize much, except at church, and most of the people there are twice my age. They have a single adult program, but I haven't had time to get involved. I haven't even been on a date for four months!"

"Oh, sorry. Well, that leaves just one scenario. This has to be bigger than industrial espionage. Ryan, tell me, just what were you working on?"

Ryan looked into the detective's eyes. Things had been hush-hush for so long, he couldn't help but hesitate.

"Ryan, look, I need to make some quick determinations here. Your life could be in danger. If you're holding out on me . . ."

"I'm not. My research is sensitive. That's all. You know, patents, trade secrets, proprietary information, that sort of thing."

"Okay, look!" Murphy closed his pad and returned it to his pocket. "Off the record, just give me an idea what you're doing. You have my word I won't tell anyone. But I need to know what I'm dealing with."

Ryan stood, glanced at the detective, then walked over to a water cooler that stood in the corner. He took a paper cup from the top of the cooler, filled it, and drank. When he turned back, Murphy's partner, Mullins, had just walked back into the room, and was staring out the window at Mol-Dyn again.

"All right; but just you. Okay?"

"Mullins is my partner. I trust him completely."

"I don't care."

Murphy twisted his mouth in annoyance, then asked his partner to leave. When the man was gone he turned back to Ryan. "Satisfied?"

"Yeah. Okay, here's the short version. I was hired by Mol-Dyn six months ago because they were interested in my work in particle physics. I have a theory that the fundamental particles of matter, quarks, are actually alive. That is, they possess some level of intelligence. Most scientists believe these particles are just . . . well, energy probability patterns, you might say, with varying charges, frequencies and other characteristics. Remember any of this from science class in school?"

Murphy nodded, and Ryan forged ahead.

"These particles are the building blocks of everything we know. They form protons, neutrons, electrons, then atoms, which form together to make molecules. Everything we see, feel, eat or breathe is a different combination of these sub-atomic particles. I wrote my doctor's thesis on the idea. Based on the data and the math, I concluded that these particles are alive and can actually be manipulated in certain ways, using . . . well, that's a little complicated. Anyway, next thing you know here's Mol-Dyn, offering me big bucks to come and work for them."

Murphy interrupted, "You mean they hired you because you believe these particles are alive?"

"Well, that's kind of an oversimplification. When my experiments began to back my theories, they started to take notice."

Murphy pondered a moment, his mind apparently struggling to understand Ryan's theory. "You mean you've proven that life exists in sub-atomic particles?"

"You catch on quick for a cop."

Murphy gave a humble shrug. "Kind of makes the word *inorganic* obsolete, doesn't it?"

Ryan smiled. He was in his element. "It's not just life really, it's intelligence! We're talking free agency, the ability to choose. Of course, we're not talking about anything on the level of human, or even plant or animal, intelligence. Their ability to choose is both framed by natural law and a factor in it. Sorry, that part's pretty complex. But it's very exciting, really. It appears that we're going to need a whole new set of equations to describe the framework . . ."

The detective looked puzzled.

"I'm losing you, aren't I?"

He smiled. "Yeah, I'm afraid so."

"Well, most of the time, physical laws keep these particles in order, or visa versa—the relationship is very complex. But, if these particles are alive or intelligent, if they have some degree of free agency, it would explain some of the behaviors we've noticed in experiments for years."

"Okay, okay. Back up here for a minute. So you prove these particles have life. What does that really mean . . . to the average guy? What are the practical implications?"

"Well, if we can affect their free agency in an intelligent way, control them, or 'entice' them, as I put it . . . Just think of what you could do if you could appeal to the agency of a sub-atomic particle! You could do almost anything. How about a cure for cancer or AIDS, the elimination of genetic defects? The sky's the limit. Of course, with control comes responsibility. There'd have to be bio-ethical standards, accountability . . . that sort of thing. Not only could you make anything your heart desires, theoretically you could destroy anything as well."

Murphy's eyes widened. "Bingo," he said in a whisper. "Ryan, how far along are you with this stuff, this manipulation thing?"

"Oh, I'm years away from any practical application. We're just learning to disorient certain quarks, modify the electron cloud slightly, that sort of thing. It's done with a very precise combination of sound, light and magnetic fields. The methodology is really in its infancy."

"But you can really do this? Now?"

"Well, yes, a little. Once they become disoriented, we plan to give them a new orientation, new laws to follow. Well, actually, it's more like another path to choose. Of course, we've only been able to induce a confused state that lasts for microseconds, but so far we haven't had much luck introducing new orders. We just haven't quite got a handle on the math yet. It's pretty hairy—takes a huge mainframe—but I don't think we're too far away."

"Well, I think I've got the gist. It's getting a little deep for a cop though." He smiled and continued. "But to get to the point, if I'm hearing you right on this, you could actually make gold from a pile of cow manure! Is that about right?"

"If we could just unlock the pattern for reorienting the sub-atomic particles, yes. All the pieces are there."

"Does anyone else know about this?"

Ryan thought for a moment. "Well, at first I wasn't taken seriously. I don't know if that means I was alone in my thinking, but my ideas were unique when I did my thesis. In fact, Mol-Dyn was the first to give it any credence at all. Then, about three months ago, some other companies began working on it too. We always assumed we were way ahead of them, but now I don't know. Maybe we're the ones behind. As far as I know, nobody has perfected a device that could fully disorient a pile of cow dung, let alone give it a new reorientation as a bar of gold. But I could be wrong. Right now, it's a mad dash to be first, I suppose."

Murphy ran his hand across his forehead distractedly. "It doesn't make sense. If the killer were after your project, why would he kill you? Wouldn't it make more sense to wait until you developed a device or a machine? They would need you to do that . . . Unless of course, *they* already have taken it to that level. In which case, they may have been trying to knock off the competition, namely you."

Murphy turned and looked out the window at the crumbling embers of what used to be Mol-Dyn's Denver facility. "Of course, the killer may have been hired to kill you for some other reason entirely."

Ryan shook his head, confused.

"Nah!" Murphy snapped back. "Someone is trying to knock off the competition. My gut tells me that's the scenario. So, who knew about your project, or had access to your notes?"

Ryan thought for a moment. "Only Mr. Graf, as far as I know. He made sure I reported only to him. He said he wanted to be the kind of boss who was always accessible, but I never actually met him! I would just e-mail my data to his computer, at an ISP located somewhere on the East Coast. We used a secure e-mail program, so I assume it wasn't tampered with. He would call back and ask questions from time to time. He was always cordial. I can't believe he'd try to kill me; I work for him! That would be counterproductive. Oh, and my assistants knew a little. They weren't involved in the full scope of the project, though. Their duties revolved around isolated experiments."

"Well, write down their names and phone numbers if you have them, anyway. For our records." Murphy handed Ryan a notepaper. "Now, what about Rusty?"

"He knew as much about physics as I do about computer programming. He only helped me with my software."

For now, it seemed better not to mention that Rusty kept copies of his notes on disks in his office.

"Hmm. Still, he had access. Right?"

Ryan stood and walked over to the window. "Yeah, but now he's dead." He looked quietly out at the Mol-Dyn fire for a moment, then turned back to the detective. "I don't know what all this means, so I'll need time to mull it over a bit. Look, Lieutenant, I'm tired. Can we pick this up some other time?"

"I suppose. I've got enough now to open a file on the investigation. You go on home. We'll be in touch later."

Ryan smiled wearily. "Are you going to ask me not to leave town?"

"I may," the detective said with a wry smile. "I haven't discounted your involvement in all this."

"Well, I'm going to be in Dallas this coming Monday at an ecological symposium. It's the one that's been in the news lately."

Murphy nodded his head. "Why are you going to this symposium?"

"One of my old college professors was supposed to give a report there, but he developed some health problems and asked me to fill in. It's a kind of obtuse theory of his relating my doctoral research to some ecological issues. I'll be back late Wednesday."

"Okay, but watch your back. Whoever showed up here tonight came for you, and he knows he missed. In fact, why don't I send one of my guys to follow you home?"

"No, thanks. I can handle myself. If anything looks out of the ordinary, I'll let you know."

"If you insist, but here, take my card. This number is my cell phone. You can reach me anywhere, anytime. Call if you run into anything."

He handed Ryan the card, shook his hand and headed out the door, joining Detective Mullins in the lobby. As they left, Ryan looked at Mullins' face. Something about him made Ryan uneasy. He was taller than Murphy, sported a heavy five o'clock shadow, and had small penetrating eyes in a very large head. He looked like a typical movie bad guy wearing a good guy suit. And it seemed strange that he never said a word. Oh well, he thought, it takes all kinds.

As the two detectives crossed the street, they approached a group of uniformed officers. Murphy engaged one of them in conversation, while Mullins stepped back into the street. Ryan could see him bend over and pick something up from the blacktop. Looking around, he dropped the object into his pocket and joined the others.

The night air was still thick with smoke and the sounds of collapsing wood and metal. Fire engines churned and men yelled. The trees took on an eerie presence as blue and red lights flashed their shadows into bizarre contortions along the sidewalk of Southshore Drive. Ryan put his hands into his pockets, walked down the steps of ModTech and headed for home.

———————

As he rounded the corner of Kenwood and Saragosa, heading for his condo at the end of the street, Ryan was in a fog, his mind preoccupied with the events of the evening. He wanted to believe that what he had just been through was some sort of warped dream. He would wake up soon and feel the sunshine touching his consciousness through the bedroom window. Rusty would still be alive, and he would report to work, as usual. But he wouldn't wake up and it wasn't a dream. He was walking, haunted by the memory of an attempt on his life.

How could this happen? What did it mean? Was Detective Murphy right? How could he have gotten himself wrapped up in so much trouble? The questions rolled over and over in his mind as his legs carried him closer to home.

He was almost there. His pace slowed to a crawl as he began to worry about safety. He was now at the entrance to his condominium complex. His heart beat faster with every step he took toward his unit.

Detective Murphy's last words ran through his mind. "He came for you, and he knows he missed!" Better to go the back way, Ryan thought.

Slipping around Building D, he moved cautiously down the sidewalk that curved and meandered circuitously around Eden's Manor. As he reached the back, an idea struck him.

In the inner courtyard of the complex was a very large garden of trees, shrubs, and plants. This might offer the perfect approach to his condo, and a convenient hiding place as well. His unit was on the ground level and could easily be viewed from the shadows of the garden.

He moved quickly toward the little forest, approaching opposite his front door. Glancing first to the right, then the left, he slipped over the rail and into the trees. When he entered the shadows, he realized his white lab coat would give him away. Fumbling in its pockets for the back-up disks, his keys and his driver's license, he realized that the license was nowhere to be found.

"Must've fallen out during all that running," he thought. Then he remembered Detective Mullins bending down and picking up an object in the street. "Great!" he muttered. Slipping out of the coat, he tossed it behind some bushes. His dark, long-sleeved shirt would be much better for sleuthing.

Hiding among the shadows, he crouched down low, stared into his front window, and waited. The place was dark, too dark to see inside. He wasn't sure what to expect, but he wasn't about to walk through the front door without first checking it out. So he stayed there and waited.

Melted into the shadows in the corner of Ryan's living room, the killer sat in a recliner, waiting. In his hand was the nine-millimeter handgun he had used on countless jobs like this. He caressed it in the darkness, allowing his mind to wander.

Yesiree, gonna make this one pay, he thought. Almost got caught by a couple of them police punks. Not gonna be a pretty sight when I'm through with this guy. Nosiree!

He couldn't remember when he first started his particular line of work, probably Vietnam. He joined the army to get away from his mother's haunting memory. But as he entered combat, he found it was the perfect venue to release a lifetime of rage. And the release was sweet, sweeter than anything he could remember. He decided then that he wasn't going to go back home at the end of his tour. Instead, he stayed on, tour after tour, molding himself into a finely honed killing machine. Eventually word got around, and he was given a few "special assignments," all for the good of the country, of course, but they always involved killing and that's what he liked about them.

"You're a freak of nature, that's what you are." his mother used to holler. "Why'd you kill that bird you little pervert?"

He remembered her grabbing his slingshot and hitting him over the head with it. "Eat all your dinner, little mister! If you don't, things will come out of the woods and eat you! That is, if I don't smack you first!"

He was all of four years old then. That was when he began to hate everything. His dad was in prison for murder, his uncle was running moonshine and always in trouble, and his younger sister was always hanging around stirring up Mamma to smack him. So he smacked his sister instead, and he began to like that too!

Later, he stole from Mamma when she was liquored up. When he was in school, which was once in a blue moon, he fought, stole and did enough mischief to make everyone hate him. But Mamma was worse.

"Come give Mamma a big kiss," she would wheedle. He would hesitate, apprehensive. "Come on now, little mister!" How he hated her kisses. Her mouth reeked of liquor, and she drooled like a diseased animal when she was drunk. "Come here, you little twerp! I'll get you if you don't. Don't make me come and get you! You know what I'll do. I'll make you pay! That's right; fifty dollars every day till you come and kiss me, then I just might have to smack you. Now get over here!"

Caressing the nine-millimeter, he waited, smiling. Gonna make this one pay, all right. "Don't make me have to come and get you, Ryan, you little twerp. 'Cause I will, little mister. Yesiree . . . I'll make you pay!"

* * *

After twenty minutes, Ryan's knees and ankles began to ache for an end to his wait. He decided to go back and check the street as one more precaution before going into the house. Keeping to the shadows, he moved toward the back of the condominium. He scanned the parking lot for strange cars, but saw nothing unusual. Luckily, no one saw him. If they did, the way he was moving through the brush, they might have reported him as a burglar. Slowly and quietly, he made his way toward the side street on the west. Sure enough, there it was . . . a red '93 or '94 Camero! And it was empty.

"I've got to think," he said to himself. "Is he in the condo? Must be. Where else would he be certain to find me? Pretty gutsy, though. How did he know I wouldn't have the police with me?" The cold insolence of the man made Ryan shudder. The best plan was simple, he decided. Just get out of there!

As slowly and carefully as he'd come, he backtracked through the parking lot toward Space 49 and his four-wheel drive. Ryan always walked to work, saving the Explorer for trips to the store and camping. Rather then use the keyless remote, which made a loud chirp, he slid the key carefully into the lock and slowly unlocked the driver's door.

Slipping into the front seat, he closed it gently behind him.

Now the tricky part. Would the killer hear the engine start? How quickly could he get there and fire off a shot? There was no time to worry about all that, Ryan decided. Starting the engine, he lumbered the four-wheeler out of the parking lot onto Saragosa, and turned east toward its intersection with Kenwood Drive.

Near the corner, he noticed a figure standing under a street light. As he approached, he saw that the figure was a man kneeling down to tie his shoelace. When Ryan pulled to the stop sign, the man turned his face toward the Explorer as if trying to make out who was driving. Ryan flicked his eyes toward the clock on the dashboard; it was 11:47 PM.

Who would be out here on the corner at this time of night? And why was he staring so hard at his car? Ryan stared back through the tinted driver's window, trying to make out features in the dim street lighting. Suddenly he recognized the face. It was Detective Mullins!

Ryan turned his head to the right, hoping the man wouldn't recognize him, and drove the vehicle straight through the intersection. Trying not to look conspicuous, he accelerated slowly, watching the man in the rearview mirror. Apparently, the detective had been unable to see in through the tinted windows. He was looking back now, in the direction of the condominium.

As soon as he was out of sight, Ryan floored the vehicle, roaring down the residential street at almost fifty miles an hour. A killer was more than likely in his condo, while a cop kept watch for him at the corner. Obviously, Denver was not a safe place for him.

He pulled out onto a main street leading toward the freeway and drove for ten minutes, trying desperately to think. One thing he could usually depend on was his ability to reason. But there didn't appear to be a whole lot of reason connected with the events of this night. What was happening? Why? What would he have to face next?

He spotted an all-night supermarket and pulled into the parking lot. Reaching into his pocket, he drew out the card Detective Murphy gave him and dialed the cell number using his car phone. One ring, two, and Ryan was startled to hear a recorded voice.

"At the tone, leave your name and number."

"Murphy, I thought you said you'd be there! This is Ryan McKay; I need a call back immediately!" He left his mobile number and hung up. Sitting back, he took a deep breath and waited. He didn't want to leave in case he was in a mobile dead zone when Murphy called him back.

Outside, a couple was loading their Van with what looked like a year's supply of food; probably going home to a normal family. More likely than not they were happy and had three or four kids. Ryan wondered if he would ever lead such a life.

He imagined himself shopping with a wife. She would be beautiful, full of energy, cheerful disposition, and they'd be wandering down the produce aisle together. Surely there was no danger in a produce aisle.

"How about one of these nice peaches?" she would say.

"How about a kiss?" he would reply.

"If you can catch me!" she would say, and off she would go, running past the lettuce.

"Brrrrreet!" He was rudely torn from his thoughts by the ring of his car phone.

"Yeah," he answered guardedly.

"Ryan, Murphy here. Are you all right?"

"Well, I'm in one piece, but no thanks to the Denver PD! What's going on here? Why is your partner watching the street just outside my condo while the killer's car is parked down the street?"

"I don't know what you're talking about. I left him off at his house half an hour ago."

"Right, and I'm Judy Garland!"

"What's going on, Ryan?"

"That's what I was hoping you could tell me."

"Where are you?" Murphy sounded agitated now.

"That's for me to know, and you and your partner to find out! Something's not right here, Murphy, and I intend to find out what it is. Who's Camero is that anyway; your partner's?"

"Ryan, I have no idea what you're talking about. Let me come to you. If my partner's out there, it's without my knowledge. I can tell you though, you're not safe! Let me help!"

"Be at the station in fifteen minutes," Ryan returned. "Right now I'm not sure who I trust."

Backing out of the parking space, he steered his four-wheeler out onto the street. Instead of turning left toward the police station and Detective Murphy, however, he turned toward the interstate.

Might be nice to get an early start for the symposium, he thought. Maybe, just maybe, some of the answers will be there, in Dallas.

Chapter 3
SYMPOSIUM

Tara braced herself against the anticipated thump of the plane's contact with the runway of Dallas-Fort Worth International Airport. She was relieved when it was the gentle touch of a perfect landing. The clouds had all been left behind, and she hoped the change in weather would be a harbinger of things to come.

"Seems you made your first flight without a hitch, Tara." Norma Welker's voice distracted her from her fears. "Though I thought for sure you might have a panic attack."

"Well thanks to you Norma, I did make it. You've been a great comfort. Thanks so much."

Before Norma could respond, the captain's voice came over the loudspeakers. "Please stay seated until the plane has come to a complete stop. We hope you enjoyed your flight, and look forward to having you with us again."

When the plane finally came to rest, passengers were already up and pillaging the overhead compartments. The aisles were jammed with men and women in business attire carrying briefcases, making it impossible for Norma to get out. Tara looked toward the back of the plane. The line extended all the way to the restrooms.

Norma turned to Tara. "I guess we're boxed in," she sighed.

"Sure looks that way."

She sat back down and looked out the window. The awful feelings had dissipated, for now anyway. She thought of her family so far away, and missed them.

"Tara? Are you all right?"

She felt a hand on her shoulder and turned. Norma's eyes expressed the concern of a mother, and she blushed.

"I'm sorry. I was just thinking of my family. I've been gone only two hours and already I miss them. Isn't that silly?"

"No, not at all! Do you have a place to stay while you're here? You're welcome to come to my place, unless of course you're one of those party animals. You're not a party animal, are you?"

"No, actually, I'm just a regular animal," she said, smiling.

"Well, you seem like a very nice animal. But I'm wondering what it is that's troubling you so much. Here, take my number."

She handed Tara a business card with an address and phone number inscribed in raised letters around what looked like an ancient Indian hieroglyphic. On one side of the symbol was a little girl's doll; on the other was what looked like an Indian kachina.

"I have a doll shop in Scottsdale, The Doll House. Have you seen it?"

Tara shrugged her shoulders and shook her head. "I'm sorry. I don't get out much."

"No matter," Norma continued. "Every year just before summer, when the snowbirds leave Arizona, I escape to Dallas. I have a nice home here. You just call the number on the back of that card if you need someone to talk to. I live alone so you wouldn't be any bother. In fact, I could use the company."

"Thank you," Tara responded, slipping the card into her jeans pocket. "You've been so nice. But I'm booked at the Harrelson Inn. The university is paying the bill, and . . . well, I wouldn't want to disappoint them." She smiled.

"That's just fine, but the offer stands as long as I'm here . . . till September 20th. I hope I'm not being too forward. I just can't help it. Every time I see someone in trouble, I have to open my mouth. I just love being helpful. Hope you find what you're looking for." She winked at Tara and squeezed her arm, then, spotting an opening in the line of people, she jumped in, waving as she left. "Bye-bye now!"

"Bye!" Tara watched, a little puzzled, as Norma worked her way up the aisle toward the exit. She replayed the woman's last sentence in her mind. 'Hope you find what you're looking for?' Did I say I was looking for something? Or is it just written all over my face? she thought. Boy, I must be really messed up!

Standing, she stretched and looked for a break in the line. A couple of the men passing by smiled at her. She was used to that, but it always made her feel self-conscious. Anxious to avoid drawing attention, she often dressed, as now, in jeans, hiking boots, and a baggy top she found at a discount store. Still, men seemed to find her attractive. Large, floppy-brimmed hats had been no help, and of course, a veil was out of the question.

A man in his thirties was making his way up the aisle. When he got to Tara's row, he stopped and gave her that look, then motioned for her to go ahead of him. She returned his smile and quickly merged with the outgoing traffic.

Carrying a small duffel bag and only one other piece of luggage, which she quickly retrieved from the baggage area, she arrived early at the Harrelson Inn. After checking in, she took the elevator to the sixth floor and located room 612. Fumbling with the door lock, she finally entered and dropped her bags on the floor.

Now what am I going to do, she thought. Walking over to the bed, she fell backwards onto the mattress and stared up at the ceiling. The symposium's not till tomorrow, maybe I'll see a movie. But first things first.

She rolled over on her stomach, and reached for the phone. Picking up the receiver, she dialed for an outside line and keyed in her long distance code, then a phone number.

"Hello Mom?

"Tara, you made it all right?"

"Yeah, I'm here. Can you believe it? I miss you guys already. Gee, what's it been, three hours?"

"Oh no, honey, it's been a lot longer than that. Why I bet it's been closer to three hours and fifteen minutes!"

"Hey, you're the ones who sheltered me all my life and never let me out of my cage, except for school. Now you've got to put up with my homesickness."

"Oh Tara, hush. You've made us so proud with your work at the university. What time's your meeting tomorrow?"

"Nine o'clock."

"Too bad the others in the group couldn't be there."

"Yeah, can you believe it. Stacy goes into labor last night, and Gene gets arrested this morning for outstanding traffic tickets. What an idiot! I've still got his plane tickets with me! Mom, I've worked so hard on *my* stuff, how am I going to present their ideas as well."

"You can do it honey! You're the smartest one in the group!"

"Well I really am excited about this. I really hope what we have will help."

"Oh it will dear. I'm . . . Oh no!"

Tara could hear the receiver drop and the muffled voices of her mother and little brother in the background. "Tara? Listen, Joey just poured sand all over the VCR. Your father's going to have a cow for sure. Call us at the cabin tomorrow, will you?"

"Sure Mom, have a nice vacation. Love you."

"Love you too! Bye!"

"Bye."

She hung up the phone and smiled. The thought of dad getting home and finding the VCR transformed into a kitty litter box somehow amused her.

A few minutes passed and her mood began to grow somber again. Recognizing the signs of an on-coming depression, Tara decided to get out of the hotel, look around and enjoy herself.

Even though this city represented just another beast to her, staying in the hotel room didn't sound good either. She had to get out, even if it meant facing the Beast head on. So she grabbed her purse and headed out the door, leaving her bags for later.

As she entered the elevator, she pushed the L button, and the doors closed. At the fifth floor, the cage stopped and the doors opened.

A tall young man, looking about her age, smiled at Tara as he entered the elevator. Instinctively, Tara looked away, but not before she noticed that he was quite good looking. He stood in the middle of the elevator, just inches from her, holding a white plastic bucket in one hand as she stared deliberately at the panel of buttons on the wall. After the usual interminable delay, the elevator started to move down again.

"Excuse me," the man said in a pleasant voice, "you wouldn't know where the ice machine is, would you?"

"No, sorry," she said, smiling to herself.

After a moment, she gave him a quick glance, then turned back to look at the buttons, as she savored the pleasant tingle of butterflies in her stomach. She wondered if he had noticed her. She hoped so.

Chancing yet another quick glance, she was disappointed to find that he was fidgeting with the bucket handle. Apparently it had broken off in his hand, and he was trying unsuccessfully to reattach it. She grinned and looked away again.

When the elevator stopped, the doors opened and the man walked out into the lobby. Tara watched, as he looked right, then left, then turned back toward Tara, shrugged his shoulders and walked off toward the front desk.

The elevator doors closed, leaving her wondering what she was doing still inside. Deciding that she wasn't ready to be out and about anyway, she pushed the sixth floor button and headed back up.

Later, as she lay in bed, she thought of what she would tell the panel tomorrow. Would she tell them of the javelina? Would they laugh at her, would they believe her at all? What would happen to her credibility if she described the event? What would happen to her integrity if she didn't?

"You're telling us that a javelina disappeared right before your eyes?" they would say.

"Were you taking drugs at the time?" some would ask.

Everyone would laugh and point their fingers at the girl from Arizona. She would return home in shame and be the laughing stock of the university. There's no way around it, she decided. Integrity is not the issue. I don't have any proof. I'm just going to give them my notes on the ants and be done with it. At least they'll be vindicated at last.

She closed her eyes and tried to push all thoughts of tomorrow and the symposium away. They turned, instead, to her family. But as she drifted toward sleep, she could no longer control them and she dreamed.

She was in the desert where her world had turned upside down. Something was out there. She could feel it. She looked, but no matter how hard she tried, she couldn't see it. She was scared and desperate, but this time, something was different; she wasn't alone. Someone was with her . . . a man. His face was turned away from her, so she couldn't tell who it was.

"Hey!" she yelled.

Her heart beat hard within her chest, as the man turned, and looked into her eyes.

"Run! Run! This way!" he said, frantically waving his arms for her to follow him.

She recognized him. It was the man from the elevator today! The fear she felt was not of him, however, but of something dark and sinister, and it was trying to get to her. She ran toward the man, but no matter how hard she struggled, an unseen force held her back.

The man reached his hand toward her. "Take my hand . . . now!"

Tara tried to raise her arm, but the weight was incredible. Something was dragging her back. She felt herself slipping. The sand beneath her feet gave way, leaving no traction for her boots. Back she went, back toward the hidden terror behind her.

"No!" she screamed, and jerked herself awake.

Sitting up in the bed, she was covered with sweat, her heart racing as she tried to clear the nightmare from her mind. The clock on the bed stand read 11:30 PM.

After several moments, she lay back down and pulled the bedspread over her. Shivering, she hid there wondering why the man from the elevator had been part of her nightmare. Who was he? She looked back at the clock, 11:31. She closed her eyes, and hoping against hope that the God she had known as a little child might still hear her and care, she slipped quietly to her knees.

"Please God. Are you still there?" she prayed. "Can you hear me? Do you know what I'm feeling, what I need? I know I don't deserve this, but I need your help. I use to believe in you, but . . . so many things have happened lately, I don't know what to think anymore. I just wish I could talk to you like I used to so many years ago. I want to know what's going on here in our world. I want to help. We're in terrible trouble. I'm so afraid, and I don't know what to do. If you can hear me, please, I won't bother you anymore. Please grant me this one request. It's not for me, God, it's not for me . . ."

Detective Mullins stared briefly into the eyes of the killer, who paced in front of him.

"Oh he's gonna pay for this one," the man in black babbled. "Now I'm gonna have to go after him."

The killer gently touched the barrel of his gun to the picture of Dr. Ryan McKay on the Colorado driver's license he held in his hand. Turning his gaze from the license to Detective Mullins, he continued.

"I oughta make *you* pay, mister!"

"You're not getting paid to kill me!" Mullins retorted. "Besides, if I hadn't found that license in the street, you wouldn't have been here so quick."

He looked into the man's eyes again. They were cold, dead, almost reptilian. I can't stand to look at this nut for more then a second or two, he thought, averting his gaze once more.

"Makes no nevermind to me if I get paid or not. But you shoulda seen him leaving. That's what *you* get paid for!"

Mullins knew better than to get into it with this guy. He would lose, and lose big. The books didn't have a category for this psychopath.

"What now?" he asked.

"Well, you wait here. He may come back, but I have a feelin' he won't. If he does, take him and hold him for me. But don't hurt him. I gotta make him pay . . . for making me track him down. You kill him and I'll kill you. Understood?"

"Sure. What about you?"

"Well now, you said Ryan had a big meeting down in Dallas, right? Guess who's gonna be there waiting for him?" The killer brushed the side of Mullins' face with his pistol, and smiled. "Remember what I said now. Tell the big guy not to worry, and to have the money waiting, cause I'm gonna make this one pay all right, yesiree. Fifty dollars every day."

He turned and walked toward the door. When he got there, he spun around and flipped Ryan's driver's license at Mullins. Reacting instinctively, the policeman caught it. When he looked up, the killer was gone.

Mullins stared at the open door. He was cold, but this guy was beyond cold; he was frozen. It was becoming obvious why they asked *him* to hire this killer. No one else would get close to the guy. In fact, no one else even knew what he looked like. Even with the big bonus he was getting, though, he wasn't sure it was worth it. He'd have to sleep with one eye open until this job was done.

Now he had to call and explain how Ryan had somehow slipped through their grasp. That wouldn't be easy. There would be questions, hard questions. Then there was his partner. Somehow, Murphy was on to him. An accident would have to be arranged, or, he wondered, was one already being arranged?

Dialing the number on his cell phone, he was soon talking to "the big guy" as their hired gun had called him. Surprisingly, it went smoother than he expected. After explaining the killer's last words, he finished the call with a personal complaint.

"I'm telling you. This guy scares me. He may be good, but I expect you to keep him off my back when this is all over."

"You'll be taken care of, Mullins," the voice at the other end of the line reassured him. "Quit worrying."

"Well, I hope so. I've really stuck my neck out with this guy."

"I know. Now get off this phone and get McKay."

Hanging up the phone, Mullins wiped off Ryan's license and tossed it on the couch, then closed the door behind him and slipped out into the night. With his hands in his pockets, and his collar turned up to ward off Denver's night chill, he made an easy target for the nine-millimeter slug that abruptly introduced itself to his forehead, and sent the only living witness of the killer's face to the next life.

It was just after noon on Saturday when Ryan drove into Dallas. He had been on the road all night, not daring to stop. He wanted as much distance as possible between himself and Denver. With his mind in a furor, the night had passed quickly. What occupied him most was the possibility of a connection between particle intelligence, the happenings of last night, and the ecological calamities occurring around the world. There had to be one, he had decided. Everything Detective Murphy said pointed in that direction. That meant someone was way ahead of him in the research. Could they be using the results in a way that was damaging the ecology? He had to find out, and hundreds of top-level scientist and researchers were gathering in Dallas for an ecological symposium aimed at providing the answers. He couldn't wait for Monday. Surely it would all come together then.

The other subject that had occupied his mind was his life, more particularly his lack of any worthwhile life. The experiences of last night had him questioning his values, his priorities, his entire life plan. Did he even have a plan any more? Six years back from his mission and he still wasn't married.

He was determined now to leave Mol-Dyn, maybe go back to the mountains of Idaho for a while. He needed to refocus. He'd put off marriage for school, but he never meant for work to become his top priority. He could see now that it had, pushing his spiritual values aside and forcing life's true meaning to flutter out of his reach. He had been left with his head buried in a lab!

He also knew now that the pot at the end of the rainbow he was seeking didn't contain gold or notoriety. As he pondered where that rainbow might be, the alarm on his watch went off. He hadn't reset it since the day before. He looked at the time. It was 12:20 PM, over twenty-four hours since he last slept. Time to find a hotel room.

Mol-Dyn had a reservation for him at the Hilton, right across from the convention center where the symposium would take place. So he definitely would not go there. The Harrelson Inn looked pretty good, and they had a last-minute cancellation—something about one of the symposium speakers, a woman from Arizona, going into labor at the last moment. Heading directly to room 532, he collapsed onto the bed and slept the rest of the day and through the night.

When he finally got up on Saturday, one look in the mirror reminded him that the only thing he had with him was what he had on, and he went out to buy some clothes. Kind of tough to pack when people are trying to kill you, he thought.

That evening, he contacted the nearest ward and learned the time of their meetings then tried to absorb himself in a lame movie on the TV in his room. Sunday morning, he went to church. It was nice, as always, but never had he felt so distracted. After the services, he returned to his room and lay on the bed, feeling like his mind would burst. He was consumed with the thoughts that had occupied his drive from Denver. He no longer questioned the connection between his research, the attempt to kill him and the world's ecological problems. It was just a matter of getting his hands on the empirical data and seeing how it fit the theoretical possibilities. He could hardly wait for the symposium to start. But he had to. He had to try and calm down, to rest, to shut down his brain. Finally, he fell asleep.

He dreamed he was in a desert, but he'd never been in a desert like this before. It was thick with exotic cacti and desert plants of every description. There was a girl there, too, but he couldn't see her clearly. Something about the dream seemed important, but when he woke up a short time later, he couldn't remember what it was.

He decided to flip on the news. Immediately he wished he hadn't.

There was a story on CNN out of Denver about an unidentified police officer who was found dead just outside the condominium complex where he lived! Switching off the TV, he decided to get some ice.

There was no ice machine on his floor, so he headed for the elevator. He was mulling over the possibility that the dead officer was Detective Mullins when the elevator doors opened. For a moment, the sight they revealed made him forget everything he had seen on the news, his theories and everything else that happened in the past few days.

Standing next to the elevator panel just to his left was the most beautiful girl he had ever seen in his life. He smiled and entered, looking at the L button flashing next to her. He wanted to say Hi, but he felt like a schoolboy, tongue-tied and foolish.

"Excuse me. You wouldn't know where the ice machine is, would you?" he finally blurted.

She glanced at him briefly and said, "No, sorry," then turned away to stare at the panel of buttons on the wall.

Well, that made a great impression, he thought, canceling his fantasy of a late dinner—and the rest of his life—with the beauty who stood next to him. He couldn't cancel the butterflies in his stomach, however. How disappointing! He would probably never see her again.

Rather than look at her, he tried to look down, fumbling with the ice bucket in his hand until he broke the handle off. Now he felt like a total dork. Struggling awkwardly, he was still trying to reattach it when the doors opened to the lobby. The girl waited inside, so Ryan stepped out, chancing a quick look and a smile at her, before he turned left in search of ice.

Back in his room, he lay on his bed and thought of the girl in the elevator. Why couldn't he have found someone like that at church this morning? Shaking his head, he tried to push her out of his mind, but not an inch of her perfect form or that exquisite smile would leave his thoughts.

Eventually, he drifted into a troubled sleep, and dreamed he was back in the desert. This time he was with the girl from the elevator. Something was wrong. She was in trouble. Someone or something was trying to kill her. He shouted for her to take his hand. Just as he was reaching for her, he jerked awake. Lying there breathless and sweating, he looked at his watch. It was 11:30 PM.

Morning came and Tara felt new life. Surprisingly, she had slept well after her little prayer. She was determined to be alive and excited today. After a pleasant shower, she put on her nicest dress—wishing it were jeans and a baggy shirt instead—and called room service for some fruit, toast and juice. Then she went over her notes. She still wasn't sure just how to present Gene or Stacey's reports, but at last she settled on reading a brief description and conclusion from each.

Despite her misgivings of the day before, she decided to be bold today. These were crazy times, and crazy times required that she tell about the javelina. If she was more worried about ridicule than finding the truth, she didn't belong in science. The world deserved the truth and nothing but the truth, and she was going to give it to them, come what may. Besides, the place could probably use a little excitement!

She put her papers together and closed her briefcase, then stood and looked in the mirror. She tried a smile.

"Come on Tara, you can do this!" She managed something a little more pleasant and imagined herself in front of the symposium. "Ladies and gentlemen, I'm Tara Johnson, from beautiful downtown Tempe, and I've come to tell you that this desertification you're so worried about, is nothing! Let me tell you about a wild pig that vanished right before my eyes! There are scientifically identifiable spots out in the Superstition Wilderness where you can get high *without* drugs . . . Right!" She laughed. Grabbing her purse and her briefcase, she left the room.

Thirty minutes later, Tara walked into the Dallas Convention Center. Hundreds of people were milling around looking for seats. She waited in line, showed her identification, got her nametag, then went to find a seat. She had arrived early enough that she was able to sit fairly close to the front. The convention floor had been arranged with round tables, about six feet in diameter, covered with white tablecloths. On each table were six glasses and a pitcher filled with ice water. Seated around each table were six chairs.

Tara noticed that most of the people were arriving in groups of two to four. She was afraid that, because she was alone, someone might come and ask her to move, perhaps to a table reserved for single attendees. But she could see no one trying to bring such order out of the chaos of arriving dignitaries, so she took a seat.

The place was electric with anticipation. Something good was sure to come from this meeting. Tara imagined that many there shared her secret hope that their presentation would prove to be the key that opened the great puzzle. Tara watched the faces as they came in talking, smiling, hoping, aspiring, and as they passed her table or near it, she looked into their eyes.

The eyes told her volumes, and the most telling were the ones in which she saw fear. There weren't many, but there were some. Those eyes spoke of terrible foreboding, the kind Tara felt in her heart, a feeling that something was not right . . . and might never be right again. In some of those fearful eyes, however, she saw a glimmer of hope. She watched those eyes particularly, as long as possible.

Twenty minutes passed before her table filled up. Two guys from a college in upper New York sat to her right, followed by a couple from an independent research firm in Ohio. Then a man from some chemical research outfit in California sat on her immediate left. Each of them was friendly and expressed the feeling that this would be an enlightening conference.

The man from California was uncomfortably friendly. His name was Hank Smithson, and he apparently felt that, since Tara was alone, he would make it his personal duty to see that she was entertained. He went on and on about California, his lab, the time that he went to a conference in San Francisco, and how, if Tara ever wanted to come to California, she should look him up. He promised repeatedly that, if she did, he would show her a good time.

It was innocent enough, Tara decided, but still a pain. What she wanted was to take in the spirit of the conference, not listen to pick-up lines. But every time she smiled and turned to look at others, he would keep talking so she would have to turn back and say, "Uh huh . . . yeah. Oh, I see . . ." or something to that effect.

She looked at her watch; it was 9:00. She hoped the meeting would start on time. As if on cue, an elderly woman, dressed so well she looked like an eighty-year-old store mannequin, took the microphone.

"Ladies and Gentlemen, on behalf of the Bureau of Land Management, the Environmental Protection Agency and the U.S. Senate Subcommittee on World Ecological Affairs, we welcome you to this first ever, Macro-Ecological Symposium on World Events. We appreciate the dedicated, painstaking time and effort put forth by each of you and your colleagues in preparing the studies that will enlighten us regarding the very serious problems facing our world today."

At first, Tara was impressed. The panel of men and women on the stage representing each of the governmental agencies were introduced. They all seemed terribly important, but as she looked into the faces of the panel members only twenty feet away, she sensed apathy, indifference and just a little pompous arrogance. Something wasn't right with this group.

There were twelve of them sitting behind a narrow table that extended from one end of the stage to the other. On the front side of the table, facing the assembly, a nametag identified each panel member and the agency he or she represented. From left to right there were four senators, with one chair empty for the woman then speaking, three men and two women from the EPA, and a man from the Bureau of Land Management. Two men in three-piece suits sat at the far right. Their nametags read "Robert Kilpack, Secretary of the Navy," and "Brett Wimple, Private Sector."

Tara wondered why she was getting vibes from the panel that didn't jibe with the purpose of the meeting. She grew increasingly nervous as she waited to see what would happen.

"And so, as your name is called," the woman continued, "please come forward, step up to the microphone and take no more than six minutes for your presentation. We may take up to four minutes with questions. Please be precise with your answers and take no more than the time allotted. We have over a hundred presentations to hear in just three days."

The woman spent the next fifteen minutes detailing the purpose of the symposium and the mission of the groups on the stage in relation to the current chaotic state of world events. Tara felt the energy of the large gathering being sucked from its collective soul as the senator continued her monotone oration far too long. Tara looked around. There were indifferent and disinterested looks now on many of the faces.

Next to her, the man from California whispered, "Why doesn't she shut up and sit down, so we can get on with the presentations?" She smiled nervously.

For her part, Tara used the monotonous speech for a last minute mental dry run. She worried that she would not be able to convey the true meaning of a yearlong study in six minutes, and guessed that others would feel the same way.

Finally the woman concluded her remarks, called a name, and sat down. Thus began a most interesting day. People from every branch of the scientific community marched one by one to the stand, made a hasty presentation and postulated a variety of theories until their precious six minutes were up.

"Thank you," the woman would announce in a perfunctory monotone, "we have no questions at this time. You may be seated." She would then call the next name.

This went on all day, the panel sitting smugly, almost unmoving, in their raised seats, taking few, if any, notes and staring stone-faced at each speaker in a way that grated on the nerves of everyone present. No one said or did anything about it, however . . . until 3:45 PM.

A man from CalTech was hastily wrapping up what had been an almost incomprehensible summary of his research, when Tara heard a slight commotion behind and to her left. She turned to see the man she had seen in the elevator the day before making his way to the front. He saw Tara and gave her a wink. His approach to the stage took him right past her, which made her a little nervous in a pleasant way. When he reached her table, he stopped momentarily and whispered in her ear.

"It's against my nature to make a scene, but I could tell you're as tired of this as I am."

Before she could respond, the man walked up to the stage. He stepped to the microphone just as the senator was telling the frustrated scientist, "Thank you, we have no questions at this time . . ." When the tall interloper took the mike, she sputtered, "Excuse me sir. I think you are out of turn, I was about to call Cindy Holcum from Maryland. You certainly don't look like a Cindy to me."

"Why thank you," he replied calmly, "I don't feel much like a Cindy either." There were titters of laughter from the crowd. Tara smiled.

"Well," she continued in a snide tone of voice, "I'm afraid I'm going to have to ask you to take your seat then, until your name is called."

He responded politely but in an unwavering tone of voice, "Not at this time, ma'am. I've got something to say, and it needs to be said now. Please take your seat and relax, I'll be brief."

The convention applauded their agreement, with a few hoots of delight from a group way in the back. Finally, someone with the courage to speak up, Tara thought. Whoever he was, he had just won her admiration.

Before he could start, however, the man sitting at the end of the panel stood. "Dr. McKay, please; this is not the way we wish to proceed."

'Dr. McKay' turned and looked at the man. "I'm sorry; do I know you? Your voice is familiar and you seem to know me."

The man looked annoyed. He was in his mid-thirties, smartly dressed, but with that engineering computer-nerd look about him.

Finally he answered. "You need to be seated, you'll be called up tomorrow. Can you imagine what it would be like if everyone stood up out of turn? It would be chaos."

"Yes it would, and I apologize to my colleagues. As I said, this will only take a moment. Please be seated. I mean no harm."

He looked out at his peers, then back at the panel members. There were no objections from the audience, so he continued. "I have sat for almost six hours here today, listening with real intent, trying to get a feel for what's being presented in the six brief minutes allotted to each speaker. I'm bursting with questions, but this panel has done nothing but sit here, apparently deaf, mute and blind!" The audience went wild with applause at this observation. "My understanding was that we came here to learn. You can't learn without asking questions. Are you interested or not? I know I am."

The man at the end of the panel grimaced. Balling his hands into frustrated fists, he exited the stage to his left as Ryan continued.

"Ladies and gentlemen, I mean no disrespect to our distinguished panel, but I feel that we, as a group, need to communicate. So, I'd like to ask the panel that we be allowed the option of asking questions if they don't. I mean, let's use the four minutes! Most of you have worked long and hard for the last year toward this end. Let's make it count for something."

Everyone, including Tara, stood and applauded. That's what she came for, all right, answers, and if there were no questions, there would be no answers.

Ryan turned to his left and then right, eyeing the panel as they conferred amongst themselves while the audience continued to applaud and pound the tables. Finally, the woman stood and spoke into her microphone.

"The panel will deliberate on the subject and make a recommendation in the morning. We thank you for bringing this to our attention Dr. McKay."

"Very good, thank you . . . but before I leave, I'd like to pose a question that may seem a little off the wall." He looked over at Tara, who smiled her support. "I work in particle physics, and some of you may think this sounds crazy, but please listen carefully. If it were possible to manipulate matter, to . . . persuade sub-atomic particles to follow a different set of rules than those that govern them now, could there be a connection between such manipulation, your field of research, and the world events we are now experiencing? If so, I'd like very much to hear about it. Thank you."

He stepped down from the stage leaving the room in a confused hubbub but truly alive for the first time since the symposium began. The senator rose and picked up the microphone in front of her.

"Ladies and gentlemen, I'm sorry. We will stand adjourned until nine AM tomorrow morning . . . when we will announce the panel's decision on Dr. McKay's proposal, then resume with Ms. Holcum."

As the convention broke up, it was obvious Ryan's little interruption had caused quite a stir among the audience. Everyone at Tara's table was talking about it.

Hank Smithson turned to her. "What in the world was that guy talking about? If you try to control or manipulate matter, you get an explosion! Ask the Japanese," he laughed haughtily. "By the way, can I give you a lift anywhere? Where are you staying?"

"No thanks, I'm just down the street. Would you excuse me? I have to catch someone before they leave."

Without waiting for a response, she turned and walked briskly away, leaving the chemist from California in mid-sentence.

She hated to be rude, but she had to get away from the guy, and she really did have to try and catch someone. She needed to talk to Dr. McKay, the man from the elevator, the man from her dream the night before and the man whose question had shot through her like a bolt of lightning, leaving her mind reeling. She had to share with him some of the thoughts churning inside her or she would burst.

As she walked, she thought. She could see the javelina dying, then vanishing. She remembered the feelings that permeated her body as she approached the coyote's skeleton and then the boulder. As she

considered these events, she rehearsed McKay's words in her mind.
"Manipulate matter, . . . persuade sub-atomic particles to follow a
different set of rules." She had to reach him. He was the only one who
might be able to explain what happened that day in the desert.

Making her way out of the meeting center and into the check-in
area, she looked everywhere. He was nowhere to be found. The place
was crammed with people trying to get out, and just outside was the
media, with their vans, mikes, cameras and personnel. Tara had
forgotten that they were banned from the symposium, leaving them to
cover the event from the outside.

The reporters reminded Tara of a pack of wolves as they swarmed
around the unsuspecting rabbits fresh from the proceedings. They
would tear at their prey with questions, while the poor creatures tried
desperately to get away.

One who didn't run, she noticed, was Hank Smithson. He was
bending one "wolf's" ear right off with his version of the events. She
wondered how he beat her to the front. Then she noticed that he was
sweating heavily, his eyes flitting from one female attendee to another.
The sight made Tara smile as she turned, still unnoticed by the
determined Mr. Smithson, and walked away in search of Dr. McKay.

For twenty minutes, Tara circled the Dallas Convention Center.
The day was warm, but a cooler breeze had begun to stir, and it felt
good. After all the time she spent in the desert, this was like paradise.
She wanted to relax and take it in for a while, but she felt driven to find
him.

At 5:30 PM, she arrived back at the hotel, and walked directly to the
young girl at the check-in counter.

"I'm sorry, but could you give me the room number for Dr.
McKay?"

The girl gave Tara a knowing glance and said, "Sure honey."
Turning to her computer console, she typed in his name. A moment
later she turned back to Tara. "I'm sorry, but we have no one by that
name listed. Could you possibly have the wrong name?"

"I don't think so. I know he's here, maybe you've seen him, tall,
very good looking, wavy brownish blonde hair. He was wearing a light
blue Levi shirt with a tie?"

"Oh, you mean Mr. Shelton. Yeah, he's a hottie. Got in day before
yesterday. Here he is, room 532: Kent Shelton. In fact, he just went up."

"Thank you." Tara turned toward the elevators as the girl grabbed her arm and leaned closer to her.

"Don't tell anyone I gave you his room number. Okay?" she whispered.

Tara nodded her head, and left for the elevators as the girl called to her, "Good Luck!" Kids have such one-track minds these days, she thought. The elevator doors opened, she stepped in, and hit the five button.

Once on the fifth floor, Tara quickly found room 532. Outside the door, she caught herself straightening her hair and primping before she knocked. She felt foolish. What if someone was watching? Glancing around quickly, she gave the door four quick knocks.

Almost immediately it opened and there he was, bigger than life. He looked at her and smiled. Tara could feel the butterflies rising in her stomach again.

He said nothing for a moment, a look of surprise on his face, then stumbled over a greeting. "Hello, ah, nice to see you again."

She smiled. "Dr. McKay, I mean Mr. Shelton . . . whatever your name is, I'm Tara Johnson from ASU. I need to talk to you about what you said today."

"Oh, yes. Great, please come in. Where are my manners?" He opened the door all the way and stepped back allowing Tara to enter. "Would you like something to drink?"

"Uh, sure."

"I hope you like water, because that's all I have."

She laughed. "Yes, water's fine."

He took two cups and tore off the plastic wrappers, then filled them with water from a pitcher.

"At least I have ice! Finally found the machine last night . . . on the fourth floor." He handed Tara the cup. "Please sit down." He motioned toward the chairs over by the window, and they each took one.

Tara felt clumsy and awkward, and it must have shown on her face.

"My name is Ryan, Ryan McKay, and I'm pleased to make your acquaintance, Tara. Relax, please; you look a little nervous. I promise I won't bite." His smile soothed her.

"I'm glad to hear that. I'm afraid I've lived a rather sheltered existence by today's standards. I don't normally go into strange men's hotel rooms!"

"You don't know how glad I am to hear that." Ryan's smile made Tara feel more comfortable about being there, but the obvious interest in his eyes made her heart race. "Would you rather we went down to the lobby?" he asked.

"No. I'll feel more comfortable discussing this with you in private. I'm just a little flustered." You can do this, girl! she told herself. No matter how attractive he is.

"Okay, then." He relaxed in his chair. "Now, just what was it that made you look me up?"

"You mentioned something about . . . manipulating matter."

"Yes." Ryan leaned forward.

"Well, something happened out in the desert in Arizona that I don't know if I can share tomorrow when I give my presentation. But I just can't shake the feeling that it may have something to do with matter manipulation. I really can't think of any other explanation for it."

Ryan's eyes lit up. "Please, tell me what happened?"

"Well, it may be a stretch. And the more I think about it, the more it seems like a dream."

"I love a good stretch," said Ryan. He stared intently at Tara, making her blush. "I'm sorry Tara, but you have the most fabulous brown eyes I've ever seen. I bet you get that a lot, huh?"

She blushed and smiled. "Not really, but as I was saying . . ."

"I'm sorry; *mea culpa*. You were going to tell me what happened in the desert."

Tara tried again to compose herself. For the first time in years she was actually pleased that a man found her attractive. If she could just stop blushing long enough to continue. She wriggled in her chair, trying to get comfortable and calm herself.

"I really don't like talking too much about it. Every time I do, I get these terrible feelings, and it takes a lot of effort to get rid of them. It's not pleasant. But I'll tell you under one condition," she said.

"And what's that?"

"That you won't laugh, or accuse me of being on drugs."

"That's two conditions," Ryan teased.

"Oh. Right."

"Hey, I'm not good at arithmetic either, but I promise not to laugh, and I definitely won't accuse such a wonderful person of being on drugs."

Did he just call me wonderful? Tara thought. Pleased but still embarrassed, she proceeded to recount everything that took place in the Superstition Mountains, from her study of the ants and her feelings of being watched, to the two invisible zones where strange feelings occurred in her body as she approached them. She finished with an account of the coyote and finally, the javelina. Ryan never interrupted her, but continued to look straight into her eyes, his own eyes widening at each new disclosure.

"Well?" she asked when she had finished nearly an hour later.

"Well, well!" Ryan turned from her and looked thoughtfully out the window.

"Come on! Am I crazy?" she asked after a moment.

"Yes, yes, it's entirely possible," Ryan said, still gazing out the window.

"What? You think I'm crazy?" Tara winced.

"Huh? Oh, no, no. I'm sorry. What you experienced . . . it's entirely possible that there's a connection with matter control. It fits some of my data. It's just on a scale I never imagined. Weird stuff! Out in the middle of the desert, you say?"

"Yes."

"Hmm." Ryan began to pace back and forth between the table and the window.

Tara grew impatient. "Well, what do you think?"

"I'm sorry Tara, I was just doing a little mental triage. I have so many thoughts to assimilate. The math is very complicated. It's a little tricky doing it in your head. But I feel confident you're on the right track. Any idea how it's being done?" He stopped pacing and stood in front of the small window, looking out again, hands clasped behind his back.

"No . . . You're doing the math in your head?"

"Uh, yes. Some of it, anyway. Sorry if it upsets you."

"No, no. It doesn't upset me. I was just a little surprised."

"Well, I could sit here and speculate till the cows come home. What I need to do is go there."

"To *my* desert? When?"

"Now, of course. Tonight!" Ryan strode to the table and took Tara by the hand, looking deep into her eyes. She could feel him pleading with her. "Can you take me there?"

"But what about our presentations tomorrow?"

"Tara, do you honestly believe we would be taken seriously? There's something not right about that so-called symposium." His eyes told her he was sincere.

"No, we wouldn't." She withdrew her hand from his and turned toward the door, sighed and turned back again. "I can't put my finger on it, but that whole panel . . . it's like they're only there to go through the motions."

"Exactly. So let's get out of here and go where we can make a difference. Let's go get some answers!" He waited for a response.

Tara knew he was right. This great symposium of ecological events was nothing but a ruse. She felt betrayed, but she wasn't sure who to blame. Something told her that this man could help her get some real answers, though the boldness of his proposal unnerved her. She turned to him. His face looked so kind, filled with life, and in his eyes she saw someone she could trust.

"Okay, let's do it," she said.

"Great, I'm already packed. I was leaving for Idaho anyway. Now, thanks to you, I have a better direction. I'll give you a head start to get your things. How long do you need?"

She headed for the door, "Give me ten minutes. I'll meet you in the lobby."

"Okay."

As she opened the door, she turned back to him. "Thanks!"

"For what?"

"For not laughing at the girl from Arizona." She smiled. Then, on impulse, she stepped forward and kissed his cheek, turned and walked down the hall.

On the way to the elevator, she paused, thinking back to her prayer the night before. Could this be her answer? Her heart wanted to believe it was, but her mind wouldn't allow it. No, not now . . . not yet.

Chapter 4
DESERT

For several minutes Ryan sat in his hotel room glowing as he tried to slow the whirl of his thoughts and the beating of his heart. The ecology, he told himself, focus on the ecology. Could there be a connection between what Tara experienced in the desert and his ideas of matter control? If so, whoever was responsible was decades ahead of him. He could hardly comprehend the magnitude of the phenomenon Tara had described. If matter control was behind it, what would he do? Would they be able to find out who was responsible? What if it was a natural phenomenon? What would that mean for the world's ecology? The possibilities were staggering.

Not staggering enough, however, to keep his thoughts from returning to Tara herself. He could hardly believe his good fortune. When he opened the door to find her there, he must have sounded like a fool. Who could deny the existence of God with women like that in the world? he enthused. Did he actually call her "wonderful"? And what was all that about her eyes? What an idiot he was!

He had to get to know this girl from Arizona. He couldn't blow this opportunity. She was definitely the kind of person found only in pots at the ends of the kind of rainbows he was searching for. Thank-ing the Lord one more time, he drew a deep breath and headed out.

With his bag slung over his shoulder, he approached the elevator. A lone man was waiting there for the doors to open.

"Howdy!" he said to Ryan. "Comin', or goin'?"

"Going, I guess. And you?"

"Oh, I'll be goin' sooner or later too! Yesiree; can't stay forever. They make you pay if you do . . . everyday."

Ryan just nodded. He wasn't comfortable with the way the man looked at him, so he averted his gaze. But he could still feel the man's eyes boring holes into his back.

The elevator doors opened and they both stepped inside. The doors closed. Ryan pushed the L button, and looked at the man as if to ask which floor he wanted. The man smiled and shook his head. The elevator began to move downward. Again Ryan could feel the man looking at him from behind and to his left.

As the elevator slowed to a stop, he turned toward the man again. This time his hand was in his coat, as if to remove something. Before he could, however, the doors opened and three people got on, laughing and smiling, followed by Tara. She had a bag over one shoulder and was carrying another. She squeezed through the others and stood by Ryan.

Looking up at him from her height of, Ryan estimated five feet seven or eight inches, she whispered, "I feel really weird doing this. I just took an elevator to the wrong floor! I must be losing it."

"I know the feeling," he said, looking over at the man in the corner. His hand was now removed from his coat, and he was smiling. Finally, the doors opened, and they walked out.

Grabbing her elbow with his free hand, Ryan whispered, "Let's get out of here . . . fast."

He escorted her through the lobby toward the front entrance. As they passed the hotel desk, Tara hesitated.

"Don't you want to check out?"

"No time!"

"Huh? What's the big hurry?"

Ryan looked behind them. He didn't see the man now, but had the feeling he should get out of the hotel as quickly as possible.

"I'm sorry. I'll explain later," he said, leading her out of the lobby to the front. The parking garage was located across the street. Catching an opening in traffic, they ran across, barely missing a couple on bikes.

"I didn't even ask if you had a car," he said to her.

"I don't. I flew in. Surely you don't intend to drive to Arizona?"

"The thought did occur to me."

"Well, I have two open plane tickets."

"Better," he said. "I'll leave my car at the airport."

He took one of her bags and began jogging toward his car. She followed, easily keeping pace with him. They reached the Explorer and he hit the button on his key ring. The chirp of the keyless entry sounded as the door locks popped up. Throwing their bags in, he jumped in with Tara right behind and started up the engine.

They didn't hear the gunshot, but the window on Ryan's side exploded with a pop. Tara screamed. Ryan reached over and pushed her down, as he stepped on the accelerator. There was another pop. This time it was the back glass as Ryan raced to put more distance between them and the shooter.

Good thing for window film, he thought. Whoever was doing the shooting couldn't see through it in the darkness of the garage, and it kept the glass in one piece, despite being shattered by bullets.

The Explorer bounced into the street to the blare of angry horns.

"Are you all right?" Ryan shouted.

Tara didn't respond.

"Tara!"

Slowly, Tara rose and spoke. "What in heaven's name is going on?"

"Thank goodness you're all right! I'm so sorry."

"Yeah, me too!" She paused momentarily. "Uh, I think this would be a good time for an explanation."

"Wait till we get to the airport. Okay? I promise, on the plane."

"Am I going to live that long?"

"Yes, if I can just get away from this guy."

No words were spoken until they reached the airport. Ryan was totally absorbed in a race through the city streets. Though it did not appear that he was being followed, his eyes were focused on the rear-view mirror most of the way. Tara sat stiffly, her right hand clenching the handle above the passenger door.

"Which airline?" Ryan asked as they approached the airport.

"America West, there!" She pointed to the right. Ryan nearly missed the turnoff, squealing his tires and almost tipping the Explorer onto to two wheels as he negotiated the turn.

Parking in the loading area, he jumped out and grabbed their bags.

"Let's go!" he urged.

"What about your car?"

"Don't worry. They'll tow it, and that way I'll know just where to find it when I get back. Probably cheaper than airport parking anyway." He smiled, hoping a little humor would calm her.

When they got to the gate, they still had half an hour to wait for the next flight. This gave Ryan enough time to tell Tara what had happened in Denver, the shootings, the fire, Detective Murphy, the red Camero, even Detective Mullins standing on the corner. "What I didn't know," he concluded, "was that I'd be followed to Dallas. I'm sorry. This caught me completely off guard. I swear to you. If I had known, I would never have involved you. Believe me, you're far too important to me . . . I mean, to jeopardize your safety!"

Tara gave him a puzzled look, but she seemed to relax.

They sat in the terminal impatiently waiting, boarding passes in hand, watching and hoping they would not see the shooter. Occasionally they stared awkwardly at each other.

"I know what you're thinking, Tara," Ryan said at last.

"You do?"

"Yeah. You're questioning your sanity, and mine, and wondering if you're doing the right thing."

"For starters, yeah. I'm also wondering why we both feel so strongly about this. Talk about wild impulse!"

"Yeah," he nodded. "That's about where I am, too."

"But I think I have an idea about it."

"What's that?"

"The will to know. I've always felt compelled to get answers. I hate loose ends . . . irrationality. You must have that trait too. Am I right?"

"Very good." Ryan smiled. "And yes, you're right."

Ryan wondered if it was divine providence that had thrust the two of them, complete strangers, together under circumstances that compelled them to trust each other like this. He hoped so.

The airport was not as crowded as usual. Only ten other people were waiting for the plane to Phoenix, two couples and a family of six. It was 8:40 PM when they finally started to board.

"Ladies and gentlemen, we will now begin boarding flight 1246 to Phoenix. All passengers may board now. Please look around you and make sure you haven't left anything in the terminal, and have an enjoyable flight."

Finally! Ryan thought. He stood, took his and one of Tara's bags in one hand, and said, "We're off."

"Yeah," Tara responded, "but to where?"

"Why, to the great state of Arizona, my friend . . . and some answers, I hope." Smiling, he was relieved when she smiled back.

Tentatively, he took her hand, and was pleased when she returned his firm grip as he escorted her down the ramp.

———❈———

My friend? Tara liked the sound of those words. Ryan was certainly an interesting guy, to say the least. She could never shake the feeling of butterflies in her stomach when she was near him, and when he took her hand in his, she could feel them in her throat. Could he rekindle the passion that had lain dormant in her heart since Devin died? It seemed all too likely. So why was she resisting? Maybe because she knew the Beast of life would take him from her the instant she let herself care.

When they were dodging bullets in the parking garage, she was furious with him. Why hadn't he told her about his past before she agreed to go with him? But had she been entirely honest with him? She never told him that people close to her usually died, or how scared she was that it might happen to him. Had she misled him into believing they could waltz right out into the desert and discover buried treasures of truth? Would they find anything there . . . but death? Only time would tell, a very short time, she thought as she shuddered with fear.

———❈———

After they reached cruising altitude, Ryan asked. "When was the last time you slept well?"

"If I told you that it had been weeks, would you believe me?"

"Based on what you've told me about your studies in the desert, yeah, I'd believe you." He looked into her eyes and saw a gleam of hope struggling in a pool of fear. "Close those big browns now, and sleep. I'll watch over you and see that no wild javelinas try to get you."

"If they do, throw these." She handed him a bag of airline peanuts.

"No chance, these are mine," he said. "I'm famished." He took the peanuts and put them in his front pocket, then stood up and opened the overhead compartment. Taking out a small white pillow, he handed it to Tara, then sat back down.

"Thank you," she said.

"Now get some rest! Doctor's orders."

She closed her eyes, and soon appeared to be in peaceful sleep.

Ryan asked a flight attendant for a blanket, which he used to cover her. She was now out completely. He looked at her, and the Spirit whispered a confirmation of his feelings. This girl was indeed a treasure, one to be guarded and preserved. Though he hardly knew her, he knew he would give his life, if needed, to see that she was safe.

But what was it that threatened her? He gazed past her, out the window into the black abyss. Someone down there had tried to kill him, someone tangible, a known and identifiable threat. Tara's danger seemed different; it was unknown, a some*thing* not a some*one*.

The lights on the plane were dim. Most of the passengers either slept or whispered quietly as Ryan stared restlessly out into the night. Dallas was long gone now. An occasional light or group of lights passed slowly below them. Must be homes, he thought. People winding down their days, getting ready for bed, safe from the monsters of life, seen and unseen. He wished for such a life, but some very real monsters waited malevolently for him, and possibly for Tara as well.

He looked at his watch, then laid his head back and tried to close his eyes. Beside him, Tara stirred, her face troubled now. Still asleep, she moved her head to Ryan's shoulder and relaxed. A warm glow washed through him, and he gazed tenderly at her peaceful face. Again he closed his eyes. In his mind, he pictured a desert . . . and Tara.

"Please God," he whispered, "help me find the answers. Help me find out what has Tara so frightened."

In his heart, he felt God would answer his prayer, but the assurance was without feelings of comfort, so it only served to feed his anxiety. He drew another deep breath and sighed as he considered the future, his heart filled with foreboding.

The killer stood in the parking garage, anger boiling in his soul. How could he have missed! Something was wrong with this hit. Maybe somebody upstairs was watching over this Ryan McKay character. It had to be! How else could he have missed him twice? Well, it wouldn't help in the end. He would get him, sure enough, and make him pay.

He would have to go back in the hotel, though, and get the name of the girl. He could get it. He had ways of making people talk. Then he would track them down like the dogs they were. He would track them down and make them pay!

Two misses as a child would have cost him dearly. His mamma would have been livid. She would have been foaming at the mouth.

"Get over here, little mister!" she would say. "And wipe that silly grin off your face! How could you have missed twice, you little twerp?" Whomp! Right on the head with a cake pan. "I think I'll lock you up in the shed so the monsters from the woods can try to get you!" Whomp! "Take that, you little creature! I'll make you pay dearly for this one, buddy, fifty dollars every day!" Whomp!

In a way, he was glad he missed. It had taken him years to realize that Mamma couldn't reach him from her grave in the woods. Surely she was squirming in her box right now. But what if she got out? Oh, she would get him then, yesiree, and make the little mister pay for all his indiscretions. That she would!

But he was driven now by something more evil than his mamma, or his fear of her. This evil had dwelt in his heart for so long it had taken up permanent residence. It was pure sociopathic evil. It drove him now like General Patton would a tank. And he liked it.

Yes, he was a tank. He wasn't even the driver! Blame someone else. He was just the vehicle of mass destruction, not the general. But now the tank was getting mad, and anyone that got in its way would be sorry.

The plane touched down at 9:05 PM Phoenix time. During the summer, a two-hour difference separated the time zones. Tara jerked awake, and rubbed the sleep from her eyes. For a moment, she couldn't remember where she was. She had slept only two hours, but it felt like a week. When she saw Ryan's tender smile, it all came back.

"Have a nice sleep?" he asked.

"Yes, wonderful." She smiled back, then added self-consciously. "But I must look like I crawled out from under a rock." She rubbed the sleep from her eyes.

"Actually, you look fabulous." His tender gaze felt like a caress. He continued, "Looks like we made it in one piece. Welcome home!"

"Yeah, home." She looked out the window. It was dark. If it were only daylight, she thought, she might be able to muster a little good cheer. Instead, all she could do was smile and say, "Welcome to my neighborhood." She sighed as they headed out of the plane and up the jet ramp. "Ever been in the desert?"

He shook his head. "Not really. I've seen it from a car, in Nevada and California."

"Well, I hope you brought a sweater; could be snowing out there."

"Really? Think I'll have time to build an igloo?" He looked at her like a little boy asking for candy.

"We're going to have to rustle us up a walrus for dinner first. Can you handle a harpoon?"

They both laughed, from which Tara drew strength, strength she knew they would need in a very short time.

In the taxi on the way to Tara's home, Ryan quizzed her about the desert. What was it like? Would a boy from Idaho survive the relentless sun if he found himself in the middle of it? She explained some basic survival skills: taking plenty of water, knowing where you are at all times, staying out of the sun during the hottest part of the day, and others.

At 9:45, the taxi turned into *Sonora Vista*, Tara's neighborhood. Her street was lined with well-manicured lawns and stuccoed two-story homes. Ryan commented on the tiled roofs. Queen palms and other landscaping outlined deep green carpets of grass as the occasional active sprinkler system sputtered and sprayed through the neighborhood.

The taxi pulled up to the curb in front of Tara's home. As they got out, Ryan handed the driver a twenty-dollar bill.

"Keep the change," he said.

"Yeah right buddy, the fare is $33.50."

"Oh, sorry, I'll get some from the house," Tara offered. The man was covered in tattoos, must have weighed close to three hundred pounds and looked like he ate physicists for breakfast.

"No, I'll get it." Ryan fumbled in his wallet. "Sorry," he said, handing the man another twenty. The cab sped off into the night, as Ryan and Tara laughed their way to the front porch.

Wiping the sweat from his forehead, Ryan said, "Man, it's almost ten o'clock and it must be a hundred degrees!"

"You'd be surprised what a person can get used to."

"Yeah, I guess."

Suddenly he turned back and tried to hail the taxi, but it was long gone. When he turned back, he said, "Blast, missed him. I forget, I'll be staying at a motel tonight."

She grabbed his arm. "I have a car; I'll take you. But let's talk first."

Once inside, she motioned Ryan into the living room. The house was well decorated in a country style. Vaulted ceilings and open spaces made it look bigger than it really was. Live plants had been used extensively. In the corners there were small trees in large pots, and in the windowsills were plants of every kind. Walking over to a large and comfortable sofa, Ryan plopped down and drew a deep breath.

"I love the plants, Tara!"

"I've always had a green thumb," she said, holding up her thumb and wiggling it. Smiling, she sat down on the chair across from him, kicked off her shoes, and pulled her feet up under her. "Don't worry about waking anyone. They're all up at the cabin. Dad had the week off, so they headed for the high country."

"Really? You have high country around here?"

"Oh yeah. The cabin sits at about seventy five hundred feet, nestled in the gorgeous pines on the Mogollon Rim, and it's only about two hours north."

"Well I'll be. I'd love to see it someday. Looks like you've got it all here in Arizona."

"Yeah, including the weirdest thing of all!" she said, referring to her experience in the desert. "But hey, before any of the strange stuff, how about something to drink?"

"Ice water's fine."

"Two ice waters, coming up."

When Tara returned, she found Ryan looking through her family photo album. She spent the next thirty minutes showing him all the family members in various poses, as well as two family vacations: one to California, the other to Mexico. When they were finished, she closed the albums and sat up.

"Okay, I want you to tell me everything about this matter manipulation stuff. I need to know how it might relate to what I saw in the desert."

"I'll tell you under two conditions." he said

"And what are those?"

"That you won't laugh, and that you won't think I'm on drugs. Also, that you tell me what that happened in the desert once again."

"That's three conditions." she reminded him.

"That's right. I guess neither of us can count. Deal?"

"Deal."

The next hour was spent rehashing Tara's experiences, followed by a nearly equal period in which Ryan went over some of his experiments on the disorientation of sub-atomic particles. Tara lapped up the details, answering and asking questions until she was satisfied with her level of understanding. In the end, they agreed to withhold any more theorizing until they returned from the desert tomorrow.

"Well Tara, I'd better get going if we're gonna get an early start."

"You could just stay here on the couch. It's pretty comfy."

"Actually, that wouldn't be wise," he said uncomfortably.

"What do you mean?"

"Well, think about it. You're alone here, but you have neighbors. What if they saw me? Knowing your folks are out of town, they're liable to jump to all kinds of conclusions. I wouldn't want to tarnish your reputation, just because I'm sleepy."

Tara looked into his eyes. He was dead serious! Suddenly, this guy wasn't just six foot three. In her eyes, he was ten feet tall. She smiled appreciatively.

"You're a pretty special guy, Ryan McKay. Not many men would be concerned about a girl's image. I have to say, you've won my respect."

Reaching over to the table, she grabbed her keys and tossed them to him. "Here. Take my Jeep. It's out on the street. If you just head out the way it's facing, you turn right at the stop sign. Go one mile and you'll see a small motel on the left. It always has vacancies."

"Fair enough. What time should I meet you back here?"

She looked at her watch. "Well, let's see. How about seven? The place we're going is only a thirty-minute drive from here. That should give us an early enough start."

He took his bag and slung it over his shoulder. "Until seven, then."

"Until seven."

She walked him to the door, and paused. She wanted very much to kiss him, but resisted the impulse. Then, to her surprise, he leaned over and kissed her gently, looking momentarily into her eyes. With a brief "good night," he turned and left as she closed the door behind him.

That night as she lay in bed, she dreamed. But this time the dream was not a nightmare. It was the dream of a young woman falling in love.

Seven o'clock came early for Ryan, but soon he was back at the Johnsons'. Tara laughed when she opened the door and saw he was wearing a thick, long-sleeved Levi shirt and loafers.

"Yeah I know, I'm not really dressed for desert travel," he said, "Everything I have is long-sleeved!"

"Not to worry. My brother has plenty of stuff. You better come in. That just won't do. You'll be suffering from heat exhaustion by noon!"

Turning, she walked into the back of the house while Ryan waited in the living room.

"Got anything to eat?" he called to her.

"Yeah, I packed a few things," she yelled from the next room.

In a minute Tara came out with a few T-shirts. "Take your pick; they're all extra large. Lucky you had some jeans. I don't think my brother's would fit. You'd look like you were waiting for a flood!"

"Yeah, this one should do." He picked a white, purple and orange Phoenix Suns shirt with the Suns Gorilla on it. "Ever since I was a kid, I've rooted for the Suns. Hope your brother won't mind."

"He's got so many he'll never even know. Here's a pair of my dad's tennis shoes. I hope they fit. They're size twelve."

"Perfect!" he said. "You drive, I'll dress."

They hit I-60 and headed toward Apache Junction. As she drove, Ryan removed his long-sleeved shirt and started to put on the T-shirt.

"I suggest you take off that undershirt," Tara offered. "It'll be awfully hot, even with just a T-shirt."

Ryan looked down at the "garments" he'd worn religiously since he first went through the Idaho Falls Temple before his mission. How did he explain them to Tara?

"Oh, uh, well. I'm a Mormon, see, and these are . . . special undergarments. We wear them *all* the time."

"I've met plenty of Mormons before. You can hardly grow up here without knowing some, but I never heard they wore 'special undergarments.'"

"Well, it's not something we talk about much."

"What are they for?"

He paused to think how he could explain. "Just to remind us of certain promises we make to God."

"Oh," she said, her curiosity obviously peaked. "Like what kind of promises?"

He smiled, "Well, one of them is that we won't tarnish the reputations of young ladies from Arizona by staying overnight at their homes when their parents are away."

"So that's it!" she responded with a smile. "I thought there was something special about you, Dr. McKay. Now I know it's just your underwear!"

They both laughed.

Leaving the freeway at Superstition Trail, she drove to Dutchman's Trailhead, where she turned the Jeep onto the trail. To Ryan, it was not much of a road, designed primarily as a hiking trail, only six to eight feet wide and filled with bumps, rocks and brush.

Ryan looked to his right. "That's some mountain; very unique."

"Yeah, that's the famous Superstition Mountain. Legend has it that back in the 1800's, Jacob Waltzer, a Dutchman, had a gold mine up there somewhere. He died leaving only some vague clues as to its whereabouts. A lot of people have died over the years trying to find it, some of them under very mysterious circumstances. They call it the Lost Dutchman's Gold Mine. Big stuff around here."

"It's beautiful out here, Tara. Oh! Look at that cactus! That's a saguaro isn't it?"

"Whoa, where'd you learn about cacti? I'm impressed."

"Well, actually, I can read. Did I mention that? And I'll read just about anything, including *Cacti of the Southwest* . . . if it's in a dentist's office. And believe me, it was a great read," he said rolling his eyes.

"I'll bet," said Tara steering the Jeep gingerly along the path. "Those winters up in Idaho must be real lonely."

"You ain't just a-kiddin'."

They drove Dutchman's Trail for about six miles when Tara turned to the right, onto a smaller version of the path they'd been following.

"Uh, you seem to know where you're going, but where'd the road go?" Ryan asked. He bounced up and down as the Jeep maneuvered around rocks and cacti and into and out of ditches and ravines, at one point almost falling out the side door.

"Not far now, then we walk."

"Actually this is kind of fun!" he said. "Do you ever just go four wheeling?"

"Sometimes, but not here. I like to keep things as natural as possible up here. You know, the way Mother Nature made them. I hate seeing people out here tearing things up. Especially now with so many species of plants and animals being lost."

"Right." he said. "We've sure messed things up, haven't we?"

"Yeah, but if we can just get a few answers here, maybe there's hope. I'm not sure that what we've been experiencing is entirely the result of man's negligence . . . And presto, we're here!"

She parked the jeep in the middle of nowhere and reached over to the glove box. Popping it open, she pulled out a nine-millimeter pistol. Ryan's eyes opened wide.

"Do you think we're going to need that?"

"Don't know, but it sure makes me feel better. Here, you carry it."

She handed the gun to Ryan. He checked to make sure the safety was on, then tucked it into his jeans. Tara grabbed the pack from the back seat, slung it over her shoulder and shut the Jeep door.

"This is it! Now just follow the yellow brick road. It shouldn't be too hard. I made it!"

The path was clearly worn, as it meandered off into the desert, and up and over a small rise.

"You must have put a lot of miles on this path, it's very impressive. How are your feet?"

"Perfect! You've just got to have the right boots. Think you can keep up?"

"Oh, I think I can manage," he said with a snicker.

They walked up the trail to the rise, and down to the riverbed. In five minutes they were at the spot where the coyote met his demise. Tara stopped and put her arm out to Ryan.

"This is it, big guy." She pointed to a spot in the middle of the riverbed about twenty yards ahead. "See that spot there in the middle where the sand makes a small dip?"

He nodded his head in the affirmative.

"All right, that's where I first noticed the coyote. Of course it's gone now, but so is a lot of the sand. That's strange; it's like the ground there has sunk in a bit."

Ryan started to move forward.

"Wait!" Tara blurted out. "Move very slowly. And don't be afraid to stop and come back. You won't be able to make it all the way to the dip."

Ryan stepped forward, slowly, while Tara watched. "You go ahead," she said. "Personally, I've had enough. I just want to see what you make of it."

The sun shone over his shoulder, and the crunch of the sand was the only sound he heard. He stepped forward about ten feet, when suddenly a wave of fear struck deep into his soul. He stopped and looked around quickly.

Tara called to him. "I know what you're feeling. Kinda' scary, isn't it?"

"Yes!" he responded, barely able to contain his emotions.

"You've got the chills, and it feels like someone's watching you, right?"

"You got it. What do I do now?"

"Move forward a little. There's a surprise for you just a couple of feet ahead."

Slowly he inched forward. Then he stopped and closed his eyes as feelings of unbridled euphoria washed over him.

Tara called out, "Now you feel a magnificent tingling feeling all over your body, and you want to stay forever, right there, right?"

"It's incredible. What in heaven is this?"

"I don't know, but if you move ahead about a foot more, I think you'll agree it's not from Heaven."

He did, and was immediately seized upon by total fear and the need to vomit. It was enough to send him running back to where Tara stood. There he sat down in the middle of the riverbed and pondered with her what he had experienced.

Tara spoke first. "It's the nausea that gets you. Right? Nausea's no fun."

"Tara, this is absolutely incredible! You say this is the same regardless of what direction you approach?"

"Yes, it's an invisible circle, like one of those force fields on Star Trek, and it seems to be expanding."

Ryan was obviously lost in thought. He sat in the morning sun with his head in his hands, eyes fixed on the spot that really wasn't a spot at all, just a dip in the sand.

"Ryan? Ryan? Yoo-hoo, anyone home?" Tara waved her hand in

front of his face.

Finally, he spoke. "The other place is bigger than this?"

"Oh yeah. It's so weird. I wouldn't be surprised if the Lost Dutchman's Gold Mine is in there somewhere." She was trying to lighten the mood.

"Lots of gold?" said Ryan eagerly.

"Ohhhh yeah. Lots!" Tara teased.

"Enough to buy me some cool hiking boots, like the ones you've got?"

"Enough for two pair! Maybe."

"Oh, then take me! Please." He stood up.

"This way."

She took the lead as they walked the remaining eighth of a mile to the anthill.

"Do NOT step on these ants!" she ordered as they neared it. "I know most of them personally."

He smiled and stepped carefully around the colony, then continued to follow her toward another small rise.

"Come on, I'll race you."

She began running, with Ryan close behind. The race brought her up the rise ahead of him. But when she got to the top, she screamed.

Where the boulder had been, there was a hole with no bottom in sight. The ground around it sloped downward in a funnel shape that reached nearly to the top of the rise. Tara's momentum had carried her over the top, and in her effort to stop, her feet slipped out from under her. She landed flat on her back, and started to slide in the sand toward an abyss that looked like the mouth of Hell itself.

Looking up, she saw Ryan reach the top. His face registered the same shock she had felt.

"Don't move!" he shouted. Dropping to his stomach, he yelled again, "Take my hand! Quick!"

"I can't move! If I do, I'll slide more! Something is pulling me down, Ryan! Please help me!"

She was just out of Ryan's reach. Taking off his belt, he flung one end to her.

"Turn around and grab my belt. It's just a foot behind you. You'll have to do it in one move!"

Quickly, Tara flipped over and grabbed the belt. She was on her stomach now. Something was pulling at her, and she could feel it getting stronger. Ryan was pulling hard against it.

Tara let go of the belt with one hand and let her backpack slip off her left shoulder, then grabbing the belt with her other hand, she let it slip off her right shoulder. The pack slid slowly down the slope. Tara watched over her shoulder as it slid over the edge where it dissolved upward into the sky just like the javelina. She looked back to see fear in Ryan's face.

"Fight it Tara! I'm pulling as hard as I can!"

Tara tried to work her feet and legs up the slope, but felt herself growing weak. The tingling sensations felt like they would overtake her. She knew she would loose the battle any minute.

"Help me Ryan! I'm losing it."

She began to feel nauseous. Her world was fading. She knew that death must be near, but she was powerless to fight it any longer. Her limbs were starting to go numb. Somewhere, as if from very far off, she could here Ryan calling to her to take his hand. She wasn't sure what she was doing or how to comply with his request.

She could barely feel Ryan's hand grab her arm. Her mind was in a strange and distant, dreamlike place. Somehow she knew Ryan was fighting for her life against an unseen force, and vaguely now, she was aware of a long and hard battle. In the end, she could tell only that Ryan had won.

For a full ten minutes he held her in his arms in the shade of the desert willows. When she finally opened her eyes and her senses began to clear, she knew Ryan had won not only the battle for her life, but the battle for her heart as well. Still very weak and barely conscious, she wrapped her arms around his neck, and drew as close to him as she could. She was too weak to fight her feelings now. Giving in to a force stronger and older than the universe, she admitted to herself that she was hopelessly in love, eternally and inseparably connected to this man from Idaho.

Finally she spoke, looking up into Ryan's eyes.

"Thanks. I'll never forget this."

"Neither will I."

"Ryan? I . . ."

"Shhh, don't say a word." He brushed the hair from her face and kissed her forehead. "I hope you're feeling what I am," he spoke tenderly. "If you are, blink twice, if not . . . smack me."

She looked into his eyes and blinked twice, as slowly and distinctly as she could. Smiling, he held her tight. As she clung to him, she felt her body gradually returning to normal.

"You just rest right here in my arms," he said, "until you get your strength back."

He hummed a little song that sounded so sweet and innocent she thought it must be a children's song he had learned at church. It helped her relax. When he was done, she asked him what it was.

"Just a little song about families and forever. It seemed like the right tune for the moment."

"It's very nice. You'll have to teach it to me one day."

"I'll do that," he promised.

"Well, what do we do now?" she asked, feeling better.

"I don't know. I'm rather enjoying the moment, actually."

"I think I can get up."

"That's good, because my legs are numb!"

"I'm sorry; why didn't you say something?" She stood, a little wobbly, and stepped away from him. "Man, my weight must have been killing you!"

"No, not really. They just fell asleep." He rolled over and tried to move his legs. "Oh dear, they're numb all the way up to my butt!"

Laughing, he rolled on the ground until Tara started to laugh as well. She gave him a playful slap on the buttocks. When his legs were finally back in working order, they decided to take another look at "The Hole," as Ryan called it, this time from a safe distance.

Creeping carefully to the edge of the ridge, Tara peered over, Ryan at her side. It was an eerie feeling to look down the funnel and into the dark bottomless chasm. As they watched, a tumbleweed rolled into it. When it reached the gaping mouth, instead of falling in it disintegrated into the air!

They both jumped back from the rise.

"Whoa! Did you see that?" Ryan said. "Just like the backpack!"

"Yes. That's what happened to the javelina!"

"I'm glad you saw it. I could hardly believe my own eyes."

"Let's get back up there."

"Yeah."

For the next two hours, they watched, captivated. At one point a snake slithered up and over the edge across from them, then down into the cavity. Like the tumbleweed, it too dissolved as it reached the mouth of The Hole.

Later, several small birds landed on the sand. They fluttered briefly, then became powerless to escape the force pulling them down to destruction.

The animals seemed not to want to leave once they entered. Ryan theorized that they experienced the same series of feelings he and Tara had. First, apprehension and fear, then a euphoric high, followed by a sickening terror. Tara described the next stage as a numbness that made it impossible to escape. All the while the force seemed to draw them down to certain death.

"Tara, in our experiments we tried various means of breaking sub-atomic particles harmlessly apart. The difference in scale is enormous, but if I were to guess, by the things I've seen and felt here, I'd say that's what's happening in our bodies when we get near these two spots. Something is causing sub-atomic disorientation. That has to be the explanation for what we're seeing here! Though they appear to vanish, they're really just being disoriented until they dissolve into pieces so small they're invisible. I can't believe you almost got dissolved yourself!"

"Thanks for keeping me from dissolving, Ryan. Now I know what the wicked witch in the Wizard of Oz must have felt when she was 'melting.'" She imitated the movie character's voice. "What an experience!"

"I'm glad you didn't melt. It would have put a real damper on my plans."

"Plans? You have plans for me, Dr. McKay?"

"Well, maybe." He smiled, then looked back at the gaping hole. "If this is expanding Tara, where will it end?"

She shrugged her shoulders, "I don't know, but I do think you've changed the subject."

"True, and I'm going to change it again. Let's get out of here. We've got some serious thinking to do. I've got to figure out what could cause this to happen on the scale we're seeing here, and I need a place where I don't have to do the math in my head."

Chapter 5
PROMPTINGS

The killer sat waiting. He was good at waiting. He was quite comfortable on the couch in the living room of Tara's home . . . just waiting, like a quiet pool of molten lava. When Tara and Ryan walked through the door, the pool would bubble over and take them. But not till he scolded them for making him have to come and get them.

It was way beyond the money now. He had gone from Denver to Dallas, and now to Phoenix. Oh the money wasn't bad; he was very well to do. In fact, he had more money than he could possibly spend. But this Ryan guy had taken him to three states, and he would have to pay, right out of his soul.

The girl at the counter of the Harrelson Inn wouldn't talk at first. But she finally did. Oh yesiree, she did. Wouldn't be talking much now, of course. They never did when he was finished with them.

He sat casually leafing through some family photo albums, until he noticed that there were no photos of Ryan. How did these two know each other? he wondered. Did they just hook up in Dallas? What were they doing together? Oh well, made no nevermind to him, they were both history now. They both made him work. They both made him come after them, so they were both going to be the icing on his cake.

He closed the album and sat back. Sometimes it was hard to control his thoughts. When he had to wait for folks, his mind tended to wander. He held the "Device," as he liked to call his nine-millimeter handgun, stroking it lovingly, as he would a kitten. "Little kitty gonna have his dinner soon," he promised. "Very soon."

His awareness drifted. There were memories, haunting memories.

"Son, what'd you do with the cat?" Margerette Sweet sputtered at her son. She had been snoring on the couch for hours when she finally jumped to life, apparently noticing that the family cat had been gone for days. "Come here little mister! You did something to it, didn't you? Why I didn't give you up for adoption I'll never know."

She reached down to the side of the couch for her shoe. Anticipating her throw, the boy ducked and ran toward the back door.

"Get back here you lying little monster, you're in big trouble now, buddy." She was sweating heavily, having just awoken from a two-day drunk. Throwing the shoe made her tired. She'd have to teach the little mister a lesson . . . later! she warned him out loud. What she needed now was another nap. The boy paused long enough at the door to watch her close her fat eyelids, and lapse into another of her drunken stupors.

She was a self-centered, self-gratifying, hugely obese, mean and abusive drunk, and the boy was tired of her stupid dreams. He knew just what she'd say in the morning. A knight in shining armor rode up to her rundown house in the woods and took her off to his castle, making her his queen. She would have to hide the boy, of course. No self-respecting knight would take a woman who was already saddled with a kid. She would hide him in the woods till after the wedding. He sobbed when she told him that part, but Mamma assured him it was only temporary.

If he were naughty, she would say that the first order of business as the new queen was to destroy all the little boys of the kingdom. She read something like that in the Bible, she said. It made perfect sense to her.

He hated that story. Watching her there on the couch the thought of it frightened him so much that he ran, crying, and hid outside. Later, when he returned, he looked into the window and saw Mamma still asleep. He watched as her dreams were suddenly cut short. She sat up and grabbed her chest, her face in pain. Is this the part where she kills all the little boys in the kingdom, he wondered? Then she slumped down on the couch. He had never seen her sleep in that position, and this time, she never woke up.

Mamma's gone now, he thought, as he stared at the plants in the Johnsons' home. She had drunk her last drink, cursed her last curse, and beat her last little boy. She left behind nothing that he could remember except a profane legacy, a three hundred ninety five-pound carcass and some memories, memories that wouldn't go away.

When the boy finally came in and found that she was dead, he ran from the little house in the woods and never came back. He had caused her death, he was sure of it then. But later, he realized he had done nothing of the sort. Others were to blame for that tragedy. Trouble was, he didn't know for sure who was at fault, so he blamed everyone. They deserved it; they all deserved it, for killing his mamma. They all made such good targets, too.

After Mamma died, he was very angry. He beat up anyone he could, but that wasn't enough. In Vietnam he learned how to shoot them. Mamma's death would be avenged. They would all pay, yesiree, every one of them.

Suddenly a car door slammed shut, and the killer moved swiftly to the window. He looked through a slit in the blinds. It was a false alarm.

Making his way back to the sofa, he took up his vigil again, a pool of molten lava waiting for two unwary swimmers.

On the way back, Tara took Ryan for lunch at Bill Johnson's Big Apple Restaurant. There, they decided to go back to Tara's home and record all they had seen and experienced. He kicked himself for not bringing a video camera, but that could wait until tomorrow.

As Tara turned the Jeep onto Cedar Street, one block from her home, Ryan felt uncomfortable. The feeling increased as she continued up the street. When they were within three or four houses, Ryan heard a voice. No, it wasn't actually a voice, he decided. It was a prompting of the Spirit, but not like any he had experienced before.

"Stop," it said, as though someone was right at his side speaking directly into his mind.

"Tara, stop the car!"

She slowed to a stop.

"What is it, Ryan?"

Suddenly he felt silly. How could he tell this girl he just had an "impression" from the Spirit? He could kiss this relationship goodbye if he told her he was hearing voices.

"Oh, nothing, sorry. Never mind."

She started up again, but she hadn't moved more than fifty feet before the voice was back in Ryan's head, this time even louder.

"Stop. Do not enter the house," it said.

Ryan put out his hand. "Stop, Tara."

She pulled over to the curb. "You better make up your mind," she said. Then, turning to him, she added, "What's the matter, Ryan?"

"Just a feeling."

"A feeling?"

"You're probably going to think I'm nuts, but I have a very strong impression that we should not go any further up this street, and we should definitely not go into your house. I think someone's in there, maybe the guy who tried to kill us in Dallas."

"But he couldn't be here. How could he follow us? He doesn't know me, or where I live. Ryan, are you sure about these 'impressions'? I mean, how could he have found us so fast? It's impossible, isn't it?"

"However, impossible it may sound, I'm certain about this impression," he spoke firmly. "I don't know where he would get your address. Maybe your hotel registration. But he could have hoped a plane and rented a car. Do you see any rental cars parked near by?"

Tara looked around, then put the Jeep in reverse and backed up until she could see more of the street in front of her house. Neither of them spoke, as they stared at a brand new Lincoln Town Car with a Hertz Rental Car sticker on it parked just around the corner on the street from which they had turned. They looked at each other, as Tara finally broke the silence.

"It's just a coincidence, don't you think?"

"Let's not take any chances."

"We can go to my uncle's cabin. No way he could trace us there. Nobody knows where it is. It's so hard to find, even my uncle gets lost."

She put her hand in Ryan's, and he gave it a gentle squeeze. "Okay. Let's go. We've got to find a safe place where we can put all this together."

"You wanted to see the high country. Looks like this is your opportunity."

Turning the white Jeep Cherokee around, Tara headed them north. Before they left the Phoenix area, however, she made one more stop—at a pay phone. Ryan got out to listen as she dialed 911.

"My name is Tara Johnson, I live at 1621 S. Cedar Street," Tara said. "There's a man in my house, I think he has a gun. He's wanted in connection with a murder in Denver. Please send as many units as you can . . . quickly! And check out the gray Lincoln Town Car with the Hertz rental sticker parked around the corner six or seven houses north of my address."

Ryan smiled approvingly. "You're good! If he's there, that ought to stir things up a bit. Shall we go?"

"After you, kind sir." she said, smiling.

Two hours later, they were north of Payson, on top of the Mogollon Rim, in the heart of the ponderosa pines. Even though the killer was somewhere behind them, and the chaos in the desert seemed like another world, they couldn't shake the feeling that it was their escape that wasn't real.

The trip, however, was wonderful. For two hours Ryan put aside the bad memories of the last few days and talked of feelings, hopes, aspirations, joys, sorrows, similarities, differences and everything that people talk about when they think they're falling in love.

He never thought it would happen like this. It felt like love had chosen him, rather than making him choose. He felt drawn inexorably to this girl. He wanted to know everything about her—everything she loved, everything she thought, everything she felt—and he wanted to know it now.

She was funny and had a smile he found irresistible. She was smart, but humble, a good listener and a good talker. She was all he ever wanted in a woman, wrapped in the most beautiful package he had ever seen. And there was something more. He sensed that she needed him, needed his protection, his . . . love. That meant a lot to him. He really wanted someone who needed and wanted him.

The only thing he wasn't sure about was her attitude toward religion. Would he be able to take her to the temple some day? That meant eternity to him, so it was something he had to assess carefully. It was the one major reservation remaining in his heart. He was confident in his missionary abilities and was reasonably sure it would all work out as he hoped, but he had to maintain his objectivity until he knew.

From what he had seen so far, she was everything he needed and wanted. She was more important to him than Mol-Dyn, recognition for his project or any material possession he could imagine. He looked over at her, wondering, hoping that she felt the same way about him.

Tara stared straight ahead at the lines in the highway. With each passing mile, she felt further away from the dark forces trying to snuff

out their lives. Now, more than ever, she wanted to live. But would the
Beast lash out again? Would it snatch Ryan away too, as it had Devin?
Would happiness elude her as it always had, leaving her alone once again
to fight feelings of insecurity, doubt and fear?

She turned to look at Ryan. He was smiling but silent, apparently
deep in thought. How could feelings for this man, whom she hadn't
known for more than two days, be so voraciously consuming her heart?
She had sworn after Devin's death that she would abandon love forever,
and disappear into her work. Could she maintain that commitment now?
Did she even want to anymore?

What about his religion? She had never dated a Mormon before,
though she knew some Mormon guys. They weren't weird like the
religious fanatics she had met in high school. Ryan, especially, seemed
rational, so . . . grounded. Yet there was something strangely delightful
about him. He had a peaceful confidence in life, a quiet security that she
longed for. Could she ever feel the way he did about life . . . about God?

There was commitment in him, too. She liked that the most. Take
the promises he spoke of on the way out to the desert. She had personal
proof that he kept them. Any other man would not only have stayed at
her house, he would have tried his hand at her locked door! Could a
religion actually inspire in a man the kind of quiet commitment to
civilized behavior she saw in Ryan, or was he just exceptional? It was
something she would have to look into.

She turned and looked again at him.

"What are you thinking?" he asked.

"Oh, nothing really. And you?"

"Nothing really. How much further to the cabin?"

"About five minutes. In fact, we turn here." She slowed down and
steered the Jeep onto a dirt road going north.

"I'd like to know what the weather's going to be, Ryan. Could you
turn the radio to the news? It's the second button from the left on the
AM dial."

"Oh, sure." He punched the button and turned up the volume.

". . . Repeating our top story today, two Mesa police officers were
gunned down while responding to a complaint from a local resident
about a possible intruder at 1621 S. Cedar Street. Apparently the officers
walked in on a gunman who is wanted by Denver police in connection
with three murders in that city. The police have no description of the

killer, who allegedly stole a rental car from the lot at Sky Harbor Airport earlier today. If anyone has information about the murders, please contact the Mesa police."

Ryan turned down the radio and looked at Tara. "That could've been us!"

"Oh, Ryan. Those poor policemen! I feel just terrible."

"You told them he was armed. What more could you do?"

She sat in silence for several moments, then said, "You're going to have to tell me more about these 'impressions.'"

"I promise, but later. When we have some time."

They traveled in silence roughly three more miles before Tara turned right at a fork, then one more mile before she pulled up in front of a beautiful log house in the middle of nowhere. The forest seemed to envelop the cabin and the surrounding road, making it almost invisible until they were directly in front of it.

It was a two-story home, with a large covered patio circling the entire structure. There were large decks upstairs, with patio furniture and a barbecue. In front, a new Chevrolet Suburban was parked in a circular gravel driveway.

"Tara, this is no cabin, it's a mansion!"

"Yeah, well, my uncle has a few bucks."

The screen door on the front patio opened, and a woman came out holding a fishing rod. "Tara!"

"Mom!" Tara called. Slamming the Jeep door closed, she ran up the steps to her mother and threw her arms around her. Ryan had stepped out and was standing quietly by as they hugged.

"Mom, I want you to meet a friend of mine." She motioned to Ryan. "Ryan, come on up here and meet my mother. Mom, Ryan is one of the top particle physicists in the world." She raised her voice as she made this statement, so Ryan could hear as he came up the steps. She thought of it, somewhat humorously, as a test of his humility, and watched him closely. As she hoped, Ryan blushed.

"Pleased to meet you Mrs. Johnson," he said, extending his hand.

"Nice to meet you too, Ryan. A top physicist, huh?"

"Not really. I'm really pretty new at it. I've still got a lot to learn."

Mrs. Johnson smiled and turned to Tara. "I thought you were supposed to be in Dallas? What happened?"

"Mom, it's a long story, I'll tell you later. Where's Dad?"

"Oh he's down fishing with the kids. I was just on my way. Have you eaten? Let me fix you something and you can tell me what's going on. Your father won't be back for an hour."

She guided them into the cabin, winking at Tara as she passed. Once in the kitchen, she sat them at the table and piled food in front of them until Ryan begged her to stop.

She spent the next twenty minutes talking to him, asking about his work, where he grew up, his family, anything and everything, with Tara listening attentively.

When the stream of questions subsided, she smiled approvingly at Tara, and winked. "I guess he passes. You can keep him."

"Mom!"

Ryan burst out laughing. Tara and her mother snickered at first, then joined him. When they finally settled down, it was Mrs. Johnson who spoke.

"Tara, now tell me why you're here. I know something's wrong, I see it in your face."

Tara looked at Ryan, as if to get the go ahead. He nodded, and hesitantly she began the story. "Well Mom, it's like this . . ."

She spent the next half-hour recapping how they met, and what happened in Dallas and Phoenix. Her mother sat silent, taking it all in. Occasionally, Ryan would fill in where Tara couldn't. When they got to the part about Ryan's premonition and the two murdered police officers, her mother stood and paced nervously, stopping on occasion to look out the big bay windows into the woods.

"Mom, I don't know how it all happened, but I don't think our family is safe. This man is trying to kill us, and don't know why. Worst of all, he knows where we live!"

"Do you think he knows about this cabin?" asked Mrs. Johnson, visibly upset.

"No way! How could he? He never even saw us here in Arizona. We just called the cops. Of course, if he's listening to the news, he might figure that we made a complaint."

"I'll have your father call the police when he gets back. Maybe they'll catch him! In the meantime, you two stay here until they do."

"Thanks, Mom. You're the greatest."

"Nonsense," her mother said nervously, "Everything'll be fine."

Tara knew her mother didn't handle stress well. She presented a calm exterior, but inside she had to be a wreck! Tara reached out and took her into her arms, giving her the best hug she could.

"Ryan," said Mrs. Johnson after Tara's reassuring embrace, "we have more room here than we know what to do with. Welcome to our family vacation." She took his hand and gave it a squeeze.

He smiled sheepishly. "Thank you, Mrs. Johnson. I'm really sorry I brought all this on you and your family. I don't . . ."

"Ryan," Tara interrupted, "it wasn't you. Besides, we're in this together now, so no more I'm sorry's. Okay?"

He shrugged and she gave him a quick hug, blushing at the electric thrill she felt at his touch. Seeing her daughter's reaction, Mrs. Johnson smiled knowingly. Tara's reddening hue deepened, and she tried to hide her face from Ryan.

Just then the door opened. They all turned to watch a small boy bound in, followed by a teenage girl and a somewhat older brother. Lastly, Tara's dad entered. He was a large man, with a big grin that made people feel comfortable in his presence.

"Well what have we here?"

Mrs. Johnson introduced Ryan, then sent the younger children upstairs to watch a movie. An hour passed as Tara and Ryan related again their experiences of the past two days. In the end, Tara's father concurred with her mother that they should stay at the cabin and wait to see what happened with the police. As long as the killer was on the loose, he said, it was the only place they would be safe, and Ryan was welcome to stay with them as long as necessary.

"We have a friend in Phoenix," Mr. Johnson continued, "who might be able to help. His name is Wil Dowding. He's a private investigator, and very good one. He frequently does stuff for our firm. I'll put in a call to him and have him check into it. If anyone can find this guy, he can. In the meantime, Ryan, you ever done any fishing?"

"Are you kidding, Mr. Johnson? I'm from Idaho!"

"Well, you'll have plenty of opportunity to brush up here, I imagine. Good to have you with us."

For the first time in many years, Ryan felt like part of a family. The members of his ward had been helpful after his parent's died, and his bishop really took him under his wing after his aging, single aunt took him in. But he hadn't actually lived with a family for years. The Johnson's accepted him instantly and made him feel comfortable, and somehow they managed to push any mention of trouble out of their conversation.

"We'll just leave such weighty matters as catching killers to the pros," Mr. Johnson said, refusing with the same vehemence Tara had expressed to hear any apologies from Ryan for the circumstances that had been thrust on their family.

It was strange, Ryan thought, how the turmoil they left in the desert was so easily forgotten here in the mountains. He felt no desire to rush down to the city and take up the killer's pursuit personally. The only thing that mattered to him now was Tara's safety. For the time being, that meant staying where they were, in the mountains, completely out of touch from the world, and that suited him fine.

In the week that followed, Mr. Johnson was in close contact with the police. They found nothing that would help them locate whoever it was that broke into their home. The death of police officers gave the case high priority, but there simply was no evidence. It was "the work of a professional," as they put it, and eventually, it had to be turned over to higher authorities. After a week, the local police were out of the loop, and the Johnson's heard nothing more about the case.

Except for brief telephone interviews, Tara and Ryan stayed out of the investigation entirely. Instead, they spent their days getting better acquainted. They walked together, fished together and spent hours talking together. Ryan never tired of being with her, and as nearly as he could tell she enjoyed every minute they were together as much as he did. He felt as though he had finally found his best friend.

Their third night at the cabin, they walked to a spot they particularly enjoyed between the cabin and the lake where the trees allowed a vision of the sky and the ground was covered with soft grass. The moon was particularly bright that night, and the starry heavens looked like a solid canopy sparkling over their heads. There they lay down side by side and stared up into space as they talked.

"Actually, I think there is a great big wall out there about . . . two billion light-years away," Tara said, "That's the end of the universe."

"Yeah, nothing beyond that wall," Ryan agreed.

"Yep, nothing. Lots of nothing, stretching out for . . . oh, another couple billion more light-years, maybe."

"Yeah," he said. "Then another wall."

Tara giggled, and snuggled closer to Ryan.

"Tara?" Ryan whispered in a more serious tone.

"Yes, Particle Man?" she whispered back. It was something Tara's little brother, Joey, had called him the second day they were at the cabin. Ever since, she had used it affectionately from time to time.

"Have you ever thought about forever?"

"Yes," she said. "I've always had the idea that . . ."

When she didn't continue, Ryan asked, "What idea, Ant Woman?" The name was his defense against "Particle Man," but Tara didn't seem to mind it. It wasn't particularly flattering in his mind, so he only used it when he wanted to tweak her.

"No, you'll just think I'm crazy."

"Too late. I already think you're crazy . . . but in a good way. Okay, maybe it's me that's crazy."

She laughed, her mouth widening into the smile he so adored. "Promise you won't . . . argue with me about this, okay? It's just the way I feel. I've always felt this way, and I can't help it."

"What way?"

"Well, somehow, I think we're all part of it, eternity that is. I know what they teach in Sunday School, but I just feel like we've always existed . . . not as human beings maybe, but . . . as something identifiable . . . I don't know. Personalities are so unique. What are they, really? What looks out of my eyes and no one else's? Have you ever thought about that?"

"Tara . . ." he started.

"I know," she interrupted, sitting up to face him, then speaking rapidly, as though she needed to relieve herself of a great burden and wanted no arguments while she did it. "You've been on a mission, teaching religion, I know. And I'm sure you've been taught that a God who exists outside of space and time created us out of nothing; that the universe depends on Him for its existence; and that we are mere creatures who began our existence at the moment of creation, and will cease to exist if anything happens to Him. I've heard it all since I was a kid, but . . ." She stopped, as Ryan placed his finger on her mouth.

"Can I get a word in here?"

"I just know how disappointed you're going to be. I'm just not a believer, Ryan. Metaphysics is a scientific impossibility. There is no evidence for it. What could be outside space? More space? I mean, does that make sense to you? You're a scientist."

She looked at him finally, quickly wiping the moisture from the corner of her eye, and waiting expectantly.

Ryan sat up and embraced her. "Do you know anything about Mormonism?"

"I know they believe in Christ. I've heard people say otherwise, but I saw that statue of him in your temple. Besides, it's obvious you guys are Christians. I mean, really; it *is* The Church of Jesus Christ of Latter-day Saints, isn't it?"

"Our 'temple'?"

"Yes, you know, over in Mesa. When I was in high school everyone would go there on Sunday night. It may seem funny, but it was *the* hangout when I was a kid."

"You must mean the Visitor's Center, next to the temple."

"Yeah. That's right. I remember now. You couldn't go into the temple unless you were a member."

"Didn't they tell you anything there about what we believe?"

"I think they offered, but we were just there to hang out. It wasn't cool to talk about religion when I was in high school. It was just a neat feeling there. So peaceful and safe, a real sense of eternity. I used to love it, before . . ." She stopped and looked at him, her face painted with guilt and sorrow.

"I think you need to know about some of the things we believe," Ryan said. "For one thing, we don't believe in metaphysics at all. Like the ancient Jews and the earliest Christians, we believe in a god who is real, that is, part of the real universe. That metaphysics stuff was imported into Christianity long after Christ died. We believe God created the universe, absolutely! But we definitely do not believe He did it out of nothing. And most importantly, Tara, we believe that we *are* eternal, just like you said."

"You're kidding. I never heard of such a thing."

"Well, I believe we're the only religion that teaches that now."

"I remember the feeling I had at the funerals of my friends. No sense of eternity there! Everything seemed so shallow . . . so incomplete. Ever since then, I've blamed God for a lot of things that have happened to me."

"What do you mean?" asked Ryan tenderly.

"Well, I was mad at him for the death of my friends. Then, when he didn't seem to be at their funerals, that was it. I thought maybe he didn't even know them, or me, or care about us at all. Everything seemed so dark in the world. I thought he just up and left us. But now I'm thinking I may have been wrong. Maybe it was just me all along."

"What made you change your mind?"

"Well, for one thing, I met you. I want to know more about him, Ryan. I want to know what you know about him. I *need* to know it. I really want you to tell me about this church of yours. Frankly, I would be interested in any organization that could produce a man like you."

He blushed and looked away momentarily. She smiled and Ryan took her head in his hands. Leaning toward her, he kissed her gently on the lips. At the touch of his lips, she threw her arms around his neck and pulled him into her embrace.

The next night, Tara couldn't wait to get Ryan alone at their favorite spot. There would be no kissing tonight, however. Instead, she was determined to learn. She felt like one of her desert plants begging to be watered as she grilled Ryan about Mormonism.

The first thing she had to know was why God let her friends die.

"The answer to that really starts with the understanding that God did *not* make us out of nothing. He merely fashioned bodies in which our spirits could grow and progress. That's the real reason we're here."

"Well, I know the Bible doesn't say He made us out of nothing. I used to drive my Sunday School teachers crazy pointing that one out."

"I wish I could've been there to see you do that."

"No you don't. Trust me."

"Well anyway, the point is, if this is true, it means that man's free agency is really his."

"'Really his'? What do you mean?" she asked.

"I mean, he wasn't programmed by a god who created him out of nothing. He really is accountable for his own choices. I had a lawyer friend who used to say that, if God created us out of nothing, he wanted to know where to file the lawsuit."

"'The lawsuit?'"

"Yeah. For . . . I think he called it 'negligent manufacture.'"

Tara laughed. "Do you think he could make that a class action? I feel pretty negligently manufactured myself."

"Sorry, no can do, because God *didn't* manufacture you. In fact, He's been trying for a long time to improve you."

"And I suppose that when bad things happen to us and our friends, it improves us?"

"In the ways that make us more like God, yes, very much."

Ryan's answer surprised her. It struck her to the very core. Maybe the Beast of life wasn't such a bad thing after all, she thought. The idea was hard to accept, but it made a lot of sense. No wonder Ryan wasn't afraid of the Beast. In his view, it was nothing but 'adversity,' a strict and demanding teacher. She had to admit it, some of the best teachers she ever had were just that type.

"What about God, Ryan? When I was a kid, I thought I knew him. But ever since, as I learned more about him . . . Well, I might as well tell you, the whole three-in-one thing seems impossible to me. It's irrational, don't you think?"

"I believe that's why they call it a paradox."

"See," she continued, "and I thought for sure I was gonna go to Hell for saying that. In fact, that's where my Sunday School teacher said I'd go."

"Oh, I can't believe that," he said.

"It's true. I swear it. Of course, I'd been badgering him to death with questions for the past year." Ryan smiled at this. She loved it when he smiled. "But the universe, the world, its ecosystem, the laws we study in biology . . . and physics. None of these are irrational. Why should we expect God to be irrational?"

"My sentiments, exactly."

"Really? But how can you say that? I know there's only one God, Ryan. I used to pray to Him when I was little. I didn't have a choice of gods then; there was only one! So what do you do with the Father, the Son and the Holy Ghost?"

"Well, we can't very well reject them, can we? I mean, the New Testament is pretty clear about that."

"No, you're right. But see, that leads us to the Trinity, right? It's so frustrating!"

"Actually, it's pretty simple. The Father is God, and the Son and the

Holy Ghost are united with Him. But only in a figurative sense. Theirs is a perfect unity of mind, will and purpose; it's not a physical thing at all."

"I don't understand. God is God, right? What do you mean by 'figurative'?"

"Okay, let me explain it this way. You're assuming 'God' is a person's name, like Joe. Right?"

"What's wrong with that?"

"Well, let's see. If we substitute a name like 'Joe' for the word 'God' in the Bible, we have a problem. In the Old Testament it says, "I am Joe, and there is no other Joe besides me. There is only one Joe, me!"

"Yeah, that's what I said."

"Well, then the New Testament comes along and says, 'The Father, Son and Holy Ghost are Joe. There are three, in one Joe.' It makes no sense. Contradictory, right?"

"Exactly! You catch on fast for a particle physicist."

Ryan laughed. "All right, but what if the Bible meant the word God not as a name, but as title, an office sort of. The ultimate presiding office in the universe! Let's substitute an office or title, like the 'Presidency,' for the name 'Joe.' Then the Old Testament says, 'I am the Presidency, and there is no other Presidency besides me. There is only one Presidency, this one.' And the New Testament says, 'The Father, Son and Holy Ghost are one Presidency. There are three, in one Presidency.' All of sudden there's no problem! Right? Of course, anyone who holds this office *is* God. At least, that's the way the word is used to indicate their perfect unity."

Tara was silent for nearly a minute, her mouth half-open in shock. "So, 'God' is an office held by the Father, Son and Holy Ghost," she said at last.

"Well, that's a little oversimplified, but, yeah, it's the basic idea."

"But that's so simple, so obvious. How could we ever have misunderstood that? Good heavens, what happened to the Christian world? Why don't they teach that now?"

"That's a very long story. Later, okay?"

"Whatever you say, but it's so perfect! No weird three-in-one stuff. I mean, even now, when I think of God, I think of him as a wise and loving father."

"Well, as a matter of fact, we believe that God really *is* our father, the father of our spirits anyway. That's why He's so interested in our progress. We're his children, fashioned entirely in His likeness. As a biologist, you would say . . . we're the same species."

She felt as though lightening had struck her twice. "I've always heard ministers say something like that, but I don't think they ever really meant it, not literally anyway . . . You really mean that someday, when I grow up . . ."

"And return to Him," Ryan interrupted.

"I'll be like Him?"

"Yes. That's the goal anyway . . . eventually. Of course, for you, there will be *one* big difference. You'll still be a woman, thank heaven!"

She smiled, but that reminded her. "Wait a minute. This is something I have to know. Will we still know each other then?" It was her most important question, and she couldn't wait to hear his answer.

"Absolutely. In fact, we believe that if we're married in the temple, where they have the authority to bind in heaven as well as on earth, we can still be married when we get to heaven."

Tears filled Tara's eyes. "You mean if *we* were married there, *we* could be together . . . *forever*, even after we die?"

"Yes," he said firmly.

"Okay, then. Where do I sign up?"

"Sign up?"

"Yeah, whatever you call it. I've never heard anything so beautiful in all my life. I want to become a member of your Church, now!"

"Well, come to Church with me Sunday, and I'll have the missionaries take you through the process. There's a lot more you have to learn."

"Okay, but you're not going to slow me down on this, Particle Man. I'm ready now. I've never felt anything like this before in my life."

"I understand. What you're feeling is the Holy Ghost witnessing to you that these things are true."

She pondered his words. "Yes, that's exactly what the empirical evidence suggests to me."

She smiled and Ryan laughed. "Ever the scientist, eh?" he said

"And a good scientist doesn't reject empirical evidence! I'm just interested in the truth . . . and Ryan, this is the truth. Thank you so much for sharing it with me."

The next morning, Tara couldn't wait to tell her family that she was going to join the Mormon Church. She chose breakfast to make her announcement. Everyone was together enjoying Mrs. Johnson's gastronomical delights. This morning it was pancakes, with fresh blueberry's and a syrup of her own making that had Ryan expressing his enjoyment at every bite.

As Tara blurted out her intentions, Ryan winced in anticipation of the family's reaction. Her mother spoke first.

"That's very nice, dear. I'm so glad you've finally found something you can believe in." Turning to Ryan, whose mouth was slowly dropping open, she continued. "She read the Bible cover-to-cover when she was nine, you know. I swear, Ryan, she almost had it memorized. But you wouldn't believe the trouble she used to cause in Sunday School. We had to stop taking her. I really thought she would turn into an atheist, what with her science studies and everything."

"Yes," her father seconded. "We haven't been able to discuss religion with her since she was twelve. I don't know what you've told her, Ryan, but I'm sure grateful for it."

Ryan pinched himself. Could it be this easy? It never was during his mission! Yet he had seen the spirit move people before. Tara was just very special that way. He knew from the beginning there was something special about her. He just didn't realize until now just how special.

"Well," Ryan offered, "we're going into Payson for church tomorrow. Would any of you like to join us?"

Tara looked at them enthusiastically, but her obvious expectations were not realized. They all smiled politely, as they made one excuse after another. Tara started to put some pressure on them, when Ryan touched her arm gently.

"It's all right," he said to the family. "Perhaps another time."

Everyone seemed relieved and smiled at Ryan, except Tara, who glared at him out of the corner of her eye, as if to say, "what are you doing?" He gave her his best it's-all-right-I-know-what-I'm-doing look, but it seemed to placate her only slightly.

Then ten-year-old Joey chimed in with a question that was certain to change the subject. He had been looking intently from Ryan to Tara and back again throughout the entire conversation.

"Do you love my sister?" he asked.

Tara choked on her pancake and her dad tried to shush him, but Ryan looked at Tara and back at Joey. For the first time he expressed openly what his heart had felt for days.

"Yes Joey, I do love your sister. She's pretty special, don't you think?"

Ryan looked at Tara, an unwavering certainty in his eyes, as she returned his gaze, blushing visibly. Mom and Dad smiled, and her younger giggled. Finally, Ryan reached over and took Tara's hand.

That Sunday, Church was heaven for Ryan, and Tara couldn't seem to get enough. Her enthusiasm refreshed him. It surprised the local missionaries too, but they agreed to come to the cabin that evening and start teaching her from the standard lesson plan.

Tara sailed through the first one and insisted that they return the next day for the second. She made it very clear that she expected to be baptized the following week. She would wait no longer. The Book of Mormon she devoured in three days, reading practically non-stop.

It seemed to Ryan that the week flew by, and the very next Sunday, there he was, at the baptismal font in the little chapel in Payson. Dressed in white, he baptized the woman he loved, as her family and other members of the local congregation looked on. He had never known such joy.

That evening he and Tara were again at their favorite spot near the cabin gazing up at the stars. Ryan felt as though the last two weeks had been a dream, so different from the terror they had known before. He knew they would have to get back to that reality and the problems that were boiling just below the surface of his consciousness. But for the time being, he decided to remain in the dream.

Tara was speaking as he turned to smile at her. "Ryan, now that I have the Holy Ghost, will I be able to hear Him speak to me too, the way he did to you that day the killer was in our house? I mean, what if I'm not in tune? I don't feel particularly different. Closer to Him than I have in years, yes, but not all that different."

"You shouldn't expect to feel all that different, either. You've always been a good person. That goodness has just been confirmed in you now. But wait till you read the Bible again, or any of the scriptures. You won't believe how the Spirit opens your understanding. But as far as His promptings are concerned, just open your heart, your 'spiritual ears.' You'll feel Him in you mind and in your heart. If you have the confirmation of both, your mind, or intellect, and your heart, or feelings—like two witnesses—then be sure to follow that prompting, and you'll always be guided by the Holy Ghost."

"But what if I . . ."

"Tara, what are you feeling right now?"

"I feel so wonderful! I can't tell you what it's like. I feel like . . . I'm ready to walk into the presence of God. I can just feel him, so close . . . even more than when I was a child."

"That's just the way you should feel, and the way you *will* feel whenever the Spirit whispers to your heart."

"I hope I'll always feel this way."

"You can. It's meant to last forever."

"I love forever! This is the feeling I used to get at the temple in Mesa. Which reminds me, I want to go there . . . tomorrow, Ryan. Can we do that?"

"Yes. Yes, Tara, but . . . you have to be a member for at least a year before they let you go into the temple. There's still a lot for you to learn."

"That's okay. A year from today, then. Will you take me?"

"I promise I will," he said.

Turning to face her, he propped his head on his arm and looked into her eyes. "And when I do, I want us to come out sealed together forever . . . for all eternity! Will you marry me, Tara Johnson?"

She looked at him for a long moment, then turned back to look up at the stars. Ryan's heart was beating so hard he thought it would burst out of his chest. This was the question of a lifetime for him. Didn't she feel the same way he did? He had thought so. Why didn't she say anything? Could he have been wrong?

"Perhaps," she said at last.

"Perhaps? What kind of an answer is that, Ant Woman?"

"Well, it's this kind of answer," she said, turning onto her side to face him again. "I'll marry you, Particle Man, on one condition."

"What's that?" Ryan asked realizing he hadn't taken a breath in over a minute.

"That you marry me next week. I couldn't possibly wait a year for that!"

Chapter 6
THEORY

Wil Dowding was forty-eight years old, and felt in the prime of his life. He'd been an investigator for nineteen years, and enjoyed every minute of it. And for most of those years his best friend had been Lonnie Johnson. So, when he received the call from Lon, he was more than happy to help out.

He and Lonnie had gone to high school together, and it was Lon who gave him his first break into corporate Arizona. When Wil was hungry and needed work Lonnie convinced management at his insurance firm that Dowding was the best in the business. Without references, they hired him on the spot for a big job, based solely on the recommendation of Lonnie Johnson. Since then, Wil's reputation had grown. He was now the most respected P.I. in Phoenix, with a staff of over twenty.

But, for two weeks now, Wil had been searching for the alleged killer from Colorado, without uncovering the faintest hint of a clue. The Mesa Police Department had turned the case over to the FBI, who also had found nothing. The killer left no cigarette butts, food wrappers, shell casings or anything. All Wil knew for sure, was that the man was wanted in connection with three murders in Denver and possibly one in Dallas.

Wil loved the Johnsons, and had always been close to the family. He wanted to do all he could to find the man who was after Tara and her new fiancé, Ryan. But something wasn't right about this mad man. Wil had assigned two of his better field assistants to tracking him, and two to the Johnson's for protection. He was pulling out all the stops on this case, working personally with the police agencies and his street connections. He spent three days in Denver, and two in Dallas, digging for information, but he found nothing. Detective Murphy in Denver wasn't much help, and his partner, Mullins, had been found dead. Even with the description Ryan gave him and all of Wil's efforts, it seemed the killer had dropped off the planet, without a trace. For him it was not only an annoying failure, it was personally embarrassing.

Off the planet, however, was not where the killer had dropped. He had taken a plane to Hawaii. For a couple of weeks he laid around on the beach trying to decide what to do next. He was angry, and needed to vent. When he couldn't take the nagging memories of his mother any longer, or the fact that he had missed Ryan on three separate occasions now, he left Hawaii and boarded a plane for Tennessee. Once there, he bought a new Dodge pick-up for a very special trip. He was going to see his dear sweet departed mamma. It would be his first trip back to the woods of his home since he ran away as a boy.

He had put it off for too many years, he decided. Before he could continue his work, he needed to exorcise that big fat demon from his soul. His mamma had been haunting his dreams, sleeping and waking, for far too long. He needed to visit her, and tell her once and for all to leave him alone.

The cabin had long since been torn down, but he knew right where to go to find her grave. Walking the hundred yards or so from Catrock Road, through the oak and hickory infested woods, he soon came to the small mounds of earth and simple headstones of the hidden graveyard. It was a small cemetery used by a few families over a period of many years. Overgrown now with vines, ivy and scrub oak, a passing stranger might not notice it at all.

"Don't make me have to look for you mamma." he said out loud, smiling humorlessly. "From where you are, there ain't no way you can pay me fifty dollars every day!"

He stepped through the mounds, not caring whether he went around or over them, and finally found his mamma's grave. Pulling away the ivy and brush, he knelt in the middle of the mound and stared at the words printed on the headstone. They were short, sweet and not at all factual:

MARGERETTE SWEET
DEVOTED MOTHER
1924 – 1966

"Mamma? Why you been hounding me?" he called out while he put his hands over the face of the headstone. "You're dead, Mamma! Can't you just be dead? Go away now; go to Heaven, or Hell, whichever will let you in. Just leave me alone, I can't do my work proper!"

"I'll proper you, you little pervert!" a voice spoke so close to his ear it sounded almost as though it were inside his head.

The killer jerked around to his right. No one was there. Had he imagined the voice? No, surely someone spoke. He looked again at the headstone.

"Mamma?"

"That's right, you little mister. Your sweet mamma's back from the grave to smack you one!"

Again he looked quickly to his right, but no one was there. The voice was coming from inside him. He wrapped his hands over his head as if a tumor had exploded inside it.

"No! Mamma no! Please go away!

"No way, boy, I'm here to stay now, yesiree, gonna help my little pervert son find his prey. Did you miss three times boy? Miss that fella Ryan and his little missy? Gonna have to pay for it if you did, you know!"

The killer threw himself across his mother's grave, a look of pain and fear twisting his face. He had come because he was haunted by her memory. Now, somehow, she had crawled inside his brain!

"Get out of my head Mamma! Get out now or I'll blow you out!" He pulled out the Device and pressed it to his temple.

"Go ahead you little twerp, do it!" he heard his mamma taunting him.

Perplexed, the killer hesitated. "You want me to do it Mamma?"

"You can't, little mister! Can you?"

"I can do it, and take you with me!" he answered, the sweat breaking out on his face.

"Then do it!" the voice screamed.

His finger on the trigger tightened, but he couldn't pull it all the way.

"See? Don't you realize why you're here you little punk?"

His head felt like it was on fire. "Yes, I came here to get rid of you! That's why!" Again he grabbed the sides of his head, and rolled on his back in agony looking up at the canopy of blue sky overhead.

His mamma's voice came again, permeating his brain like a wave of low dose electricity. "No, no boy, you came to get me! You need me! You came, because two heads are better than one, well, a head and a half if I have to count yours."

"What?"

"Yesiree, this job you're doing needs a little help from your old Mamma."

"How you gonna help?"

"Look in your back left pocket, twerp," her voice said.

He stuffed his gun back in his pants, and pulled out the small book from his pocket. He had taken it from Tara's home weeks ago. It was the girl's address book. He fumbled clumsily through it. There were many names and addresses. Friends and acquaintances, he assumed, but no clues as to her whereabouts.

"You done looking in it fool?" Her voice was as mean as ever, but in a sick way, it comforted him. He nodded his head. "Okay, here's what we do . . ."

After the wedding, Tara's father took an extended leave from work and the family left for Canada, not to return until just before school started. They had been planning something like this for years, but it took a killer to make them actually follow through. Hopefully by the time they returned, Wil Dowding, or the police, would have caught the madman, or at least made it safe for them to return.

Tara and Ryan stayed on at the cabin and honeymooned. It was wonderful, but like any new bride, Tara was growing increasingly concerned about how long they could afford to remain away from work. On their second morning as husband and wife, she turned over in bed and gazed adoringly at Ryan.

"I could stay here forever. What about you?"

Ryan smiled back at her. "I wish that were possible."

"Yeah," she said. "I suppose we'll soon run out of money and have to return to reality."

"Actually," he replied with a knowing look in his eye, "money is not the problem."

He turned and sat up. As he fumbled with something on his bed table, she objected.

"What do you mean? Money is always a problem!"

Having apparently found what he was looking for, Ryan turned back to her. "Not always," he said, handing her a bank statement that bore his name and hers as "Tara J. McKay."

Seeing her married name for the first time in print gave her a thrill. "Oh that's nice. You opened an account for us."

"You might want to check the balance, wife."

Tara's mouth dropped open as her eyes located the figure on the paper in front of her. There was over seven hundred thousand dollars posted at the top of the page.

"Where did all this come from?" she asked. "Did the bank make a mistake?"

"It's no mistake. It came from my parent's life insurance . . . and my rather ridiculous salary at Mol-Dyn. I got the inheritance when I was twenty-one, but I never really needed it for anything, what with scholarships and all. Do you want me to send it back?" He gave her an obliging look.

"Not on your life, husband!"

She hugged him then looked back at the statement. "It's just like you not to place importance on this kind of thing. I love you so much, Dr. McKay!"

The money really put Tara at ease. They would not have to rush back to Phoenix after all. The very idea of returning made her shudder. She hadn't thought of the city or that day in the desert when Ryan saved her life, for nearly a month now. She wished they could stay forever in the blissful heaven they enjoyed in the mountains, and now it looked like a realistic possibility.

Eventually, however, she knew that reality could not be denied. And sure enough, that afternoon Ryan asked her if they could go back to the Superstition Wilderness to record the ever-growing hole in the desert. Reluctantly, Tara packed what they would need and the next day they left early.

The site was undisturbed, except that it had grown slightly larger.

Using the video camera, they were lucky enough to record a few small animals, which entered the area and paid for their curiosity with their lives. When they were done, they immediately drove the two hours back to the cabin.

"Do you think we should report this to the authorities?" Ryan asked her. "That hole is awfully dangerous."

"I agree," she responded. "But reporting it to the authorities would have exactly the wrong effect."

"What do you mean?"

"In the year and a half I've been studying at that site, I've never seen another human being, not one, anywhere near the place. If we report it to the authorities, that'll all change. No matter what the authorities do to block it off, it'll become a magnet for the curious. I'd much rather it remained completely unknown."

"I guess you're right, but it makes me nervous. For now, it'll remain our little secret . . . like the Lost Dutchman's Gold Mine."

"Yep, our own little gold mine, only instead of gold, we mine fear." She looked soberly down at her hands, folded tensely in her lap.

Back at the cabin they began to theorize about the world, their predicament, and the problems at hand. Knowing that they couldn't escape the incessant gnawing in their gut much longer, she began a slow and reluctant return to reality.

Her need to find answers compelled her to write down their theories, while Ryan got out the disks he had taken from Rusty Phillips' office and installed them on her laptop. He then spent hours in mathematical calculations that she found completely bewildering.

That evening, Ryan had Tara read a list of the major elements of environmental degradation that formed the basis of the theorizing she had been doing. It included:

1) Lowering of sea levels, once not a major concern, now a real threat.
2) Drastic erosion of the world's topsoil, including the strangest erosion of all, The Hole.
3) Worldwide extinction of many plants and animals.
4) Dwarfing of many other plants and animals.

Ryan listened carefully and sat in silence for several minutes.

Finally, he asked, "Do you remember that paper at the conference about changes in cosmic radiation at sea level?"

"Yes," she said, trying to remember the details.

"What was the bottom line percentage change he reported?"

"I think it was 27.35 percent," she answered, pleased at her recollection of so obscure a figure.

"That's my brilliant wife," Ryan remarked, writing the figure down. "I guess it wouldn't be too hard for you to remember that girl's related report on changes in the atmosphere's polarization of the sun's radiation."

"I have that in my notes," she said, as she dug them out of the pile of material next to her and handed them to her husband

Ryan took the notes and turned to Tara's laptop, where he performed some calculations using the data. After several minutes, he turned back to Tara.

"Okay, there's a theory that explains all this. It's not the only theory, but it fits the all data . . . if we make a few interesting assumptions."

"Out with it, Particle Man. I'm dying of curiosity here."

"Okay. Here it is. I think somebody is manipulating the elements that compose our biosphere. It's happening on a scale I find incredible, but hear me out before you toss the theory, okay? Think about that hole of ours. Its expansion and relatively recent appearance couldn't account for the global effects these calculations are showing. I'm thinking there have to be more. Many more similar sites! Now we haven't heard of anyone stumbling across any, so what do you think of this little idea . . ."

"I'm listening," affirmed Tara.

"Good. I think sites similar to The Hole are either located in remote areas on land, like your desert, or in the oceans. What's the probability of that, if it's a natural phenomenon? Pretty small, I think. Given the worldwide concern, someone would have found one of these sites long before now if they were natural. But if they're not natural, then the best bet would be to place them in remote places, especially in oceans, where they wouldn't be easily detected, which by the way, would account for all the sea level changes."

"Okay. I follow you so far."

"These sites are destabilizing the surrounding matter, disorienting it and shooting it up into the atmosphere, where it remains, an astronomically valuable resource, until it can be reoriented. All that disoriented matter is still there, of course, even though it's invisible, and it's affecting the radiation levels reaching the planet's surface. That," he continued, "would explain the deterioration in the various plant and animal species."

Tara paused, thinking through Ryan's explanation. "That's a great theory, Sherlock, but have you considered the implications? What are these sites? How are they being hidden? And most important of all, who would do such a thing? Are we talking aliens from another galaxy? Surely no one on this planet would set out to intentionally destroy life, as we know it! Are you sure this isn't just a natural phenomenon?"

"Well, first, let me make some things clear, the numbers are all subject to exact mathematical determination, and are within 0.3 percent of the data. That's a pretty tight theory if you ask me. I can't answer your other questions, but I'd bet my life that's what's going on."

Tara looked at him for a minute, then walked over to the table where he sat. "Let me see that data, Particle Man."

For the next half-hour Ryan explained how the data fit the finer points of his theory. At the end of the session, she sat back. "Well I don't fully understand all this. Physics never was my strong suit. One thing is certain, however. I have great faith in you. So what if you *are* right? What do we do next, notify SETI?"

"I don't think we can attribute this to little green men. That hit man was a real human being and he's definitely a part of this."

"And it couldn't be a natural phenomenon?"

"It has the smell of man to me, greedy and eager to cash in on something, with no regard for the consequences. As hard as it is to believe, I'd lay the blame on our own species, though I have to say, this is greed on a scale I would never have imagined!"

She shook her head. "We may be the only ones who know this. We have to stop it, Ryan . . . and get our matter back! Or is that even possible?"

"Should be . . . theoretically. But I have a lot more work to do on the reorientation aspect before I can tell you anything for sure. If we can just get our hands on the equipment they're using . . . well, for starters, turning it off would be a good idea."

Tara laughed. "I think you have a gift for understatement, my dear. Who do you think could be doing this?"

"I think we have to admit this couldn't have been done without the government either cooperating, or closing an eye to it. Someone is getting a lot of money or power from this. You can bet on it. I hate to think our own government is involved, but do you remember that panel at the symposium?"

"Oh yes, I see your point. Something was definitely not right there."

Ryan sat in frozen silence for several minutes as the implications of his theory settled in Tara's mind. "This could be very dangerous, Tara. The level of involvement this data suggests is frightening. These will probably be powerful people. The hit man who's after us could be just the tip of the iceberg."

Tara wasn't smiling any more. "Ryan?"

"Yes?"

"I'm afraid. Something inside . . ." The fear she felt began to swell within her soul. It rose from deep inside, where she thought they could repress it forever, and threatened to destroy her new happiness.

"It'll be all right. I feel it too Tara, but it'll be all right. Somehow, maybe with God's help, we'll lick this thing. I'm sure. Come here."

Tara snuggled into him as he wrapped his arms around her. Nothing could tear her from the feelings she had been experiencing the last three weeks. For now, love would win out. She would successfully repress the forces of darkness one more time.

Softly, Ryan spoke. "Why do nights like this have to end?"

"So that we can have more wonderful and exciting tomorrows?"

"That's my girl. Are you scared?"

"Yes, and you?"

"If I said no, I'd be lying." Ryan replied.

"So lie to me!"

"What, and spoil my perfect record of twenty-seven lieless years?"

Tara punched him playfully on the arm. "Ryan McKay, you're too good to be true! Come on, one lie, just one, let's hear it buddy!"

She jumped on him and they wrestled for several wonderful, minutes. Finally Ryan pinned her and forced her to say uncle, then held her tight and covered her face with kisses.

Somewhere in the distance, coming closer, was a malevolent force, boiling and seething, consumed by hatred, and ready to kill. Tara could feel it, but she would ignore it again tonight, and accept instead nothing but Ryan's love.

The next day, however, the morning paper contained news that would no longer allow her the luxury she had taken the night before. According to an Associated Press release, four prominent physicists had either come up dead or missing. After reading it to Ryan, she dropped the newspaper on the table, and looked across at the man she loved so much.

Ryan stood and stretched his muscles. "You know Tara, if we could get this guy to try and kill us—under controlled circumstances, of course—I bet he could lead us to the men behind this conspiracy."

"So what do we do, take out an ad in the Phoenix paper?"

"Nope. We go back to my condo in Denver and wait for him to find us. If he still wants us that is."

Tara stood and paced nervously.

"What is it?" asked Ryan, concern painting his face.

She pondered for a minute then said, "Ryan, before you came along, I wouldn't have hesitated to run off and do something wild like this—rushing off to track down a killer or expose a giant government conspiracy. But now . . . It's just too big a risk! I don't want to lose the happiest time of my life. I just know that if we leave now, somehow the Beast will find us and take it all away?"

"The Beast?"

"Sorry. Over the last few years, I've come to refer to the world, life, as a beast. It's a personal thing I guess I have to deal with."

"Well I agree. It is a beast and not a pleasant one to be sure. But we can't hide from it, can we?"

"I don't know Ryan. We're safe here. Maybe the thing to do is let Wil and the police find the bad guys, and we'll . . ."

He put an arm around her shoulder and pulled her close, speaking softly. "You getting soft on me, babe? What happened to your determination to know the truth?"

"Hey, give me some slack. That was before."

"Before what?"

"Before I found the most wonderful man in the world, and married him!"

"Well, I admit I am wonderful," he teased. "But Tara, unless we do something, how do you suppose this will end? More people dead, or missing? A dead planet? The world is falling apart you know . . .

rapidly!"

Tara pulled away from him. "Ryan, besides my family, everything I've ever felt love for has been taken away from me, until you came along. I . . . Oh I give up, you wouldn't understand."

Ryan frowned at her.

"I'm sorry. Of course you'd understand. Forgive me, honey." She threw her arms around him and held him tight.

"Nothing to forgive. I just want you to know that I really do understand what you're going through."

"I just don't want to lose you." She stroked his face with her hand.

Running his fingers through her hair, Ryan spoke soberly, "Tara, we'll be together forever, and that's a long time. Nothing will keep us from the temple. I promise!" He smiled at her. "But if we don't try to help out, what future is there for us, or *our* family?"

She looked back at him stubbornly holding on to the beauty that had been their life for the last month.

"Look what they're doing to our planet," he continued. "I've never been a save-the-world freak, but this is different. Somebody has to stop this, and I don't think the government or the police will do it."

Neither spoke for several minutes. Finally Tara broke the silence.

"Well, when do we go?"

They walked out to the front porch and he kissed her reassuringly. Holding on to him, Tara tried to reassure herself that everything would be all right. Rocking gently in the porch swing, they watched the wind blow through the trees. To Tara, the sound it made seemed to whisper a chilling threat. "Leave here, and you'll die!"

But she knew Ryan was right. If they stayed there and did nothing they could also die, and with them, quite possibly, the rest of life on their little planet. They had to go first thing in the morning, leaving behind the peace she had found in the mountains for a bleak and uncertain future.

Chapter 7
DISORIENTED

The next day, they met Wil Dowding at 10:00 AM in his office in Phoenix. As they walked into his seventeenth-floor office overlooking the Valley of the Sun, Tara gave him a hug.

"Thanks so much for what you're doing, Wil," she said.

"Are you kidding? For you, I'd do anything." He looked at Ryan and smiled, extending his hand. "This is a wonderful young lady you've got here, Ryan."

"Yes sir, she sure is," he agreed.

Ryan liked what he saw in Wil. Slender of build, and sporting a nicely trimmed gray beard, he looked more like an engineer or college professor than a private investigator. But his piercing gaze and serious nature convinced Ryan he was not a man to be trifled with.

"Call me Wil. Why don't you two sit over here and tell me what's going on this morning, and why you're here." He motioned them over to a plush high-back couch as he took a chair opposite them.

Tara started. "Wil, we think it's imperative that we find this killer. To do that, we may need to go back to Denver. We both . . ."

"What makes you think *you* need to find this lunatic?" Wil interrupted.

"Because we know why he's trying to kill us," Ryan offered, "and we think he can lead us to the people who hired him."

Tara added, "We think these people are behind the problems that are plaguing the environment. It's deeper than just this hit man."

"You're a physicist, Ryan. Tara, you're a biologist. You two aren't prepared to deal with a man like this or the kind of people who would hire him. He could easily kill you both."

Wil's demeanor was very serious as he stood and paced in front of them. "I've got some of my best men on the job looking for this psychopath right now. So far, we've come up with nothing. How are you two going to capture him?"

"There's only one way, Wil," Ryan said. "And I think you know what I'm talking about. We've got to be the bait. If we're together in Denver, I think he'll find us. But that's where we need you. We can lure him in, but you'll have to step in and nail him."

Wil stood and walked to his desk where he paused, looking out the window. "There's one small problem with your plan, Ryan, besides the obvious danger for the two of you."

"What's that?" Ryan asked.

"He's not in Denver." Wil turned to face them. "He's here, in Phoenix."

Tara sprang from the couch. "You found him!"

"Not exactly, Tara. Please sit down."

She hesitated, then obeyed.

"Did you have an address book of some kind at the house?"

"Yes, I did, but it's been missing. Why?"

Wil stroked his beard then pulled his chair over in front of the couch. He appeared uneasy. "Tara, Gene Anderson was killed yesterday. Shot through the heart. The bullet matched the one I took from the headliner of your Explorer, Ryan."

Tara leaned back into the couch, and exhaled a deep breath. She looked ready to faint. Concerned and puzzled, Ryan took her hand and looked into her eyes.

"Gene worked with me at the university," she explained. "He was supposed to go with me to the Dallas Symposium." Leaning forward, she asked. "How could this be, Wil?"

Wil shook his head as he got up and walked over to his desk again. Reaching inside the top drawer, he pulled out a slip of paper. Turning, he offered it to Tara. "This is a copy of the note they found pinned to Gene's body yesterday."

Ryan and Tara read it together.

DON'T MAKE ME COME LOOKIN FOR YOU, TARA. THIS ONE'S THE FIRST, BUT I'LL GO THROUGH THE WHOLE ADDRESS BOOK FROM A TO Z AND WHACK EM ALL IF I

HAVE TO, LITTLE MISSY. AND BY THE WAY, BRING THAT
MCKAY FELLA WITH YOU OR I'LL MAKE YOU PAY SO BAD
YOU'LL WISH YOU WAS NEVER BORN.

Tara dropped to the couch, and buried her face in her hands. "Oh
Ryan, he's got my address book." Ryan put his arm around her and tried
to console her.

"Don't blame yourself, Tara," Wil assured her. "This guy is nuts.
There's no way anyone could have known. I tried to call you this
morning, but you'd left already. The police got a call last night around
midnight. The guy confessed to the whole thing, including everything in
Denver, as well as the pot shots he took at you in Dallas. But we still
can't pin a name or any form of ID on him. Have you talked to the
police, Ryan? You're the only person who's ever seen this guy."

"I spoke to the Mesa police when Tara's dad first contacted them,
but it was hopeless!" he growled. "I only got a brief look at the guy;
hardly a glance. White male, mid-forties; that's all I could give them.
We've just got to get this guy, Wil! Alive! He simply must be taken alive.
It's crucial." He brushed the hair away from Tara's face and touched her
cheek gently. "He dies, and so do our chances of finding whoever's
behind this thing."

"That may be difficult, but we'll do everything we can. I don't know
about your plan, but it may be our only chance." Wil stood and walked
over to the window again. "We've got to act fast. We have no idea of his
timetable with your address book. Back at your house . . ."

"I won't let Tara go there," Ryan interrupted.

"I'm way ahead of you, Ryan. I plan to send a decoy in for Tara. I
think we can get away with it. But with you, I'm afraid he knows you.
We fool him there, and he's liable to go off and kill some more of Tara's
friends, just for spite."

"Agreed." said Ryan.

"No way, Ryan!" Tara protested, jumping from the couch.

"Tara, this guy is loony tunes, not to mention a professional. He's
followed me through three states. You don't think he knows me?"

"That's not the point!" she said.

"It's precisely the point. He's got to be caught! We both know that.
And I'm the perfect bait to do it." He took her hand and looked deep
into her eyes. "Tara, what we have is special. But it means nothing if we

let these people destroy everything around us. I love you too much to not do this."

"Well, I can't love you if you're dead!"

"Tara stop. Do you remember looking up at the stars those countless nights in the mountains? How we talked about forever?"

"Of course."

"Well, there's nothing this guy can do to tear us apart. We were meant to be together, and we always will be. I promise."

Tara looked into his eyes. "Ryan, you're so important to me. I don't want to lose you!" Then she sighed, resignation in her eyes. "But I know you're right. It's just that it's so hard."

"Yes, but I feel good about Wil's expertise here, and I know that we'll have help from above. You feel that too, don't you?"

"Yes, I guess so. Wil, please watch him for me. Okay? I couldn't bear it if anything happened to either of you."

"You have my word, Tara," Wil promised.

Tara turned to her husband and put her arms around him. "Ryan, I swear, if anything happens to you . . ."

He held her close, then took her face in his hands and looked into her eyes. "The good always win, don't you know that?"

"No Ryan, not always. You're forgetting my past."

"This isn't your past. This is now. The good guys are going to win this time!"

The plan, Wil explained, was to have Ryan and a policewoman posing as Tara go to the Johnson home. There they would act as if they had just returned from a trip. Wil and his associates would be hidden in the house with taser guns, hoping that the killer would come after them. If they could pull it off without a hitch, they'd nab him, alive. It wasn't perfect, but it was the best chance they had.

After wasting Gene Anderson, the killer went out to eat. He parked the silver Dodge Ram pick-up he had purchased in Memphis in the well-lit parking lot of an all night cafe in Tempe and went in to order. He needed lots of energy. Tomorrow would be a big day.

Mamma was clever. If she was right, dead as she was, Ryan and Tara would be back in their home by tomorrow night. But he was smart too! There could be tricks, and he knew how to handle tricks. And he wouldn't spare no one who got in his way. Nosiree, they would all pay, big time.

That night he didn't sleep well. In between visions of his dreaded mamma, he found himself in the desert. The girl, Tara, was there and he wanted her, wanted her bad. He was going to make her pay for dragging him out there. But something else was there that made his icy heart race. It terrified him. It was trying to kill him. He ran, and ran hard, but he couldn't get away!

Jolted from his sleep, he sat up in bed, sweating heavily, and looked at his watch. It was 11:30 PM. He reached for his gun, and put it under his pillow. It was a comfort, he thought, but it didn't stop the pounding of his heart.

The next morning he rose late, had a big breakfast, and headed for Phoenix. The address of Dowding Investigations was in Tara's little book, and that made him curious. The office was in a big high-rise building downtown. He parked the car across the street and went inside to the lobby.

He wondered if Dowding might somehow be involved in Tara's case. It made sense, what with all the phone numbers she had for the guy, and he was an investigator, a private cop. So he figured he'd check him out. He smiled at the thought. He was nothing if not thorough!

The directory said Dowding Investigations was in Suite 1701. As he rode the elevator to the seventeenth floor, he felt relieved that his mamma hadn't bothered him today. So far his mind had been able to keep her out. But he knew that it wouldn't be long before she made her stinking presence known.

The elevator doors opened, and he was again in a large lobby. Dowding Investigations took up the whole north side of the building. The walls were glass, allowing him to see well into the offices.

Cautiously, he looked around at the people inside. Most of them were young men in their mid-twenties, clean cut, with an FBI look about them. The women were equally young, with the exception of a woman at the front counter, who was somewhere in her fifties.

A series of offices with wooden doors surrounded by plants lined the left wall. In the middle, was a group of desks arranged in a way that made the place look like a newsroom. To the right were a very nice arrangement of artsy pictures, and one door. As the killer stared at the door, it opened. To his surprise, a man with a beard, whom he guessed to be Dowding, walked out, followed by Tara and Ryan!

What luck! But then his hunches usually did prove right. Oh, how he wanted to pull out his Device and plug them all, right there. But there were too many. He didn't like the odds. Wil and the others were talking as though they were in no hurry to leave, so the killer decided to leave before he was seen. He turned casually to the panel in front of him and pushed the elevator button. The doors opened, and he stepped inside.

Exiting the building, he hurried to his truck where he could watch the front entrance without being noticed. It didn't take long for Wil, Ryan, and a couple of the young guys to come out. They were met by a police officer and another woman who looked very much like Tara.

"So, it's the old bait and switch," he sneered. But where is Tara? Still in the office, no doubt. Well, the little missy was history now; that's for sure.

"You just gonna' sit here and sweat like a pig in this truck?" blurted his mamma's voice.

The killer twitched involuntarily then began fidgeting in his seat. "She's in the building Mamma, relax, I'm gonna get her!" He looked around to see if anyone noticed that he was talking to himself.

"Mamma?" he asked, but Mamma didn't answer. He was alone once again.

The cool of the truck's air conditioning helped soothe him, but he could see it was time to go. Reaching for the keys, he shut off the ignition and pulled the handle on the front door. Looking around him, he headed back up to the seventeenth floor, and went into the lobby's restroom.

He was a master at breaking and entering. Without skipping a beat, he was into the crawl space above the restroom, maneuvering through it toward Dowding Investigations. Finding no firewall between himself and Suite 1701, he was soon over the area of the front desk. Through an AC intake vent, he could see and hear everything.

From his vantage, he peered through the open door into the office presumably occupied by Dowding himself. There, he saw Tara talking to one of the man's cronies. Moving like a snake, he slid silently over to the vent above Dowding's office and listened.

"You'll be staying in Mr. Dowding's office, Tara," said Steve. "Everything you need is right here. The couch makes out into a bed. Marge is bringing a blanket and pillow for you, and some food to put in the fridge in case you get hungry. Feel free to use the TV."

"Thanks. I'm not sure if I'll be in the mood for much TV."

A chill came over her as she moved over to the window. She wished that Ryan were by her side now.

"Steve?"

"Yes?"

"Could you have Ryan call me?"

"I'll see what I can do." He smiled and walked out the door, closing it softly behind him.

Through the window, Tara watched the city below. People and cars were buzzing around, engaged in their daily tasks. At this height, they reminded her of her ant colony out in the desert, meandering to and fro' in their little world far below.

She could see for miles both north and east. As was typical on a bright and warm October afternoon, she could see beyond the East Valley all the way to Superstition Mountain. Its majestic silhouette was clearly visible as it stood like a sentinel to the madness it guarded. Even from her perch twenty miles away, Tara could feel the familiar chill creeping up her back. Somehow, she hoped, the madness would end and Ryan would return to her. Then the chill would leave forever. She turned back to the couch and sat down, waiting for the phone to ring.

Sensing an angry presence, Tara looked around, her eyes focusing momentarily on the metal grill above and behind her. But she could see nothing. She wrapped her arms around her shoulders to ward off the chill and continued to wait.

This was not going to be easy. Ryan had left barely thirty minutes ago! Could she stand the wait? She walked over to the phone on Wil's desk. Picking up the receiver she dialed her home number but quickly hung up.

"Oh please, Ryan, call!" she said out loud.

Suddenly the phone rang, startling her. "Hello?"

"Tara?"

"Ryan, I needed to hear your voice."

"Hey Desert Rat, you're hearing it now, and on Wil's fancy little cell phone to boot! They said it was a matter of national security that I call. You all right?"

"No! I'm terrible. We should be doing this together. Is everything okay over there?"

"Well, seeing as we've only been here for roughly, two minutes, I guess it's okay." He chuckled softly.

"Ha! Very funny." She turned and looked around the office. "Come back here and get me. We can go back to the desert and get all the gold from the Lost Dutchman's Mine, and buy ourselves an island." Making fun about their 'gold mine' had become a running joke for her and Ryan. The little fantasy helped ease the fear they each felt.

"Tara, you're melting my heart here. How can I ease your fears?"

"I don't know. Just talk to me?"

"So tell me again, honey, how much gold is stashed in your little anthill?"

"Well, there's gotta be several billion dollars worth, at least!" she said excitedly. "Enough to . . ."

"Tara?"

"Yes, my prince?"

"You're the greatest. Hang in there. We're going to get him, I know it."

"I wish I shared your optimism," she answered.

"Why do you say that?"

"Something's not right here."

"What do you mean?"

"I don't know. I can't quite put my finger on it. It's just a feeling I have. I can't explain it."

Ryan didn't respond immediately. "Listen Tara, hang in there and give the plan a chance," he said at last. "It's got to work."

That kind of optimism reminded her of her high school friend Anne. It was comforting, but not very reassuring. "Okay, I will," she sighed. "But you call the second anything happens."

"You'll be the first, I promise. I love you, sweetheart."

"I love you too," she responded. "Bye now."

"Bye."

Tara put the receiver back and turned to the chair at Wil's desk. It felt like eyes were staring at her from somewhere in the room. She could feel their evil, but she couldn't see them, and there was just nowhere for an intruder to hide. She was scared and alone, so she said a silent prayer that she and Ryan would be able to see each other soon, and that everything would be all right. When she opened her eyes, she felt a calm begin to sweep through her body.

"Is that you, Heavenly Father?" she asked out loud. Feeling reassured she rose from the desk and went to the couch where she laid down. Closing her eyes, she envisioned herself with Ryan under the stars at her uncle's cabin. She thought of forever, and how they spoke of spending it together. How she looked forward to the temple and the day when Ryan would take her there. Remarkably, she found peace, and drifted off to sleep.

The sun had been set almost an hour and the employees at Dowding Investigations were long gone. Only two men were left to guard Tara, and they were watching a ballgame on the television in the foyer while she slept. In Wil Dowding's office, just above the door, the screws holding the vent in place slowly began to turn.

"Slowly now son, don't wake the little missy," said Mamma's voice.

"Not now Mamma, I got work to do!" the killer hissed. "Go away!"

"Don't mess up now son. If I could, I'd whop you on your head. You know that."

"Well, you can't, Mamma. So shut up!" the killer snapped back in a loud whisper.

On the couch, Tara stirred. Her dreams were of the desert again, and of Ryan. Also voices, a man's and a woman's. Rousing herself from sleep, she gasped when she saw in the darkness before her the silhouette of a man.

"Steve? Is that you?"

"'Fraid not little missy."

Tara sat up quickly. She reached for the light on the table next to the couch and clicked it on. In its feeble light, she could see that the man in front of her was holding a gun.

"Oh my Lord!"

"Nope, not him neither."

Tara turned toward the door and yelled. "Steve!"

"I'm 'fraid he's sleepin' now. I think he and his partner have a very bad headache."

Her heart raced. She knew she was face to face with the man who was trying to kill them, a maniac, totally unstable and sociopathic. But he didn't look at all like her concept of a murderer. Of course, she had never met a killer before, but this guy looked like somebody's brother.

By now he had clicked on the overhead lights, and as her eyes grew accustomed to the full light, she could see he was clean cut, fairly good looking, in his mid-forties, with dark hair and dark eyes. Pretty normal, she thought, except that something in his eyes struck fear into her very soul. She had never seen cold death in someone's eyes before, but there it was.

She tried to muster what courage she could and asked, "What are you going to do with me?"

He stared at her for a moment, then said, "Well, I was going to kill you right here. You've been a real pain to me little missy. Yesiree, you've been a really bad girl."

He stood up and stepped over to Tara. Before she understood what was happening, he struck her on the side of her face with his hand. "There now, how'd that feel. Don't make me have to whop you again."

Tara had never been hit in the face before and the shock of it left her seething. She wanted to strike back, but she knew that if she did, she could die in an instant.

"Why are you doing this? What have I done to you?"

"You haven't done nothin' except get in my way, so just stay quiet or I'll plug you right now. Understand?"

"No, I don't understand. What are you doing this for?"

"I'm doing this for Graf, not that it's any business of yours."

"You mean 'graft'? But why?" Tara was rubbing her cheek trying to stay calm.

"None of your business!" yelled the killer. "Now get over here!"

Grabbing Tara by the arm, he threw her toward Wil's desk. She crashed into its side with enough force to put a bruise on the side of her leg.

Wincing in pain and sick at the idea of being so powerless, she thought again of fighting back. But since meeting Ryan, her desire to live had pushed all thoughts of risk-taking out of her mind. Now she just wanted to do what this madman said, and hope somehow he would let her live. She looked up at the killer. His cold, dead eyes stared back at her. They were like a snake's eyes, devoid of human feeling. She felt like a small mouse in his cage. Her heart was pounding wildly. She knew he was there to take her life, and she needed to act quickly. There had to be something she could do or say that would divert him.

"Do you have a family?" she asked, as she tried to rub the pain out of her leg.

"What?" he responded in surprise.

"I mean, does your family know what you do?"

"What are you talking about? I got no family!" He stopped moving toward her, and his face took on a new look of bewilderment. "Why would you ask me that, little missy?"

Tara grasped for any idea, any straw she could use to keep this man from hurting her. "Well, I just thought you look so nice. You must have come from a good family. I mean, violence seems out of character for you," she lied.

"I grew up with violence, girl, and dishin' it out is what I do best. In fact, I been dishin' it out since I was a kid." He stroked his gun and pointed it at Tara. "POW! Just like that. All over the world."

Tara flinched when he mockingly shot at her, but quickly regained her composure. "So, what did your mother think of all that violence?"

A new look crossed the man's face. It was a look of guilt, or shame, she couldn't be sure.

"I don't have a mother!" he yelled.

"Oh yes you do you little twerp!"

"Shut up Mamma, you're not supposed to be here!"

"Your Mamma goes where she wants to, bub. How would you like a smack to your stupid head?"

Tara watched in shock. Somehow she had pushed the killer into a schizophrenic conversation with himself. The scene took on a surreal ambiance, as the man waved his gun and paced back and forth carrying on a warped discussion. She was in an office, seventeen floors above the world, with a raving lunatic.

Tara knew she had to use her head if she was going to stay alive. There has to be some way to take advantage of the situation, she thought. But it was all she could do to keep from crying and giving up.

She focused on Ryan and her family, while the man argued with his "mamma." Closing her eyes, she said a silent prayer, and felt a little better.

The killer backed away from Tara a step. "Mamma, please leave me. I need you to leave. Now!"

He looked like he was ready to cry. Tara was amazed at the way his voice changed back and forth from a normal man's voice to a high falsetto, as though it were a woman's.

"No way I'm leaving, sonny. You'll only mess things up. Ask her about the gold, you little pervert!"

"Forget the gold Mamma. I don't need it."

"Your Mamma needs it, you fool. You may think you got enough, but you can never have enough. Now sit back and watch your Mamma."

At this point, Tara was frozen in fear. A tear escaped down her cheek. She couldn't move or speak, and even if she found the strength, she couldn't think of a thing to say.

"Okay, little missy, let's talk." The killer walked right up to her, and slapped her hard across the face again. "There now. Mamma's got to show you who's boss. You understand? Now, where's the gold?"

Tara had no idea what the killer wanted. "What are you talking about? What gold?" She tried to back away, but was stopped by the desk.

He hit her again. "The gold in the desert, little missy! I heard you talking to your honey about it on the phone. Don't make me have to ask you again."

Finally, Tara understood. The killer must have been hiding in the office or nearby, and overheard her and Ryan teasing each other about the Lost Dutchman's Gold Mine. She couldn't believe he had taken her seriously. She looked into his eyes, not knowing what to say.

"Listen, you little hussy, you made my boy have to chase you all over tarnation, now it's time for you to pay, baby, fifty dollars everyday. 'Course, a little gold might help me to forgive you. So, do you think maybe you could just tell Mamma where to pick it up? I'll only take a little."

Suddenly, Tara felt something new, something that was familiar and warm, but much stronger than anything she had experienced before. It impinged ever so gently on her mind, like a still, small voice saying, "Make them believe there is gold."

Of course, she thought. It was the only way to buy more time. The killer and his "mamma" were bent on evil. But it was the mother part of his schizophrenia that seemed less violent and more greedy. She liked to hit and belittle, but the killer reveled in murder. Somehow she had to keep Mamma around.

"So, you heard about the gold. I wish I could tell you just where to get it, but it's way out in the desert. If I show you, will you let me go?" A desperate plan was beginning to form in Tara's mind.

"Oh I'd have to talk to my son, but I bet I could talk him into lettin' you get off easy." The "mamma" character wiped the drool off her/his mouth and eagerly watched Tara for a response.

Suddenly the killer returned from his mental hiatus. "No way Mamma. She's going, and Ryan has gotta go too!"

"Now how you gonna do that you miserable twerp?"

He stepped back toward Tara. "Pick up that phone!" he yelled in his own voice.

Tara did as she was ordered.

"Dial your house, and tell that Ryan fella to meet you at the gold mine. Tell him to lie through his teeth to Dowding or you'll be dead when he gets there. He comes alone, you understand? And let me tell you little missy, I'll blow a hole in both of you so big you'll be able to park a bus in it if you try anything stupid. Got it?"

The killer caressed Tara's cheek with his gun. His look reminded her of a snake ready to strike.

"I got it," Tara said, moving her face slowly away from the gun. "But he's only been there once," she lied. "I'm not sure he'll be able to find it alone."

"For your sake, he'd better."

She dialed the number and waited. One ring, then two. Suddenly the killer grabbed the phone, and hung it up. His eyes flitted to the cell phone on the desk, and he reached over to grab it.

"On second thought, we'll call after we have a head start. We don't want him getting' there before we do."

Fifteen minutes later, they were heading east through Mesa on the Superstition Freeway when the killer had Tara dial home again.

"Hello?" answered Ryan.

"Ryan, it's me."

"What's wrong, Tara? Why do you sound like you're in the car?"

"He's here with me Ryan, the killer. He's going to kill me if you don't do exactly as I say. He knows about the gold."

"The what?"

"The gold. He must have heard us talking earlier," she said. "He wants you to meet us there alone, in one hour, or he'll kill me."

"Tara, are you telling me to go to the desert?"

"Yes. Can you find the place?"

"In the dark?"

"In one hour," she said.

"Tara, can he hear me?"

"No."

He paused. She was terrified, but she could almost hear the wheels of his mind turning.

"If you're thinking what I'm thinking," he said at last, "this may be our best chance. I'm on my way. Hang in there."

"Hurry, Ryan!"

The killer grabbed the phone from Tara and turned it off, then the mamma character returned.

Tara was driving, but this didn't stop "Mamma" from grabbing her by the hair.

"No tricks, little missy, or I swear, I'll take care of your man real ugly! You hear?"

Ryan was frantic. Grabbing Wil's arm, he explained the phone call as they ran for Tara's Jeep. Driving like a maniac, he headed east on the I-60 toward the Superstition Wilderness. It was 10:40 PM, and the freeway was mostly clear. He had roughly forty minutes to get to Tara's spot in the desert. That should have been plenty of time, if only he could remember where to go. But he wasn't sure he had paid close enough attention on his earlier trips with Tara . . . and those trips had been in daylight.

Wil looked over at him, then down at the speedometer. A quick glance downward told Ryan he was going 90 miles per hour.

"Slow it down just a little, Ryan." Wil said. "I know most of the Highway Patrolmen here and they'd probably understand why you're speeding, but we have to get there alive if we're going to save Tara."

"I'm worried Wil. This guy's nuts. He's liable to do anything. And what if I can't find the place?" Ryan was near hysteria.

"We'll find it. I know you can do it. Tell me more about this place."

Ryan gave him a quick version of the hole where the boulder had once been, and how everything going into it dissolved.

"It's crazy, Wil. First it scares you, then it gives you this wonderful euphoric sensation, then while you're basking in the high, it saps your will to live and sucks you into oblivion."

"And this killer thinks there's gold there?"

"Yeah. Tara and I kid around about the Lost Dutchman's Gold Mine—just a little game about 'The Hole' unearthing tons of gold. He must have been listening to us on the phone. Tara's smart. She's luring him right where we want him. Man, I love that girl. Just pray I can find the place."

Wil scratched his beard, then turned to Ryan. "This is dangerous, Ryan. I don't need to tell you why he wants you both out there."

"Of course not. He want's us dead. But I think we may have a little surprise for him, if he'll just take the bait."

———◆———

Tara put the truck in park, then stepped on the emergency brake out of habit. "We walk from here," she said. The killer had made her drive so that he could keep the gun trained on her. Surprisingly, neither he nor his dear mamma had spoken a word after the phone call to Ryan.

"Step out my way, slowly," he said after he got out. "And don't try anything. It's dark out here, and I'll shoot you if I need to."

"I won't. Just remember, I show you the gold, and you let me go, right?"

He didn't answer her, but gave her a push, and made a motion with his gun for her to start walking. Tara knew he meant to kill her. She also knew why he wanted Ryan out there. She only hoped she could get him first.

It was dark, but the moon was almost full and it hung straight above her, giving them enough light to make their way through the desert. Fifteen minutes later, they were at the riverbed.

———◆———

Ryan and Wil finally found Dutchman's Trailhead at about 11:10 PM. Ryan turned the Jeep onto the trail, and headed southeast.

"This is it! I remember that big saguaro right there." He pointed to his right, showing Wil the towering giant. "It's a bumpy few miles. The hard part will be finding where we turn off. Keep your eyes open Wil, there's a little ditch on your side where we turn. I can't remember exactly how far, and we're running out of time."

"We'll make it Ryan, and when we do, we'll nail this jerk. We've got to keep our heads about us, though. I've seen his kind before. As crazy as he may be, he knows exactly what he's doing. So, don't panic. Let's not give him any advantage."

Ryan looked down at the odometer. They had gone three miles. "So then, Wil, what do we do when we get there. Will he be waiting for us?"

"Possibly, but I think not. My bet is that he's had Tara take him to the hole. But to be safe, I'll hide down in the back seat until you've left, just in case he's watching. When you get out, leave your door open. I'll follow you to the spot. I'm actually pretty good at night tracking."

Ryan thought about Tara with the killer. Would she try to lure him into The Hole? What if she tried and failed? What if he pushed her in instead, seeing there was no gold? He had to be there. He had to save her! His life had taken such a wonderful turn when he met her; he couldn't bear to think of where he'd be without her. All his life, he had dreamed of this. Now a moron with a gun was threatening to destroy that dream.

The Jeep bumped along in the desert night, both men deep in thought. Ryan checked the odometer again . . . five and a half miles. He checked his watch. It was 11:18 PM.

"We're getting close!" he said out loud. "Come on, where are you?" He was scanning the sides of the trail. "What if I passed it? Please God, help us, don't let me mess this up."

The road was rough, and time was racing swiftly by. Nothing looked familiar. Ryan couldn't help but think of the wicked things this nut might do to his wife. He never hurt a man in his life, but right now he wanted nothing more than to send this maniac to the lowest depths of Hell.

"There! Ryan is that it?" Wil was pointing to a spot thirty feet in front of them and to the right.

"Yeah! It looks like it. God, help it to be the right one." He turned the Jeep onto the path and drove out into the darkness.

"Boy, this is not much of a trail, are you sure this is it?" Wil asked.

"That's exactly what I told Tara when we came here the first time. But to be honest Wil, I don't know. It seems like it, though."

"Whoa!" Wil cried out, bumping his head on the roof. The Jeep hit a small ravine with a thud. Suddenly their movement halted, as the wheels began to spin in the sand. "Hold it Ryan, don't get us in any deeper!"

Ryan slapped the steering wheel in frustration, and looked at his watch. It was 11:23. His grip tightened on the wheel. "Come on, come on!" he shouted, slipping the Jeep into four-wheel drive.

"Okay, ease it out!" Wil said. Slowly, the Jeep crept out of its position in the ravine, and they were off again.

Several minutes passed before they saw a new Dodge pick-up ahead in the moonlight. "This has gotta be it!" said Ryan, "Stay down."

He parked and jumped out into the shadowy desert night, not knowing what to expect. His heart was racing, as he stood in the moonlight, motionless. The night was so still, the only sound he could hear was his heart bumping wildly in his chest.

He cupped his hands to his mouth and yelled.

"Tara!"

Tara and the killer had been listening to the Cherokee's distinctive engine sound as it stumbled through the desert then stopped. They were just passing the riverbed where the coyote died when she heard Ryan yell her name. He was only a couple hundred yards away. The killer and his dead mamma were carrying on a whispered argument, seemingly preoccupied.

Tara knew she could probably ditch the man. She knew the area so well, even in the darkness, she was pretty sure she could get away, leaving him to mumble in the night with his dear old mamma. But she couldn't risk it now, with Ryan so close.

"So," the killer muttered, now alert, "looks like old Ryan found his way after all! Move it, girl!"

Tara picked up the pace. She knew she had to act fast. If Ryan showed up before she could take care of the killer, he could be gunned down in an instant. Two minutes passed before they reached the ant colony.

"We're here," she said, turning toward the killer.

"Good! Now sit down," he ordered, "and we'll wait for your honey."

"Don't you want to see the gold?"

"No."

"I'm sure your mamma would like to see it. Besides, she promised to let me go if I showed her."

"Shut up!" demanded the killer. "I'm not going to give up killing your boyfriend for all the gold in Fort Knox.

Tara knew she had to appeal to the mother's greed now, or she and Ryan were dead. She took a deep breath, hoping that what she felt prompted to say didn't earn her a bullet.

"Look, I know if your mamma knew about the diamonds and other gems, she'd want to see them now. The Lost Dutchman's Gold Mine actually contained more priceless gems than gold. I'd be willing to let you have it all, right here, tonight, if you just let us go."

"Did you say diamonds, little missy?" came the greedy voice of Mamma. She smacked Tara across the face. "Git your butt over there and show me where they are! Move it or lose it darlin'!"

The gamble had worked.

"It's up there, just over that rise," said Tara, pointing toward The Hole.

"You first, little girl. And no tricks!"

"I promise, no tricks." Tara actually enjoyed lying to the fiend. "But there are so many diamonds, you've got to let me take just a few back with me." She was trying hard to keep Mamma around and her son trapped in his own mind.

Tara stepped up to the edge of the deadly pit. It was dark, but there was no denying what lay before them. She felt enveloped in fear, fear that her own end had come. She could hear Mamma talking of how she would finally be able to buy that castle she always dreamed of, as the killer stepped up beside her.

Lying before them was what seemed an endless expanse of gloom. A whisper of death was in the air, and it seemed to be calling to Tara.

"Don't fight it, young one. Step out into my hungry bowels, and end it all," it seemed to say. It knew it would be fed tonight. A chill swept up Tara's spine, and she prayed for strength.

"Where are them diamonds, little missy. Don't make me have to look for 'em, or you'll pay with your life, Dearie."

Tara started to shake at the thought of what she was about to do. But she knew it was now or never.

"They're right there, Mamma!" she shouted.

With all her strength and speed, she jumped behind the killer and shoved him toward Hell. The gun went flying, but somehow, as he fell, he was able to twist around and grab Tara's leg, then hold on tight. Both of them slipped over the edge. Flipping around to her stomach, Tara managed to grasp a root at the base of what was once a beautiful desert willow. She hung on with all her strength, the killer dangling from one of her legs.

"That was rude, little missy. How would you like a smack on your stupid head?" cried Mamma in a slurred voice.

Tara could feel the killer struggling to climb up her leg and shook him back down.

"Shut up Mamma!" he cried. "Can't you see she tricked us?"

His life's being sapped out of him by the second, Tara thought, but she was starting to feel it too, and she couldn't shake his death-grip on her ankle.

"Sonny? Something's not right here. Something's a matter with my legs. If you don't get us out of here now, sonny, you're gonna pay."

"Not now, Mamma! For once will you just shut up!"

Tara was already beginning to feel the effects of the euphoria. She fought it with all her might.

"Ryan! Ryan! Help me!" She yelled as loud as she could, tightening her grip on the plant.

She could hear him now, just over the rise. He must be at the ant colony. Finally, he raced up to the rise, and knelt above her.

"Tara! Grab my hand! Grab my hand!"

She did, but her weight, with the killer holding on to her ankle, was too great. When Wil arrived they each grabbed one arm, but they kept slipping in the loose sand. The killer would not let go. He was gradually pulling them all down toward death.

At that point, Ryan did something that made Tara's heart stop. He jumped out into the darkness, landing on top of the killer. Holding on with one hand, he raised his free hand and started beating the man with all his might.

The shock of Ryan's action made Tara miss the desert willow root she was trying to grasp again. Wil struggled to hang on to her in the sliding sand. She felt a sense of impending horror, as she heard Wil shout, "I'm loosing her Ryan!"

Fear, courage and above all, love, gave Ryan the strength he needed. He knew now that he would have to give his own life to save the one he loved. A strange peace came over him at the realization. Fighting off the numbing fear, he reached up and grabbed the thumb of the madman's hand where he held relentlessly onto Tara's ankle. With a jerk, he twisted it until it broke. Screaming, the killer released his grip on Tara and they broke free. At first slowly, then faster, he and Ryan slid toward the center of The Hole.

"We're going to Hell Mamma!" the killer shouted. "We're going to Hell!"

Looking up, Ryan saw Tara, her body limp and lifeless, being pulled to safety as euphoria filled his heart. Tears of joy welled up in his eyes. "Take care of her, Wil!" he shouted as he disappeared with the killer into the blackness and oblivion of disorientation.

Chapter 8
PARADISE

Everything was feeling. First blackness, serene and peaceful; then, ahead, enlightenment, like a pinhole, but growing. The sensation of ultimate speed eclipsing the blackness. Speed beyond that of light, rushing and pushing toward a light at the end of . . . a tunnel; light growing, growing; the need to reach the light, growing, transcending all desires. A strange vibrating hum permeating mind, heart, entire essence. Thoughts, memories, a lifetime in an instant, bright as the days they occurred. Peace, the light growing, enveloping entire soul, pushing out darkness. Kindness, tenderness . . . perfect Love!

Everything was sight. In the middle of the light, a figure stood alone, waiting. Unrecognizable, but growing more familiar. Comprehension, understanding grew to . . . perfect knowledge. Outstretched arms reached to embrace.

"Ryan, welcome home. I've missed you so much."

The words were smooth, spoken with perfect love; tears flowed, his heart swelled.

"Dad! You're alive!"

"Of course, son. I've always been alive."

"But I thought you were killed in the car crash."

"I was."

"Then . . . I don't understand."

Suddenly, total recollection. The desert, his struggle with the killer, and . . . his own death. He stepped back from his father.

"No, Dad. No! I can't be dead. I've got to go back. Tara needs me! She's in danger. Please Dad, how can I go back?"

"Relax son, and think about how you died. Tara's fine. She's all right for now. You saved her life by giving up your own! I'm so proud of you."

Ryan looked at his father. The two of them appeared to be about the same age, which surprised Ryan greatly. He could feel the stature of his father while they embraced; he was large and muscular. All the pictures he had of his father showed a man of medium build.

"Oh no! I just realized. I was . . . disoriented, right?"

"Well yes, son, in a manner of speaking. But as you can see, you're not really dead!"

"No, of course not. But Dad, you've got to help me. There were some really strange things going on there; I need to be with Tara. She needs me. Her life is still in danger . . . isn't it?"

"Yes."

"In fact many more lives are in danger if we don't get to the people causing these problems, right?"

"My, how you've grown and matured. You get right to the point now, don't you?"

"It's all a matter of time, Dad. And Tara's going to run out of it soon if I don't help. Isn't there some way I can go back? Can you help me?"

"Come with me, son. Let's walk a bit first. I have some important things to tell you." He stopped and put his hand on Ryan's shoulder. "You can relax, Ryan, everything's fine for now. But there's a lot for you to learn."

He gave him another hug, longer this time. And for a while, Ryan couldn't let go. He sensed that his father possessed great power and knowledge. He couldn't believe that they were together again, and he wanted to soak up the moment. But he had no intention of staying long if he could help it.

It had always been a dream of his to know his father. Suddenly, still in his father's embrace, he began to absorb knowledge about him. It was miraculous; his mind could hardly accept it at first, but it was very real, more than anything Ryan had ever experienced before. He felt like a sponge, consuming his father's mortal experiences, his memories of their family. In what seemed like an instant, they were assimilated into his own consciousness.

How odd, he thought. There is no sense of time. His father's life played out for him in the brief seconds of an embrace, moments that felt instantaneous but could as easily have been centuries as nanoseconds.

It was as though he were present, watching himself be born, learn to walk, talk, dress himself, and always feeling his father's pride. The events were seen through his father's eyes and felt with his father's heart. He took his first steps, caught his first fish and hiked his first trail; even felt his father's pain when he was taken from mortality, leaving his son behind alone.

Surprisingly, the experiences didn't stop with the end of his father's earthly life. He felt his father beam with pride at his high school graduation, and sensed his admiration as he watched his son through his college years. He felt his father's love for him when he left home for his two-year mission, and experienced the overwhelming joy his father felt at his marriage to Tara. How wonderful to know how much his father loved Tara.

He let go and stepped back. "What was all that?" he asked.

His father smiled. "Oh, just a little gift from me to you."

"It was wonderful! Thank you." After a pause, he added, "Can I see Mom?"

"Not just yet, Ryan. Come, let's walk."

He put his arm around Ryan's shoulder, and guided him through the most beautiful forest Ryan had ever seen. Majestic trees that looked like pines, but had no needles lying around them, cascaded down rolling hills through a grassy, park-like setting. It was neither too hot, nor too cold. Birds flew, creatures walked; everything was perfect.

Ryan looked around, marveling at the world he saw. It had everything earth had, but all its beauty was intensified. All living things seemed in perfect harmony with the many people Ryan saw milling around, talking, reading, even learning. Then he noticed a man standing to their left, next to a magnificent tree awash in shades of purple and green. The man was watching them.

"Dad, who's that guy over there? He seems pretty interested in what we're doing."

"Oh, he's just someone a lot like you and me."

The man was smiling. Ryan couldn't help but smile back and wave before turning his attention back to his father.

"Ryan, knowledge is a wonderful thing. I was so pleased that you chose science as a profession. As a little boy, you had a sense of wonder about everything. I knew you wouldn't settle for a world without answers. When a man puts enough pieces of a particular puzzle together, he can imagine the picture before it forms. This is vision. But as he continues to work on the puzzle, he will eventually achieve total clarity. You left before you could put all the pieces together, Ryan. You have vision, but you don't have total clarity. Not yet. The truth is, you're needed here."

"Dad, are you telling me that I was brought here for some purpose, leaving Tara behind to fend for herself?"

"Yes, and no. Again, you are seeing a vision, but without total clarity."

"Dad! Tara is alone now. With me gone like this, she'll be hiding from . . . 'the Beast' for the rest of her life!"

They stopped walking, and Ryan's father motioned for him to sit on a magnificent marble bench. "Let me give you a little more of the picture, son. You're troubled, I know, but I think we can help you. First, let's try to achieve some clarity for you, okay?"

"Okay, Dad. I'm sorry."

"Nothing to be sorry about," he responded, waving his hand in a dismissing gesture.

He sat back and looked intently at his father. He was everything Ryan had ever imagined him to be and more, a thousand times more. He looked around in awe. This new world was more brilliant and alive than anything he had ever seen. Colors he had never imagined tantalized his eyes, bathing them in brilliant hues. Delightful new scents permeated the air. His senses were heightened so that everything dazzled him, screaming out to his ever-inquisitive mind for closer inspection.

But Tara's situation gnawed at him, distracting him from the beauty of his surroundings. As he thought of her, he could hardly focus on anything else. Somehow he had to get back to her. He struggled to compose himself as he turned back to his father.

"Your particle intelligence theory was right on the money, son," his father said. "All particles are alive and have intelligence. If it weren't so, the world could never have been organized as it is. In fact, worlds without number are being organized right now, always using the same small building blocks you refer to as sub-atomic particles. One who is much greater than you or I gives these particles life and imparts the law that governs them. Indeed, this One is the law by which *all* things are governed. But, as with all living things, these particles have free agency within the sphere of their existence. That means they can be disoriented, as you call it—deceived, really—and thus they will disassociate for a time.

"Normally, these particles are absolutely obedient to the One who gave them life, but recently a group of troubled folks have been trying to get them to obey someone else."

"Are you talking about Satan, Dad?"

"Actually, the person who is spearheading this particular effort is someone they call The Merchant. You might call him Satan's Manager of Sales and Marketing, a very evil and powerful individual. The first step in his plan is to 'disorient' and collect living matter from the earth. He believes this will give him the raw material he needs to create physical bodies for himself and his followers. He knows also that it will cause great chaos and damage to the Earth."

"How do we stop him?"

"With people like you and Tara. You see, there are two groups of people causing most of the problems you've run into. As you surmised, the first group consists of powerful men on earth. They've set up the technology that destabilizes the sub-atomic particles. These particle destabilizers, for lack of a better description, are set up all over the world now—usually in the oceans, so as not to be detected. These are very wicked individuals, situated both in and out of many different governments. They have sold the earth's inheritance for personal gain. I had hoped you could find them as a mortal, and bring them down. But . . ."

"I died!" Ryan finished his sentence.

"Yes, son, and very heroically, if I may say so."

Ryan hung his head. His mind struggled to find the clarity he had been promised, but he could not stop thinking of Tara.

His father continued. "Remember now, these are living particles, and once they become disoriented, they disassociate from each other. They're in a dazed and confused state, much like what you felt just before . . . coming here. The only thing in the physical realm that is not affected by these machines is light. So, after these particles have been disassociated, they're attracted like a magnet to the only stable thing around them . . ."

"The sun!" Ryan exclaimed. "They follow the sun's light. But my calculations indicate that they don't leave the atmosphere."

"That's right son. They are also attracted to the massive body of life they feel from the Earth. They never actually venture out into space."

"Well, that confirms my calculations. Um . . . but what happens to them then?"

His father looked at him with a near-divine tenderness in his eyes, and continued. "Not many understand this process as well as you do. In fact, most of the mortals behind this don't understand what's really happening. All they know is that, for creating what they consider some minor chaos in the world's ecological system, The Merchant compensates them with everything they want. Information can be very addicting, son, and it can give its possessor a sense of unlimited power as well as control over others. In this case, not just individuals but entire countries!"

Ryan shook his head and sighed. "I knew it. Greed on the grandest scale imaginable!"

The senior McKay put his hand on Ryan's shoulder. "Yes. And that's why they came after you, son. They can't afford to have honest, concerned folks, like yourself and Tara, discovering their little secret."

"So what happens to the disoriented matter?"

"Here's where the second group is involved. They are even more wicked than the men on earth. They are spirits, in form like you and I, but they work with The Merchant. Some are in the process of collecting the living matter. Others try to control the disoriented matter. They hope to gain complete control in the physical realm. Without physical bodies, they can only operate here."

"That's terrible! So how are they doing? Is it working?"

"Actually, they haven't had much success. The truth is they'll never be able to turn that matter to their own purposes. It simply will not obey them. It knows the difference between God and Satan. It may be disoriented for a time, but it will eventually realize what has happened. It simply will not follow evil in the long run."

"So . . . what you're saying is that I could never have turned lead into gold?" Ryan smiled resignedly.

"I'm afraid not, son. The universe doesn't work that way."

"I figured there had to be a catch somewhere. But doesn't The Merchant know this? What does he hope to gain through this plan of his?"

"The Merchant, and his followers refuse to accept the Truth that governs the universe. They think they can thwart the plan of the Creator, and invent their own rules. They have no desire to live according to the plan of God, or become part of any free and orderly society. They would like nothing better than to destroy everything associated with God's plan. They want to live a pirate's life through the eternities, taking what they will and leaving in their wake sorrow and ruin."

Ryan smiled at this father, who continued. "Right now, you and I are spiritual. Although spirit is matter, it is very . . . refined, and is not able to control or manipulate physical matter with any degree of ease. Nor is it susceptible to the same kinds of manipulation as, say, sub-atomic particles. As a scientist, you might be able to grasp the situation by thinking of Einstein's formula equating matter and energy. Physical matter is something like 900 trillion times more energy-dense than spirit matter. It's impossible, at this time, for those in the physical realm to even perceive the spiritual realm, though, if they employ the power of their own spirits, they can hear and sometimes even see us."

His father paused momentarily, allowing Ryan to take in the ramifications of what he had said. Ryan could tell his father was just skimming the surface, and marveled at the depth of his understanding.

"There will come a time," the senior McKay continued, "when you and I will be reunited with physical matter, joined together forever by the Creator in a perfect union of power and glory. The Merchant and his servants will never have this opportunity. Long ago, they chose not to be a part of the God's plan. Now they see mortals dying and progressing on to great things, and they want the same for themselves . . . without actually earning it, of course. For their choice, God decreed that they would not progress. They're filled with hate because of that. They want to destroy Earth and everything associated with God."

"So this is kind of a two-pronged attack?" Ryan asked, his mind studying the situation that would continue to plague his wife.

"Yes. They think they can give *themselves* bodies and worlds of physical matter. At the same time, they want to bring disorder and chaos to Earth. They'll never achieve their first goal, but they're doing quite a job with the second!"

"Haven't they realized yet that they can't really succeed?"

"They're angry men, and just won't admit the truth. They focus only on the success they are having amongst men, and will continue in their efforts until we stop them. They enjoy the prospect of destroying the earth, even if they can't do anything with the matter they've disoriented."

"Couldn't you just stop them? I mean, it's pretty obvious God has the power to do that."

His father looked deep into his eyes. "Son, He does *not* interfere with man's free agency. He works only through normal channels of persuasion, though He will occasionally step in where men have surrendered their agency to chance. The agency of man is sacrosanct. The power of an individual to bring change to a world, for good or ill by choosing one path over another is fundamental to existence itself! Of course, He tries to be as persuasive as possible. And we're constantly working to counter the negative decisions of our fellow men both here and in the physical world. But it remains the classic battle of good and evil, and countless individuals like you and I fight it every day on every world in the universe. God must allow people to choose evil as well as good. Otherwise there is no freedom, and without freedom, who would follow God? It is through freedom that character is built. Indeed, without freedom—and accountability—there is no character."

"But then how can God be sure that Satan and people like The Merchant, won't win?"

His father smiled knowingly. "There are always enough good men and women to balance out the effects of evil . . . always. With God's guidance, the good will always prevail. But I'm probably saying more than I should right now. Suffice it to say, I'm involved in the work of stopping The Merchant and his group here in the spirit realm. You have been brought back to help. Your service in this cause will be very beneficial for you and for Tara, as well as the rest of mankind. Besides, someone has to do it," he concluded with a gleam in his eye.

"Boy, I don't know, Dad." He stood and turned to face his father. "How are you and I going to do this? It seems bigger than two people."

"Oh, it is," reassured his father.

"Well, I don't want to seem presumptuous and all, but, if this is up to us, and God isn't going to interfere . . ."

His father interrupted. "I didn't exactly say that, son. God will not interfere with man's free agency. He expects us to fight our own battles, but He definitely has a plan, and the power to carry out that plan. It's just a lot more . . . complex than you would imagine."

"So it's like Brigham Young said: 'When you're on your knees, pray as if everything depends on God, but when you stand up, work as if everything depends on you.'"

"That's always been good advice," his father replied, smiling.

"But what I'd like to know is just how many of these followers of The Merchant there are. Ten, twenty, a hundred? What are we fighting? I mean, what're we up against?"

"Numbers are not the issue, son. We are up against evil. And know this: you are very significant in this particular battle. You have been called as a leader, to provide crucial assistance in bringing this chaos to an end."

Ryan stood and walked a few steps away. He was deep in thought. Finally he turned. "Dad, I've dreamed of this moment, when I could see you again. And I would be honored to serve at your side; to help in whatever cause is just. I love you so much . . . but I can't. Not until I can help Tara find a safe and happy life. Dad, I love her. I would do anything for her. And I fear for her. She's been hurt so much by life. My death has to be the last straw for her. I've got to get back. I have to! Can you possibly arrange it?" He reached for his father's hands and took them into his own squeezing firmly. "Please Dad, you've got to get permission from whoever you have to so I can go back."

His father drew him close and hugged him. "I already have, son. In fact, you can go now."

Ryan was overcome by the news. Weeping, he felt overwhelmed by the tenderness, foresight and power he sensed in this being he called his father.

"There are some conditions for your return, however."

"Conditions?"

"Yes, rules if you will."

"Dad, I'll do anything if I can just go back." Suddenly a thought struck him. "Wait a minute. You're not saying I can go back as I was, are you? I didn't just die; I was disintegrated. There's no body for me to go back to . . . I, I can't go back as a mortal, can I?"

His father sighed. "You can go back now, son, just as you are, in spirit. Tara will be able to see you. But one of the conditions is that she will only be permitted to see you twice. The first time will be during your initial visit. The next time will be when you bring her home."

The look of shock and puzzlement on Ryan's face produced a sympathetic smile from his father. Putting his hand on Ryan's shoulder, he continued.

"On your initial visit, you should explain to her that when she no longer sees you, she will still be able to hear you. But she must listen with her heart, where you'll be able to speak to her and help her. She'll have to feel for you, for the promptings you give her. These promptings will guide her, and help her in what she has to do. Let her know that she'll have to exercise more faith than ever before to get through the ordeal that will face her. It will all be up to her.

"Remember what I told you about spirits. You will not have sufficient power to interfere with the world or its people directly, unless it is given to you by proper authority. You can travel around, learn about those concerned with this chaos, then, through your promptings, you can guide Tara in her journey.

"And while you're there, guiding her, you too will have to exercise faith. It is not the same as being here. You will never be alone, but the physical realm, where you will be, is different from this realm. We'll be on your right hand and your left, sometimes seen, often unseen, but always giving you and Tara the strength you will need to carry out your mission. I can't tell you who *we* are, but you will see other spirits from time to time. Don't be alarmed. Concern yourself only with Tara and her safety as you work with her to complete your assignment. You'll be like a guardian for her until this mission is completed."

"How will I know what to do?"

Placing his hand on Ryan's chest, he said, "You'll know right here, son. Don't worry, and remember, whatever happens, do not lose focus on what life is all about. For Tara, it's not just about finding those who are trying to do this terrible thing to the earth. She will have other concerns as well. She must remain faithful to the truth she has received, and continue to learn and serve until she too crosses over. Do you understand?"

Ryan nodded, then asked, "How do I get back?"

"Oh, that's the fun part. All you have to do is think of where you want to be or who you want to be with, and you're there. It's that easy!"

They embraced one last time. "Thank you so much Dad. I love you."

"And I love you, son."

Ryan stepped back. "I guess I'm ready. Is she?"

"Everything's been taken care of," his father assured him, motioning to the man who had been watching them.

Ryan couldn't help but notice the grace with which this person moved. As he drew near, Ryan saw that he was about the same age as him and his father. He was a large man, too, strong and handsome. Though he seemed young, his countenance portrayed the same unfathomable depths of knowledge and power he sensed in his father.

"Ryan, I'd like you to meet Brandon. He'll be guiding you back, just to make sure you get where you need to be. Wouldn't want you to end up on the moon," he laughed. Both Brandon and Ryan smiled.

Ryan extended his hand to Brandon. "Nice to meet you."

"I'm honored," Brandon said, as he took Ryan's hand.

Ryan took one last long look around.

"You boys should go now," his father said. "God speed."

"Dad?" Ryan asked.

"Yes?"

"Is this Heaven?"

His father smiled. "Not quite, son, but close. This is Paradise."

Ryan smiled back, closed his eyes, and thought of Tara.

Chapter 9
INITIAL VISIT

The steady rain pitter-pattered gently against the window as Carol Johnson stared aimlessly ahead, looking at nothing in particular. Outside, flashes of lightning illuminated a blurry water-soaked world. This was not the usual summer monsoon, lasting a short but violent fifteen or twenty minutes. It was a full-blown storm. A December hurricane off the coast of Mexico had pumped a lot of moisture northward into Arizona, giving more than enough rain to the parched and thirsty desert. This was the third day of the storm and the sun was nowhere to be found.

Behind her, the door opened. Lonnie Johnson and Wil Dowding walked in, each greeting Carol with a comforting hug.

"What's going on?" Lonnie whispered as he turned his gaze toward the woman in the hospital bed.

"The doctor thinks she's coming out of it! He just left but he feels it could happen any time. All the tests he's been doing indicate a big increase in brain activity. He says it's just a matter of time. In fact, he's not going home until she comes to."

Lonnie Johnson gave his wife's hand a squeeze. "This is fantastic! I'm so glad you called. Jeff is gathering all the kids together. They'll be here shortly."

Outside, the rain eased to a drizzle. Carol, noticing the change, glanced toward the window. "Look Lonnie, maybe there is hope."

They looked down at Tara's face. Even though she had been in her coma for over six weeks, she looked as beautiful as ever. Carol combed her hair every day, and babied and pampered her in every way she could.

When she was first brought in, Tara looked like death. But with the constant nourishment of the I.V., and her family's unfailing attention and love, she had improved. She seemed ready now to be reborn. It was as if she had been in a cocoon, ready to emerge a beautiful butterfly.

Carol looked at the men. "The doctor says her vitals are strong, that she's built up strength. He feels sure she'll make a full recovery."

"And the baby?" asked a concerned Wil.

"According to the doctor, everything's fine. Of course it was touch and go the first couple weeks, but he says the baby seems to be doing fine, thank God."

"I'm so glad!" said Wil. "She's a strong willed girl! I brought her a Poinsettia for the Christmas season!" He looked around for a spot to put the plant among the myriad of others, then gave up and set it on the floor. "Looks like a dang botanical garden in here!" he commented.

"It just wouldn't be right if she didn't have plants to wake up to," Carol sighed.

As she turned back to her daughter, the mood turned somber. Silence filled the room as if they were all hit with the same thought at once. If Tara awoke soon, how would she tell her about Ryan? Several minutes passed, then Carol spoke.

"Lon?"

"Yes dear?"

Knowing that people in comas often hear what is said around them, she spoke very softly near his ear. "You think she knows? How in the world are we going to tell her?"

"Shush now. We'll cross that bridge when we get to it," he reassured.

She looked deep into her husband's eyes, soothing and comforting him with her gaze and receiving the same from him, as only two people in love can do. Wil interrupted them.

"Lon, Carol, I think you have an audience."

They turned to look at Tara, and to their astonishment, her eyes were open. Carol grabbed her hand.

"Tara? Oh, Tara, you're back!" She leaned down and kissed her cheek. "We were so worried, but you're back now! We love you so much! Tara, can you hear us?" she asked anxiously.

Tara gave a weak smile and nodded her head.

Lon reached over and gave her hand a gentle squeeze. "It's good to have you back honey. The kids will all be here in a few minutes. What a wonderful Christmas gift this is!"

"Welcome back, Tara," Wil said, then added, "I'll step out and let you have a little time together."

He left, but reentered only a few minutes later with the doctor. Carol was chattering away as they entered, telling Tara about all the kids and showing her the plants, being very careful not to say anything about Ryan or his death. As yet, Tara hadn't said a word, she just lay there half smiles, looking weak and confused.

The doctor moved in and started to check her over. He checked her heart rate, blood pressure, reflexes, eyes, ears, nose and throat. He spoke calmly to her, asking her to move her fingers, toes, arms and legs. Finally, he turned to her parents and smiled.

"Well, looks like she's in good repair. I have a few more tests I'd like to run, but I'll come back a little later. If you have no questions, I'll talk to you then."

Tara felt a little groggy, but she was fully awake and could see and hear everything happening around her. There was one thing she had to do. Before the doctor could leave, she pulled at his arm. Looking up at him, she spoke in a whisper.

"Doctor?"

"Yes," the doctor said, leaning closer.

"May I see you alone for a moment?"

Confused, but smiling, and with tears of joy in their eyes, the group reluctantly backed through the doorway into the hall.

Someone said, "We'll be right outside the door here. Can we get you anything, Tara? A magazine, book?"

She smiled and shook her head. When the door closed, she turned to the doctor and tried to sit up. But she was weaker than she realized, and fell back on her pillow with a gasp. Looking around the room in confusion, she turned to the doctor again.

"Yes Tara, how can I help you?"

"Where am I?" she whispered.

"You're at Desert Mercy Hospital."

"How did I get here?"

"Now that's a little more complicated. We can talk about it in the morning. But I can tell you this, you've been in a coma for six weeks, and I'm very glad to see you're finally awake and smiling. What else would you like to know?"

She whispered a little more strongly this time. "Who were all those people in my room?"

After Tara was released from the hospital, two months passed with no change in her condition. The world around her picked up the pace toward total chaos, but she was oblivious to it. She couldn't remember anything that happened before she awoke in the hospital. Nor could she remember her studies at school, or any of her friends or professors.

But to her, the greatest mystery of all was the fact that she was pregnant! How could that possibly be? she wondered. How in the world could she forget a man whom she apparently had loved enough to marry, and with whom she was having a baby? She was wearing a wedding ring, but who was he and where had he gone? No matter how she tried, these mysteries were tucked away into the farthest reaches of her mind, locked in a mental vault with no key in sight.

The psychologist working on Tara's case, informed the Johnson's that this was not uncommon in cases of severe emotional trauma, and that it was important for her to come out of it on her own. They were not to force the issue by telling her things that she wouldn't be able to handle. She had built mental walls as an emotional defense, an escape from the horrible events her subconscious mind would not allow her to remember. Even in a coma, these walls could be erected. She assured them that Tara would eventually find a trigger on her own that would start the walls crumbling.

"When that happens," she said, "you be there for her! Give her all the love and support you can. It will not be an easy time for her."

Tara was very much aware of her parent's trepidation. She knew how much they wanted her to remember, and they were very careful how they answered her questions. The psychologist advised Tara to be patient with them, and not to be worried about the way they looked at her. She was told to ask questions as things began to go from fuzzy to less fuzzy, all the while hoping the whole jumbled mess would clear up soon. Above all, she was to remain patient until things started getting familiar to her.

She was beginning to see things differently now. It was like trying to remember a dream. In the past, when she wanted to remember her dreams, she would shift around in bed until she found the position in which she was laying when the dream occurred. At the same time, she would relax her mind and try to remember. When she found the right position, the dream would often flood back. Sometimes, if she could fall back asleep, it would continue. She thought it strange that she could remember this old method of hers, but not the people who called themselves her family, regardless of her location in the house.

As the sun came up each morning, however, the faces around her took on a certain familiarity. They even began to feel right. It seemed to her that she was almost ready for her memories to come back.

It was about one o'clock on a Sunday afternoon when clarity reentered her world. Her family had gone to church, while she opted to stay home. Something didn't seem comfortable to her about the church where they'd been taking her. It was familiar, but oddly unfamiliar at the same time. That bothered her, but all she told them was that she wasn't feeling up to snuff, with her pregnancy and all.

There were other reasons she didn't go to church with them this particular Sunday. She felt as if something was going to happen. It was like she was in position and ready for the dream of her life to return. She didn't want to alarm her folks, in case her premonitions turned out to be false. But she felt something was just around the corner, and she wanted more than anything to be at home when it arrived.

The phone rang, interrupting her thoughts. Leaving her seat at the kitchen window, she walked over and picked it up.

"Hello?" she said.

"Hello." said a man's voice on the other end. "Is this the Johnson residence?"

"Yes it is." replied Tara.

"To whom am I speaking?"

"This is Tara. Who's this?"

There was a click and Tara found herself listening to nothing but a dial tone whining in her ear. She shrugged her shoulders, hung up the receiver, and went back to her seat at the bay window.

Sitting there in the kitchen, she nibbled saltines, occasionally glancing into the backyard when suddenly she noticed two men. They were standing quietly in the shade of a mulberry tree watching her.

It startled her at first, but as she looked at the man on the left, she could feel walls beginning to crumble. Somewhere deep inside a key was found and a vault was opened. Slowly at first, as if reticent to enter a new world, her memories began to drift back, permeating a mind she thought would never be hers again. Tears welled up as total recall pushed the blackness of amnesia from her soul. She stood up, a little shaky, and yelled at the top of her lungs.

"Ryan!"

———◆———

Outside, Ryan steadied himself. The speed of his trip from the spirit world to the spot where he now stood had been unnerving. When he closed his eyes in the spirit world and thought of Tara, her exact location appeared in his mind. He decided on the backyard at the Johnson home, hoping he could see her through the window before he made contact. The instant he made this decision, he was there. That's going to take some getting used to, he thought.

"It's always toughest the first time," his traveling companion assured him.

"Did you read my thoughts?" Ryan asked.

"We communicate through intentional thought. Most of the time we move our lips, but sometimes we don't. I thought you were commenting on the trip. Sorry."

"Oh, no problem, Brandon." He turned back to feast his eyes on Tara.

"I've always thought so too," Brandon said.

"What?"

"Oh, sorry. I thought you were talking to me again. I'll have to watch your lips after this. I didn't mean to embarrass you . . . But you're right. She is beautiful."

Ryan smiled. "Will I know what she's thinking, too?"

"Yes. Pretty much, if you listen carefully. We can keep our thoughts private, of course, but mortals don't do that very well."

"Have you ever been a mortal, Brandon?"

"Not yet, Ryan, but soon. I'll be going soon!"

Ryan sensed his excitement and wondered at it, then turned back to look at Tara.

"You're basically on your own from here, Ryan. She'll be able to see you now, just remember what you were told, and be wise with your time."

It was then that Tara shouted his name. Seeing her come to the window, Brandon turned to Ryan and smiled.

"So now it begins. I'll see you from time to time. It's not going to be easy, but I'll be here for you, for a while anyway." He took Ryan's hand and shook it. "Oh, by the way, it's been four months since your death."

"What?"

"Spirits don't have the same sense of time mortals do. It'll all be clear soon." He smiled. "Good luck."

Before Ryan could comprehend what he meant, Brandon was gone. The back door of the house opened and Tara was running toward him, sobbing and yelling his name. As she approached, he held out his hand for her to stop.

"Tara, please stop . . ."

"I thought you were dead!" she cried. Then, apparently hearing his words at last, she slowed to a stop just a few feet in front of him. He could tell she sensed something was wrong. Her thoughts were open to him. She wanted to rush in and hug him, but she was watching his hand in the air in front of her.

Then, as Tara moved to within inches of his hand, an awareness enlightened him. She was pregnant! He didn't know how he knew, he just did. She wasn't even showing . . . or was she?

"Why don't you want me to touch you?" she asked. "What's wrong?"

"Oh, I do Tara, more than anything, but there are a few things we have to talk about first."

"What is it, Ryan? What could possibly keep us apart?"

He extended his hand toward hers. "Take my hand."

She reached out, but her hand passed right through his. Her eyes opened wide and the blood drained from her face. She tried again and again to take his hand. Finally she gave up and buried her face in her hands.

"Tara, I died in the desert. You know that, and even though you know my spirit's not dead, it's sort of a shock to see it for yourself." She was speechless as Ryan continued. "I've been sent here to help you. And I want you to know how very much I love you."

Ryan sensed she was weak, close to fainting. "Tara, sit down here in the shade. I have so much to tell you."

"You'll have to do more than that, Ryan!" she managed at last. "I'm not sure what's happening to me. I've had amnesia up until about two minutes ago. Now I think you better tell me I'm not going insane." She looked up at him, tears pouring down her cheeks.

"Oh Tara, please don't cry," he pleaded.

"Ryan. You *are* dead! I remember now. A few minutes ago, I couldn't even remember my own name! Now I'm sitting in my back yard talking to my dead husband!"

He wanted to take her in his arms and comfort her. "I wish it weren't so, Tara. But I'm here, and I'm not really dead! I mean, I haven't ceased to exist."

"I know, but I want so much for you to hold me! I think I'm going to pass out. This is too much! The Beast has won again. How can I live the rest of my life without you?" She dropped her head, then looked up at him again. "How long will I even be able to see you?"

"I don't know. This is all so new. For me, only a few hours have passed since we were in the desert. I just came from my father, and . . . Oh, he was great! He . . ."

"Wait, Ryan, please wait. Why don't you tell me what happened to you first. What happened out in the desert?" She added in thought, *"If I can believe any of this is really happening!"*

"Tara, I assure you, this is really happening." A startled look came over her face. "Yes, I can read your mind, Ant Woman. Well, sometimes." He smiled and continued.

"In the desert, I jumped on the killer while he was hanging on to you, dragging you into The Hole. He and I slid down into it, and the next thing I knew, I was headed through a dark tunnel toward a light. When I got to the end, I met my dad. We talked about how he died, about you, and about the people involved in all this mess here."

"The people involved? Does that mean your theory . . ."

"Tara, please, this isn't easy. Don't let your analytical mind take over just yet. Hang in with me for a minute, okay?"

"I'm sorry. Go on."

"Tara, it was so awesome! It was Paradise, really! My dad hugged me and I felt the most incredible warmth, it was unbelievable. In fact it was he who got me back here to help you. I don't know what he had to do, but here I am! A little later than I would've liked . . . and a little lighter . . . but here, nevertheless."

"I don't know what to say. I would've been killed too. I'm overwhelmed that you would pay such a price to save my life."

"I would pay it a hundred times over. You have no idea how important it is for you to be here."

"Right now, I just wish I could hold you."

"Eventually, honey. We'll be together . . . in time."

"I don't like the sound of that." She paused, looking up at him. "But it's wonderful to see you. Are you sure I'm not dreaming? I know we believe in an afterlife, and all, but . . . it's just, well, I never really expected to see a spirit actually standing in front of me."

"You're not dreaming." he confirmed.

Tara was quiet for a moment, struggling for words. "Ryan? I, uh, well, I'm . . ."

"Yes I know. And it's a boy." The latter information popped into his mind an instant before he said it.

"How did you know? . . . It is?"

"Yes. But it's kind of hard to explain how I know. I just seem to know things. It comes to me naturally somehow, like sunshine; you just soak it in. I can't really explain it."

"Sounds perfect for a physicist."

"It's handy, but I'd give anything to be with you, in the physical world. This spirit stuff sure has its limitations."

"Well, you look wonderful," she said. "Oh, I miss you so much."

For a moment, they stared at each other, Ryan reflecting on the brief but joyous time they had spent together and contemplating the things they would no longer be able to share. Then he grinned.

"What?" Tara asked.

"Oh nothing."

"Come on!" she insisted, "Give it up, Particle Man. What are you smiling about?"

"I know what you're thinking, and it's just like you!" He stroked his chin, and nodded approval. "It's a good sign too."

"Ryan, tell me!"

"Well, besides the obvious frustrations and sadness you're feeling, your mind is at it again. You're wondering about this spirit in front of you. You want to study it, weigh it, take a sample, measure its limitations. Half of you is convinced our life is over, the other half wants to find out more."

She smiled sheepishly.

"That's not all!" he continued. "While I was speaking just now, you were wondering about Anne, your friend who died when you were in high school, which made you think again about what's happening to our world. Then, and here's why I love you so much, you wondered just how you and I could bring down the people who are causing all this anarchy and destruction. You want to go after the freaks who stole your husband from you and your unborn son. How am I doing?"

"You are really amazing. But answer me this, if you can, Superboy, how could I have gone from total amnesia, to total recall, just by seeing you here?"

"The time was right. The amnesia was there to protect you . . . until I could get here and . . . explain things. It was probably a protection for our unborn baby, as well. Let's face it, you might have done something stupid, like try to join me, or worse yet, go off half-cocked to find the perpetrators."

She nodded in agreement. "Yeah, you're probably right."

"Actually," confirmed Ryan, "it is true. That, uh, sunshine thing, you know. Can't help myself. Wish I'd had this ability when I was . . . "

"Can anyone else see you?" asked Tara.

"No, just you. But that'll have an end."

"An end? I knew it! When?"

"I was told that you would be able to see me only during this, my initial visit, and . . . well, one more time . . . later. Much later, I hope. I wasn't told how long the initial visit would last. But after it's over, and at least till we put the bad guys away, I'll still be able to talk to you. You just won't be able to hear me with your ears. You'll have to discern my whisperings through your heart, by listening closely to your impressions."

Tara's eyes glazed over in thought.

"Yes," Ryan continued, "just like that impression you had in Wil's office, when you were dealing with the killer."

"How'd you . . . I'm not sure I like this mind reading stuff."

"Sorry. But remember, you'll have to listen very closely, and rest assured, I'll be with you all the time, until the end."

"Are you telling me, that I won't be able to see you after today?"

"Maybe . . . I don't know, really. I was just told 'during my initial visit' you could see and hear me, and the next time you would see me, I would be taking you home, with me, if you catch my drift."

"Ryan, that isn't fair. I won't help anyone put these bad guys away unless I can see you longer than that!" She stood and looked angrily up into the sky. "Do you hear me?" she shouted. Looking back at Ryan, she continued. "They can't take you away from me and expect me to put myself and my baby in harm's way.

Ryan sighed. "Honey, please. I didn't make the rules."

"And another thing. The last time I received an impression, I listened with my heart and did what I was told. Do you remember that? All it did was get you killed! How can I ever trust my feelings after that?" She turned away from him and burst into tears.

Silently, Ryan moved closer to her. He longed to hold and comfort her. Sensing his presence, she turned. Reaching out, she tried to hold him, but to no avail. Frustrated, she turned back and ran into the house. There she heaved herself onto the couch in the living room and cried into a large pillow.

"Tara?" Ryan had stuck with her like a shadow. He knelt beside the couch. "Tara? You did the right thing in the desert, following your heart . . . following the Spirit. My father said I had 'vision' now—only a part of the whole, not 'total clarity.' So I don't understand why this all happened, but my 'vision' tells me it was meant to be. I know it was right! You and I have loved each other as much as any two people can. Now we have to love each other on a higher level. You know I'm alive. I'm right here. I won't leave you. We'll be together someday, I promise. I've seen things in Paradise that would knock your socks off! And one day, we'll be there together, and we'll hold each other, and . . . Tara, please look at me."

She raised her head, and gazed into his face. Ryan reached out his hand, and stroked her hair. She wouldn't be able to feel anything, but he hoped the sight of it might comfort her.

"Someone upstairs loves you very much," he said. "You're known there. They have a lot of faith in you. You and I must exercise the same kind of faith in ourselves. You know this is what we have to do. I know we can do it. I'm as upset about the situation as you are, but somehow we have to rise above self-pity and do this thing. In the end, it'll all be worth it. I feel that stronger than anything."

She lifted her head from the pillow, managing a weak smile. "Self-pity? I don't think you understand. I've lost everyone I ever cared about. I just wanted a normal life with you, and children someday."

"You didn't lose your parents!" he said soberly.

She started to cry. "Oh, Ryan, I'm so sorry. I'm being so selfish. This whole thing must be tearing you up as well. I just don't have your 'vision' yet, I guess."

He smiled at her and reached for her cheek. "I'm here for you, my darling. I always will be. It's not what we wanted, but we've got to put our feelings aside. Right now, we're needed for bigger things."

"Can you tell me about it? I won't cry anymore, I promise. Just tell me everything from the moment you met your father till the time I saw you in the back yard." She sat up, and gave him her full attention. "I really want to know. My family won't be back for a while yet."

"Yes, I know."

"Oh yeah, I forgot. You already know everything."

"Not everything," he corrected.

"Still, that 'sunshine thing' sounds pretty cool. So go ahead, tell me what you know."

He started at the beginning, with his drive out to the desert and his struggle with the killer, and worked his way to the conversation with his father. He told her about The Merchant and his connection with unscrupulous men in various governments, and finished with an account of his trip back to her. Tara sat silent, soaking it all in.

Her thoughts were an open book. He could see that she was already settling into the situation. Her natural curiosity, scientific background and ability to accept discovered truths, whatever their character, was serving her well. But for that nature in her, he realized, she might have had a mental breakdown.

Instead, there she was, talking to her dead husband—not a figment of her overwrought imagination, but a real, live personage of spirit whom only she could see. He sensed her inner strength, a solid, powerful character that filled him with admiration. She had accepted his death, and was ready to move on . . . but only if the future included him. He had to think of some way to stay visible longer.

"Ryan, when I looked out the window and saw you, you were with another man. Who was he?"

"You saw him?"

"Yes."

"Hmm. Do you have any ideas?" he asked knowingly now.

"Just a feeling, that's all."

"Tell me."

"No, it's kind of silly." she said sheepishly.

"Well, you're right! He's our son."

"But how can that be? I feel him moving in here all the time." She had her hands on her tummy.

"My guess is, that he comes and goes. I know he's to be our son, our earthly son anyway, but he said he'd be back to help me out when I need it. So my guess is that he can come and go while his body is still in the womb. Handsome fellow isn't he?"

"Oh yes, he's a hunk." Tara leaned back on the couch and looked up at the ceiling, a warm smile on her face. "Imagine! I saw my son! I can't believe it. I think I'll name him Ryan Junior."

Ryan smiled at the compliment. "I think maybe Brandon would be better. What do you think?"

"Brandon? I like it, Ryan, really. Okay," she agreed, "our son's name is Brandon. That's a wonderful name." She looked at Ryan, staring deep into his eyes. "Why am I feeling so good? I should be dying right now, but I feel great, so alive!"

Ryan paused, allowing himself to feel the spiritual ambiance that surrounded him. "You're feeling the support of God's Spirit. It's his 'peace.' It brings comfort and hope. You're feeling some of that hope right now, and I must say, it becomes you, Mrs. McKay."

"Why thank you Dr. McKay," said Tara with a fake southern accent. "I do believe I'm blushing."

They both laughed, and for a minute, he forgot their peculiar situation. But he was still worried about his time with Tara. He wanted a plan for her safety as well as a plan to find those who were working with The Merchant, and he wanted it to play out while he was still visible to her. Although he was able to discern almost everything around him, sense spiritual things and perceive great moral truths, he was at a complete loss when it came to the length of time he would be visible to Tara.

His father said she would see him during his *initial* visit. Did that mean she would see him as long as the visit lasted, or as long as he didn't leave her sight? Was there a specific period for this visit? He tried to get a feel for the answer, but he could discern nothing.

"Tara, we need to talk about something else for a moment."

"And what would that be?" she said still giggling. He saw that her thoughts were those of a mother anticipating her first child, and smiled briefly.

"We need to consider your safety."

"But Ryan, the killer's dead, remember."

"Yes, but I also remember that the killer was *hired*, by someone who isn't dead. We never did find out who that was, remember. I have a feeling that whoever did it, will want to finish the job."

The giggling stopped. "Are you saying the baby and I are still going to be hunted down by these animals?"

"I don't know that for sure," he said, trying not to alarm her too much. "But we have to assume that it's a possibility. Let's face it, if it were only me they were after, they'd be finished. But the killer was trying to kill both of us. If he passed his information on to whoever hired him, there's a chance they'll think that you know what I knew. So let's be safe and get you out of here."

"But Ryan, I can't just up and leave my family after what they've been through. And what about their safety? Surely they're at risk too?"

Suddenly her eyes widened.

"What is it Tara?" Unaware, she was hiding the thought from him.

"Oh, maybe nothing. I received a strange phone call just minutes before you got here. It had an odd feel to it. Was it them?"

"I don't know. Wil had your parents admit you to the hospital under a different name, didn't he?"

"Yes, he did, but I told the caller I was Tara."

"Mmm. The threat may be closer than I thought."

Neither spoke for a moment. "How did you know what Wil did?"

"Because on some level, you must have thought it. I seem to be able to perceive thoughts on different levels."

"Very handy."

"But not totally reliable. Anyway, about your parents, I don't think these people would want to draw undue attention to themselves. The only ones they're likely to be interested in are you and Wil. I think your family will be safe, as long as you're not here."

"Okay, let's assume you're right. Now, how do we find out who is behind all this? I hope you're not planning to dangle me as bait! I will not let anything happen to this baby." She spread her hands protectively over her stomach.

"I don't think anything will happen to Brandon. He'll get here safely. I don't think you need to worry about that. I'm here to protect you now anyway, I won't let anything go wrong."

"Ryan, this baby and my family are all I have left. I want to get the people who took you away from me, but how can I take care of both?"

"By trusting me. Those who are with us are greater than those who are against us."

"I believe that, I really do. I feel much stronger now. I don't know if it's you, the baby or the things you've told me, but right now I think I could do anything. Still, I'm afraid. I don't want anything to happen to my baby."

Ryan looked at her approvingly. "It's all right to be afraid. But I promise, I won't let anything happen to you, or our baby."

She spoke cautiously, but with a look of enthusiasm in her eyes. "What do we do first?"

"Let's consider our leads. Did the killer say anything about who he worked for? A name? A company?"

"No, I don't think so. Let's see . . ." She tried to recall everything that happened in Wil's office before they headed for the desert on that fateful day four months ago. "I remember just after he hit me, I asked him why he was doing this. I was pretty sore at the time, but I remember him saying it was for graft, which was no surprise, really, even if it was bad grammar."

"Graft?"

"Yeah, you know, greed, corruption? He pronounced it 'graf,' but you know how charming them hillbillies can talk," she grinned, imitating the killer's accent.

Ryan's eyes opened wide. "That fits. I think I know part of the 'who?'"

"You do?"

"Yes. We're going to need Wil's help on this. I think we can trust him with the truth about my involvement. We're going to need a good plan to pull this off, girl. But with a little luck, the Amazing McKays can do it!"

"'The Amazing McKays?'" she repeated. "I don't know about that. But I guess we do make a pretty amazing couple right now!"

The sound of the garage door opening signaled the return of the Johnson family. They must have gone on a drive after church to give her some extra time, Tara thought. They probably hoped she would go through the box of pictures and the albums they left on the table. Her amnesia had been pretty hard on them. The box of pictures was a little obvious, an act of desperation perhaps, but she appreciated their concern.

Alerted to their return by Ryan, Tara readied herself for the big moment. She sat nervously on the couch, while Ryan stood near the window. Finally, the door to the garage opened and the family began to pile in.

"Hey Tara!" said Joey. "Man, you shoulda come with us. It was way cool!"

"Yes," Mom repeated lightly, "it was 'way cool!'"

Denise, Tara's younger sister by eight years, came up to her with her hands behind her back. "I couldn't help but pick these for you, I knew you'd love them." She brought her hands around, revealing a beautiful bunch of purple flowers. "We found them up around the McDowell Mountains where we use to go on family hikes. I thought it would be too cold for flowers, but here they are. I know you like purple."

"Oh thanks Denise, they're beautiful." She took the flowers and smelled their fragrance, while memories of the family hikes flooded her mind. How wonderful that she could remember. She placed the flowers delicately in the already full vase on the table before her. Most of the family went for the kitchen in search of food, while Mom and Dad stayed back to talk to Tara. Carol was the first to speak.

"It was a great service today, I wish you would come with us next week."

"I'm sorry Mom, and thanks for inviting me . . . but you know I go to the Mormon Church now. Still, I'm glad I stayed home today. By the way, did you see the Nelsons?"

"Yes, of course . . . Hey! You remember the Nelsons?"

"Why wouldn't I?"

Tara couldn't help but play with them a bit before giving them the big news. Smiling, she glanced quickly at Ryan, and the Johnson's followed her gaze, a perplexed look on their faces. He shrugged his shoulders and smiled back. Then, invisible to them, he walked over and stood behind them.

"Tara? Are you getting some of your memory back?" asked Carol hopefully.

"No, Mom." She smiled, trying to hold back her excitement. "I've got it *all* back!"

She rose from the couch, and held out her arms. Both her parents rushed in to hug her, puzzlement, surprise and gratitude mixed in their eyes. Tara began to sob openly. The kids from the kitchen came out to see what the commotion was about, and Ryan slipped unnoticed back into the corner.

"How did it happen?" said Mom.

"How'd what happen?" Joey chimed in.

"Your sister has her memory back!" exploded Dad.

Tara noticed that Ryan's eyes had filled with tears as he watched the tender scene. She thought how hard this was on him, being unable to participate in a normal family life, and smiled tenderly. The family all prodded for an explanation, but Tara hid the real answer, saying it all just came to her. Well, in a way that was right, she thought. It *had* just come to her. She just wasn't about to mention that it came when she saw the ghost of her dead husband in their backyard, at least not now. There would be enough time for them to think she was crazy later.

Finally, when all the hoopla died down, Tara dropped her new bombshell.

"Mom, Dad. I need to leave."

"Say what?" her father stammered.

"I know this sounds crazy, but my life is still in danger. I . . ."

"Tara," interrupted her mother.

"No, wait Mom. Dad, I need you to call Wil and ask if he can come by. He'll understand. I know this all sounds frightening, but unfortunately, it's true. There's a legitimate reason, and if I could just get the three of you together, it'd all make sense."

"I can do that, but it's not going to make sense. How about if I have him come over right now."

"Well, it would be better in the morning, after the kids go to school. I know it may be inconvenient, but it'll be worth it, I promise."

Ryan watched nervously from the corner of the room. She knew he probably wouldn't like what she was up to.

"I'll set it up," he said, and headed for the phone.

"Tara, this is unnecessary," her mother said. "The danger is over. The psychologist didn't want us to tell you everything. She was afraid you could have a breakdown. But . . . do you remember what happened in the desert?"

"Of course Mother, and yes, I know the killer is dead. I also know what happened to Ryan." Her calm demeanor obviously perplexed her mother, but Tara continued. "This is much bigger than the psychologist knows. There's much more I have to tell you. I hope it'll help you understand."

"Tara, honey, are you feeling all right?"

"Mom!"

"No, really, I'm not trying to patronize you, I just need to know, if you're feeling like you're back to your old self?"

"Actually Mom, no, I don't feel like my old self. I feel a lot better, better than I've felt for a long time." She smiled over at Ryan.

Her mother looked briefly in the direction her daughter had smiled and breathed a confused sigh, then managed a smile herself as her dad reentered the room.

"Mom, Dad, for the first time in a very long time, I feel like I really have something to live for. I have hope. On the one hand, I'm terribly saddened by the fact that I have to spend the rest of my life without Ryan. But in some ways . . ." she looked over at him, "I've never been more at peace. Just trust me."

She began to weep, and threw her arms around her mother, holding her tight as the rest of her family looked on compassionately, not knowing what to do. She then excused herself, promising to tell them more in the morning, and went up to her room.

It was seven-thirty in the evening now, and dark outside, but it would be hours before the family got tired and headed for bed. The privacy of her room was what she wanted. She had to be alone with Ryan. Below them, in the family room, a Sunday Night Movie began to play on the television, it's muffled sounds drifting up the stairs and through the crack under her door.

"Come sit next to me," she said, patting the bed softly. Ryan walked over and took his place beside her. "I'm so mixed up right now. I need you to talk to me, to be with me. How are we going to get through this?"

"We'll find a way, honey," he spoke softly.

The effect of his assurance was soothing. She was going to need a lot of that. All she had was his presence and his words of comfort. She hoped it would be enough.

"Hold out your hand," she said. As Ryan lifted his hand, she lifted hers and tried to feel his. "It's amazing! I can see you, but I can't feel anything. Can you feel my body?"

He shook his head. "No, but I can feel your spirit, and it's wonderful."

"How does it feel?"

"It glows with warmth, comfort . . . love. It feels like home. I know these are ambiguous terms, but, for a spirit, they're very real."

He gazed intently into her eyes.

"What?" she asked.

"You. You're amazing. You never stop, do you?"

"Never stop what?" she persisted.

"Trying to find out the answers to everything." He smiled. "We're so much alike you and I. One of the first things that my dad said to me was how proud he was of my always wanting to get the answers. I think that's one of the qualities he and I both find so appealing about you. You want to try something?"

"If it's with you, I'm game. What do you have in mind?"

"Just stand up and close your eyes, and concentrate on what you're feeling in your heart, I'll do the rest."

Tara closed her eyes. "Don't leave me," she implored.

"Never, my love. I don't know if this'll work, or if it's even permitted, but I have to try it. Here goes!"

She caught her breath, and tears began to flow down her cheeks. She opened her eyes.

"Ryan?" She whirled around to see him step away from where she had been standing. "What was that?" she exclaimed.

Ryan smiled. "Did you feel it?"

"Did I feel it? Wow! It was fantastic! It was you . . . right here." She placed her hands over her heart. "In fact, all over. I could almost touch you! It was like . . ."

"Like we were one?" he said finishing her sentence.

"Yes! Yes, like we were one. Like you were side-by-side with every fiber of my soul!"

"Okay, I've got another experiment for us. Want to try?"

"Absolutely!"

"Good. Spoken like a true scientist. Now, we've got a lot to talk about right?"

"Oh yes."

"Okay." he said. "You remember that I can read your thoughts?"

"Right."

"All right. You also know that only you can hear me speak. So I was thinking, if we're going to be up late talking, your parents are sure to hear you and think you've had that mental breakdown the psychologist predicted!"

"I know where you're going with this Ryan. I speak, silently, that is, in my mind, and you answer me out loud. That way, no one knows that a very wonderful conversation is taking place! Right?" Tara grinned like a schoolgirl.

"That's right."

"Okay, so how's this. Am I not the coolest girl you ever met?" she thought.

"Yes you are. Never a cooler woman in all the world." he responded.

"Ryan, do you know what we could do with an act like this?"

"Yeah, we could use it to find the people behind all this mess."

"Oh yeah . . . that's right. You sure know how to turn the mood around."

He laughed and soon she joined him.

Chapter 10
WHERE THERE'S A WIL
THERE'S A WAY

Two of his best men were dead. The thought consumed Wil Dowding as he sat in his easy chair, staring out the window at the carefully landscaped backyard of his home.

These were not just his employees, they were his friends. He had trained them, and brought them up in the investigative business. They were like the sons he never had, the family he never knew. When his wife left him only two years after their wedding day, he vowed to go it alone in life. That was twenty years ago. He had no idea then that he would become so attached to these young men in his employ. Their deaths left a void in him that still gnawed after four months. Like a nagging ulcer, the hurt in his soul craved relief . . . but there was none.

For three months now, he had been struggling with his emotions until he felt like he was losing control. He couldn't stay focused. Life was loosing its meaning, if it ever had any . . . besides revenge.

As a boy growing up in Colorado, his world was full of meaning. He had a good family and nice neighbors. He was the fastest runner in his school, and later, the star of his high school track team. He loved running. He loved school. He loved life.

But then he turned eighteen, and graduated. It was 1969, and Vietnam was gobbling up all the eighteen-year-olds it could find. His father was retired military, and he encouraged Wil to enlist in the Navy. It was, according to Dad, the safest of the armed forces at the time. The added bonus of an education and money toward college made the enlistment well worth it, he thought, so he joined.

But war made no sense to him. Death was not something to be taken lightly. It was one thing to protect home, family and country, but the needless killing that went on in Vietnam sickened him. It was all he could do to bide his time until he got out.

In the meantime, when opportunities to take classes in investigative techniques came up, he jumped at them. He enjoyed those classes immensely, and took all the education the Navy would offer on the subject.

At the end of '71, he was given the opportunity to transfer ashore, to take part in a special investigation course. Eventually, he was assigned to a unit investigating internal affairs. This was where he met his wife. They were married in '72, but by '74 she had run off with a naval officer from Annapolis. Distraught and depressed, he left the Navy in early '75. He went into private investigation then, and struggled hopelessly until Lonnie Johnson gave him his first break.

Now he had a large office, a successful business . . . and was involved in something that had taken two of his "family," plus Tara's husband! The only thing he felt more than depression now was a burning desire to get his hands on someone's throat.

The fact that Tara was alive, and out of her coma, with a good prognosis from her doctor, had given him some relief. Lonnie's family was his family. She was like his daughter. Her husband had given his life for her, and Wil was still stunned at her loss.

He was determined to avenge them all, his boys and Ryan. It was his personal commitment, his consuming goal in life. If he went broke doing it, or ended up like Ryan, giving his life for it, he didn't care. But Tara was his only lead, now, and she could remember nothing. So he sat alone, burning with emotion on a cloudy Sunday afternoon, wishing for nothing more than a hint of opportunity, when the ringing phone broke his trance.

"Hello." he answered softly.

"Wil, Lon here."

"Oh, hi. How's . . ."

"Good news, man! Tara's got her memory back!"

"Oh Lon, that's fabulous!"

"She wants to see you first thing in the morning, Wil. She says she has some important stuff for us, and really she wants you there."

"I'm at your disposal, Lon. In fact, this is news I've been waiting for a long time. Just tell me when and where."

"How's our house, say about eight o'clock?"

"Great! I'll be there tomorrow morning. Give her a big kiss for me, will ya?"

"Will do. Thanks man."

There hadn't been a ray of sunshine in his life for months. Maybe this was the break in the clouds he'd been waiting for. Wil sat back in the easy chair and stared again into the backyard, thinking about what he would do when he caught the men responsible for his and Tara's loss. His thoughts were dark and filled with vengeance, but for a short time anyway, they made him happy.

***

Carol, Lon, and Wil sat in the family room of the Johnson home. Before them sat a box of doughnut holes Wil had brought over. They were each munching as they waited for Tara to come down from her room.

"I don't think she slept too well last night," said Carol wiping the white doughnut powder from her mouth. "She had a hard time getting up this morning."

"Well, she's had a rough time lately," Wil said, an edge of emotion in his voice.

"You can say that again." Lon chimed in. "But I gotta tell you Wil, yesterday she seemed so, so . . ."

"Happy." finished Carol.

"Yes, happy. It's as if she knows something we don't. Something big, exciting. I can't explain, but she's not at all down or depressed like I thought she would be."

Wil stroked his beard. "This is interesting. Very interesting . . ."

"What's interesting?" asked a puzzled Tara. She had come down the stairs earlier and was standing behind them all along.

"Tara!" Carol jumped up and ran around the couch to give her a hug.

"Nice of you to join us, Tara," said her Dad with a touch of sarcasm.

"I'm sorry, I slept in. But I had a lot to . . . think about last night. Besides, I've been down here for a while, but you didn't notice me. Good morning, Wil!" She came around in front of the sofa and gave him a hug.

"Glad to have you back, Tara," he said.

"Glad to be back, and I'm even happier that you came."

"Wouldn't miss this for the world. It's so good to see you smile. Look, I brought your favorites," he replied.

"Right on, doughnut holes! No wonder you guys didn't notice me." Tara reached in and grabbed a handful of the little round puffs and sat down on the fireplace hearth, facing everyone. "Okay, I guess you're all wondering why I called this meeting?" She looked past them and smiled.

Ryan, who had come down with her, was standing just behind her father. He had been with her all night, and she could still see him. His father had said that she would be able to see him for his initial visit only, so he had decided not to leave her sight. The hope was that this would extend their "initial visit" indefinitely. The argument made sense to her. So, as difficult as it might prove for Ryan, they had decided he would always stay at least in the same room with her.

They realized too that it would be useful in their plan. With direct communication between them, and Ryan's ability to read thoughts, they could more easily find the men responsible for what was happening to the planet.

"Okay!" blurted her impatient mother, "are you going to fill us in, or just eat doughnuts?"

Tara swallowed and smiled sheepishly. "Sorry. Okay. Yesterday, as you know, a most amazing thing happened. My memory returned! I remember everything now: the desert, the killer, even what happened to Ryan. But what I'm about to say, is going to sound a little off the wall, so I want you three to just sit and listen until I'm finished. Deal?"

They all nodded in affirmation.

"Remember, wait until I'm finished." *I don't know about this Ryan,*" she thought.

"Go ahead. They'll believe you," he said, boosting her confidence.

She took a deep breath and began. "This is going to take a little faith on your part, but it's essential that you believe me. Otherwise you'll never go for the rest of the plan." Tara tried hard not to worry about the blank expressions on their faces. "Yesterday, while you were in church, I was sitting in the kitchen by the bay window, wondering if I would ever get my life back. I was staring out into the backyard, when all of a sudden . . . I saw Ryan. Now remember, you promised, not a word."

Her mother had her hand over her mouth, looking bewildered. Lon and Wil had blank expressions on their faces.

"Mom, Dad, I swear to you, I saw him! I ran out to him, but he stopped me before I could touch him. He explained to me what had happened to him, how he had died, and that he had permission to come back and help me." *"Now would be nice, Ryan!"*

"You're doing fine," he assured her.

She took her eyes off him, and continued. "Now, before you ask, yes, he's here with us now, but only I can see him. Now bear with me on this. Mom, he's so wonderful. He knows what we're all thinking, and he wants you to know, for my sake, that I'm not crazy."

"Tara," Ryan said, "tell your mother that you would rather she didn't call the psychologist about this."

"Mother, Ryan says to tell you that I would rather you didn't call the psychologist about this." The implications of the message took a moment to reach Tara's consciousness. "Hey, Mom! What are you thinking?"

"I'm sorry, dear," her mother replied, her eyes wide.

"Don't you dare call her!"

Her mother whispered, "You mean he's really here, now?"

"Yes, Mom. That's what I said. And he really can read our thoughts."

"Tara," said Ryan, "tell your dad he wants to know if you can tell him how much change he has in his pocket. He knows he's got eighty-five cents in his front left pocket. Tell Wil that he should go ahead and make that call to his office, and let them know he'll be a little late."

"Okay Dad, your turn. You wanted to know if Ryan could tell you how much change is in your left front pocket. He probably wouldn't be able to tell you except for the fact that you know. Therefore, he knows you have eighty-five cents. And Wil, he says to go make that phone call and tell your office you'll be later than you expected."

No one moved. All three just sat, apparently in shock, their eyes wide and their mouths open. Finally Wil broke the silence.

"Tara, understand, this is all new to us, well, at least to me anyway. But I believe everything you're saying. It's more of a feeling than anything else, I guess, but I just feel you're telling the truth."

"I thought you'd be the easiest to convince. Believe me, we're going to need your help the most. Thanks Wil, for believing."

Her mother, tears welling up in her eyes, spoke next. "Tara, I knew something miraculous happened to you for you to recover the way you did. How was he able to heal you?"

"He didn't heal me, Mom. Ryan thinks I was in a coma for my own protection. Same with the amnesia. He says that someone upstairs has a plan for me, and I was protected until the time was right, until he could get back and help me. I guess they knew I wouldn't be able to cope without him. I probably would have done something stupid. Anyway, when he got here, the amnesia just lifted."

Her dad's eyes looked glazed over. "Boy, it really puts things into perspective, doesn't it. I mean, I always believed in God, but now, the whole idea of an afterlife is so real, so here and now. It's . . ." He took hold of Carol's hand and shook his head in amazement.

"It's everything we've always believed in, honey," said Carol, "but with an in-house, personal touch."

They both smiled.

"Tara," interrupted Wil, "you said you needed help. I want nothing more than to provide that help, if I can. What's going on, and where's Ryan right now?"

"Well, he's here, next to me. And he's smiling. I wish you could see him." She looked at Ryan who spoke softly to her.

"Ryan wants me to tell you all how much he loves each of you. He wishes he could give each of you a big hug. He also wants you to know, that he's not leaving my side until everything is safe, and maybe not even then."

"Sounds just like him, but what do you mean safe?" asked Lon.

With the help of Ryan, Tara spent the next hour explaining her studies in the desert, "The Hole," Ryan's studies of particle intelligence, and how "The Merchant" and his group of spirits were using mortal men to steal matter. She even told them of the strange phone call she received, and was surprised to learn that others in the family had reported similar calls.

Surprisingly, they lapped up all the information, without question. They had a remarkable degree of faith in her objectivity, it seemed. Tara knew that their beliefs in God and an afterlife would make it easier to accept and understand what she was telling them.

When she finished, Wil stood up and gave her a hug. "Tara, I want you to know, you have me, my agency, and all I possess to help you with this. I'll do everything in my power to see this thing through with you. You're not alone."

"Thank you, Wil."

"I don't know what to say," Lonnie moaned. "Wil, I'm not leaving all this to you. I'll . . ."

"Lon . . . " interrupted Mrs. Johnson.

Frustrated, he continued. "No Carol, this whole thing . . . I mean, I believe Ryan is here, but all this running. Why do they have to run? I'm not going to just stand by and see my daughter . . . Wil, help me here!" Lon turned to Wil looking for support, a look of anger and frustration on his face.

"Lonnie," Wil said calmly. "In all seriousness, you know you have to think of the rest of your family. If you'll take care of them, guard them, I'll do everything I can to assure Tara's safety. I have every resource necessary to help her right now, and you know it. I believe her with all my heart, just as you do. With Ryan on our side, it'll work out. Tara will be safe."

Lonnie stood silent for a moment, then turned back to Tara. "I love you honey." He stepped over and hugged her, then spoke quietly, "I guess he's right, I don't like it, but he's right. You call me if you need anything. I'll drop everything and be there, once the family's safe. Wil is a good man, and with the help of God, you'll be fine."

"I know, Dad. Thanks so much for everything you do for me. I wouldn't leave for a minute if I didn't think it was the right thing to do." She started to cry.

"When do you think you'll be leaving?" asked Carol quietly.

"The sooner the better for everyone," Tara said. "I can't tell you where I'm going, but I will be in touch. The less you know, the better off you'll be. Please tell the kids I love them. And thank them for their patience these last few weeks. Okay?"

"They'll understand sweetie. Don't you worry about them!" assured Dad. Turning to Wil he asked, "I'll be able to get hold of you, right?"

"Absolutely! Wherever I am, I'll leave word with the office that your messages are to be put through."

"Thanks."

"Ryan doesn't feel any of you are in immediate danger, and that carries a lot of weight with me," Tara assured them. "But, the longer I stay here, the more it'll put you in danger. Besides, we need to get

started on our plan, otherwise, who knows how far things will go. I
promise to stay in touch. I won't leave you completely in the dark. And
I'll call you the minute you become grandparents!"

"Oh please, must you remind us?" sighed Dad. "We're too young to
be grandparents!" He laughed, then added, "But you better call the
minute that child arrives!"

"It's going to be a boy, Dad, and his name is Brandon."

It took a few moments longer to discuss how Wil would be
involved and make Lon and Carol feel as comfortable as possible.
Finally, Carol stood and took Tara into her arms.

"Take good care of her, Ryan, we miss you so much!" She was
looking toward the fireplace as she spoke.

"Umm, he's over here Mom."

<hr>

From the moment he left the Johnsons' house, Wil felt as though
he had come out of a dark cave, into full sunlight. For the first time in
years, a feeling of hope lit his spirit. He had a cause! Never before had
he felt part of so noble an effort. Even the heavens were backing this
one, he thought, and it felt great! He had an opportunity to help save the
world. For the first time since his marriage failed, a sense of gratitude
filled his heart. He was especially grateful for the feeling that he had
been released from the demons within him, the anger that would surely
have brought his demise. This was much better than revenge, he
thought.

At Dowding Investigations the atmosphere was electric. He had
called an emergency meeting for late that afternoon, and all personnel
were called in from the field to attend. All current assignments were
given lower status, as the "Disorientation" file was officially opened. By
four o'clock, everyone was in the conference room, ready to listen.

"Okay guys, thanks for being here," Wil started. "I'm going to give
you a brief description of our latest case. This is going to sound a little
far fetched, but if you just hang with me, I think you'll see that it's the
most important matter the firm has ever handled.

"You're all aware of the current chaotic trends in the earth's
ecology? Well, in short, here's why the world is so screwed up. I've been
given reliable information that suggests some person, or group of

persons, has found a way to break down the atom, peacefully, to manipulate sub-atomic particles for financial gain. I don't fully understand the concept, but with the help of a particle physicist, I've put the best description I can in the files on the table in front of you.

"You all know Lonnie Johnson's daughter, Tara." Wil motioned toward Tara sitting quietly at the back of the room.

"Her life is in grave danger. A contract has been taken out on her because of her knowledge of this particle manipulation scheme. We don't know who's behind it, but her husband, Ryan, died at the hands of the same sickos who killed Steve and Josh. We're not only going to find them, we're going to bring an end to the worldwide ecological chaos these people are causing. Any questions so far?"

Jim Simons, Wil's senior investigator and field manager, was the first to venture up a hand.

"Yes Jim?"

"Are you saying that the people who killed Ryan, are the ones behind all the stuff we've been hearing about in the news?"

"Yes."

"That's big, Wil, can we do this?" he queried.

"Yes, we can, and to be frank, we have to!"

"Can we get some help on this Wil?" asked Art Bonny, Jim's protégé and assistant.

Art's greatest desire in life was to work for the FBI and Wil knew he would relish the thought of bringing them in on the project. So he was very firm in his answer.

"No. We have evidence of government involvement in this conspiracy. So, at this point and until we find out otherwise, we don't know who to trust. Do not, and I repeat, do not, communicate with law enforcement on this project unless I instruct you otherwise. We'll be going it alone."

Somewhat deflated, but managing a smile, Art shrugged his shoulders, "Oh well, I tried!"

"Yes Art, you did. Someday, I promise, if we get to rub shoulders with the FBI, you'll get the assignment."

"Well, I'm your man!" Art joked.

When the snickering died down, Wil continued. "Everything, and I mean everything, will take a back seat to this work. Each of you could be involved in one way or another at some point in time. I want each of you to read the file in front of you tonight and become thoroughly familiar with it. When it comes time for you to participate, you *will* drop anything you're working on and jump on this."

Wil looked into the faces of each member of his staff. To a man, or woman, they would die for him, and he knew it. He would do the same for them, many times over if he could.

"I'm not going to sugar-coat this. It's going to be dangerous. Read the list of people recently killed whose deaths we have been able to connect to this case, and you'll see what I mean; it's in the file. I will be doing most of the heavy stuff myself, but the need for total confidentiality is a must. Nobody is to know a thing about this until I give the word. Outside this office, the case doesn't exist! Understood?"

Each of them nodded their agreement as he forged ahead.

"Tara and I will be leaving town, incognito. I'm not even sure we aren't being watched now, so I'm taking all precautions. The less you know about this part of the plan, the better. Jim here will be in charge while I'm away. Keep working your current cases, until he lets you know differently."

Assignments and last minute preparations were made, and the meeting was adjourned. With Jim's help, Ty Richards and Jacqueline Hanks were made up to look like Wil and Tara. Acting as decoys, they left the building through the main entrance, while Tara and Wil slipped into disguise and left by another route.

Lonnie Johnson had assured Wil that he would raise whatever capital was needed for the project. He had many corporate friends in high places who, he said, would be glad to help. Though his agency was very successful, Wil had no idea how long it would take to complete the project or how many of his resources would have to be employed. He would have sacrificed everything for the project, but he was grateful for any help his friend could provide.

<hr />

It was nearing 10:40 PM when they pulled into the driveway of a very posh home in one of the many upscale neighborhoods that make up Pasadena, Texas. The front of the home was well lit, illuminating the red brick and vine-covered facade of the large Spanish-style house. The driveway was reddish brown Spanish tile, and the front patio was laid in

a smaller rock of varied color. It was decorated with white cement
benches, graceful light fixtures and a white wrought iron patio table and
chairs. The home had to be twenty years old, but it was immaculate and
adorned with beautiful plants of all sizes that hid its age, giving it the
timeless look of an old Mexican hacienda. As Tara and Wil approached
the front door, an inside porch light went on and the door opened.

"Tara Johnson!" Norma Welker greeted her enthusiastically, her
warm smile conveying genuine hospitality. Again, as on the plane, it
spoke peace to Tara's heart. "I'm so glad you called!"

Tara smiled back. "I'm so grateful to you for opening your home to
us, Norma. And this, by the way, is Wil Dowding, the private
investigator I spoke to you about on the phone."

Norma's eyes lit noticeably at the introduction, and she extended
her hand demurely, an attractive expression on her face. Tara could see
Wil's eyes widen appreciatively too as he accepted her hand and shook it
gently. After the introductions, Norma led them into the house, and
closed the door behind them, shutting out the night.

Norma made them feel comfortable in the living room as she
offered a tray of hors d'oeuvres. Her warm and charming demeanor put
Tara at ease and set the atmosphere for the conversation that followed.

When Wil asked Tara if she knew someone in Dallas, the spot
where he wanted to begin their search, she told him of her experience
with Norma on the plane, and Norma's offer of a place to stay. At first,
he was skeptical, but Tara told him there was something unique about
the woman, something worth trusting. Obviously, Wil was now happier
than ever that he had accepted her recommendation. Tara gave him a sly
grin, a matchmaker's gleam in her eye.

"Okay now," Norma started, "suppose you two fill me in on your
troubles. And by the way, that apple cider you're drinking is a secret
recipe handed down from generations of cider-maniacs. It's non-
alcoholic, but it'll put you at ease, and as my mother says, your words
will flow like melting butter. Hope you like it."

"Actually," said Tara, "it's the best I've ever tasted!"

"Me too!" added Wil, enthusiastically.

"I wish I could have some of that stuff," said Ryan from his
position just behind Tara.

"Quiet Ryan, you'll throw me off here!"

"I think it's Wil we have to worry about, not you," he said, trying to hold in a chuckle. Snickering with him, Tara choked on her cider.

"Are you all right, dear?" Norma asked.

"Oh, yes, yes," she answered, trying to cough without laughing.

"Good." Norma smiled. "Tara, ever since I left you at the airport, I haven't slept well. I knew you had something eating at you, and it's been haunting me for months now. I'm so happy you called. If I can be of any assistance to you and your friend, I'm yours, and my house is yours." At the words "your friend," she glanced approvingly at Wil.

"Thank you Norma," Tara responded. "But I feel I have to be straight with you."

"You must be in some kind of trouble," interrupted Norma, "that much I can tell." She was nodding now, eyes piercing both Tara and Wil. "In fact, you look like your life is in danger. Am I right?"

"Yes, Norma. Good heavens, are you psychic?"

"Oh, foolishness, no! But I've always believed very strongly in the spiritual realm. And there's something here that seems associated with that realm, something I'm feeling. What is it Tara?"

"It's me Tara." Ryan was looking into Norma's eyes. "Somehow, she feels my presence. She can't see me, but I think she senses I'm here. She's a very spiritual person."

"Can I trust her?"

"You know you can, Tara."

For a moment, Tara had forgotten to trust her feelings about people. She remembered the peaceful feeling Norma exuded when she first met her. It was time to start trusting that feeling again.

"Well Norma . . ." Tara picked up the pitcher of cider, and refilled her glass, "Do you believe in ghosts?"

Lieutenant Eddie Sitton had been in Naval Intelligence for over a decade. He met Wil in Phoenix two years ago when some nut was stalking his daughter, Meg, while she attended ASU. He hired Wil to augment police efforts to catch the guy. It turned out the nut was a serial killer, and Wil was the only one able to figure it out. While the undermanned and underpaid police were forced to add the case to scores of others they were already working, Wil quickly and methodically broke it open. He traced the evidence to a store clerk where his daughter shopped. The man was caught, convicted of murder and now sat on death row.

With his daughter's life saved, Eddie vowed he would do anything in his power, personal or professional, to help Wil, should the occasion arise. He was a man who could pull a lot of strings. All Wil had to do was ask. On Tuesday, February 18, at 8:30 AM Eastern time, the call came.

It was pleasant enough, but the tone in Wil's voice gave his request a sense of urgency. When Wil asked him to call back from a pay phone, he had Eddie's full attention. Of course he would do all he could to help, he reassured. He was given a number where he could reach Wil directly. No one was to know what he was looking for, no one. That was imperative. Anything but total and absolute confidentiality would mean Wil's certain death. Eddie promised, and Eddie Sitton was a man of his word.

So when he finally got to the pay phone and heard Wil's request, he assured him that it was not a matter of *if* he could help, but *when*.

Wil was generally pleased with the investigation so far. Tara was safe. Norma had accepted the girl's dilemma with open arms. She also had no trouble accepting the fact that Ryan would be hanging around the house as well, which was no small surprise to Wil. Ryan had assured both of them, through Tara, that Norma would be a valuable asset. He was right. Nobody but Tara and Wil knew who she was. She had no relationship to Tara or her family, and she was free to help Tara with her pregnancy.

Wil offered to pay her, but Norma would have none of it. She had more money than she knew what to do with, she said. This was her chance to do something that really mattered. Her store in Scottsdale was profitable, and her mother loved running the place in her absence. All she wanted was the opportunity to help.

The plan was for Norma to continue going back and forth between Dallas and Scottsdale, as was her habit, until June. She would then remain in Dallas, as she usually did, to be with Tara until she delivered in

July. The remainder of the summer would be spent helping with the baby.

Tara would wait until after the delivery to enter the fray. Sure, she would go nuts sitting and waiting, but everyone wanted to give her and the unborn child the best possible chance. His safety came first, and strong as she was, Wil would not have Tara running around in her current condition.

So far, Tara could still see Ryan. According to her, his spirit had not left her side for a minute. She expressed some guilt about extending the initial visit this way just to keep him around, but as Wil understood it, Ryan had assured her that he was supposed to go with his feelings, and these were his feelings. If his initial visit were to last, say . . . a year or two, Wil thought, what difference would it make? Spirits didn't seem to perceive time anyway, according to Ryan. Besides, they were in love and growing closer every day. What could be wrong with that?

On February 20, it was time for Wil to leave. After last minute instructions, and a lengthy briefing from Ryan, delivered vicariously through Tara, he said goodbye. Norma had proven a truly unexpected light in a life that had experienced precious few of them for the last twenty years. He hoped he would have more opportunity to see her, and thanked Tara again for her insistence that they use her place as a safe house. For now, it was off to start the groundwork for what they hoped would be the downfall of The Merchant's pawns. He had a hot tip from Eddie Sitton, and was anxious to see where the chase would lead.

Chapter 11
MECHANISM

By late May, it seemed to Tara that the world was getting more lethargic with every passing day. Mother Nature was slow to bloom. Even though spring had officially sprung some time ago, the trees were just beginning to bud, and only a few flowers were breaking the ground, struggling to rise and meet the sun.

Tara and Ryan were in the back yard chatting. Two women, assigned by the local bishop to watch over and help Tara, had just been by, leaving a wonderfully aromatic loaf of homemade bread behind. Bishop Merrill was aware of Tara's need for protection and helped her feel at home attending the local ward. Except for the Ward Clerk, who was sworn to secrecy, everyone there knew her as Jenny Sargent.

"That's hard to believe, I mean, I don't doubt you," Tara assured him, "but it's amazing."

"It really is," Ryan continued. "I see them, and I know they see me, but it's like . . . I don't know, like they've all got their own missions or assignments to carry out."

He was referring to the many spirits he had seen during his time as Tara's guardian. He didn't realize at first that the spirits were there, probably because he was so wrapped up in what he was doing. But now that he had some free time, he was amazed at the interaction between the physical and spiritual worlds. Spirits were coming and going, helping, warning, comforting those in need, with the mortals not knowing and often not feeling their presence.

"What do they look like?" asked Tara.

"Just like you and me. Maybe a little different. Confidence. I think that's the difference. Here it seems people are weighed down by self-

175

pity, low self-esteem; you know, all those taboo things we know we shouldn't do but never seem to overcome. But the spirits I see are wonderful. I wish you could see them too."

"No wings?" she teased.

"Just on the birds."

"The what?"

"The birds," he said matter-of-factly. "There are birds here too."

"Oh. Speaking of birds, I haven't seen many around here." Tara was looking at the trees, and the three vacant birdhouses sitting on poles at the corners of Norma's property. "Do you suppose they're just leaving the area, or joining the ranks of extinct species?"

Ryan followed her gaze. "A little of both I'm afraid. It's a nasty world out there. Whoever's doing this is picking up speed. I can feel it."

"I'm scared Ryan," she said soberly. "What kind of world will be left for Brandon when he's born? At this rate, there'll be nothing left by the time we can help."

"Have faith, honey. I know it seems like we're doing nothing, but Wil is on to something. And when the baby is born, we'll jump right in. Time is of the essence, I know, but it'll happen soon, I promise."

"Ryan?"

"Yes?"

"A thought just occurred to me."

"Really? That's a scary concept in itself."

She swished her hand through his immaterial body. "Seriously, Ryan, what do we do when we find these people?"

"We'll let Wil worry about that. He'll know what to do . . . I hope."

They stayed in the back yard for another hour, speaking little, thinking a lot. Tara nibbled on the still-warm bread while Ryan looked on with envy.

Later that night, as Tara slept, Ryan had a visitor. It was Brandon, the young man who would come into the world in July to be his son. Ryan stood watching Tara breathe in the slow, deep rhythm of sleep, pondering the nature of his being. He marveled that he did not feel the need for sleep, that he constantly remained in a state of perfect alertness, never feeling pain, hunger, indigestion or headaches. Not the slightest physical discomfort. In a way, he missed some of those senses, and envied Tara for being able to sleep and shut out everything around her.

In the middle of these musings he felt someone approach. Knowing immediately who it was, he turned to meet Brandon.

"Hello, son. I've been waiting for you to return. I wanted so much to talk to you."

Brandon smiled. "They keep me pretty busy, Dad. It's a crazy world out there."

"Yeah, I know what you mean."

"I've come to offer my assistance. It appears you may need it."

"I do, son."

"What would you like me to do?"

"Could you check in on Wil Dowding? He's been gone for over six weeks. I'm not sure where he is."

"That won't be a problem," Brandon assured.

"I'd do it, but I can't leave your mother."

"I know. So does Grandpa."

"Is he upset with me?"

"Oh no. He said he would have done the same thing under the circumstances. In fact, I think he half expected you to do it. That's why I'm here, since you can't roam around."

Ryan glanced at Tara's sleeping form. "Aren't you suppose to be in there?" he said, gesturing to the baby growing in Tara's womb.

"Oh, no. I go in on occasion, to get the feel of my new physical body, but I'm not due to make it permanent until July twelfth. So for the time being, I'm at your disposal." His smile was soothing, gracious, and Ryan took heart in his confidence.

"I have so many questions about life after life, Brandon. It's all so intriguing."

"In due time, Dad. I'm sorry. I'm not supposed to discuss anything unless it pertains to this world and what you're working on. I hope you understand."

"Well, I'm not sure I do, but whatever you say," Ryan acquiesced, his eyes now on Tara. "Let me know as soon as possible about Wil, and good luck."

"I'm on my way. And Dad, I love you . . . and I'm so glad you love mother."

Ryan turned and hugged his son. "I love you too, son."

After the embrace, he was gone. In less than five minutes, however, he was back, startling Ryan out of his reverie.

"Speed of thought, remember?" Brandon remarked.

"Oh, yes, I remember. Just not used to it. What did you find?"

"Wil is sleeping in a small motel in a little seaside town called Aqua Sublima. It's in Jalisco, Mexico, on the western side of the country. He's dreaming about Norma, I think."

"Our Norma?" Ryan inquired.

"Yes," Brandon smiled.

Ryan couldn't help but laugh. He always thought Wil and Norma made a good pair. He'd have to share with Tara in the morning.

"Tomorrow, when he's up, I'll return and get a better read on what he's doing. I'll report my findings to you in the morning."

"Thanks, son. That would be terrific."

"Until then, have a wonderful night." he said.

"Do you have to leave right away?" Ryan implored.

"Actually, yes. Seems I'm everyone's errand boy today. Grandpa has me running all over creation. But that's okay, I enjoy it, really."

Brandon's pun about running all over creation made Ryan smile. Spirit world humor, he mused. "Then tell my father thanks for understanding."

"I will. And Dad, it truly is an honor for me to be of service to you. I begged to get this assignment."

"Gee, thanks Brandon," he said, a little surprised.

They embraced briefly, and Brandon was gone.

Ryan stared into the void where Brandon had been. He longed to be able to follow his inquisitive nature and go with his son, but he knew his place was next to Tara. His love for her was stronger than any yearnings he had to explore the galaxies.

The hours passed, and the world spun toward morning. Through it all, as he had for months, Ryan stood sentinel over his sleeping beauty, a devoted but lonely guardian.

Before Tara awoke the next morning, Brandon appeared again.

"Hi, son," Ryan greeted him without having to look. "Any news?"

"Yes, Dad." He stepped to Ryan's side and joined him, looking down at the woman who would soon be his mother. "Wil is planning to call you today with an update. He has a positive lead."

"Great," Ryan responded turning to look fondly at his future son. "Thanks for your help."

"My pleasure, Dad." He turned from Tara. "I have to go now. See you later," and he was gone.

When eight o'clock came, Tara and Ryan were in the kitchen. She was having breakfast. It was a beautiful morning, and the sun shone through the windows brightening an ever-darkening world.

"I've been eating like a horse these past few months. I think I'm going to enter a hot air balloon race. Nobody'll know I'm not the balloon!"

"Nonsense! You're as fit as the day I met you. You just have another person inside you. And believe me, Brandon is no pygmy!"

Tara laughed. At seven months, Ryan thought she positively radiated beauty. For the first time, he understood what people said about that look in the eyes of a pregnant woman. It was a sparkle that exuded joy, and symbolized everything about life that was good.

He had been able to hug his unborn child, a thrill that Tara wouldn't have for another two months. He couldn't wait for the time when she would snuggle her newborn baby. He wanted so much to be part of that physical embrace, but he couldn't think about that now.

"Oh, by the way," he said to Tara, "Wil is going to call us this morning. He has a positive lead."

"That's good to hear. But, ah, if you were here last night, how do you know?"

"Your son told me."

"You saw Brandon?"

"Yes, briefly."

"Oh, you have to tell me everything."

Ryan shrugged and launched into a rehearsal of his brief visit the night before.

Wil had only called three times since he left: once from San Diego, once from Denver, and once from Washington. Each time, his lead had been a dead end. The calls came to Norma who relayed the message from her store in Scottsdale. They were trying to avoid any kind of trace, but Ryan always suspected there was more to it than security.

This time the call was direct. At eight-forty, the phone rang, and Tara picked it up.

"Hello, Tara. This is Wil."

"Wil! How are you doing?"

"I'm doing great, but how are you feeling? Taking it easy I hope."

"Oh sure, you know me."

"Well, you take it easy girl. Is Ryan there?"

"Yes he is," assured Tara.

"Great! Can you put the phone on speaker, so he can hear too?"

"Oh that won't be necessary. He's got terrific hearing." She looked over at Ryan who nodded in the affirmative. "Go ahead, Wil. What have you got?"

"Guys, after three months of digging, I think we've finally struck gold. I checked out every member of the panel in that symposium you guys attended. All but two were fine. The first name to raise any red flags was Brett Wimple, the guy representing 'the Private Sector.' He's completely dropped out of sight! I've had my best men on it and he's just disappeared, nowhere to be found. Nobody, and I mean nobody, knows anything about him. The name may be an alias, but at this point we just don't know. By the way, your boss, Marv Graf, is missing too. Actually, Graf disappeared before Wimple.

"The other name, Robert Kilpack, was a real nugget. He's Secretary of the Navy! Serves under the Secretary of Defense. He was appointed two years ago.

"When I called Eddie and asked about any quiet projects involving strange equipment or apparatus, he dug a little and found out through a Navy Seal friend of his that the Navy conducted a clandestine 'search and rescue' operation near Jalisco last summer. The strangest thing about it was that the person giving the orders on this particular mission was supposedly a civilian, no name. Nobody liked the guy. He was a real power nut with an ego the size of the ocean. Turns out, it was this Kilpack fella. Never told them he was Secretary of the Navy!

"Anyway, he was looking for a piece of equipment supposedly lost at sea and drifting toward Jalisco. It was a big hush-hush deal, but they never did find it. It was real strange, though, to have the Secretary of the Navy personally taking charge of this kind of operation, especially in Mexican waters!

"So, anyway, I went straight to this little fishing town called Aqua Sublima. After snooping around, and of course using my wonderful charm and my entire repertoire of Spanish, I befriended an old man here named Borrego. He told me about a Mexican fisherman who disappeared early last summer. He went out fishing one morning and never came home. After a few days, the locals organized a search party. When they found him, they found something very strange as well. His boat, the *La Luna*, was almost half gone!"

"Tara, ask him what the severed edges looked like."

She looked at him curiously. "Wil, Ryan wants to know what the severed edges looked like, can you describe them?"

"Absolutely, I've seen it! The edges are smooth, as if the boat was . . . dissolved in half. They've got it here in a barn that belongs to a woman named Rivera."

"Ask him about security, Tara. How many know about this?"

"What about security there, Wil? How many know about the boat?"

"Don't worry, Tara. This is a tiny town, and the people here are strong willed. They're not letting anyone have it or even know it's here. I guess they trusted me. But they think it all has something to do with their fishing problems. This afternoon, they're taking me out to where it was found. I'm going to do some diving, see what else I can find. Maybe the other half of the boat, or whatever it was that cut it in half."

"Be careful, Wil," warned Tara. "Tell me you're not going alone."

"Nobody here knows how to dive, Tara! Its just me, myself and I. I'll call if I find anything."

"We wish you luck, Wil."

"I'll need it kids. Thanks! Bye now."

Tara hung up the receiver and turned to Ryan. "Well, what do you think?"

"I'm not sure. This could be the break we've been looking for. On the one hand, I thought Mr. Graf was the man we wanted, but now . . ."

"You don't think he is?"

"I don't know. Oh, I think he's involved all right, but obviously there are others in the chain. It doesn't sound like there are that many, though, and that's reassuring. Let's just get our baby here, so we can help."

"Yes, the baby. Ah, Ryan?"

"Yes dear?"

"Tell me again about last night . . . about our son, Brandon." She leaned forward, wide-eyed, eager and smiling from ear to ear.

On July twelfth, Brandon Ryan McKay entered mortality. Tara was admitted as Jenny Sargent into Dallas General Hospital at two forty-five in the afternoon. She was prepped and hooked up to various monitors, then began doing her breathing exercises.

When Norma stepped out for a moment to get a drink, Tara tried an exercise that required her to concentrate on an orange mark taped to the wall, with a black dot in the middle. Ryan was kneeling next to her, encouraging her, when Brandon appeared to him. Ryan and he communicated thought-to-thought, so as not to distract Tara.

"Looks like it's your turn for mortality son," said Ryan

"Yes, I'm very excited." Brandon replied.

"Are you scared?"

"No, not scared. We're all assured, at the time of birth, that there'll be many on this side ready to help. But I am nervous."

"Why can't I remember about my life before I was born? It's still like a veil is over my eyes, I can almost see . . ."

"When you make the crossover permanent, it'll all come back rather quickly," assured Brandon.

"Make the crossover permanent?" Ryan asked.

"They'll explain later, Dad."

"Well, I'm gonna miss our little visits." Ryan admitted.

"Me too."

"I want you to know, that I'm proud of who you are Brandon, and that I will always be there for you. I know you won't remember me, but I want you to know that I love you more than I could ever convey in words."

"I love you too Dad. And I promise to try to remember. I've waited so long for this moment, but you mean so much to me that leaving now is not easy at all."

"I know it doesn't look like much, but there's a wonderful world out there for you, you'll do just fine."

"It's time now, Dad. Tell Mom how much I love her, and that I feel it's one of the greatest honors of my existence to have her as my mother."

"I will," said Ryan. *"God be with you."*

"And you, Dad. Till we meet again."

Brandon smiled and then slipped into the little body in Tara's womb. Immediately, she groaned and grabbed her stomach.

"Ryan get the doctor, I've got to push now!"

"Sorry dear, my hands are kind of tied."

"Oh yeah, I forgot."

Tara grabbed the cord next to her and pushed the button on the end. In seconds, a nurse appeared. Thirty minutes later, an exhausted Tara held the most exquisite little baby boy in her arms. Tears streaming down her face, she talked openly to Ryan, not caring if anyone thought she was crazy or not.

For the next four weeks, Norma helped Tara care for the baby. Diapers were changed, nursings took place, and tummies were burped. Brandon was a strong and healthy baby, and was growing fast. Norma was a big help too, and twice Tara's parents were secreted in for a few days to spend time with Tara and Brandon. Of course, for security reasons, they never came to Norma's house.

For a time, Tara felt lost in a world of peace, love, babies and diapers. But on the horizon, and closing fast, was a clamor that stirred feelings long suppressed. It grew closer each day, until she could no longer stand to ignore it. She and Ryan both heard and felt it, and their anxiety was growing with each passing day. She felt like a captured wolf, locked in a cage while outside, just beyond the tree line, the pack was calling to her, calling her to break the chains of captivity and rush out to run free in the moonlight, never again to be tied down by fear.

But it was not really to freedom she was being called. The call had the stink of death to it as well as the promise of victory. Somehow, she had to sneak around those that intended her harm, to destroy them before they could destroy all the innocents of the world. The call was to danger, but it was her calling, her mission, and she knew that even though the odds were against them, she and Ryan had to be victorious. Heaven help them, and all creation, if they failed!

She arranged for Norma to care for Brandon while she was gone. Norma was ecstatic about it. She never had children of her own and felt wonderfully challenged by the role. Still it was hard for Tara to go when the taxi came to pick her up.

"Tara, Ryan, I can't tell you how much I appreciate this. I promise I'll take care of Brandon as though he were my own!"

"We know you will, Norma. It's just so hard to leave him. I don't know if I can bear it."

"Don't you worry, dear. He'll be just fine, but you hurry back here, so he can have his real mommy with him! Okay?"

Tara cuddled her son. What a marvelous thing he was, this person that she and Ryan had created together! She had always dreamed of being a mother, and was pained to have to leave such a remarkable little wonder. But if she were selfish and stayed behind, his world would crumble around him. She had to do this, for him!

"How long do you think this will take?" Norma asked.

"I wish we knew. Ryan seems to think it could be weeks, maybe months. I don't think I could stand it that long."

"Don't worry. I'll show him your picture every day." She held up an eight-by-ten she had taken recently and laughed. "I'll even show him the video I took last time I was down, the one of you and Brandon in the backyard. He'll remember you, I promise."

Tears welled up in Tara's eyes, and she hugged Norma with her free arm. "Thanks, Norma, you're the greatest."

"Nonsense, you're the one taking the risks."

"I'll try to get back soon enough that he won't forget me."

"When you do, you think Wil might come with you?"

Tara laughed. "That'll be easier to arrange than you might think."

"Really? That sounds interesting. Can you tell me more?"

"Sorry. Not supposed to, but I'll bet he'd like to get better acquainted with you when this is all over."

"Well, you make sure you bring him back with you then! Okay?"

"I will. By the way, Ryan wants me to tell you that you'll have some extra help here after he leaves. You won't see anything, of course, but if you listen with your heart, and follow your impressions, you'll be protected. And apparently the guy they're sending is a very large and strong fellow. Ryan says you're in good hands."

"You know, I believe that. Thanks, Ryan." She paused briefly, looking on either side of Tara, then added, "wherever you are."

Tara held her son close and kissed him one last time, then handed him to Norma. Without looking back, she ran to the waiting cab. Ryan spoke words of comfort to her as she jumped in, and as the taxi sped away, Tara wiped the tears from her face, determined to meet the challenge that lay ahead. She wasn't sure what that would involve, but she knew it started in Mexico.

<hr />

Wil met Tara and Ryan at the Guadalajara airport. He was driving an old Volkswagen Beetle, year unknown. It was a rather beat up rust bucket, with only one front seat, but it had a back seat and it ran. He had borrowed it from his friend, Borrego. It was a two-hour ride to Aqua Sublima. That gave them plenty of time to catch up on his efforts.

"Okay kids, I have an idea. I thought about this one night when I couldn't sleep. It was hot and all I could think about was talking to an invisible Ryan. Anyway, how about if you, Ryan, try and stand, or sit, to Tara's right as much as you can, and that way I can look at you when I talk. At least that way I'll know where you are, and won't feel like I'm talking to the air. It'll help me carry on a more meaningful conversation, even though I can't see or hear you."

"I like the idea, Wil!" Tara exclaimed. "And Ryan likes it too."

Wil smiled and winked at the empty spot to her right.

"So, are you going to tell us what you found or are we going to have to guess?" Tara prompted.

"For that my dear, you're going to have to guess. I want to surprise you guys, see the look on your face. It's big, so be ready to be dazzled. Ryan, if you're reading my mind, stop it! I want you to try and hold off on that for just a bit longer, okay?"

"Ryan says it's too late," said Tara, laughing.

Wil smiled and shook his head. "Okay, but no fair telling Tara!"

"He said he won't, Wil."

When they finally arrived in Aqua Sublima, the route to the warehouse led directly through the town.

"This place once had a population of twenty five hundred," Wil remarked. "Most of the residents were dependent on fishing for their survival. As the fishing crisis deepened, at least half of them moved away toward the cities, where family and friends could help them find work."

Tara and Ryan stared out the windows of the VW in wonder as they listened to Wil tell of Agua Sublima's recent economic woes.

"Two years ago," he continued, "this town was like many American fishing villages. These homes were neat, and everything was gorgeous. I saw pictures and believe me, it was a different place then."

The streets were lined with very small but neat homes; most of them painted blue or tan. Many of them had white picket fences surrounding the front yards. With the grass growing up and around the slats of the fences, and windows boarded up, it was obvious which of the homes were vacant now. The occupied homes were neatly painted, their yards trimmed and their flowerpots blooming with plastic flowers.

"This is so sad Wil," said Tara. "This town must have been beautiful in its prime. Where are the children?"

"What children?" answered Wil. "About the only people left are the hard core fishermen. They refuse to leave. They go out for weeks at a time, returning with little to show for it. The town is drying up fast."

The business district consisted of a market, a bank, a five and dime store and a mercantile of some sort. Other small businesses made up the balance of the street, which couldn't have been more than five hundred feet long. Wil turned west at its end, and drove a quarter of a mile out of town into the jungle. Finally, he stopped in front of a large barn.

"This is it!" he said. "Now Ryan," he gazed to Tara's right through the rear view mirror, "I think you'll find this very interesting."

They got out of the car and walked up to the front door. Wil gave a few quick raps with his fist, and the door jerked open a few inches. Inside, a dark figure, peering through the crack, recognized him and opened the door further, allowing them to enter.

The lighting from a single bulb near the entrance was very dim. The man who let them in walked to the wall on the north side of the building and started up a generator. Suddenly, the place came to life as some twenty additional bulbs, hanging from the rafters thirty feet above them, illuminated the whole structure.

The barn or warehouse was approximately one hundred feet wide and a hundred and fifty feet long. It had concrete floors and paneled siding, and was completely empty except for two objects in the back that took up about one third of the building. These objects were covered by large tarps of some kind.

"Borrego, I want you to meet a very dear friend of mine. This is Tara McKay. Tara, this is my best friend in all of Mexico, Borrego Vialobos, who, by the way, speaks wonderful English."

Tara shook his hand. "I am very pleased to meet you Borrego."

"The pleasure is all mine Señora McKay. Any friend of Wil's, is a friend of mine."

"Thank you for waiting, Borrego." said Wil.

"It is nothing. Here is the key. I will see you two in the morning."

"Gracias amigo."

"De nada. Hasta mañana." Borrego called out as he left through the front door.

Wil turned to the objects in the back of the warehouse. "This is it guys. Don't move. I want to see your reaction."

He walked over and one by one pulled the coverings off, exposing a most extraordinary sight. Tara walked over and stood in awe.

On the right, was a complicated piece of equipment, looking much like a television antenna or a light beacon used to divert ships from shallow water or rocks. The bottom was in the shape of a satellite dish, approximately thirty feet in diameter. Just above the dish, was an intricate set of mechanisms, each with wires and metal strips extending from their centers to a circuit board close to the center of the dish. In the very center, a metal rod extended up about twenty feet. It was braced on all sides by a metal frame.

Underneath the dish was a computer, apparently the brain of the creature, which had obviously been damaged. Around the dish on the underside were three mounts, which looked like they had been stripped from whatever mooring originally held the thing in place.

To the left of the antenna structure, was a more disturbing sight. It was a thirty-five foot wooden fishing boat, missing most of it's starboard half. Forty percent was completely gone, as though it had vanished.

"Oh my . . ." Tara looked at it in bewilderment. "I guess I didn't quite get the picture of this when you described it earlier."

She raised her hand and traced the lettering on the rear of the boat. *La Luna* it said, but the "a" in *"Luna"* was half gone.

"Look at this, Tara," Ryan was looking at the edge of the wood. "Look how the edge is almost polished, not torn or ripped."

They spent the first several minutes inspecting the boat and it's contents, then turned to the strange mechanism.

"It took me over a week to drag this thing up from the bottom of the ocean and get it into this warehouse. I tried to place it in a way that would reconstruct the incident. As you can see, it looks like the *La Luna* floated into this thing. The collision broke the gizmo loose from it moorings, and then it sank."

"What about the fisherman?" asked Tara.

"I didn't want to tell you about that. The remains of Luis Rivera, or what was left of him anyway, were found on the boat along with a dead seagull. He was gone completely just below the chest. They thought sharks had gotten him, but it was just like the boat. The edges of the bone, his clothing and what was left of his flesh were as smooth as marble. It was as if half of him had vanished . . . really eerie."

"Tara, ask Wil if the Navy is still looking for this."

"According to my friend in Naval Intelligence," Wil answered after Tara's reiteration, "the search for this thing was put to rest last year. Nobody's going to show up looking for it now. They figure it dropped into the deepest nether-reaches of the sea, where even Jacques Cousteau couldn't find it. Funny thing is, I found it in just two hundred feet of water! Since I discovered this thing, the town thinks the Mexican and U.S. governments are behind it, and they're really angry. I told them that my job was to try and trace it back to whoever made it and bring them to justice. Now they love me."

"Two hundred feet of water? That's too deep for skin diving," Tara noted.

"I had the equipment I needed, and I was able to go down with only Borrego topside. But the thing wasn't that easy to find. The current had washed it into a deep crevice. It must have continued to work for some time after it went down. It cut a hole through the rock that kind of followed the path of the crevice northward for as far as I could see. But I figure the current battered against it and eventually broke the thing. It didn't seem to be working when I got there."

Tara said, "Ryan's wondering exactly what direction it was pointing when you found it."

"Sort of west of north and downward a little, I think."

"I see where you're going with this, Ryan," she said. "Wil, could this thing have been projecting its signal through a fault line?"

"I'm no geologist, but I wouldn't be surprised if it was," Wil responded.

"I know the San Andreas comes up through California from Mexico. If this was following a similar crack, it could easily have come out in the Superstitions just east of Mesa!"

"You could be right," said Wil. "I'll have one of my people go out and see if that phenomenon is still going on out there."

"They better be careful, just in case we're wrong."

Tara turned toward the machinery next to the boat. "Were you able to find any serial numbers, patent numbers, or manufacturers names on this contraption?"

"Good question. Borrego and I scoured the thing to no avail. We hesitated taking anything apart, though, until Ryan could get here. We didn't want to set anything off."

"Yeah. I'd hate to come all the way down here to find half a Wil. I'm under strict instructions to get you back to Norma in one piece."

"What?" asked Wil.

Tara smiled at the air to her right, then looked back at Wil. "Oh, I just think she might be kind of interested in seeing you, that's all."

"Now, whatever gave you that idea?" Wil probed.

"Oh, maybe the fact that she said so, that's all!" Tara reached over and nudged him in the shoulder with the tip of her finger. "Are you blushing, Mr. Dowding?"

"Hush girl, you're embarrassing me. Ryan?"

"He's over by the machine now . . . there, in front of the dish," said Tara pointing.

Ryan was transfixed as he gazed at the machine in front of him. It was surprisingly similar to the equipment he'd been developing, but in some respects it was light-years ahead. Theories for its function were racing through his mind.

"Ryan, I've been all over this thing, as much as I dare," Wil interrupted his thoughts. "I hope you can help. Just tell Tara what you'd like me to do, I've got tools."

"Tara, you and Wil sit for a spell and visit. I think I can do this myself, without tools."

"You're in luck, Wil," Tara telegraphed. "Ryan says to sit for a while. He's gonna' see what he can do by himself."

The two made themselves comfortable near the boat as Ryan inspected every square inch of the mechanism. To his surprise, he could see inside whatever he examined. He had no idea what powers he possessed, as he tested his limits for the first time. It was as though he could perceive the organization of the living matter in the circuitry, the motors, through and around everything. He wondered if it was a property of the matter itself, or if it was actually communicating to him as one living thing to another. When he was done, he had obtained not only several traceable serial numbers and company names, but also a solid understanding of how the device worked.

While Tara translated, Ryan explained what they had in front of them. Though his father had told him what was happening, in general, this was his first opportunity to see how it was actually being done. He pointed out each element of the device and explained its function. Blank stares from both Tara and Wil suggested a more elementary summary was needed.

"My work focused on the connection between the elementary waves and the various quantum particles. This mechanism is directed entirely at the particles themselves. It's a direction I was just starting to explore, but it's been fully implemented in this design. Very clever. Like the influence of God's Spirit and the opposite, temptation, the focus is on individual behavior. It disorients the particles by spinning them into what could only be described as a euphoric frenzy. In that state, they cease to take their cues from the elementary waves, and fall out of phase. I don't know if that makes any sense, but a frequency shift occurs as a result of changes in their spin, orientation and other characteristics." He looked at Tara. "That didn't help either, did it? Well let's just say it makes the fabric of their reality seem to disappear."

Tara smiled, and Ryan continued. "The dish also serves as a receiver for satellite signals. Those signals could turn the unit on and off, vary its output and power, even cause it to self-destruct. Luckily, it was damaged somehow. It's totally inoperable now." Ryan turned to look at the mechanism again. "Wouldn't take much to fix it, though."

"Okay," said Wil after Ryan's remarks were transmitted to him, "first thing we do is trace the components to the buyers. We already know it's military, and possibly high government, so we'll work it from both ends, try to come up with some names and signatures. I'll get my men on the civilian end, and ask Eddie to work the military end."

"Where would we be without you, Wil?" Tara commented.

"Well, this is only the beginning," he reminded her.

"Yes, but it's a solid one. So where do *we* begin?"

Wil paused to think, and Ryan took the opportunity to answer Tara's question himself, "I think you and I should follow up directly on the military end. That's going to be where we need my resources the most. It won't be easy, but I feel the Amazing McKays are up to it. What do you think?"

After a moment's hesitation, she answered, "I think I need a Tylenol."

Chapter 12
ANSWERS

In a rented office in Bethesda, Maryland, two men in dark conservative suits spoke in low tones. The room was sparsely furnished with a desk, a phone/fax, a computer with all the trimmings, a small refrigerator, and a Lazy Boy reclining chair. There were no plants and nothing on the walls. The third man, to whom they spoke, was dressed in Levi's and a Redskins T-shirt, and sat at the desk.

"Do you have any idea how close we are?" the man at the desk asked. "And now this!" He threw a report on the cluttered surface in front of him. "Tell me; how do I spend the kind of money I do for a job, and it gets so botched up? How does that happen?"

"Well, the man we hired is the best, the absolute best," said one of the suits. "There was no way of knowing this would happen. We have to assume he's dead. It's been too many months."

"We've been working this project for over three years without a glitch," the man at the desk snapped. "I have no patience for glitches; do you understand me?" He was speaking now in a raised, though controlled, tone. "Your heads will roll long before any more glitches occur, that much I can assure you. For your sakes, I hope the girl is as dead as McKay. We can't afford any mistakes. I will spare no expense to protect what we have. Now, as to this Wil Dowding character, kill him. It's that simple. Just do it! Now go! Get outta here!"

The suits left, and the man at the desk leaned back in his chair. He thought back to the day he hired Ryan McKay. The young man created quite a stir at the university with his dissertation on elemental intelligence. He had hired him quickly, and sequestered him away in his own private lab to keep him quiet. At first, hiring was the thing. Now, he just erased anyone who happened on to the theory of sub-atomic manipulation. It was quicker, easier and much cheaper.

He marveled at how powerful he had become since he entered the information trading business. Most of his life, he had been regarded as a nobody by his peers. In fact, he wasn't even regarded! He had done a lot of things to get attention, mostly cheat and lie, but for a long time that only made things worse. Cheating and lying grew on him, however. He enjoyed it. And now he had power! Power from on high. Well, maybe not so 'high,' but it was power, and that was all that mattered. Whoever said cheaters never prosper didn't really know how to cheat.

He tilted the Lazy Boy up and reached for the phone, dialing a number in Washington.

"It's me . . . Yes, we're on top of it . . . Yes, I understand. It's a go. This Dowding character is history . . . No, the girl is nowhere to be found. We think Dowding hid her, but we'll get to her soon . . . Proceeding is not a problem . . . No, nobody else has a clue . . . Tomorrow night, then. Okay, after the dinner . . . Eight o'clock, right. Bye."

The man placed the phone in its cradle and sat back in the Lazy Boy. He thought of the phone system he had engineered with a little help from The Merchant, and smiled. All his calls were free, untraceable and even undetectable by the phone company.

Knowledge is a wonderful thing, he thought. Yes, wonderful. He closed his eyes and fell into a trance, repeating his special mantra, searching and searching again for The Merchant.

Tara and Ryan left Mexico a few days after Wil showed them the sub-atomic disorientation device. Ryan shortened it to SADD, which seemed such a fitting acronym, that the term immediately stuck in Tara's vocabulary. Their goal was to track down its components and see what governmental agency or official had purchased them. To make their task easier, Wil took a couple of days before they left to train Tara in the art of disguise. He had a complete kit sent down from Phoenix— wigs, make-up, latex body and facial parts, clothing, everything he thought she might need.

Ryan laughed hysterically the first time Wil made her up into a completely different personality.

"It's a good thing nobody can hear you," she thought at him.

"But not such a good thing that everyone can *see* you," he managed between fits of laughter.

Each time she talked to anyone, she was supposed to be a different woman. As Wil explained, this would completely sever any connection between their investigation and Tara Johnson McKay, or Jenny Sargent. Hopefully it would also avoid arousing suspicion.

At first, the effort was totally against Tara's nature and personality. But as she practiced, Wil's polite chuckles and Ryan's rolling gales subsided, and the skill of acting became more natural to her. She even began to enjoy it.

The first leg of their journey was a flight to Miami. At the ticket counter, Wil almost purchased a ticket for Ryan, he was so accustomed to the spirit's presence. With a hand on his arm and a quiet snicker, Tara reminded him that she was the only one who would need a seat. He accompanied her and Ryan to the gate, where he sent them on their way.

***

After a week in Miami, Tara finally met with Eddie Sitton. It was in a hotel restaurant overlooking an indoor water fountain. Ryan stood next to his wife, quietly observing. The meeting was short and to the point.

"I'm so pleased to meet you Mr. Sitton, Wil speaks so highly of you," Tara said as she rose to greet Naval Intelligence officer.

"The pleasure is mine Tara. Believe me, any friend of Wil's, is a friend of mine . . . for life." He shook her hand firmly and placed an envelope in front of her on the table, then gracefully slid into a chair across from her.

Tara was expecting to meet a man in military uniform. She was surprised, as he approached the table, to see he was dressed in Levi shorts and a white tank top that accentuated his short but muscular physique. His blonde hair, bright blue eyes, and infectious smile won Tara over instantly.

"So tell me, how did you know who I was?" she quizzed.

"Are you kidding? Wil is nothing if not thorough," was all he said before he jumped into the package in front of her. "We don't have much time. I have to catch a flight to San Diego. But I managed to get you enough to keep you busy for awhile." He had the envelope open and was pulling out pieces of paper. "These are the names of the companies who supplied all the micro-processing chips and whatnot. As you can see there are quite a few. The names on the purchase orders are all fake, however. So are the P.O. numbers."

"P.O. numbers?"

"The purchase order numbers. They're written on an order book that isn't even military! However, the invoices there have the names of the salespeople who made the sales for each of the companies. If you can get to those guys, maybe they can tell you who gave them the P.O.s." He shuffled through the pile of papers and pointed to several forms. "Those are copies of invoices that don't even exist any more."

He pulled his hand back and looked Tara in the eye. "Whatever you and Wil are up against Tara, please be careful. I risked a great deal to get this stuff. It no longer exists in any records I've been able to check. The military was pretty thorough in covering this up. These transactions never occurred, if you get my drift. But that doesn't change the fact that these are authenticated copies. Understand? This is admissible evidence, so guard it with your life. I think I've pushed as far as I can on the military end. Now it's up to you and Wil."

"Mr. Sitton, thank you so much," Tara said as he slipped the papers back into the envelope. "We know you've gone above and beyond what . . ."

"No, no, Tara. It was the least I could do! Wil has more integrity than the entire Navy. It's just that there *is* nothing else."

"I understand. I'll tell Wil. We really appreciate your help," she said, trying to show her gratitude. She knew that Eddie had a family and had gone way out on a limb for Wil. She wanted him to know how grateful she was.

"Tara, I have a good feeling about this. I'm here for you. If there's anything else I can do, just call. Right now I gotta run, though. Duty calls. Follow the leads there, it'll pay off for you, I'm sure of it! One of those leads has to be a nugget!" He stood and shook her hand again, smiled and waved as he made his way to the restaurant exit.

Tara turned to Ryan. *"Well, what did you think?"*

"He's a good man. I believe he gave us what he could. Let's just hope it's what we need."

"If we can connect these papers to some actual people, like Kilpack, will that be enough?"

"Depends on how high up we can connect the chain."

"Yeah, but can we do it?"

"We'll never know till we try, right?"

"Right." She started toward the exit. *After you, ghost man.*

They followed the leads Sitton gave them like Hansel and Gretel following breadcrumbs, through Miami, Phoenix and San Francisco. Tara asked the questions, and let Ryan read the minds. They made a good team, but it got them nowhere. Not one salesman had actually seen or spoken with the person or persons making the purchases. They were all made through a now defunct government Internet site. The invoices where mailed to a thoroughly befuddled Navy Purchasing Department, where copies were made. Then the originals were sent back apparently unpaid.

But Sitton proved to be right in the end; there was a nugget, but only a small one. A salesman in San Francisco produced a fax with a smudged phone number. It was clear enough to read, however. It was a Washington, D.C. number, and rang in the office of the Secretary of the Navy.

On October 1, six weeks after they left Dallas, their plane touched down in Washington. To Tara, the cool autumn air was a refreshing change from Mexico, Miami, and Phoenix. It was especially welcome because this time she was disguised as a middle-aged, somewhat plump and frumpy English teacher named Mrs. Emerson.

From the airport, she and Ryan went directly to the Pentagon. Though they knew they couldn't trace the San Francisco fax number, they had decided on a direct approach to the one government official who seemed to be involved in the scheme. Insisting upon directions to the office of Robert Kilpack, Secretary of the Navy, Tara eventually arrived at a very impressive anteroom where she sought an interview, ostensibly for her middle school class.

A pleasant Hispanic woman in her mid-thirties, who claimed to be Mr. Kilpack's personal secretary, explained that he was out of town on business. This visibly disappointed "Mrs. Emerson," who then asked a myriad of questions about the Secretary, his activities and his whereabouts. To placate her, the secretary spent close to ten minutes answering most of these questions, her mind obviously churning out far more information than she divulged to Tara.

"Thank you very much," Tara said at last, "You've been so kind."

"Oh, you're most welcome, Mrs. Emerson," she smiled. "I'm sure Mr. Kilpack would be delighted to speak to you if he were here. Those kids back in Nebraska are very lucky to have a teacher who would come all this way, just to learn about the Pentagon and the Navy."

"Tara, ask her about Brett Wimple. She seems to be linking that name with Kilpack pretty heavily."

"You getting much?"

"She's trying to protect Kilpack, though she genuinely doesn't know where he is, but this Brett fellow keeps coming into her mind, and she's scared to death of him.

"By the way," Tara added as though it were an afterthought. "I was told to talk to Brett Wimple by a man across the hall there. He said that Mr. Wimple might be able to answer some of my questions."

The secretary's eyes widened. Tara could almost hear her thoughts churning, which was exactly what Ryan would want.

"I'm sorry," she stammered, "I don't know who you're talking about."

"Oh, that's all right, I have no idea what the man across the hall had in mind anyway. Well, I'm running a bit late. Thank you for your patience."

She and Ryan turned and walked back out into the hall. Tara tried to walk away like an older and heavier woman, but she could hear Ryan snickering.

"What's she thinking? Has she seen through my disguise?" she asked.

"No. She's standing back there in a stupor with the address of Brett Wimple flowing through her mind!"

"Great!"

"Not if she notices that shuffle of yours. I can hardly keep from laughing."

"Good thing they can't hear you."

"Yes, but they can see you, and that's definitely not going work."

Tara increased her speed as they passed the information booth at the front of the building, at which point Ryan started to laugh. It was all she could do to stifle her giggles until the got past the guards at the exit of the building. When they were out of sight, she burst out laughing and nearly lost part of her disguise.

"You were great Tara, but that little shuffle down the hall just about put me away!" He continued to laugh for several seconds.

"Hey, I did my best, but it's hard knowing that you're laughing at me!"

Finally he caught his breath. "I'm sorry, honey. I'd hate to blow your cover."

"You couldn't blow my cover. Haven't you noticed? I've become quite the actress."

"Yes, you have!" he confirmed.

"Besides," she said on a more serious note, "I appreciate your sense of humor. I really need it right now, the way things are."

"Anything I can do to help," he reassured her. "As long as I don't get too carried away."

"Not to worry, dear husband, you didn't. So, do you think I missed my true calling in life?"

"Well, you're quite the woman, that's for sure."

Tears welled up in her eyes, as she tried desperately to smile through a frown. "I love it when you look at me that way. Especially through this make-up!"

He stepped toward her as if to take her in his arms, then stopped and looked down at himself. "Hey, I'll get my body back one day you know." His voice strained to sound light hearted.

"Yeah, I know." She succeeded in forcing a smile, and decided to change the subject. "Ryan, the Secretary of the Navy is a pretty important guy isn't he?"

"Very. And I see where you're headed with this. How can he just disappear and nobody know his whereabouts?"

"Exactly! If he were such an important guy, wouldn't he have meetings, an agenda? I mean, if not at the Pentagon, maybe at the White House?"

"Good question. Strange that his personal secretary would have no answers. Let's find Wimple and see if we can get some from him. But before we do that, there's something you should know."

"What's that?"

"That woman was scared of Wimple. I mean deadly afraid. In fact, when you mentioned his name, she feared for her life." Ryan paused in thought. "Let's be careful on this one. Okay?"

"Good advice."

As they drove down the street following the route he had gotten from the secretary, Ryan watched for indicators to Tara's mood.

"Ryan, these trees are beautiful! I never got to see this in the desert. The reds, the golds, they're fantastic!"

Ryan smiled at her outward cheer. He'd been aware of an underlying sadness that had been building within her for some time. He was discreet about mentioning anything, but he could, after all, discern her thoughts. She was lonely. Even with him beside her, she missed him and dreaded the day he would have to leave her completely. He understood her feelings. He missed her to! He wanted so badly just to hold her.

With every passing day her depression had been growing stronger. She tried to hide it, but Ryan knew, and it tore him up. She longed to share the simple things in life, like the colors of autumn, with a husband and a son. Instead, she had a ghost for a husband and her baby boy was almost two thousand miles away.

He knew, too, that she still wondered if this was all that life had in store, her dreams crushed and her hopes dashed to pieces by a dark, cruel, unrelenting world. Soon, he feared, her depression would affect their work, and Ryan needed to stop it before that happened, before it overwhelmed her.

"I know what you're thinking, Tara, and you've got to stop! What life has for you is still out there somewhere. In the end it'll all be worth it. I'm certain."

She glanced quickly at him without the smile she had been forcing all too often lately. "I suppose you're right, but . . . I don't know, it's so frustrating. I want to be able to touch you, hold our son together . . . I miss you! I miss my boy!" She struggled against the tears Ryan saw in her heart.

He wanted to reach out somehow and hold her, perhaps move over to where she was sitting and coincide with her briefly. But he could do nothing. She was driving and couldn't be distracted without causing an accident. He really needed to help her before they made what could be their most dangerous contact. What could he say or do? She was right, after all. Life was a Beast, and it would not let her go.

Suddenly, he was overwhelmed by a communication that could have only one source. The feeling was so powerful that he thought for a moment he would be transported out of Tara's presence in that instant, ending his 'initial visit' with her then and there. When finally he could speak, he did so in a whisper.

"Tara," he said, as he turned to her still burning from the experience. "I have a message for you."

"'A message'?" She perked up at the unusual news. "For me? Who is it from?"

"I think you'll know when you hear it."

"Well," she prodded when he hesitated for a moment. "Give it up, Particle Man."

"Okay, but I don't know how you're going to take this." Ryan tried his best to deliver the message in the same way it had come. Moving to her side, he spoke slowly, resonantly, directly into her ear.

"My precious daughter, remember your prayer to me in Dallas. Take heart, and know that I love you. I have given you all that you asked of me. What greater blessing can you receive?"

Tara pulled the car quickly to the curb, tears filling her eyes. When the car came to a stop, she leaned on the steering wheel and sobbed uncontrollably for several minutes. When finally she could speak, she turned to Ryan.

"That was from . . ."

"I know."

"He did answer my prayer, Ryan, the one I offered in Dallas when I wasn't even sure He existed! He's answering it now. He's been answering it ever since that day! But I've been so blind and selfish I couldn't see it. Oh Ryan, I'm so sorry. I'll never complain about my problems again. I promise."

Though her eyes were red, there was a joyous smile on her lips, the happiest he'd seen since he returned to her from Paradise. In fact, Ryan could not remember when she had looked so beautiful, or when he had felt such joy.

She started the car again, a look of determination in her eyes that told him that his own prayer had been answered as well. His joyful thoughts were interrupted, however, when he almost missed the turn.

"Ooops! Sorry. Turn here!"

Tara quickly wheeled the rental car, a silver Ford Taurus, onto Mill Street.

"Good job, for a biologist masquerading as an actress."

She smiled.

"Are you all right?" he asked after they had gone some distance in silence. Suddenly he was concerned. Could she still see and hear him, or were his fears about the termination of his 'initial visit' justified?

"Better than ever," she answered finally.

"That's a relief. For a moment there, I thought you couldn't hear me."

"No problem there, my precious husband."

"Good," he continued, "because Wimple's in an office, less than a mile from here. Are you sure you're ready? What's the next character's name?"

Checking a list she received from Wil, she tried the new character, Kristin Taylor, by simply changing the tone of her voice to one of prim efficiency. "As ready as I will ever be, Particle Man. So, how do you think we should approach this gentleman?"

"Good, good. That's really amazing. But I'm not sure on the approach yet. Let's just go there, let me read his thoughts, and I'll steer you from there."

"You've got it!"

Five minutes later, they turned a corner and pulled the Taurus into the parking lot of an office complex. It was small, rectangular in shape, and contained only twelve business offices. Beautiful oak, maple and elm trees, gloriously colored and shedding lightly, surrounded the complex. A thin layer of fallen leaves carpeted what used to be grass.

Not knowing just *how* he knew, Ryan pointed to an office on the southeast corner of the building. "He's in there."

Tara looked at him, smiled and shook her head. "I wish you could've done that when you were alive. Life would have been even more interesting."

"What do you mean, I'm still alive."

"You know what I mean."

She parked the car next to a blue Suburban, and turned the ignition off. Outside, a small breeze was picking up leaves, sending them cartwheeling and stumbling into each other.

"Ryan, I'm so glad you're with me. There's no way I could've done this without you." She drew in and exhaled a deep breath. "Okay, what's my gimmick."

Ryan thought for a moment. "At first, I thought maybe Kilpack's secretary might have called him, maybe to tell him that someone was asking questions, but that's not the feeling I'm getting. Let's assume he's unprepared for you. Tell him that you have a message for him from Kilpack. No doubt he'll be surprised. I'll snoop out a few thoughts from his mind, and tell you what to say from there." He looked over at her, and smiled. "How's that sound?"

"Like a plan from heaven," she said smiling back. Unbuckling her seatbelt, she started to open the door.

"Hey! Aren't you forgetting something?"

Ryan's question obviously startled her. "What?"

Looking at the glove box, Ryan raised an eyebrow for effect.

"Oh yeah. But I thought you hate guns?"

"I do . . . except when it comes to your safety. Remember, there's little I can do to help you physically. All I can hope is that I'll discern any thoughts of malice before you're in danger. But you're the last resort, so be ready."

Tara took the nine-millimeter and its clip from the glove box. With ease, she slapped the cartridge in place, and clicked off the safety. Wil had taught her well, he thought. With the gun in her purse and the snap undone for easy access, she opened the car door and stepped out onto the blacktop. In a few short moments, they were at the unmarked door of suite 103.

As Tara knocked, Ryan noticed a shadowy figure leaving the office at high speed. It went right through the wall and around the side of the building. Obviously a spirit, Ryan thought, but the feelings he got from it were very disturbing. He couldn't catch the face, and dared not leave Tara to follow it. Not wanting to alarm her, he said nothing.

"You sure he's in?" asked Tara.

"He's in."

Ryan could sense the person on the other side of the door almost as if the barrier wasn't there. "Tara, it's Marv Graf, my old boss! He's Brett Wimple! That explains a lot. You'll recognize him from the symposium, where he used the alias of Wimple. He's about to open the door, so don't look surprised. And use the Wimple name, apparently that's the one he's been using here!"

At that moment the door opened, and a man in his thirties, wearing a Washington Redskins T-shirt spoke. "What is it?" he asked.

Sure enough, it was the man from the panel, looking a bit more relaxed without his expensive Italian suit. "Oh hello, Mr. Wimple, I'm Kristyn Taylor, I was sent by Mr. Kilpack with a message." Tara clutched her purse and it's hard contents close to her.

The man's thoughts started to flow as he reacted to the unexpected visit. Ryan could almost see them and his intentions. The man was puzzled. Kilpack had never sent a messenger before. His phone was totally untraceable and secure, so he wondered about a personal visit in the open like this. Scanning his mind, Ryan came up with volumes . . . and none of it pleasant. This man was evil to the core, totally wrapped up in power and monetary gain. He would do anything to achieve his concept of wealth. Mostly, he had others do the dirty work, but he gave the orders, and knew very well what he was doing. Ryan marveled how none of this had come across during his conversations with the man while at Mol-Dyn.

Perhaps most disturbing, however, was something Ryan could now sense about him without knowing exactly how. He had been in contact with the other side! In fact, he was in contact with the very spirit about whom his father had warned him! Ryan would have to be very careful, very careful indeed.

"Tara, tell him that his meeting tomorrow night has been changed to eight-thirty, and that he should be very careful, because somebody is on to them, then wait for a reaction." Ryan wanted more time to fully download everything the man knew.

'Kristyn Taylor' relayed the message, and stood silent, waiting for a response.

"Why the delay?" he said finally.

With Ryan's coaching, Tara said, "He needs the extra time to lose somebody. Walk carefully, Brett." She turned then and walked back to the car, leaving the man completely off guard. They were half way to the car before Ryan heard the office door close.

"What was all that about?" asked a bewildered Tara.

"Seems our Mr. Wimple has an important meeting tomorrow night with Robert Kilpack. When he shows up late with the story of your message, they'll both get so worked up, they'll think of every possible problem. I should be able to find out everything they're up to then. It's nice to finally see the man who hired me. Boy, if he only knew I was standing there!"

"So who is he really? Graf or Wimple?"

"Graf. Wimple is just an alias."

"Ryan, that felt very weird."

"It sure did. Come on, let's get hold of Wil."

They stopped at a phone booth and Tara put in a call. It was agreed that Wil would arrive in Washington the next morning and meet them at their hotel.

As they drove back, Tara questioned him about Graf. "So, what do you think. Is he as bad as you thought?"

"No, he's worse. He's the one behind all the murders. He thinks he's the top man, but," he paused, "the truth is he's just a cog in a bigger machine. Still, he's a very highly placed cog!"

He looked at her, absorbing her thoughts. She was stunned. For the second time in her short life, she had come face to face with a ruthless killer.

"So what's next?" she finally asked.

"We're going to a meeting." he replied dryly.

They passed the rest of the drive in silence, both lost in thought. Something was nagging at Ryan. The spirit he saw leaving Wimple's office . . . there was something familiar about it . . . something dark and sinister. An uneasy feeling came over him, and again he looked over at Tara. He didn't like what he was thinking; it did not bode well for their future. He was going to have to stay very sharp. If only Brandon, or his father were there to help.

Later that night, as Tara slept in her hotel room, Ryan, the lonely guard, stood the silent sentinel again, watching, waiting, unable to leave her side, restless and worried.

Marv Graf sat back in the Lazy Boy and took a deep breath. Today had to be his worst day since his introduction to The Merchant three years ago. He closed his eyes and tried to expel his anxieties. He thought of the two men who had been there in the morning and mentally shot them.

Then there was the strange spiritual visitor who interrupted his meditations earlier, making him think strange and unnatural thoughts. He had been expecting The Merchant to come and give him new ideas, and inventions, but instead this intruder had almost scrambled his brain. He imagined tying a spirit grenade around the stranger's neck and pulling the pin, then pushed him from his thoughts hoping he would blow away forever.

Last but not least, had been the unexpected female messenger with an even more unexpected message. Who could possibly be on to them? Why was his meeting tomorrow night being put off thirty minutes? It had never happened before. If there were problems, why wasn't he consulted? After all, he was the one holding all the cards. Well, most of them anyway. He was the one selected by The Merchant for this great mission, the only one able to reach him. He shouldn't be treated like this. He would have to have a talk with Kilpack, remind him who was at the helm.

He started to hum the strange mantra that began the whole affair years ago. He had invented it himself, based on some off-the-wall research done by a local "institute," and he had practiced it for months. It soothed him, helped to put him in just the right state to reject his physical self and leave his body behind. Well, not entirely. It was a blissful condition devoid of any earthly cares where he could retreat and find peace, out of body.

The Merchant had been looking for a soul such as his three years ago when he spotted Graf during one of his earliest expeditions. He had been told that he was about to discover the secrets of the universe. Back then, meeting The Merchant face to face in the astral realm frightened him more than anything he had ever experienced on earth. But he was assured that all would be well, that because of his open mindedness and willingness to explore the limits of freedom, he would be rewarded beyond his imagination . . . and he had a very vivid imagination.

From that day on, Marv had been on top of the world! He had made contact with the other side! It wasn't psychic hype or new age channeling. This was the real thing. And he alone held the key, a key to vast wealth that he could unlock for the marginal price dictated by The Merchant. All he had to do was position a few technological devices around the globe, cause an insignificant 'glitch' in the ecology of the planet, and the world was his!

The Merchant still frightened him, of course, but his little retreats into the netherworld were well worth those few moments of stark terror. Just look at his bank account! Look at the people in the government who sought his expertise and compensated him handsomely for it!

Contented, he continued to hum his mantra, searching for the road to the spirit realm where he could leave his body behind and find his mentor, The Merchant. The vibrations finally came, as expected, but this time, as he projected out of his body, someone else projected in, and as the startling and impertinent interloper entered, it dragged Marv back in with him. A brief struggle ensued. With a cry for help, Marv wilted and gave in to the stronger and more wicked invader. His body was now an unwilling slave of the intruding ghost.

The new Marv Graf stood up and looked out the window toward an empty parking lot.

"So, the little missy came a looking. Well now, she's just gonna have to pay for sending me down that hole in the desert. Her and that fella of hers! She's gonna' pay all right; both of them! Fifty dollars every day! Don't worry Mama, I found me a new Device!"

He looked down at the hands of his host body, and squeezed them into fists. Inside, lava began to boil, slowly bubbling and seething, ready again to burst forth upon the world. And somewhere inside, deep within that lava, a man screamed.

Chapter 13
LAVA

The day was getting late, and Wil was tired. After days of searching, he finally found a truck large enough for the task. He was at the wheel, heading back to Aqua Sublima to arrange for the safe removal of the SADD to a warehouse in Phoenix. He wasn't sure he and Borrego could pull it off by themselves, but right now, he needed to get back and make sure everything was safe and ready to go.

The hour-long drive to town was uneventful, except for the usual magnificent sunset that fell gently on the Mexican Riviera. It was dark as he pulled up in front of the secluded warehouse that belonged to Señora Rivera. Using the key Borrego gave him, he opened the padlock and slipped inside. Flipping on the light switch, however, resulted in nothing.

Suddenly the silence of the night was shattered by a gunshot, and a slug slammed into the wall two inches from Wil's head. Instinctively he dropped to a squatting position, his gun out. Instead of firing it, however, he ducked and slithered through the crack of the door and headed for the jungle as more shots rang out behind him.

By the time he reached the tree line, bullets were zipping past him like tiny bolts of lightning, tearing at the jungle growth and smacking into tree trunks. He didn't have time to think as he ran a jagged course into the bowels of darkness. Bullets continued to zing past him, until he dove behind a fallen tree, gasping for breath.

He knew there was no time to rest, not even enough to catch his breath. He could hear several men running toward him from the direction of the warehouse. Springing to his feet, he ran as fast as he could toward the river. If the men behind him had night vision goggles, the time he had left could be counted in seconds. He had to make the river!

Without regard to noise, he ran for all he was worth, knowing that if he could get to the river, it's current would take him quickly away from these death-wielding strangers. Bullets continued to race past him in random patterns as he drew closer to freedom.

Suddenly, and without warning, the jungle disappeared from around him and he was falling. Flailing wildly, he fell some twenty feet, before splashing down on the silent, but swift current of the Rio Chongo, headed for the sea.

He heard no more shots as he sank into the Chongo's depths struggling madly for air. He had hit the water before he could take a breath, and he had been laboring for air because of his run. He could not survive more than a few seconds underwater! He needed desperately to hit the bottom so he could push off and reach the surface, but there was no bottom. After several desperate, interminable moments, he kicked his way to the surface and gulped in the life-giving air above it.

Silently, he made his way across the river hoping the shooters couldn't see him, and dragged himself up onto the bank and into the jungle. In minutes, he was far away from the threat behind him. Without knowing his location exactly, he followed the river's sound to the sea. Keeping within the tree line that hugged the beach, he continued to walk until he finally found his bearings.

All Wil could think about now was his promise to Tara's father to keep her safe. The SADD was gone, that was certain. He had to find a place where he could hide out for the night. He was exhausted, muddy, bruised, and had a cut just above his left ear, which was still bleeding, but he only had two things driving him: find safety and protect Tara. Of course, the thought of a very attractive woman from Scottsdale also intruded briefly on his mind.

He continued on for two more hours until he stumbled upon a small inlet of beachfront vacation homes, most of which were vacant now. Within minutes, he was safely tucked away for the night.

At sun-up he showered. Finding various toiletries in the bathroom, he shaved his beard off, and changed into a fresh batch of clothing he found in the closet. They were not a perfect fit but close enough. He then put the finishing touches on a disguise made up entirely from the women's make-up he had found in the bathroom. When he was finished, he paused to look at himself in the mirror. "Oh yeah, I look good!" he said smiling, then turned and limped out to a waiting car.

Borrego had responded to his early morning call with gusto. He borrowed an old limousine from a cousin, and within two hours he had Wil in Guadalajara. Pulling into the airport's passenger loading zone, he handed Wil two packages from the back seat and shook his hand.

"Good luck, Señor Wil," he said in his heavy accent.

"Gracias mi amigo," Wil returned. "When this is all over, I will fly you and your family up to the States for a nice long visit. You've been a wonderful friend."

"Vaya con Dios. It is too bad they burned the barn down last night. I hope these videos will be enough to do what you must."

Wil looked at the packages Borrego handed him. "Yes my friend, I hope so too. By the way, tell Señora Rivera not to worry. My office will wire her enough money for a new barn."

"No, no. It is not necessary. The people in town are very grateful to you already. We will rebuild the barn, and we will pray for you every day!" Borrego's smile was big and genuine.

"Thank you Borrego, we will definitely need your prayers."

Tara responded to the knock on her hotel room door by first looking through the peephole.

"Ryan?" she spoke in a puzzled whisper.

"It's Wil," he stated flatly.

"Uh, I don't think so. I don't recognize this man at all!" She was more than a little worried.

"He's in disguise, Tara. It's him . . . I promise."

Tara opened the door tentatively, and there in front of her stood a clean-shaven man who looked to be in his thirties, wearing sunglasses and smiling from ear to ear.

"Tara!" the man yelled, tossing a backpack into the room and sweeping her off her feet with a hug.

"Wil? Is that you? I've never seen you without a beard, and you look so . . . young! What in the world?"

"It's a long story. I thought it wise to incorporate a new disguise as I traveled. These stretchers pull the skin tight around my eyes. They're hidden under the hair piece."

"Well, this is a good one! I would never have recognized you without Ryan's help."

"We must be having an effect. Some very nasty people want me dead and are pulling out all the stops to accomplish that goal. What I don't know is just how far up the political ladder this goes."

"I think we could be in a position to find that out very soon," Tara offered enthusiastically.

"Good," he said. "Because it's clear my connections in the Navy have been compromised. My last message from Eddie Sitton was that an inside All-Points Bulletin has been issued for both of us. There are also rumors that some warrants are being issued based on a bunch of absurd charges."

"What are we going to do about that, Wil?" Tara asked, suddenly concerned.

By midnight, Tara, Wil and Ryan had fully briefed each other and discussed some possibilities for the following evening. Wil leaned back in his chair at the table. He looked nervous, which worried Tara.

"You realize we're going to have to leave the country after this."

She looked over at Ryan, as if to get confirmation, then back at Wil. "You think that'll be necessary?" she asked.

"You thought it was bad having a hit man after you? Try the country's whole armed forces. Then there's my greatest fear: the FBI, the CIA, the police and anyone else they can think of. It's only a matter of days before those warrants hit!"

"Wil, this is crazy! What are we going to do? Even if we get what we want tomorrow night, we aren't finished. I mean, we have to stop these people. Right? We can't just give up. Ryan?" She looked over at him. He had gone over to the bed.

"He's right, Tara," Ryan responded. "We've stumbled onto something very big, as we knew we would. We're about to get the goods on them, and now they're striking back. This whole affair goes very high in the government. High enough to get you and Wil erased!"

"Hey! We didn't come this far just to run away! We've got to finish what we started. You know the Lord wants us to succeed here!" After the message she got through Ryan, Tara knew God was on their side, and didn't believe anyone could stand against them. She stood up, her face turning red, her grip on the tabletop tightening like a vice. "I've got a little boy at home who would like a normal world to grow up in. I'm not going to let him down! I'm not going to give up and run just when we learn who's behind all this!"

"I wasn't saying we'd quit," Wil interjected. "But we can't very well stop these people if we're dead. Remember, the best part of a good offense is a good defense." He paused. "Talk to her Ryan!" Wil directed his last remark to Tara's right.

"Sorry, Wil. He's not there, he's over on the bed."

"Since when did spirits need to rest?" Wil asked looking over at the bed. "Can you tell her where I'm going with this, Ryan?"

Ryan stood up and walked over to Tara. "He's right you know. We need to think of your safety, too. You think you're invincible right now because God is on our side in this battle, but it doesn't work that way. They're going to be all over you and Wil. There'll be no escaping if you don't get out soon. Besides, Wil has a promising plan."

"Okay," said Tara plopping resignedly into a chair on one side of the small table, "what's your plan, Wil?"

Wil smiled. "What we need is some help from a higher power," he said leaning over to pick up the backpack he had brought with him.

"I thought we had that," Tara interjected.

"Not that high of a power. Something a little more mundane, and I think this may get us just the help we need."

Opening the backpack, Wil dropped a large manila envelope on the table. It was overstuffed and ripping out at the seams. He dumped the contents out on the table.

"This is our ace in the hole."

Tara picked up a video that lay amongst the documents and other items, and looked for a label.

"Excellent," said Ryan. "It's almost enough."

"What do you mean 'almost'?" Tara responded.

"Wil's done a good job collecting all this evidence. He's almost there."

"Ryan says you're 'almost there,' Wil. What does he mean? How do you plan to use this stuff?"

"That video you're holding shows all the equipment and the boat we found in Aqua Sublima, as well as testimonials from the locals about the owner of the *La Luna*, Luis Rivera. There's a complete section in there from the medical officials who did a post-mortem on Rivera's remains, complete with close-ups. Pretty graphic stuff."

"Those I don't need to see." Tara pulled her hand back, her face tightening into an expression of disgust.

"These computer discs I got from Eddie Sitton; they document the placement of fifteen so-called submarine detection devices. They all bear a striking resemblance to that device we found down in Mexico. A private company from California, which went belly-up recently, placed them at various locations in the Pacific and the Atlantic. The company officers all died mysteriously last August. Here are their death certificates. Here are copies of the P.O.s and invoices Eddie gave you documenting the sale of the components. A nice little package, except for one or two things."

"Like names of the military purchasers. Right?" Tara interjected.

"Well, we have a lot of circumstantial evidence implicating Kilpack. We do need more on this Graf/Wimple character. At least you two know where he is and what he looks like. Still, it seems like there's an important element missing."

"What do you mean?" asked Tara

"Well, what's their motivation? The way I see it, the Secretary of the Navy has to be in it for the money. Same for Graf. So where's the money coming from, and who stands to benefit enough to shell it out? There's got to be someone higher up. Somebody who's using these guys, and paying them big! I'm just not sure who that is yet."

"Okay, so we find out how far up this goes tomorrow night, then we turn in this packet of information. But where? Who is this 'higher power' you're talking about, Wil? The courts?"

"Not on your life. We've got to go much higher than the courts. We turn over a copy of this to every news agency that'll take one! Then let them do the rest. A lot of people are going to be interested in what we've uncovered. The world is hungry for answers to this crisis. The media will go right for the jugular. All we need to do is get those names, establish the connections and let them do the rest. But we need to complete our investigation and get this to the right people before whoever is at the top of this food chain catches up with us."

"Now that sounds like a plan, Wil!"

"Tara," Ryan interjected, "to do what you have to do here will burn the bridges that lead back to a normal life. Media reaction to this evidence should stop the matter disorientation problem itself, but to stop the personal attack on you guys is going to take a lot longer. You and Wil could be at the wrong end of somebody's gun sights for years. You'll have to go into hiding. Are you ready for that?"

"What's he saying?" Wil asked. "I'm trying to follow your expressions, but I need some help."

"Just a minute, Wil," Tara said as Ryan continued.

"Ask Wil about the other packet."

"What other packet?" she asked.

"Just ask him."

Tara looked sympathetically at Wil. "You look tired, Wil. I'm so sorry I involved you in all this. You're so much like Ryan, so dedicated . . ."

"Hey, no apologies. I'm glad you asked me."

". . . and so sneaky," Tara completed her sentence with a smile. "So where's the other packet, Wil?"

"What makes you think there's another packet?" he asked trying to look innocent.

"Give it up Wil. Where is it?"

He blew out a deep breath and rolled his eyes. "Oh, that packet! I'm going to get you for this, Ryan." Smiling nervously, he reached down into the pack and pulled out another, less bulky envelope.

"Well, I was waiting for the right moment, but I guess Ryan figures the right moment is now."

He brushed the contents of the first packet to one side on the small table, and emptied the second. It contained Social Security cards, drivers' licenses, photos, I.D., both Canadian and U.S., birth certificates, everything needed to give four people new identities, topped off with four plane tickets.

Tara looked through them with a blank face. "I guess I sort of figured it would come to this," she signed, then she noticed something about the documents. "Why have you included Norma?"

Wil hesitated. The look on his face made Tara nervous.

"Two days ago, Norma called our office and said that someone had been watching her home. We pulled her and Brandon . . ."

"No!" Tara gasped jumping from her seat next to the table. "Is he okay? Is he safe? Where is he?"

"Whoa, whoa! They're both fine, I swear." Wil held up his hands trying to calm her. "They'll be here tomorrow. But the day we moved them out, not only did her Scottsdale house blow up, but her store was burned to the ground as well."

"Ryan, are they okay? Please tell me they're okay!" Tara pleaded, turning toward him for comfort.

He smiled and nodded his head, confirming what Wil had said. "Yes, honey, they're in good hands. It's okay."

His smile reassured Tara as nothing else could. But she wondered if he understood how much she ached to see her baby and hold him, to know for herself that he was safe. The pain was something she felt only a mother could truly understand.

"A father's pain can be just as sharp," Ryan added, a knowing smile on his face.

Wiping a tear from her cheek, she asked, "Why are they coming here?"

"Like I said, Tara, we have to get out of the country. I think this has to be our plan: Tomorrow night we go to the meeting with Kilpack and Graf. From what Ryan said, it's a dinner-type affair, thousand dollar a plate stuff. You know, a chance for the common folk to mingle and hobnob with the political folks. Kilpack should be there. So will Graf, if your information is accurate. That must be where they're holding that meeting you told me about. If this is what I heard about on the news coming over here, the dinner was designed to bring in money for political wannabes, party-liners who agree with the President's defense ideas, that sort of thing. It's open to the paying public, so we'll just pay and go."

She paused to consider the plan. "Let's see. These people have the armed forces, the FBI, the CIA, the police and heaven knows who else after us and we're just gonna walk into their little party and sniff 'em out."

"Yeah," Wil nodded. "That's about it. They won't be expecting that. Besides we won't look anything like ourselves."

"Well, if we can get into the dinner, Ryan can mosey around and pick the brains of everyone there. That could give us what we need to tidy up your little media package." She turned a skeptical eye to her husband, "What do you think Ryan?"

"It's risky, but I think it's the best we can do."

"What does he think?" Wil asked.

"Looks like it's a go," Tara responded.

"Okay dollface, let's figure out how to get you and me made up so we're unrecognizable. We'll find a campaign headquarters somewhere tomorrow. Shouldn't be that hard. Give the dirty dogs two grand, then head out for an evening of fun and adventure. Sound good to you?"

"No," she sighed, then smiled, and nodded yes.

"Good then, let's get started."

—⊰⊱—

Mr. and Mrs. Jenkins arrived at the fundraising dinner at 5:45 PM, he in a plain black tux, and her in a full length, slit to the knee, black evening gown, offset with costume jewelry. It was padded to give Tara the appearance of a much older woman. The other guests were dressed to the hilt in an effort to attract attention, so hardly anyone noticed the older, relatively unpretentious Jenkins couple, as they quietly moved across the room toward their assigned table. Of course, nobody but Mrs. Jenkins noticed the six foot three spirit walking next to her, studying each face as he passed.

"I feel so uncomfortable here Ryan," Tara thought, as they maintained a silent conversation.

"I think you'd be surprised how many of these people feel the same way. Many wish they could be part of this lifestyle, even though it goes against their nature."

"By the way, Wil sure cleans up nice, doesn't he?"

"He sure does! Only I wish I were taking you to dinner tonight. You know, I could sure go for a cold drink. I can't remember the last time I had a soda! It's strange how I crave something as menial as that . . . especially when I'm not even thirsty!"

Tara couldn't help laughing at this, which prompted Wil to ask what was so funny.

"I'll tell you later," she whispered, looking around her to make sure no one had noticed.

A five-piece woodwind orchestra was playing some light music up on the stage. From their vantage against the west wall, near the back of the room, Tara marveled at the opulence of the setting and the haughty patrons in attendance. She had never been to anything quite like this, a major fundraiser in the heart of the nation's capital. The air was thick with a false sense of power, as though the attendees thought their presence actually gave them some real influence. She chuckled at the concept of paying $1000 for a plate of chicken.

At six o'clock promptly, carts were wheeled out from the kitchen with plates full of hot, steaming Fettuccini Alfredo. Baskets were brought out, and placed in the middle of each table. The aroma of freshly baked garlic bread wafted through the cloth covering, tantalizing the taste buds. Members of Congress, high-ranking military personnel, and local politicians, all dressed as waiters, entered the room bringing a round of applause, and began serving the tables. It was a unique touch to an otherwise boring gala.

"Well, hello folks!" said a man in a white jacket standing next to the cart of food that appeared at Tara and Wil's table. "I'm Jim Harris, Congressman from Delaware. I'll be your waiter this evening. I'd take your order, but since we're all having the same thing, this'll have to do." He laughed.

Everyone at the table laughed politely. Tara sighed and shook her head. Looking at the man intently, she decided he was a phony. It was something about his eyes. She knew Wil hated politicians and was paying absolutely no attention. At her side Ryan rolled his eyes.

Congressman Harris made small talk as he served their table, then took his cart and ambled back toward the kitchen. Wil was talking about the nation's economy with the man to his right, and Tara pretended to follow their conversation. She smiled and nodded agreeably, while she conversed silently with Ryan.

"Okay Tara," Ryan said. "I'm going to roam around a bit. I saw Kilpack at one of the tables near the front, but not Graf. Whatever you do, don't leave the room, not even to powder your nose."

"Don't worry," Tara replied, *"you're not leaving my sight. By the way, do I look interested in what Wil and this dude are saying? Watch me . . . a smile and a chuckle here . . . and a 'uh huh' there. You know, I really should have been an actress!"*

"Yeah right! Have your fun. Call me if you need me. Remember, I can hear your thoughts, but I'm not sure how far away. We'll see. Catch you in a bit."

———❊———

Ryan left Tara and began making his way around the room, listening to the thoughts of the dinner patrons. Gradually he moved toward the front where most of the politicians were seated. Ever watchful of Tara, he turned frequently and waved.

Listening to their thoughts was hard at first. It was like being in a crowded room where everyone was speaking at the same time, loudly! Thoughts and words, words and thoughts, each battling for his attention. For some time, he found himself focusing on the spoken words, unable to concentrate on the thoughts. Gradually he improved his ability to focus, tuning his mind to their thoughts as he would a radio. Once he learned how, it was easy.

Most of the people were thinking about the food.

"A thousand dollars for this!"

"Look at this crud! Shoulda' gone to that party with the Winters!"

Comments on the food persisted for most. Some, however, bounced from topic to topic:

"Whoa! Look at her! What I'd give to exchange this tub of lard I married for her!"

"Jeez, I'd love to take that stud home. This pig I'm stuck with is gonna' die of a heart attack . . ."

"I hate tuxedos. I look like a flaming moron!"

"I don't get it. What are they going to do with all this money anyway? I'll bet some of it's going in that guy's pockets . . ."

"Would you look at that! Betty looks ridiculous. I wonder if she's noticed my dress . . ."

"I'll bet we're the best dressed couple here . . ."

"Why'd they sit us next to these losers . . ."

"Make this whole blasted crowd pay fifty dollars every day. That's what I oughta' do!"

Instantly, Ryan stopped. Where did that come from? He turned to his left. There, sitting two tables over was Marv Graf lost in thought. He wasn't eating, but instead was looking around as if he expected someone. Ryan moved in closer.

"All right little mister, just smile and look stupid, as you no doubt are. Let me do all the thinking. If I gotta' talk to these people much longer, I'm gonna' up and kill 'em, that's for sure. We'll meet with your Kilpack friend, see what's on his mind, then I gotta get someone. Yesiree, a little missy, that's for sure!"

There was something frighteningly familiar and disturbing to Ryan about these thoughts, but the situation didn't make any sense to him. They seemed to be coming from Graf. He couldn't quite put the picture together.

". . . dollars every day, the little pervert. Lucky for me that Ryan fella is dead. He was a real pain. Killed me deader than a doorknob. Lucky I found you Marv old boy . . . gave me new life . . . gave me a way to finally get that girl. Never thought I'd have to come back from the dead to get her though. Okay, okay. If you'll stop pestering me about who's got you possessed, I'll tell you. I'm the guy you hired all those months ago to snuff out Ryan McKay. You know, the guy you hired to keep him quiet. I'm also the guy who's gonna kill you eventually. So shut up and enjoy the ride. Gonna make you pay for this, making me have to possess you. Gonna make little Missy McKay pay too, if I can find her."

Before the killer finished his thought, Ryan was standing next to Graf, listening. Now he understood the situation clearly.

"Oh Ryan, I'm already missing you, can you hear me?" Tara broke into his thoughts from across the room.

Ryan turned to her, wondering for the first time if spirits sweat. He was standing between the woman he loved, and the man who intended to kill her. What could he do? He managed a smile and waved to her, then said, "I miss you too dear, stay put, don't leave your seat. I'll be back in a minute."

Tara smiled and flashed her beautiful brown eyes at him. He could see through the makeup she was wearing. It was the beautiful girl hidden beneath the older woman's disguise he saw smiling at him. Could the being who stalked her see that girl too? His concern intensified, as he considered what to do.

He turned back toward Graf, and his heart sank. The man was gone! Feeling the tension rise, he looked around the room. He fought to keep from thinking that he would like to find Graf. It could have transported him to the man, with disastrous results. If he left the room, he and Tara would almost certainly be separated permanently!

That's where he needed to go, he thought, back toward Tara. Everything was all right for the moment, and would continue that way if he could just keep a close eye on her. He moved from table to table, looking into faces, searching for Graf but coming up empty.

Minutes passed, and not a sign of him. Had the man gone to the restroom? Ryan knew he had to stay alert. Then he turned again to look at Tara. Danger was standing directly to her left. It was Graf, wearing a white jacket and bent over in conversation with her. In less time than it takes to think, Ryan was next to them.

" . . .the phone is in the next room. If you'd be so kind as to follow me," he was saying, "I'll take you there."

"I can't leave now," Tara responded. "Can you just take a message?"

He knew she had recognized the man as Marv Graf. She turned casually toward Ryan. *"Help me out here!"* she thought.

"Miss, it's your son, there's been a terrible accident, and . . ."

"Tara, he's lying!" Ryan said. "Don't believe a word he says!"

A tear began to form in one eye, and a look of bewilderment crossed her face. Wil was standing now, ready to approach Graf.

"What do I do Ryan?" Tara pleaded.

"Nothing! Be calm and ask him to leave. He's recognized you somehow, and he's trying to get you out of here."

"I couldn't stand it if anything really happened to my baby, Ryan. Are you sure?"

"Yes!"

Tara turned and put a hand on Wil's chest. "It's okay, honey," she said, "Obviously, he's mistaken us for someone else." She turned to Graf. "We have no children, sir. I'm sorry."

Suddenly, Graf looked toward Ryan! The man's physical body prevented the killer from actually seeing him, but apparently, his spirit could still sense Ryan's presence.

Looking back at Tara, Graf smiled. "That's okay little missy, whoever gave me this message'll have to pay . . . big time. Yesiree, sorry to bother you and the mister." He smiled at Wil, and turned again toward Ryan. "Another day perhaps," he said, then slowly and walked back into the kitchen.

Wil put a hand on Tara's shoulder as she slumped down, and dropped her head on the table. "What was that all about?" he asked.

"Oh, please no . . ." was all she could mutter.

Wil sat back down and put his arm around Tara, patting her shoulder as he comforted her.

"Tara, Brandon and Norma are just fine," Ryan reassured. "He was trying to get you out of this crowded room. He knows who you are, and somehow . . . he knows about me."

"What can we do?" she asked, her thoughts flooded with despair.

"We can stay calm. We came here to do a job, and we still need to do it. Can you hang in there for just a little longer?"

She sat up and took a deep breath, then spoke out loud, "Yes, yes, I'm all right. I'll be okay." *"But that voice . . . what's going on, Ryan?"*

The others at the table were looking on in idle curiosity. Wil motioned for them to continue eating. Reluctantly, they turned back to their plates.

"What's going on, Tara?" Wil whispered.

She put her hand on his and gave it a pat. "That was him, Wil. Graf! But I'm okay now." She looked up at Ryan. *"Help me Ryan, please. I need your strength."*

Ryan knelt in front of her. "Tara, the strength is in you. I promise you, Brandon is fine. We can do this!"

"But I'm so confused. That was the voice of the man who killed you. How could that be?"

"I'm not entirely sure, but I intend to find out."

Wil sat silently, with his arm around her shoulder. She turned to him and smiled, acknowledging his efforts to console her.

"Tara?" Wil said quietly. "Our man is back."

He motioned toward Graf's table. The man was in his black tuxedo jacket, as if he had just been out for a stroll, and sitting beside him was the Secretary of the Navy, Robert Kilpack. They were in quiet conversation, while the rest of the table's occupants were staring in the opposite direction at the man who had taken the podium.

In an instant, Ryan was beside the pair. He listened for several minutes, while the Congressman from Virginia told a few jokes and introduced the topic for the evening and their guest speaker, the Vice President of the United States.

Before the Vice president reached the podium, Ryan was back to Tara. "Let's get out of here, before our man gets done over there. We've only got a few minutes to get away clean. I've got all I need."

Tara whispered something to Wil, and left the table. Wil followed seconds later, as the Vice President stepped to the podium. Once outside, they took a series of cabs on a wild path to their hotel, in hopes of warding off any tail. They said nothing in the cabs, or to the drivers. Washington cabbies were always suspect, according to Wil.

They didn't speak again until they were in Tara's room, at which time she filled Wil in on her silent conversation with Ryan in the cab. She also explained that the killer who took Ryan's life in Arizona had somehow come back from the dead, possessed Marv Graf and was now bent on hunting her down.

Everyone was silent for a moment. Finally Tara expressed her frustration. "This is crazy! I feel like we're in some kind of nightmare and can't get out."

"Yeah, me too," Wil sighed, "and worse yet, I feel like the nightmare is about to blow up with us in it!"

The killer walked aimlessly through the night with no particular destination in mind. He was thinking now. His conversation with Kilpack had proved intriguing, even if it did kind of throw a wrench into his plans. He had intended to kill Tara Johnson and Wil Dowding that night, and put an end to this business once and for all. But Tara wouldn't go outside with him, so he had been forced to stay at the dinner. That's when things began to turn and twist a bit.

In his mind, he replayed his conversation with Kilpack as the man sat next to him at the table.

"Man," said Kilpack, "you look terrible! What have you been doing with yourself?"

The killer almost reached out and strangled him right there. But he decided to heed the ravings of the twerp whose body he had taken and listen instead. By the time Kilpack had finished talking, a very interesting thing had happened. The lava boiling in his soul had subsided. He was a new man, with a new body. Of course, it wasn't brand new, but it was new to him. He could care less about the host trapped in its recesses. All he cared about was the fact that now he could move around and carry out his own designs.

A new man! Yes, things were going to be different now. The new man had some new plans! Tara and Wil would have to wait a spell. A bigger fish was going down. The biggest fish of all, in fact! And he was going to set the hook himself. Yesiree . . . he was going fishing! The only good fish was a dead fish, he thought, and he was the master of death. Why, he was even dead himself!

The thought made him smile. He soon found himself thinking such delightfully obsessive thoughts of killing that he lost all control of himself. A maniacal laughter sent him to his knees. The streets were crawling with people, but all he could do was hold his sides and laugh, ignoring those who looked at him with disgust. They would just think he was another well-dressed drunk in Washington. The thought made him laugh even more as he lay on his side in the middle of the sidewalk chuckling and giggling like a child.

He wasn't sure how long he remained in his manic state, but most of the people were gone when he finally stood up. His watch had stopped during the dinner, but judging by the lack of people on the streets, he estimated the time to be around midnight. Oops! Time to be moving on! he thought.

For years now, he had been doing minor hits for others. Others who cared only to use him to crush some small obstacle in their way. He didn't mind so much, he was paid well and he always enjoyed his work. But now it was different. Something this big only came along once in a lifetime. No, once in several lifetimes!

Yesiree, Tara would have to wait, not long mind you, just a little while. Maybe the two lamebrains working for Graf would actually find them and finish them off, sparing him the trouble. Who knows? When he was finished with the big fish, he'd worry about the pesky little fish. If she was still alive when he was done fishing, he'd finish her too, and make her pay! Yesiree, pay big time. Way more than fifty dollars a day. Way more!

He felt like a kid in a candy store. It worked him into a frenzy just thinking about it. Walking and giggling, sweating and mumbling, he ambled toward Graf's place. Thoughts like these could sustain him for miles, if need be. He was in heaven, and a little bit of heaven was just what he needed. Yesiree, just what he needed!

Chapter 14
THE MERCHANT

After the dinner, Robert Kilpack had his driver take him to the Riley Hotel. As the dark green Suburban pulled up to the curb, Kilpack took a last, long drag on his cigarette.

"I may be a while," he told the driver. "It's late. I'll catch a cab."

"Yes sir. Goodnight sir," said the young naval officer.

Kilpack stepped out onto the sidewalk and closed the car door behind him. Entering the hotel, he made his way to the elevators where two security officers stood.

"Evening Mr. Secretary," said one of them. "He's on the fourth floor."

"Thank you," he spoke tersely.

Stepping into the open elevator, he pressed four. He was worried tonight. Something ominous was just around the corner, he could feel it, and he wasn't sure he was ready for it. The elevator rumbled to a stop and the doors opened. The hallway was crawling with Secret Service. A young woman Kilpack knew as the Vice President's personal secretary greeted him.

"Good Evening, Alice! Working a bit late aren't we?"

"A woman's work is never done, sir. He's expecting you." She smiled and escorted him to room 430. Knocking twice, she opened the door and let him in.

"Thank you Alice," said the room's lone occupant. "Why don't you knock off for the night. I think we can take it from here."

"Thank you sir. Here are those files you've been waiting for." She handed him two folders and a note. "The note is from your wife. I'll see you in the morning."

"Very well." The Vice President rose from the couch and held out a hand for Kilpack.

"Good evening Bob," he said, "come on in." When the door closed, he motioned Kilpack to take a seat near him.

"Great dinner tonight," Kilpack observed mindlessly.

"Bob," he started in without preamble, "I've worked hard to get where I am, and I don't expect to have my plans go awry."

"Everything's a go Richard. The President will be dead before the weekend. I . . ."

"He better be! Before tonight, there were only two people who knew about this; you and I. Now you have Graf involved? What were you thinking, man? Marv Graf?"

"Look, I know this sounds odd, but he's given us everything we've asked for up till now. He's a strange guy, to say the least, but he *is* gifted. Whatever he wants, he usually gets. If he can't deliver, I'll take care of the boss myself. But at the dinner tonight . . . I've never seen him so focused. I tell you, he's the perfect killing machine."

"All right then, we give him till the weekend, but after that . . . Well, you know me, Bob, I have no conscience about these things. He takes care of the boss, then you take care of him. Understood?"

"Absolutely."

"You've been richly rewarded for placing those devices for us. You get the President for me, and take out that private eye who's on to our little venture, and I smell a Vice Presidency in this for you."

"I was assured that Dowding had been taken care of already!"

"Well, somebody goofed, Bob. My source is always right. Dowding is close to cracking this, and The Merchant is not happy about it."

"Look Richard, you've been telling me about The Merchant for months now, I have no idea how he can know more than we do about this."

"Trust me, he can." He sat back and eyed Kilpack before continuing. "Ever heard of the Devil, Bob?"

"The Devil? As in Satan?" Kilpack's voice registered his surprise at this turn in the conversation.

"You know, Bob, when I was a young man, I used to go to church all the time. I was very active, in fact. Can you imagine that? Does it surprise you?" He didn't wait for an answer. "But I've always liked to lie and cheat. I've always been really good at it, too. Know what I mean?"

He flashed Kilpack a wicked smile and a mischievous wink. Kilpack smiled back knowingly.

"Anyway, I found that the more I cheated and lied, the further I got in this world. Oh, you have to do it cleverly, of course, but I decided it was the way of life I preferred. I thought, maybe I'll go to Hell, but who knows, that could happen anyway. The here and now is all I know for sure. That's what's certain, and certainty is so much more valuable than an unknown future. But you know what? I still go to church on occasion with the little woman. Do you find that odd? It's a good place to study hypocrisy, you know."

"Yes, I know," he smiled, "and you're the master, Richard! But this 'Merchant' guy. What does all this have to do with him?"

"I'm getting there. This is very important, Bob. You need to listen carefully." He paused to look at him again. The look made Kilpack nervous. "I learned something very important while serving my country in Vietnam. I learned how to meditate and go out of body. That's where I met him. Yes, Bob, I know what you're thinking, but I'm serious . . . out of body!

"At first I was scared, of course. I never really thought that spirits existed. You know, just more of that hogwash they feed you in church to keep the donations pouring in. But . . . Now don't roll your eyes, Bob! This is no lie. I learned that devils are real. Yes. They exist right here, with us, but in . . . another dimension or something. Hey, I don't understand it, they're just here.

"Well, The Merchant is one of the top devils, Bob. He's the one leading their effort to collect this matter they want so badly, the matter Graf's devices are destabilizing, or whatever you call it, thanks to you."

"Hey, all in a days work," replied an increasingly agitated Kilpack.

"This guy, The Merchant, believe me, he's no picnic. I swear, every time I talk to him I think I'm going to die. But one of these days, when they get enough of that matter, they'll have their own bodies, or so they tell me. I figure it's just another cause like the ones we chase every day in politics. But at least this one pays well. Anyway, he knows everything that's going on, all over the planet, practically the minute it happens!"

"Is that where you get all your dirt on everyone? From the Devil?"

"Bingo, Bob. Satan and his bunch have been around since Adam and Eve! They know every piece of dirt on every human being in every country in the world, and I alone am privy to that. Can you imagine a president with so much power?"

"Yes, I can . . . as long as I can get a piece of that action. But why don't you just pull out some of that dirt on the President?"

"Unfortunately, the man has no dirt; at least not enough to oust him. That's why you and I had to initiate Plan B."

"Why didn't you just get The Merchant to kill him?"

"Bob, you have so much to learn. They can't. They can influence people, but they can't kill anyone . . . well, except maybe to scare them to death!" He laughed. "We have to do most of the killing for them! They're handicapped, you see, at least when it comes to the physical world. That's why they want physical bodies!"

"Hmm. Well, believe me, if anyone could be influenced by demons, it's Marv Graf. He's as nutty as they come!"

The Vice President smiled at Kilpack. "You don't have to be nutty, my friend. You're as much influenced by them as he is. And me! They influence everyone, every minute of the day, and we all like it! You know that. We've become so accustomed to it that we do their bidding without even knowing it anymore."

Suddenly the room went cold. Kilpack stood and looked around him. He was scared. He felt an overpowering urge to run. He looked at the Vice President, who just sat by calmly with a knowing smile on his face. Kilpack was confused and frightened. He felt goosebumps cover his entire body. Turning, he looked toward the closed bedroom door as a shadowy figure moved *through* it and stood there alone, glaring at him. Kilpack jumped to the other side of the Vice President and sat down behind him, but the figure continued to glare at him, emanating pure evil.

Turning to Kilpack, the Vice President grabbed him and pulled him around, forcing him to face the dark figure.

"Bobby boy, I want you to meet The Merchant!"

In the darkness of their hotel room, Wil and Tara slept as the knob of their hall door began a slow, almost imperceptible turn. The only sound emitted was the tiniest of clicks as a key was inserted ever so carefully into the lock from the outside. However slight the disturbance, of course, it was more than enough to alert Ryan. Ever watchful, always guarding his love, he moved quickly to Tara.

"Tara! Wake up! Someone's at the door," he spoke loudly, knowing only Tara could hear. "Tara!" he shouted.

Slowly, Tara stirred. "What is it?"

"Shhh! Wake Wil! There's someone trying to get in!"

Instantly alert, Tara sat up and stepped to Wil's bed. She didn't have to say anything. He must have heard the stirring. He was already awake.

"What is it, Tara?"

"Shhh, someone is trying to get in."

Immediately, Wil brushed her to the ground and grabbed for his gun. He leapt silently to the door just as it began to open. A single gunman stepped into the darkness of their room, shutting the door behind him. When the door was closed, ensuring the man was alone, Wil ordered him to drop his gun.

Instead, the man whirled and fired a shot. He wasn't as quick as Wil, however, and his recalcitrance cost him a silenced .38 caliber slug to the chest, while his shot punched harmlessly into the couch.

Wil stepped quickly out into the hall, gun poised. Through the opened hotel room door, Tara could hear the door to the stairwell closing. Someone else must have been there as well! Wil jumped back into the room. The man on the floor remained deadly still. Wil looked at Tara, who was watching from behind the bed.

"We have to get out of here. Grab your things, we have very little time."

"What about Brandon and Norma?" Tara implored.

"Trust me, they're safe. We'll pick them up at noon."

Before he finished his sentence he was in his clothes and throwing on his shoes. Tara responded by doing the same, not even bothering to go into the bathroom to change.

Tara's heart was racing, but her mind was clear. In fact, it felt clearer now than at any other time in her life. A man with a hole in his chest lay dead on the floor in front of her, but she didn't even see him. In her mind she held only a picture of her son. She had to be safe for him. She had to be there for him. To do that, she had to get out of the room before another attack occurred, and she trusted that Wil would know what to do.

In what seemed like an instant, she was dressed and packed. Wil had the evidence packet, as well as their new identities safe in a bag, and they carefully stepped out into the hall. Tara glanced back into the room. Only now did she look at the man on the floor. One glance and she turned away, quietly shutting the door. The maids will have an interesting round this morning, she thought.

Wil moved like a cat in the night. Tara tried to move as silently, but it was still hard for her, even with Ryan's encouragement. Wil reached out and felt the elevator doors with his open palm.

"It's still," he whispered, pushing the down button. "Step toward the wall."

Tara silently obeyed. *"Ryan, is everything okay?"* she thought.

"Yes dear, everything will be okay. Just follow Wil."

Tara imitated Wil as he stepped against the wall on the other side of the doors. The only sound now was the gentle hum of the elevator as it raced on its way to meet them. On reaching their floor, its unwanted "Bing!" shattered the silence. It was uncomfortably loud, and Tara looked around quickly to see if anyone had stirred.

Wil's attention was on the doors. As they started to slide open he lunged forward with his gun ready. Nobody was inside. Quickly Wil pulled Tara in and pushed the button that would stop them on the second floor. When the doors opened again, he peered out, looked both ways, pressed the sixth floor button, and stepped out, escorting Tara to room 246. Once inside the hotel room, he left the lights out so as not to be detected by anyone. Not until then did he breathe a sigh of relief.

"Wil? I thought we were leaving the hotel?"

"We are, but not just yet."

Ryan turned toward Tara and spoke softly. "Wil knows what he's doing. Watch."

"Are you okay?" Wil asked tenderly. His look of concern prompted Tara to hug him. "It'll be okay, I promise," he said, patting her on the back then giving her a quick squeeze for good measure.

"My heart is racing, Wil. It just won't stop!"

"That's understandable considering what you just witnessed."

"I don't think its nerves. It's . . . well, the adrenaline I guess, but my mind is clear; I'm not really scared. You and Ryan have a lot to do with that, though."

Wil plopped down on the couch exhaling a deep breath and dropped the bags to the floor. "In times like this," he explained, "denial kicks in so the brain can operate on preconceived plans. Actually, it's a great feature. But that's why planning is so important. The brain will block out what it can't comprehend, in order to maintain a rational flow of thought. At such times, if you haven't done any advance planning, the brain goes into what I call ad-lib mode. That's when things get really scary!"

"I can see that. This room, keeping the lights out, its all part of a preconceived plan?"

Wil nodded. Tara sat on the edge of the bed, deep in thought. "Wil," she asked at last, "how do we pick up Norma and Brandon?"

"They'll be brought to another hotel in the morning. For now . . ." he bent over and opened his bag, taking out the disguise kit. "You and I have about five minutes to change before I set off the fire alarm."

Tara smiled as Ryan watched them change identities. "You're wonderful under pressure, Tara," he observed. "I love you."

His look was one she had seen many times before. *"I love you too, my dear departed husband. What do you think of all this?"*

"I trust Wil."

She watched as Wil stepped out into the hall. *"Yeah, me too!"*

The fire alarm let out a blaring siren, as Wil ducked back. He and Tara were dressed in robes concealing their regular clothing. A minute later, they stepped out into the hall with all the other patrons, and shuffled anonymously down to the lobby and out onto the street. As the crowd grew, and the fire engines arrived, they unobtrusively doffed their robes and hailed a cab to their new lodgings, at the Riley Hotel.

<hr />

It was very late when Robert Kilpack stepped out into the hall closing the door to the Vice President's room softly behind him. He walked over to the elevators and forced a smile to the Secret Service agents. One of them held the door open for him.

"Goodnight sir."

"Goodnight," Kilpack returned.

When the doors closed, he wiped the sweat from his forehead with a handkerchief and gently tucked it back into his lapel pocket. He looked at his hands. They were shaking uncontrollably. He clenched them a few times trying to rid his soul of the night's experiences.

"Ding!" The gentle tone of the elevator indicated that he was at his destination, and the doors opened to the main lobby. He hesitated a moment, then stepped out and headed for the lounge. There he ordered a stiff drink. Sitting in the corner at a secluded table he thought of the horrible mess he was in.

After a few drinks and feeling the relative safety of the darkness in his little corner, he reached into his inside jacket pocket and turned off the recorder. Then he sat back and assessed what had just transpired.

Why didn't The Merchant know about the tape recorder? he wondered. For a moment in that terrifying presence, he thought he would be fried for sure. They must not be able to read minds, he decided. He had come face to face with the Devil, or at least one of his top henchmen, and lived to tell about it! It was an experience he would never forget as long as he lived.

The man had no horns, no cloven hooves, no pointy tail! He looked just like a man for crying out loud! But he was by far the scariest thing Kilpack had ever seen. He looked down at his hands. They were still shaking. He wondered how he had ever survived.

What a mess! How in the world was he going to resolve this problem? His mind raced, striving to find an answer. He looked at the glass of alcohol in front of him and stuffed the napkin into its half-empty remains.

"A drink isn't going to help me now!" he grumbled out loud.

Suddenly, through the front door he saw a couple he thought he knew. From his little table, he could see them walk past the front of the lounge and head for the check-in stand. As quietly as he could, he rose and walked toward the saloon's entrance to get a better look.

Something began to stir in his heart. It was renewed hope. He thought of the pictures the Vice President had shown him from the files upstairs, and superimposed the couple at the front counter on them. Sure enough, it was Wil Dowding and Tara Johnson!

He breathed a sigh of relief, then went back to his little table in the dark. Maybe now things will work themselves out, he thought. He looked at his hands again. Even in the darkness, he knew they had stopped shaking.

"Tara, why don't you take the room over there, and I'll take the couch. That way, you and Ryan can visit in private."

"Well that would be just great, Wil, but Ryan says no go. You take the room, and I'll take the couch. That way, our watchdog will be here to see who may come in the door."

He smiled and winked. "Gotcha. Makes sense to me. See you in the morning then. Sleep tight guys."

"Goodnight Wil. Oh, and Wil?" He stopped and turned to her. She stepped to him and hugged him tightly. "Thanks for everything. I can see why you're not only the best private eye in the world, but the best friend as well!"

"Thanks, Tara." He hugged her back, a touch of moisture wetting his eyes. "Get some shuteye now, its going to be a long day. It'll be about six or seven hours before we see Norma and Brandon." He released her and turned toward the room. "Nightie night!" he called out as he closed the door behind him.

Inside, a very tired Wil dropped to the bed. He had been working for months now without adequate rest. He had been on the run, shot at several times, and generally called upon to use every piece of expertise he had ever learned just to keep himself and Tara alive. He was dog tired and ready for some real sleep.

As he lay down, he started to ramble through his mind to make sure everything was in order. His last thought was of the evidence packet. Something was missing he knew. Even with what they knew now, it just wasn't enough. Worse yet, even if it brought the people behind the plot into custody, would the evil spirits leave or stop what they were doing? Would he ever really find out who they were? The thought of Satan and his minions frightened him. Quickly he offered a little prayer that somehow it would all work out.

Suddenly, he felt distant and alone. He thought of the mess Tara was in, and realized for the first time how much of it was his fault. Her life was in danger and it really was his doing! He was worthless as a friend, and if he couldn't help his friends, what good was he as a professional? He wondered if his life would ever make any sense.

The thought of all the money he was spending to work this case also hit him. His business would be ruined, despite the help Lonnie Johnson was providing. He wouldn't be able to survive. Suddenly he felt embarrassed that he was thinking about money when his friends lives were in danger. He really was a complete failure.

He got up from the bed and sat on the chair in the corner of the room as a sense of bleak agony filled his soul. His thoughts turned darker and more hopeless.

Maybe he should just end it all now. There had been nothing in his life for years. He would never be missed. Who really cared about him? No one! In fact, with the insurance he carried, everyone would be better off if he died! He was definitely worth more dead than alive. And if he were gone, they might even leave Tara alone. Suicide wasn't always a bad thing. Maybe it was the key to a happy ending this time.

He reached over and found the handle of his handgun in the dark. Gripping it, he brought the revolver close to his heart. Everything within him shouted that this was the way out. His life was nothing! He was a loser. His demise would be a benefit to everyone. After his experiences with Tara and Ryan, he knew there was definitely a spirit world. Maybe God would have a happy ending for him there. He certainly didn't have any happy endings for him here!

He brought the revolver up to the side of his head. Pulling the trigger was the only sensible thing to do. In fact, he would be a complete fool not to pull it . . . now!

Suddenly the door flew open and the lights turned on.

"Fight it, Wil!" Tara cried. "It's him. It's The Merchant and he wants you. Ryan felt his presence here, but it took so long for him to wake me."

"Tara," pleaded Wil, "It's the best thing I can do right now."

"No, Wil, it's not! You're our only hope here! You can't give in to him, not now, not ever!"

"Wil, Brandon and I need you! Ryan says you have the strength to resist. We need you. Norma needs you!" Tara was kneeling now on the floor in front of him.

Norma, yes, he'd forgotten about Norma. Wil closed his eyes and thought of her. She was the first breath of hope he had experienced in his personal life since his twenties. He knew how she would feel if he were harmed. He thought of Ryan, and his willingness to give his life for Tara. Shouldn't he be willing to save his life for Norma?

Suddenly he felt detached from the depression that had engulfed him. He could sense the unseen force outside him trying to snuff him out. He threw his gun onto the bed.

"What am I doing? Tara, what's happening here?"

"Wil, it's The Merchant. He's very real and he's in here now. He wants to stop us and he's trying his best to do it by stopping you."

"I can't believe I would even consider shooting myself. That's not me."

"I know, Wil. It's him." She wrapped her arms around her shoulders and shivered. "Ooo. Why is it so cold in here?"

"I think it's The Merchant, Tara." Wil took her hand. "I felt it earlier."

"I can feel him in this room . . . right next to me!" she cried. "What do we do? I've never been so frightened in my life."

Ryan felt the presence before its actual arrival. He had become used to seeing spirits coming and going, and never really paid any attention to whether they were good or bad before now. He knew there were evil spirits, but never thought he would have to deal with one. Now one was here, and it was after Wil!

"Tara! Wake up, Tara!" he yelled. Tara barely stirred. He yelled louder, "Tara! Wake up, please! Wil needs you!"

Eventually Tara opened her eyes and sat up groggily on the bed.

"Tara, don't be alarmed, I don't know how to say this but there is someone in the next room trying to get at Wil. He's a spirit, the one I told you about called The Merchant. We have to go help Wil. He's in serious danger."

As soon as he pronounced the spirit's name, Tara was on her feet. Ryan shouted to her, "You realize who he is and what he's doing with Wil. He wants you and Wil to stop interfering with his plans. He knew I was protecting you, so he's going after Wil with every fiber of his miserable being."

As Tara bolted to the door, her thoughts were instantaneously present in Ryan's mind. *"This means we're close, Ryan. To think, the head of this project, The Merchant himself, would try an act of desperation like this."*

At last they were inside. Ryan could sense the demon's fury and frustration, and as they entered the room, he could see him standing next to Wil, whispering into his ear. The being paid no attention to Tara at first, but when he saw Ryan, he paused, but then continued his attack on Wil.

Ryan felt sick in his heart. The demon was assaulting his friend. He wanted to attack it, beat the devilish thing senseless, but inside he knew that wasn't the answer. Instead, he closed his eyes and prayed for strength and deliverance. At that moment, Wil threw his gun onto the bed.

The Merchant moved to Tara's side. She shivered, then dropped to her knees and started praying out loud.

Wil stood up and shouted defiantly. "Get out! Get out now! I'm not listening to you any more. Leave us alone!"

The Merchant wavered for a moment then continued his assault. But it was useless now. Wil was standing his ground in defiance as Tara continued her prayer. The demon was growing frustrated.

Now Ryan could see a force growing around Wil and Tara. Its effect was to shield them from The Merchant's spiritual attack. Soon it was apparent that they could no longer feel his presence at all. He stepped back burning with anger.

Ryan felt cold as The Merchant's anger grew. The darkness immediately around the person of this malevolent being started to deepen until the entire room was filled with the clouds of his hatred. But the blackness was ineffective against the light that surrounded Wil and Tara. Still, it spread from the evil spirit's presence until it was nearly palpable to Ryan. The Merchant rose in the air and turned menacingly toward him, his eyes burning cold with evil.

The visage was more frightful than anything Ryan had ever imagined. Yet oddly, he felt no fear. As the darkness grew, he noticed something he had not observed before. From his own spirit body, light glowed. He realized now that the glow had always been there. It had just been too subtle to recognize. Now, in the presence of this being's stark rage, it increased until it pushed the darkness back, filling the room with light. It was a spiritual light, and particularly bright immediately around his person, but Ryan could tell that neither Wil nor Tara perceived it.

As the light grew, Ryan became aware of a power he had not previously sensed in himself. He could tell that this power actually came from outside, but it was very real. With it came information too, the knowledge that he, long ago, as a young man, had been invested with authority to act for God, and that he should do so in this specific situation. The feeling pierced him to the core. At that moment, he knew that he was the all-powerful agent of an unseen but almighty Principal.

The feeling of power associated with that agency increased in his heart until the room, except for immediately around The Merchant, was filled with a light so blinding Ryan thought it must certainly have been visible even to the human eyes in the room.

Fear now gripped The Merchant's face. He cowered in the corner of the room, shielding his eyes from the light and backing away from Wil in an effort to get away from Ryan. This evil thing, which moments before looked so terrifying and fearless, was now a pitiful, cowering man, a man without a body, a frail fiber who had just botched the most important mission of his miserable career.

When he could back no further, the being spoke to Ryan. "Please, have mercy. It is not the time, yet. Let me go!"

Ryan looked across at the cringing demon and spoke the word he felt impressed to say.

"Depart!"

Trembling, the creature turned and raced from Ryan's presence, through the wall and out into the night. He ran like a coward, with a fear in his eyes Ryan would never know but could never forget. There was no question in his mind, The Merchant would never return.

As quickly as he was gone, the chill in the room disappeared. In its place was a bath of warmth that permeated Ryan's soul. This he knew even Wil and Tara could feel.

The Merchant's power dismissed, and his influence no longer discernable, Tara stood and embraced Wil. After several moments, the detective spoke.

"Thanks guys, I'm not sure what just happened, and it may take me a while to fully appreciate it, but thanks. I can't believe I got so depressed in so short a time!"

"Ryan, I felt something incredible in here. What did happen?" Tara asked.

"The enemy is vanquished, Tara. The Merchant is gone!"

"Why did he leave so quickly?" asked Wil.

Tara looked at him, then at Ryan, in stunned silence. She had not repeated Ryan's words.

"He is a coward, Wil. He left because your spirit was full of faith and so was Tara's. He left because God loves you, and The Merchant can't deal with love. He and his kind have none of that commodity to offer. It was accomplished through the power of God, and it chased him away like a roach running from the light."

"Tara," Wil stammered as tears welled up in his eyes. "I just heard Ryan! I heard him with my own ears! Ryan, are you still there?"

"I'm here Wil, right in front of you."

"Ryan?"

"He's in front of you Wil," Tara spoke through her tears.

"Ryan, speak to me" he said.

"Thanks for all you've done, good friend."

"I can't hear him now," Wil said, then added after a pause, "but I can feel him. He just thanked me."

"Yes he did," said Tara.

"Thank you, Ryan," Wil whispered gratefully.

For a moment, none of them moved. They just stood and basked in the spirit of peace and love that continued to warm the room, a stark contrast to the cold, dark thoughts that preceded it.

"Tara, Ryan," Wil said at last. "This incident proves one thing. We're very close to solving this little puzzle." He paused for a moment then added, "One piece, that's all we need. Just one more piece."

Norma and Brandon were brought to Washington by two men from Wil's office. At noon, they were secreted up to Wil and Tara's room at the Riley Hotel. Tara and Wil had been up most of the night talking with Ryan about the spiritual realm, the incident with The Merchant and what it meant. Finally, exhaustion had forced them to bed where they slept till late in the morning.

The first thing Wil did when Norma stepped into the room, even before speaking to his men, was to take her in his arms. What she saw in his eyes must have been everything she hoped for, because she was immediately and completely lost in his love.

Tara cradled Brandon to her, kissing him repeatedly as she stood next to Ryan. A light in the baby's eyes when he turned in the direction where Ryan stood took her by surprise. Could he see Ryan too? she wondered. Then, seeing Wil and Norma, she smiled wistfully. The men who came with them just smiled and quietly took a seat on the couch.

It was a long time before anyone spoke. When they did, it was to discuss their immediate plans. While Tara spent time with Brandon, Norma helped Wil and his men put together copies of the evidence packet. Photos, quotes, purchase orders, invoices, naval reports, computer disks, videos, descriptions, everything had to be duplicated, assembled and addressed. The equipment to accomplish that feat had come with Wil's men. It was quickly retrieved from their car and set up in their suite.

Just before 2:00 PM, there was a knock at the door. Wil stepped cautiously toward the entrance and peered for an instant through the peephole, then jerked away and to the side. The action looked like a trained reflex, but what he saw showed on his face as shock.

"Tara, step back please. Tanner, Evan," he urged his men, "be ready." His assistants drew their weapons and stood on either side of the door. Carefully, and with his gun hidden behind his back, Wil opened it.

"Wil Dowding?" asked a man dressed in a smart conservative suit.

"Well, Mr. Robert Kilpack. How can I help you?"

"I have something you need." Kilpack reached into the pocket of his suit and withdrew an audiocassette tape. "I think you'll find this interesting. May I come in?"

"Are you alone?" quizzed Wil.

"Yes I am."

Wil nodded to his counterparts, and, as the Secretary of the Navy came in, they went out into the hall to stand guard, closing the door behind them.

"Well I must say Mr. Kilpack, this is a bit of a surprise."

"Yes, for me too Mr. Dowding. But I can tell you that, after what I've seen and heard in the last twenty-four hours, nothing will ever surprise me again."

Tara listened from the bed, with Ryan and Norma at her side. Brandon had fallen asleep.

"Okay, I'll bite, what's on the tape?"

"A conversation I had last night in this very hotel with the Vice President of the United States. It details his . . . and my involvement in a plot to murder the President."

Wil's eyes widened. "Okay, and why are you doing this? Please, I'm at a loss here."

"Look Dowding, a couple of years ago, I made a big mistake. I got involved in something way over my head. I'm not a religious man, but after what I saw last night, I may look into it. All I know right now is I don't want to spend eternity rotting in Hell, not with the likes of whatever it was I met last night! I think when you hear this tape, you'll know what I mean. It, and the other evidence I believe you've collected, should help you put a stop to this, before a very evil man becomes President of the United States. I may have already gone too far to save myself, but it will be worth something if I can stop it now."

"Mr. Kilpack, you're telling me that this tape implicates the Vice President of the United States in a plot to kill the President?"

"Yes; him, myself, and a man named Marv Graf. I believe he is . . . or, was Ryan McKay's boss."

Wil nodded in the affirmative.

"I also understand that you know why all this is taking place, about the matter collection devices, and the individuals who are behind the little problem of our collapsing ecology. At least that's what The Merchant told me."

"You've met The Merchant?"

Kilpack took out his handkerchief and wiped his forehead. "Yes sir, I have. And I can tell you sincerely that I never want to meet him again."

"On that, sir, I can heartily agree with you."

"Then you've met him too?"

"In a manner of speaking."

"Well, then you'll understand when I say that . . . I guess I've been scared straight, so to speak."

"Yes. And if this is what you say it is, and I have no reason to disbelieve you now, we need to go to the authorities immediately."

"Nope, sorry. I know too much about the system. You literally can trust no one out there right now. I would never see the light of another day if I went public about this. When I leave here, I'll be gone for good. No one will know where I went, and no one will see me again. I would advise you to do the same. Whatever you do, do not go to the authorities yourself."

"Surely the fake warrants that have been issued against Tara and I would evaporate in the light of the evidence on that tape."

"I'm afraid not, Dowding. Last night, the Vice President showed me a file on you and Tara. You two have been implicated in a string of robberies and murders from here to California. Yesterday afternoon, 'shoot-to-kill' warrants were issued on both of you. I'm sorry to say those warrants included Norma Welker, who is described in them as an accomplice."

Norma gasped. "No, Wil, they can't do that to you, to us."

"If you're taken peacefully, the plan is to have you killed while in custody, to keep you from telling whatever you know. Those files have been disseminated to every law enforcement agency in the country from local to federal. As far as they know, you two are armed and dangerous killers. And there are a whole lot of people in this too deep to back out now."

Wil closed his eyes for a moment and drew in a deep breath.

"Dowding, as I see it, you add that tape to the rest of your evidence, turn it in to the media, then run for the hills and go deep undercover for a few years till someone can clear you. I don't see it happening soon, but trust me, if you come in with this now, you'll be dead by this evening."

"Actually, disappearing was our original plan, though I didn't have any idea it would be for so long. What about Tara's parents?"

"Nothing on them or your employees, Dowding. Not for now, anyway. And the powers-that-be won't be able to make anything stick after all this gets to the media, so I wouldn't worry about that. But the files on you three are a done deal. Sorry."

"Okay. Just one thing, though. I'd like to know how you got hooked up with Graf?"

"He was a money hungry, greedy little science nerd that Richard, the Vice President, heard about. He and his buddy, The Merchant, were looking for someone just like him for this matter collection project. They hooked him, made him believe he was all-powerful and almost immortal, then sapped his creative genius. The VP asked me to help Graf implement the plan, and I did. They paid him very well. I skimmed from the top. Pretty simple."

"Where'd the money come from?"

"Not from any traceable government source, as I'm sure you've been able to confirm. It was drug money seized by the DEA . . . millions." Kilpack wiped his forehead again. "Anyway, you get the idea. I planned to tape our meeting last night because I was afraid my days might be numbered after the President was gone. I wanted a leg up. But . . ."

"How will the media know you're telling the truth, Mr. Secretary?" Wil challenged.

"The facts will bear me out. Listen to the tape and decide for yourself. For me, I'm going to disappear, and hope that there'll be enough time in life for me to be forgiven. I know that sounds funny . . . well, to anyone who knows me, that is. But after last night, I'm a different man, Dowding. I have a very different perspective now." Kilpack stood. "Don't try to stop me," he added as Wil rose with him.

"Wouldn't think of it, Mr. Secretary."

"Thanks for all you've done. You brought this to a head. I'm not sure I ever would have learned what I did last night if it weren't for you. I want you to know I appreciate it, as I'm sure these women do." He gestured toward the bed. Reaching for Wil's hand, he shook it, then left the room unmolested.

After he was gone, Wil, Tara, Norma and Ryan all gathered around Wil. They were all in a state of shock. The reality of their situation was harder for Tara to accept than she had expected. All Wil could do was express his regrets.

Finally she spoke. "Wil, all I have to say is . . . thank heaven you plan ahead!" The reaction seemed to lighten the mood.

Together they listened to the tape. It was everything Kilpack had said, everything but the part about The Merchant. There, the conversation sounded as though it were between three people, the Vice President, a frightened Kilpack, and a third person, but the third person could not be heard. If The Merchant had been there, no one would know. He wasn't recorded on the tape.

On the reverse side, Kilpack had recorded a fifteen-minute confession telling about the entire project and his involvement with Graf and the Vice President. It was complete with the locations of all the remaining SADDs, and details on how to deactivate and destroy them.

With little time to spare before they had to go into deep hiding, they all went to work copying and assembling the evidence packages. The evening was spent dropping them off at various TV stations, newspapers, and magazines. It took longer than anticipated because of the need to avoid the police, but by 11:00 PM, Eastern Time, the national media was abuzz.

Watching from the increasingly dangerous vantage of their hotel room, Tara felt some satisfaction over the results of their work. Channel 10 was reporting, "Vice President implicated in plot to murder President!" From Channel 6 the news was "Vice President behind world atrocities!" Norma and Tara both patted Wil approvingly on the back as they all exited in full disguise with the television still blaring behind them.

No one recognized Tara, Brandon, Norma or Wil as they waited casually at Ronald Reagan Airport for a flight to Canada. Even Brandon, dressed conspicuously as a little girl, seemed to sense the need to be quiet. Ryan was next to Tara as always, but the other's kept a safe distance so they would not appear to be travelling together.

A television broadcast emanated from the TV visible in the waiting area near the gate. Tara watched as film crews beamed back to stations across America live video coverage of some of Graf's strategically placed devices at ocean locations near the Atlantic coast. They were calling them Sub-Atomic Scramblers. She liked SADDs better, but she wasn't there to tell them.

Later on the plane, in-flight news reports carried a story about a nut apprehended on the lawn of the White House over the weekend. He was carrying a gun and blubbering something about making the President pay fifty dollars every day. According to one report, an anonymous tip helped to thwart the assassination attempt, and the man was caught in the nick of time. No one could explain how he got past White House security. An investigation had been ordered.

Two days later, still in disguise, the group gathered for breakfast at a cafe in Montreal. There they watched, as a beleaguered Vice President was lead away in handcuffs from a secluded cabin in upstate New York to an awaiting FBI van. The news was met by applause from many of the restaurant's viewing patrons.

"It's amazing how fast the media jumped on this!" Tara said.

"You haven't seen anything yet," responded Wil. "Wait till all the finger pointing reaches its pinnacle. This will filter down and spread overseas. Mark my words."

"Wil! Look!" Norma was pointing to the television. A picture of a disheveled Marv Graf was being shown as a Canadian newsman gave his report.

" . . .and so during one of his moments of lucidity, Graf gave his computer password to American authorities which reportedly unlocked scores of files containing information and intelligence implicating top officials in governments throughout the world. Associated Press is reporting that Graf had millions in Swiss bank accounts, and untold resources in the form of schematics and blueprints for various as yet unknown and unidentifiable devices. It is unclear where this information came from, or how it was to be used."

"If they only knew!" breathed Wil. "And I might add that my words have been vindicated already!"

They all laughed.

"It's going to take years for the earth to recover from the rape of its natural resources," Tara observed. "Years!" She looked at Brandon sleeping in his carrier and smiled. "But thank heaven the time will come."

"Tara? What will become of the evil spirits that worked on this project?" Norma asked. "Are they still trying to collect matter?"

"Ryan says they've moved on to other projects, all part of their continuing plan to obtain material bodies and destroy the plan of God. But apparently, the matter disorientation thing has been abandoned."

"Do you mean they actually want physical bodies, like ours, that much? It's so sad."

Norma's kindness never ceased to amaze her. She would have a kind word the Devil on the Day of Judgment, Tara thought. "Norma," she said, "until we've left our bodies, I doubt any of us will appreciate the advantages of having one. The Merchant and others like him simply can't be trusted with the power that's possible for physical bodies to command. Ryan says they've been denied that privilege forever. In the meantime, thank heaven for those, like him, who watch over this world and the spirit world to ensure that their evil plans are thwarted."

"Well," said Norma, with a beaming smile. "I believe there's always help for God's children. He'll never fail them."

Tara smiled. "I believe that now myself, Norma. With all my heart."

"Ryan, Tara," Wil interjected, "when we get to where we're going, I want to know more about your church. I need to hear about a religion that teaches the beautiful things you guys believe in." He looked over at Norma. "I especially want to hear about that eternal marriage stuff. Okay?"

"Oh, that's a promise Wil," Tara answered enthusiastically. "One that I'm happy to make!"

Chapter 15
SWEET

Somewhere in the Canadian Rockies, in front of a two-story log cabin bordering a forest of pines, Brandon Ryan McKay played innocently in the fresh new grass of spring. On the porch, watching him attentively, were Mr. and Mrs. Wil Dowding fresh in from a morning jog.

"Spring is such a beautiful time of year," Norma sighed. "Too bad it can't last forever."

She unlaced her running shoes and kicked them into the jogging cart they used to pull Brandon along behind them. Wiggling her toes through her socks, she chuckled at the sight of a little toe peeking at her through a small hole on the left.

Wil smiled. They had been married for just over three years now, and for the first time in twenty he felt truly alive. His time with Norma was the highlight of his existence despite the fact that they had spent the last four years in hiding, and had been married under false names. The fear of an at-large killer and the wrath of every law enforcement agency in the United States had been swallowed up by his love for this wonderful woman.

"You know, Norma," he said, "I always thought I'd be ready to run back into life the instant I could. But this time with you . . . I never thought married life could be so fulfilling. I mean, in spite of all the hiding, these have really been the best years of my life!"

Norma looked into his eyes, as a cool breeze skirted the trees and wafted up onto the porch, caressing her tanned face and tossing her hair. She seemed out of place to him, here in the oft-frozen wilderness, like a lizard in an igloo, but she seemed to love it.

"Come here, wife," Wil demanded with a grin. Norma demurely obeyed and leaned into him. He looked into her eyes, marveling at their beauty and the light they radiated. She graced him with another of those irresistible smiles he found so alluring and he kissed her. For several minutes they held each other.

"Do you like being here, I mean really like it?" he asked at last.

"I've never been happier Wil. Talk about life in the fast lane! Until I met all of you, I was buried in it! This is great. The peace, the tranquility . . . you. I wouldn't trade it for anything."

"Well, I'm glad to hear that. When I first met Ryan, he and Tara had just come down from the mountains after their honeymoon. I can't explain it, but I had a feeling then that something dramatic was going to happen to change my life. In a way it frightened me. I knew I was setting out on a path that would tear me from my old life forever. But the strangest part was this: Without even knowing you, I knew you were out there somewhere . . . waiting for me. Then . . ." he let out a whistle, "when I saw you in Dallas that first night, I felt so ridiculous. Could you tell? I couldn't take my eyes off you."

Norma closed her eyes, then slowly opened them and looked up into his face. "To me it wasn't ridiculous. I was just so pleased that you were looking. When I looked at you that night I could see a man on a mission, and I had a feeling that somehow I was going to be involved in that mission. Strange, isn't it?"

"Yes, but . . . so right." He brushed her hair with his hand, and kissed the top of her head as she snuggled her face into his chest.

"But we're not going to hide any more. Right?" she whispered cautiously.

"Nope. No more," he breathed back. "Now that the law is finally off our backs, it's time to face our other fears. Let the killer come and get us if he can. Together, the five of us can take him. Right?" He looked steadfastly into her eyes.

"Absolutely!" she said, her tone reassuring them both. "After all, he's just a ghost. And we have a mighty fine ghost of our own, don't we?"

He smiled. "We sure do."

"Mommy and Daddy's coming home!" a small voice called out from the front lawn. Brandon was lying on his back, gazing up into the sky. He had a piece of grass between his teeth sticking out like the farmer in one of his favorite children's books.

Wil and Norma looked down the road through the woods. They could see the pavement for almost a quarter mile as it went down a valley and disappeared around a hill, but no one was in sight.

"I'm sure they are, buddy. I'll tell you when I see them," Wil called out, then he turned to Norma. "I'll be danged if I know how he does that."

"He's special, Wil."

"Yeah! It's amazing how he seems to know when someone's coming. If I could do that as a detective . . .ah, the possibilities!"

"People like him only come along once in a millennium."

"And the fact that he can see and hear Ryan! What I wouldn't give to be able to do that!" said Wil enviously.

"Well, I like you just the way you are!" Norma reached up and tweaked his nose in fun, then gave him another enthusiastic kiss.

Ever since Brandon started displaying his unusual abilities, Wil and Norma speculated that a molecular change might have taken place in his unborn body when the killer dragged Tara into The Hole back in Arizona. There was something about the way his mind worked. It was quicker and more efficient than other kids his age. Something had happened to him out there in the desert; they were sure of it.

"There they are now," said Wil, pointing down the meadow.

A bright blue pick-up had just turned into view through the trees and began the drive up the road through the open meadow to the cabin. No sound was heard at first as the hills and the woods absorbed the truck's engine noise, but soon the vehicle could be heard lumbering along the road toward the cabin. Finally pulling in, it proceeded up the driveway and stopped in front of a large log they used as a parking stop.

"Mommy, Mommy!" Brandon scrambled to the truck, calling excitedly. The door opened, and Tara jumped out, scooping him up in her arms and administering hugs, kisses and tickles.

"Daddy, Daddy!" he called next, squirming out of his mother's arms and scurrying around to the other side of the truck.

As he approached a spot near the door, the child seemed to run gleefully *through* his daddy. Then he doubled back and started making small circles around the spot where Wil thought Ryan was standing, invisible to all but the boy and his mother.

Wil's eyes started to tear. He knew it was the highlight of Ryan's day, and would have given anything to allow Ryan just one chance to hold his son! But, despite the lack of any physical contact, Brandon obviously loved his daddy very much, and had his own way of expressing his affection. It was a delightful scene to witness. Wil had never been around children much, but he had to admit it was an unusual pleasure to have this child living with them.

And the boy was certainly getting a special education, Wil thought. Ryan would tell him stories and teach him about life in a way that no other father could. Brandon would often roll on the floor of the cabin and act out whatever story his dad was telling. Sometimes Ryan read the stories and Brandon would flip the pages. Wil could sit and watch the little boy interact with his invisible father for hours.

"So how were the love birds while we were away?" Tara teased as she walked up the steps of the porch and plopped down on an over-stuffed chaise lounge.

"We've just been sitting here enjoying the morning. Did you bring me any treats?" pleaded Wil.

"As a matter of fact, I did!"

Tara held out a bag and Wil grabbed it. Reaching into it and pulling out the contents of the small package, he displayed his present to Norma. "Look, honey. Tara bought me some fuses!"

Later that evening, Tara sat with Wil and Norma on the porch. Brandon played at her feet with one of his toy action figures, while Ryan stared out into the expanse of wilderness lying before their little cabin. The sun had just set, and darkness was quickly moving in, pushing the last remnants of light from the sky. In a matter of minutes, the stars would begin to sneak out one by one, until they had all come forth, billions of them, sparkling and frolicking in the Canadian heavens.

"Ryan?"

"Yes?" he answered, turning to face her.

"You seem lost in thought. What's on your mind?"

"Me? Lost?"

"Yeah buster, what's going on in that brain of yours? You've been pretty preoccupied lately. Is something bothering you? Come on. Give it up!"

"Oh, *that* 'lost.' Well, since you asked, do you remember a couple years ago when we found out that the disoriented matter was coming back?"

"Of course! More rain, rising sea levels, thicker forests. It's been slow, but things seem to be getting back to normal." Tara turned to see that Wil and Norma were intimately involved in a conversation of their own, paying no attention to her and Brandon.

"Right, but it seems to be more then just that," Ryan continued. "We heard last week that fishing is making a totally unexpected comeback. There are some interesting implications to that story. According to my calculations . . ."

Distracted by her son, Tara looked over at Brandon. He had walked to the railing of the porch and was gazing out into the woods.

"What is it son?" asked Ryan.

Brandon turned toward his parents.

"Tell Mommy what you're looking at son," Tara asked with concern.

"He's coming."

"Who's coming?" Ryan asked.

"The bad man. Why is he coming here, Mommy?"

After his attempt on the President's life using Graf's body had failed, the killer was forced to leave that shell behind and find a new one. It wasn't difficult. He was amazed to see how many in that area left themselves open for possession in one way or another. Before he was through, he had bodysurfed his way through six more botched attempts.

Finally, when the President announced plans to retire in the face of an unprecedented seventh attempt on his life, the killer walked away satisfied. This was as good as a kill, he thought. Maybe better. He really made the President pay, big time! A lot more than fifty dollars every day.

Besides, he had other work to do. He had to get the wife of the man who killed him. That would be the best, so he had saved it for last. Now he just had to find her.

He would, too, that was for sure. He was the best finder in the world. Especially now that he was freed from the confines of a body. He could travel at the speed of thought! That allowed him to flit from coast to coast with no effort at all.

Trouble was, she had dropped out of public life. He couldn't find the slightest trail to lead him to his prey. Even her parents didn't seem to know where she was. They communicated with her over the Internet occasionally, but there was no way for him to trace that. Other spirits like that McKay fella had access to some kind of information about where everybody was, but he never got any help like that. So it wasn't easy, and he couldn't find Mamma anywhere to help him either.

Patience, he thought. That's all it takes, patience and a plan. And boy could he be patient if he wanted to. He knew it wouldn't be easy, but what he'd do with her once she was found, that's what kept him going.

For nearly four years he searched. He scoured the country, then went down into Mexico. He tried Hawaii, the Caribbean Islands, the Florida Keys, even South America, everywhere he thought a girl from Arizona would go. Then it dawned on him. Canada! Sure, why not? What a fool to think she'd stay in a warm climate!

Once he figured that out, the rest was easy. He simply criss-crossed the North until he stumbled on Wil Dowding in a small town in British Columbia. The private investigator wasn't very good, was he? He was just walking down a sidewalk in plain sight, his arms loaded with bags from the local grocery store.

The killer hung out there for weeks, watching carefully. He learned that Wil, Tara, and Norma would pop into town regularly for supplies, to visit the doctor, go to church or just visit here and there. But until he knew more, he didn't dare get too close. He didn't want that dead husband of her's to spot him . . . and the twerp never seemed to leave her side! He hated that. But he would just have to stay in town and wait, watching from a distance and hatching plans.

Then one day, as he hovered over the roof of the bank across the street from the store, he saw Tara and her dead husband drive up in her pick-up. She parked in the lot next to the town's largest shopping area, and a little boy got out with her. He couldn't have been more than four years old.

Now what have we here? he thought. The little missy went and got herself a little one? Ooo, this changes everything, everything indeed. Now she gets to pay big time. Oh yes, he thought, life is getting sweet!

With this news, he scrapped all his old plans and hatched a new one better than all the rest. He'd get to do what he loved most, bring pain and death to someone who really deserved it. Big time, boy! Big time! All he needed now was a body. But that was no problem. He'd just start with a little visit to the doctor.

Doctor Ellis was a family man in his fifties, kind and loving to all his patients. To possess him would be down right impossible, he decided. Next, he checked out the sheriff. Too bad, Sheriff Cope was as useless as Doctor Ellis. The whole thing made him sick. The sheriff could have given him the tools he needed for his plan. Oh well, maybe a deputy. But that didn't work ether. Even the sheriff's deputies were good men, all law-abiding and sober. In desperation, he decided to try the dentist.

Rick Silvey was a young man of thirty. He had no family. He had been the town's only dentist since Joe Kashwatim left to pursue the good life of retirement. That was just a year ago, but now he had all the town's business. Though Stone Creek was only a town of five hundred, the outlying area brought him enough work to keep his Corvette running and his slightly overweight body well dressed. Everybody seemed to like Rick, especially the kids, but Rick had a little secret.

Nitrous oxide, laughing gas as it was called back where the killer grew up, was Rick's Achilles' heel. Whenever occasion would permit and his assistant had left for the day, Rick would lay back in a chair and strap on the old gasbag. He would set a timer he had devised and forget about life for a while. When the timer went off, the gas stopped, and Rick would come back to reality, tidy up and drive his fancy Vette home, where he would spend the rest of the evening in front of his television.

It was a cool day in April when the killer entered Dr. Silvey's office, passing through the front wall. It was late in the afternoon and, as he expected, Rick was in a nitrous oxide stupor. He had seen this many times before. He had tried to enter the bodies of people in dentist's offices, under general anesthesia or even when they were just asleep. But they always seemed to be guarded by unseen beings of light that wouldn't let him approach. But he had no problem using the bodies of those who abused drugs or alcohol. The beings of light seemed to leave when people abused themselves in these ways.

Sure enough, a quick look around showed no protection for good old Rick, so the killer made himself at home, slipping quickly and easily into the man's body. There was a brief struggle, but Rick was weak from nitrous oxide. The killer ruled and Rick Silvey, the dentist beloved by children, soon found his body taking orders from somebody else.

***

Several days passed after Brandon's startling announcement, but the killer never showed. Though they trusted Brandon's instincts, Tara and Ryan couldn't be sure. As time passed, so did their defenses. A week later, when Tara suggested they run into town together for Brandon's check-up, no objections were raised.

It was an eight-mile drive along a dirt road lined with gorgeous pine trees and some of the most beautiful mountains in the world surrounding them, capped in glacial ice. These were the subject of their conversation today, as they had often been in the past.

"Here it is almost June," Tara said, "and just look at those mountains! I bet that ice wouldn't last ten minutes back home!"

"I don't know how you lasted so long in all that heat yourself. What did your mom say, 122 degrees last August?" Ryan reminded her.

"Is that hot, Daddy?" asked Brandon.

"Boy, is it, son! Why, you could take one of my Idaho potatoes, and just lay it out on the sidewalk. In five minutes, presto, baked potato!"

"Is that how you cook potatoes, Mommy?"

"Nah, Daddy's just fooling you. But it is hot, that's for sure. Say young man," Tara said, changing the subject, "are you ready for the dentist?"

"Yep! See?" Brandon opened his mouth wide. "I been brushing my teeth like you said."

Tara took a quick look then returned her eyes to the road. "Oh, they're gonna' look great when you see Grandma and Grandpa next week!"

"Will little boys cook if they get on the sidewalk there?" he asked innocently.

Tara and Ryan laughed, then explained how people keep cool in Arizona. They didn't get a reprieve from Brandon's questions, however, until they pulled into Stone Creek and headed up Main Street.

As Tara parked in front of Dr. Silvey's office, his assistant, Shauna Stewart, stepped out to meet them.

"Good morning, Tara, Brandon!" she remarked cheerfully.

"What's this Shauna, curbside service?"

"No," she laughed. "Rick just asked me to meet Brandon out here so you could go do your shopping. Our last appointment skipped out on us. We've just been waiting for him. Rick wants to do some fishing today. So go and have some fun, and give us about thirty minutes."

"Cool!" exclaimed Tara. "I could get used to this. I'll just be over at Tina's Cafe."

"Great, see you in a while," Shauna said.

"Okay."

Tara opened the door of the truck, as Brandon bounded over her and out to Shauna. He knew her well, and had always enjoyed his visits to the dentist. Tara knew that he considered this special treatment to be extra fun, and appreciated Shauna and Rick's thoughtfulness.

Shauna took his hand and waved goodbye to Tara. "Say goodbye to mommy, Brandon," she said. Brandon waved to his mommy, and Tara smiled and waved back.

However, he did not wave to his daddy, even though Ryan was waving to him. From the age of two, Brandon was taught not to wave to his daddy in public, or to even make eye contact. Tara and Ryan didn't want people to ostracize their son for talking to invisible people, so they trained him to recognize Ryan only when they were alone or with the Dowdings. It wasn't easy at first. He didn't understand why only he and his mommy could see his dad. But Ryan decided to make a game out of it and after that he caught on fast. Now he followed the rules without being reminded.

Occasionally, Ryan would slip Brandon a wink when no one was looking, and Brandon would grin. Everyone around just thought he was a happy boy.

Tara continued to wave until Shauna and Brandon disappeared through the front door of the office, then she steered the truck across the street and parked it in front of Tina's cafe. Tina's was one of only two places to eat in Stone Creek. The other was the Rusty Gold Pan on

Main and 7th. That was where most of the town ate, so it was where Tara didn't. She preferred Tina's anyway. It was a dive, a true grease pit, but the food was great. Best of all, however, the lighting was poor. Tara could talk to Ryan for as long as she wanted and no one was the wiser.

After ordering a burger, fries, and a glass of milk, she turned to him. *"All right. Out with it. You promised when we got to town, you'd tell me more about those calculations you've been working on."*

"I did?" he teased.

"Yes, and I'm not saying another word until you tell me what you've been up to!"

"You haven't been saying a word anyway!" he teased again, then continued. "Okay Sweetie, I'll tell you under two conditions."

"I'm listening."

"First, you can't laugh, and second, you can't think I'm nuts. Also, you have to remind me what a hamburger tastes like!"

"That's three, goofball! You never have learned how to count!"

"This is true. Laplace Transforms I can do in my head; simple arithmetic, forget it. Anyway, I've been giving this a lot of thought. If I'm right, there's no reason why every particle that was destroyed, or I should say 'disoriented,' by those devices won't be coming back. Ever since they found those things and turned them off, I've been watching, and I think I'm right about this."

"Okay, so what're you right about?"

"Well, follow me for a minute. Each of these wonderful little particles originally had a set of rules it followed. While the machines were on, they got disoriented. But when the machines went offline, their 'confusion' started to wear off. One by one, they've been reverting to their original orientation, the set of laws that governed them before!"

"Okay." Tara was hanging on every word now.

"Okay, so this is great, because according to what I've worked out in my mind . . ." Ryan stopped and paused in thought. "You know something?"

"What?" asked a puzzled and impatient Tara.

"It just occurred to me that since I've been dead, my memory is perfect! I've been doing a lot of math in my head for years now, and I've never had to use paper or pencil. Not that I could if I wanted to, of course, but . . . so, where was I?"

"You're nuts, Ryan McKay, but I still love you. You were saying that according to your calculations . . ."

"Right, sorry dear. The reorientation period is what I've been watching. It seems to be a constant function of time. The matter appears to be reorienting in the same chronological order in which it was disoriented! If my calculations are right, the period of disorientation lasts about 54 months. Watching sea levels return to normal over the past four years has helped me with this."

"54 months?"

"Yeah, well it's a bit more precise than that: One thousand, six hundred forty-two days."

"Okay, I think I'm still with you."

"Of course you are, Desert Rat." He smiled and returned to his line of thought. "Now, in their disoriented state, these particles are all roughly the same, but after one thousand, six hundred forty-two days, they revert to the condition they were in before they were disoriented! Of course, each of these particles was part of a larger system—atoms, then molecules, elements and ultimately, in many cases, large, complex organisms, like plants or . . . fish!"

"Fish?" she repeated.

"Yes. Like the fish in that news story. Now here's what I've been thinking . . ."

Suddenly, Shauna burst through the door of the cafe. She was crying and looked terrified. Looking around quickly, she ran to Tara's table.

"What's wrong, Shauna?" Her motherly instincts made her next question a plea. "Is Brandon all right?"

"Oh, Tara. I don't know what happened! Rick went crazy!" Shauna sobbed.

"What are you talking about? What happened?"

"He was talking like a mad man. He said he knows about someone named Ryan, and that if either of you try to follow him, he'll kill Brandon! Tara, he was ranting some nonsense about making you pay fifty dollars every day. I don't know what . . ."

Tara jumped to her feet, knocking over her chair. "No, no, not Brandon! Oh God, please help us!" She ran to the front door.

"Tara, stay calm! It's him, but we have to stay calm! Do you hear me?" Ryan was standing in front of her, waving her back inside. "Tara, he won't hurt Brandon if we do what he says. It's us he wants. Please stay here. We'll get him back, I promise!"

"No, no, not my little boy!" she cried. "I can't take this, Ryan! Not my little boy! Please get him back for me. Please!"

Out of the corner of her eye, Tara noticed Shauna looking at her with her mouth open, and realized she'd been screaming at the air in front of her, talking to someone named "Ryan." She turned to explain, to calm the girl, but she backed away, then collapsed at the table sobbing.

"Tara, please, you need to talk to Shauna. Take a deep breath and relax! She's ready to flip out. I can't go get Brandon right now. You know that. All I can do is help you get him! And I will, you'll see."

"I'm trying Ryan, I really am." Tara closed her eyes, and took a deep breath, then another, fighting for control.

"Looks like our man found us, honey, even surprised us. But we'll get him. Please believe me."

What do we do Ryan, Please help me to know that everything will work out, I have to know that." Tara had regained enough composure to speak in thought, but her heart was beating fast, and her mind was swimming.

"Walk over to Shauna, and let's get her to relax and think. She had nothing to do with this, but she may have some answers for us."

Yes, yes, I think so."

Tara stumbled over to the table and sat next to Shauna. The poor girl was shaking like a leaf. Tara took her hand and held it, trying to calm her.

"Shauna, dear, did Rick say anything else?"

"No. Uh, wait. Yes."

"Shauna, please, I need to know!"

"I'm sorry. He said, if you follow him, or send 'Ryan' to follow him, he'll kill Brandon. I told you that, didn't I?"

Tara nodded.

"Then he gave me this." She handed Tara a piece of paper folded in half twice. "He said if I didn't give you this, he would hunt me down and kill me. He also said he would do the same if either of us goes to the police."

Tara took the note and unfolded it. It read:

TIME TO PAY MISSY, YESIREE! TIME TO SEE IF YOU AND THAT IDIOT HUSBAND OF YOURS ARE WILLING TO KEEP YOUR SON ALIVE. DO NOT GO TO THE POLICE, DO NOT PASS GO, DO NOT COLLECT TWO HUNDRED DOLLARS! LET'S SEE IF YOU KNOW THE MEANING OF SACRIFICE! ALL I WANT IS YOU AND THAT BOZO HUSBAND OF YOURS. TIME TO MAKE YOU BOTH PAY WAY MORE THAN FIFTY DOLLARS EVERY DAY! WAY MORE! TIME TO SEND YOU TO THAT BIG OLD PLACE IN THE SKY, TARA. I'LL LET THE BOY GO FREE AS A BIRD. YOU HAVE MY WORD, AS A GENTLEMAN (REALLY). HE CAN LIVE WITH THAT NIMROD, DOWDING. JUST FOLLOW THE MAP TO A SPECIAL LITTLE PLACE WHERE YOU CAN GO NIGHTIE NIGHT FOREVER!

PS: NO COPS, GUYS. YOU KNOW I AIN'T FOOLIN!

PPS: NO TRICKS LIKE YOU PULLED IN THE DESERT MISSY! MAMMA'S GONE, AND I DON'T NEED NO GOLD WHERE I LIVE!

PPPS: DON'T MAKE ME HAVE TO COME AND GET YOU, I REALLY HATE IT WHEN I HAVE TO DO THAT!!!

SINCERELY, RICK, THE EVIL DENTIST

Tara sat in stunned silence for several seconds with Ryan reading over her shoulder. She needed strength. What were they going to do? A dead man, who wouldn't go away, had just kidnapped their son. If Ryan went to follow him, he could be leaving Tara for the rest of her life. And even if he did leave her, there was nothing he could do. He was, after all, only a spirit. Their chances in the physical world, as always, would rest on her . . . and Wil.

At the bottom of the note, a crude map had been drawn showing the way to a cabin outside of town. It was only ten miles, and the roads seemed clear enough that they shouldn't have too much trouble getting there. The words *Be here at 6:00 tonight*, with an arrow drawn to the porch of a hastily sketched cabin, were written in red. Tara looked at her watch. It was eleven forty-five AM. Six hours were all they had.

"Tara, ask Shauna what Rick's been up to the last few weeks."

Tara took another deep breath, and looked Shauna in the eyes. "Shauna, tell me what Rick's been up to lately. Has there been anything strange going on in his life?"

The girl paused for a moment. "Well, yes actually. For the last month or so, he's been acting real odd. He used to be a pretty boring guy, you know, just went home at night, didn't do much. But lately he's been studying a lot and going to Vancouver to buy things."

"What kinds of things?" Tara inquired.

"I don't know. He never told me. He would drive down there on weekends and come back with all kinds of books and electronic stuff. He never used to be interested in stuff like that before. "

Tara was silent, listening to Ryan. Finally she spoke. "Shauna, you mustn't tell anyone about this. Do you understand?"

"Yes, yes. I'm telling you, Tara. He changed. He's not the same old Rick. I believe him, when he said he'd kill me. I don't want to die."

"Then don't say a word. When we get Brandon back, we'll call the police. For now, just go home, and remember, not a word."

They stood and Tara put her hands on Shauna's shoulders. Her look of kindness and self-control seemed to relax Shauna a little. Then Tara gave her a hug and she left. After watching her walk out the door and down the sidewalk, Tara turned to Ryan.

"What are we going to do?"

"We're going to get this guy once and for all, and save our son, that's what!"

"I certainly hope so!"

"We will, Tara. But I'll bet he's gotten hold of one of those devices somehow."

"What? How? Why would he do that?"

"Come on, think. You know what he'd do with it, don't you?"

"Yes," she thought grimly. *"He wants me to die the same way he did. Am I close?"*

"I think so. "

"So what are we going to do?"

"Get Wil, for starters."

———⁂———

Brandon sat and watched the killer from his corner in the cabin. He was tied to a leash, and had only about three feet to move around. The man who looked like his dentist was working with a machine in the middle of the cabin floor. Brandon fought hard to keep from crying.

"You're not really Rick, are you?" he asked flatly.

"Well now, you're a pretty smart little boy. Tell me then smart fella, who am I?"

"A bad man."

The killer turned and looked at him. "Yeah, that's right, I'm a bad man. I'm the boogie man that comes out and gets people like you and your mamma and makes them pay big time."

"You're not a boogie man. There isn't any boogieman. My mommy said. You're just a bad man."

The killer stopped what he was doing and stared at Brandon. Something about the boy was familiar. Shrugging off the feeling, he went back to the circuit board in front of him and entered in some numbers.

"What's that machine?" asked Brandon.

"Why this here machine is a very special Device. It makes things disappear. And I'm gonna make someone very special disappear. Now shut up, or I'll smack you one!"

"Are you going to hurt me?" asked Brandon.

"Maybe. If you don't shut up I will."

"Who showed you how to make it?" the boy asked, pointing to the machine.

"I didn't make it, I just sort of fixed it."

It still amazed him how much he learned from the people whose bodies he possessed. Oh, he didn't learn everything they knew, but after one night in Rick's body, he had no trouble pretending to be a dentist. He just thought of what he needed to know, and there it was.

When he pretended to be Marv Graf at his meeting with Kilpack back in Washington, D.C., he just thought of what Kilpack wanted from him, and poof, there it was! He learned lots of interesting things, like the secret location where the damaged sub-atomic destabilizer from Agua Sublima was stored. And not just the location, but a lot of other stuff, stuff about how it worked and how to fix it.

"Are you going to make it go?" inquired Brandon.

"Oh, it'll go all right. Now stop asking me so many questions, little mister, or you'll pay too, you little twerp. Shush now!"

Brandon decided not to say any more to the bad man. Instead, he watched as the bad man shook his head and went back to work on his "disappearing" machine.

———

Back at their cabin, Tara, Ryan and the Dowdings feverishly made plans. They all knew this man was capable of killing mercilessly, so the trick would be to get Brandon away from him before he could hurt the boy, then take their best shot. Any way they planned it, Brandon's safety was the biggest concern.

"You know Tara, if they're in the cabin, I'm going to have to go in there without you."

"Yes, I know. That's been on my mind constantly."

"More than likely, that will mean our separation."

Tara closed her eyes as a tear escaped and ran down her cheek. "Oh Ryan, I hope not. I'm so afraid of losing you. I don't know what I'd do."

"I'm afraid too, Desert Rat. But we better face it." Ryan's eyes filled with tears, as he watched Tara struggle with the reality.

"I don't know if I can. That . . . person has destroyed my life. He killed you once, and now he's going to do it again. It's either you or my boy! I can't take it!"

"Listen you two," Wil interrupted, "Norma and I will get a few things ready in the other room. You need some time together. Don't worry, we still have three hours. For what it's worth, I feel very confident our plan'll work."

"Thanks, Wil." She managed through her tears. "You guys have been the greatest."

"You too, Tara." said Norma, smiling tenderly. "We'll get Brandon back, you know we will!"

"I'm praying," returned Tara.

The Dowdings left the room, and Tara and Ryan stood facing each other.

"I can't lose you Ryan, what little I have left of you."

"Tara, even if that happens—and maybe it won't—I'll always be at your side, and I promise that you'll feel me . . . here." He reached out his hand and placed it over her heart.

Tara turned away. Ryan knew what she was thinking, and she was right. It' wasn't enough for him either.

"Perhaps you should lie down."

"Yes, Ryan," she said, "I need to be as close to you as I can right now." She lay down and closed her eyes.

For the next hour, he lay where her body rested, coinciding with her spirit, each drawing from the strengths of the other and feeling totally as one. It was an hour of peace and harmony, of love and the sense of eternity, soothing and comforting, a final preparation for what Ryan hoped would be their final stand against the evil that had stalked them for so long . . . without being their final hours of life together.

Tara was talking calmly to Ryan when Wil came back into the room carrying two pistols and a rifle.

It was five o'clock, and the killer was nervous. It wasn't like him to be nervous. But actually, it wasn't like him to have this kind of enthusiasm about a job either. This one was different. This was the biggest hit of all. A first! He had always done it for someone else before; first for his country, then for whoever could afford his price, but this one was for him! And it should have gone down a long time ago, yesiree, he thought, a long time ago.

"Are you waiting for somebody?" asked Brandon.

"Yeah, you might say that."

"Is it my mommy?"

"Maybe. Now shut up!"

"Are you going to show her your machine?"

"Oh, yeah, she'll get to see my Device all right. Her and your daddy."

"Do you know my daddy?"

"Yesiree, I know him." The killer pulled out his other 'device,' a nine-millimeter handgun just like the one he had used so many times before. He checked the clip.

"What's that?" asked Brandon.

"It's a gun twerp! Haven't you seen a gun before?"

"Yeah. My uncle Wil gots a gun."

"That's nice. But didn't I tell you to shut up?"

"Yes."

"Then do it!" the killer shouted.

Something wasn't right about the kid, he decided. He couldn't look at him. It made him think weird thoughts.

———◆———

Brandon huddled in the corner, afraid to speak. Instead he thought about his mommy and daddy. He wanted to go home, but he knew they'd come for him. He even knew *when* they came. It made him happy to know that, to know his mommy and daddy were outside the cabin now. But he knew his daddy wouldn't want him to say anything to this bad man, so he didn't. He just waited and watched.

———◆———

It was exactly five-fifteen, when Ryan entered the cabin. He had his finger to his mouth, signaling Brandon to be quiet. He knew Brandon would obey, and he did. They were playing their game now and Brandon was very good at it. He only looked at Daddy when the killer turned away.

Ryan was relieved to find that the killer couldn't see him. He had been counting on the physical body of Dr. Silvey to act as a barrier to the killer's spiritual eyes, and was relieved to find that it did! With the freedom to move around, Ryan walked toward the center of the room and checked out the machinery sitting in the middle of the floor.

It had been set to turn on at the touch of a remote switch, which he found sitting on a small table about six feet from the door. This was good. If they could just get to the remote before the killer did, they might have a chance.

He expected Brandon to be tied up, not tethered in a corner. This was not a good arrangement. With the child on the far side of the cabin and the machine between him and the door, it would be much harder to extricate him.

"Brandon, can you tell the man you have to go potty?"

"I'll try Daddy," the little boy thought.

"If he lets you go, you stay in the bathroom and don't come out. Understand?"

"Okay, Daddy."

"Go ahead, ask him now, and remember, stay in the bathroom if you can."

"Mister? I have to go to the bathroom."

The killer looked at his watch. It was five seventeen, but even he understood the call of nature. "Okay boy, you got two minutes. If I have to come looking for you, though, I'll make you pay, you understand?"

"Yes sir."

He unhooked the leash from the wall, and led the child to the bathroom.

"Remember, two minutes, then you get to coming out, or I'll get to hurting you, got it?"

When the killer started to unfasten the boy's leash from the wall, Ryan went outside. Instantly, he was at Tara's side.

"Now Tara! Go! The remote is on the table inside, six feet to your left!"

But Tara didn't go. She didn't see him. She didn't hear him. As they feared, his "initial visit" had finally come to an end.

Tara looked at her watch; it was five twenty, five minutes since Ryan left. He was supposed to have been right back. With a sinking feeling, Tara looked to her right then to her left. She looked at the door where Ryan was supposed to be standing, but there was no Ryan. She felt a sense of panic rising within her.

"I don't see him Will!" she whispered.

"Then feel for him!" he whispered back. "Tara, we knew this could happen. Stay calm. You've got to feel with your heart now. Trust in yourself, honey. Listen for what Ryan has to say, but not with your ears. And, uh . . . you better do it quickly!"

Tara closed her eyes, and took a deep breath. Saying a silent prayer, she pleaded for the faith she would need and struggled to dispel any feelings of anger, self-pity or self-doubt.

As she felt the peaceful influence of the Spirit, she thought of Ryan, and tried calmly to listen for him with her spiritual ears. Almost immediately she sensed words that seemed to come from outside of her own thoughts into her heart and mind. They permeated her like nothing she had experienced before. It was Ryan, she knew it, but now she heard him with her spirit, not with her physical being.

"I'm ready now, Wil!"

Wil readied his rifle. Quickly but quietly, they stepped onto the porch. Wil moved quickly to the window, while Tara approached the door. She looked over at Wil and got a thumbs up. As quietly as she could, she turned the knob and entered the cabin. No one was in sight. She looked to her left. Sure enough, there was a small remote control box sitting there within her grasp. Skimming across the floor as lightly as a butterfly, she snatched the remote from its resting place and turned.

"Well now little missy, you can stop right there," she heard behind her.

Startled, Tara spun around to see the killer standing at the mouth of a hallway, with Brandon in one arm and in the other, a nine-millimeter handgun pointed at her.

"Brandon!" she called.

"Mommy!"

"Oh, isn't this sweet," the killer mocked. "Now you just hold it right there, missy. I had a suspicion something wasn't right here. So you thought you could try a little stunt? Well, that was really dumb, missy."

"What do you want from us?" Tara demanded.

"Oh I think you know. Now hand over that little gizmo."

"I won't, not until you let Brandon go."

Outside, Wil should have had a bead on the killer by now. Why didn't he shoot? Was he afraid the man might get off a shot at her before he died? Tara didn't care if she died, and wished she could say something to Wil. Then she felt a distinct impression. She could almost hear Ryan telling her to stay calm.

But events turned for the worse. The deranged man put his gun to Brandon's temple! That was too much. Wil couldn't take a shot now. She waited breathlessly, praying that nothing would happen to her baby.

"Please let my boy go. He hasn't done anything to you. Let him go!" Tara pleaded.

"Oh, you're right, he is innocent. But don't be fooled, I'll take him out right now if you don't do exactly as I say."

Again Tara was feeling words in her mind. They told her to do exactly as the man said, and not to worry, that there were other forces at work.

"All right. What do you want?"

"Put that gizmo on the floor and step away from it."

Slowly Tara laid the remote on the floor and backed away. Without taking his eyes off Tara, the killer backed into the hallway out of Wil's line of sight, and set Brandon on the floor.

With the gun still pointed at the boy and his eyes on Tara, the killer said, "Now, little mister, you walk over there and get that little gadget for me, or your mommy will get hurt, understand?"

"Don't hurt my mommy!"

"Then go and get it for me!"

As Brandon went, the killer held onto the leash around his neck, allowing only enough slack for him to reach the remote. Brandon strained at the rope, wanting to be with his mother, but he could go no further.

Then he did something that completely surprised Tara. He winked! Could he still see Ryan? she wondered. Was it possible?

"Brandon, if you can see Daddy, wink again." Tara almost heard the words, still and small in her heart! It was Ryan!

Brandon struggled at the end of the leash to pull away from the killer, while he looked just to Tara's right and winked. Again and almost imperceptibly, Tara heard her husband.

"Great son! Great! Now go back to the man, he won't hurt you. You can help Daddy by going back to the man now, but don't let him see you look at me. Remember our game."

Again Brandon winked. It was a childish wink, both eyes closing, with his right cheek raised and his left eye struggling to stay open, but a wink nonetheless. Slowly, he turned and walked back to the man. When he reached him, he was scooped back up as the killer stepped back into the room. Promptly, the killer tied Brandon to the wall, all the while keeping the gun to the boy's temple.

Once again, Tara thought of Wil outside waiting, his finger on the trigger, ready to squeeze. Was he waiting for the man to turn his attention to Tara? She was sure of it. When he swept his gun from Brandon to Tara, Wil would drop him!

She felt another impression now. It was like the others, but it told her to take an action that she questioned. Could Ryan really be telling her to step in front of the window? Why would he want her to block

Wil's view? She hesitated for just a moment, then decided to trust her feelings. They were all she had left now.

Slowly, she stepped to her right, two feet, then three, positioning herself between the window and the spot where the man was tying up Brandon.

"Yes! I knew you could do it Tara!" she heard once again. *"Brandon, talk to the man. Ask him why he would do such a thing."*

"Why are you doing this to us?" the boy asked obediently.

"Shush now you little twerp, or I'm going to smack you!"

"No!" cried Tara. "Please don't hurt him. He's just a boy."

"Then tell him to stop talking to me or I will!" the killer demanded angrily.

"What have we done to you? I don't understand. Who are you?" Tara pleaded.

"I'm the evil dentist," he blubbered, "raising havoc on the world!"

"No your not," said Brandon. "You're just a bad man."

At this, Tara sensed something in the killer. It was just a glimmer, but it was there. She could see it in his eyes. She looked deep and hard. Yes! Even in the black heart that was buried deep in the killer's chest, for just a moment, an infinitely small ray of light had shone. Tara knew it, she felt it, sensed it, as she had sensed things in people on countless other occasions. But she also knew it would not burn long.

Brandon's statement was so completely honest it caught the killer off guard. It was the third time he had heard the boy say it, and he knew now that it was exactly what he most wanted the kid not to say.

He turned and looked at the small boy on the leash. For an instant, something flashed through his mind. It wasn't Brandon he saw. He was watching himself as a boy, tied up in the corner of his little home in the woods, his fat mamma swearing at him and threatening him. The irony stung. Now he was the fat old mean mamma, with an innocent and frightened little boy in front of him. Is that what he looked like all those years ago? His mind staggered at the thought.

Memories, haunting memories. Again Brandon disappeared from before him. There was another little boy standing there, a child of five.

"Why I ever had you is a mystery to me you little twerp." his mamma was saying. "Why I outta make you pay fifty dollars every day of your miserable life for making me miss out on my life. Now you stay tied up and count yourself lucky if I even feed you."

Mamma was in one of her moods again. All the boy did was leave a book on the floor. For that he would miss his meals for two days! He struggled at the end of his leash all night after mamma fell asleep in her drunken stupor, but he couldn't break free. So he cried.

Again the scene changed. Now Brandon was back in front of him, with tears in his eyes. At this, the man fell to his knees, sobbing. He hated himself for doing this to an innocent little boy. The feelings he felt as a child were flooding his body. He reached out and untied the boy. Was it Brandon or himself he was untying? He wasn't sure. All he knew was that a boy needed to be freed, and it was the only thing he could do.

Seconds passed like minutes. He thought of how terribly he had been treated as a boy. How could he treat this boy the way Mamma treated him? He was sickened at how easily he had fallen into a trap of hate and meanness. It wasn't his nature. It was his mamma's nature.

Yes, that was it. He understood now. It was his mamma who needed to be taken care of. Mamma was bad. All mammas are bad. He would fix her. Yes, he would fix her big time . . . after he freed the boy. He had to do that first, and he had to hurry.

Fumbling with the knot, he struggled to untie it, but he was having trouble doing it with one hand. He would set the remote control on the floor for just a second, and use both hands.

When the leash fell to the floor, Brandon ran into his mother's arms. As Tara knelt to pick him up, a shot rang out, shattering the glass behind her. She looked at the killer; he had fallen in a heap to the floor.

Suddenly, the machine in front of Tara sprang to life. Lights went on, and a high pitched sound emanated from deep within its center. The room began to take on a bizarre, shimmering, mirage-like appearance, and everything felt like a dream. Dr. Silvey's body had fallen on the remote.

Moving as fast as she could, Tara shoved Brandon through the door. Then she tripped. An eerie, but familiar, sensation washed through her body as she fell to the floor.

"No, not again! Ryan!" was all she could say before everything went black.

A second shot rang out from the direction of the cabin window and the killer's machine was dead. Ryan moved to Tara's side and knelt beside her body now lying still on the cabin floor. Her face wore an expression of peace, and though she was unconscious, Ryan knew she would be okay.

He turned his attention toward the body of the dentist lying in a crumpled mass across the room, and knew that he too would be okay. That's when he saw the man standing next to Dr. Silvey. He was a handsome fellow, with a penetrating stare, and he was smiling at Ryan. Only he wasn't fully a man, he was a spirit.

"So, we meet again, McKay. I'm still going to make you pay, you know, big time!" he said, his smile turning into a smirk.

Ryan stood to face the killer's apparition. "Your time here is done, but where you're going, the only one paying will be yourself. And the payment will be substantial, that I promise."

"You think I'm done?" shouted the killer. "I've only just begun to wreak havoc on you and the little missy. You can't stop me; you could never stop me! All I need is another Device, and you can kiss that little woman goodbye!" He laughed and turned to leave through the cabin wall, but in an instant Ryan was there blocking his way.

"You will not leave, you will stay right here." The words flowed from Ryan's lips with such serenity and peace that it shocked the killer to a standstill. Ryan watched as the killer hesitated, seemingly aware of the light around Ryan for the first time.

"You can't do this to me!" he finally blurted out.

"Yes I can," Ryan returned gently. At first anticipating a real fight with this man, Ryan was now filled with the knowledge that a conflict would not be necessary. The light surrounding his body had grown to fill the cabin now. It was the same powerful light he experienced that day in the hotel room back in Washington so long ago. This time however, it manifested itself by holding captive the sinister spirit of another lost soul.

"Why can't I move? Who are you?" the man pleaded. "Let me go!"

"I can't do that." Ryan responded as Wil entered the cabin and gently carried Tara to safety.

"I don't understand. What's happening?" said the now frightened spirit.

The room was filled with light. The darkness immediately surrounding the killer was shrinking away, and the killer had begun to cry.

After watching his loved ones leave the cabin, Ryan felt impressed to say something more to the killer.

"Thank you for letting my son go. I won't forget that."

The man looked up at Ryan in disbelief. "Yeah, well, maybe I didn't know what I was doing."

"Yes, you did."

"That ain't like me, you know?"

"Life is filled with choices, and this time you chose to do good. I don't fully understand all there is to life, but I know a kind act like that will have its reward."

Ryan could see the darkness around the man fading as more light poured into the room. Maybe, just maybe, he thought, some of that light will make its way into the killer's heart, and there will be a small measure of mercy for him.

Suddenly, a strong impression entered Ryan's heart. This meeting was not so much for the killer's benefit as for his. If there was to be complete mercy for Ryan McKay, there was something *he* would have to do.

"Who are you?" the killer asked again.

"Right now, I may be the closest thing to a friend you've ever had."

"You? A friend? After all I've done to you and the little missy?"

"I'm trying . . .I really am," Ryan said, struggling with his feelings. The light permeated everything in the room and filled his heart with perfect love. He knew he had to exercise compassion and forgive the man. The words were hard, but they felt so right.

"I want you to know that I forgive you for all you've done to me and against my family."

Ryan could see the man's heart as it reacted to his words. Walls were crumbling inside this despicable entity, walls that had been erected decades ago when he was still an innocent child.

"I'm sorry McKay," he said at last. "I've never said that to no human being as long as I can remember, but I mean it."

The darkness withdrew, and light enveloped the spirit of the killer.

"What's happening to me?" he said. "I feel so strange. Am I going to Hell? Will I burn forever? McKay, come on, tell me, man." He dropped to his knees before Ryan. "Is there hope for my wretched soul?"

"I don't know the answer to your questions," said Ryan, "but hang on to those good feelings, and you may not burn . . . at least, not forever."

The killer looked up at Ryan, a thin smile on his face. Ryan wondered if this was not perhaps the first time in his miserable existence that the man ever had a reason to smile.

"What is this?" the killer asked. "I never felt nothing good before in my life. What is this, McKay?" Ryan looked down at the man and watched forty years of tears stream unabated down his cheeks.

Suddenly there appeared two bright and powerful personages of spirit on either side of the killer. The man looked up at them. "Go with me, McKay!"

Ryan knew the command was a plea. Could it be that this one-time killer was now looking to Ryan as a friend, an advocate? Was Ryan the only human being in this man's sorry life who had ever shown him any compassion or forgiveness? Surely the man knew he was going to some kind of spirit prison to pay for his murderous life. Still, he was prepared to go willingly and face the consequences! Ryan wondered how, or if, mercy would apply toward this murderer and instantly realized that it was not his place to know or to make that decision. He could see a ray of light in the man's heart, and he wanted Ryan to accompany him on his journey. That was all he needed to know.

Ryan looked at the killer. His hatred for the man was gone now, replaced by compassion. At last he truly felt the forgiveness he had expressed earlier. The weight of anger and vengeance lifted from his soul as the light immediately about his person increased to an intensity he could not have imagined as a physical being. He needed to go and help bring healing to the wounds in this man's soul, especially where they had effected his own life.

Looking to the spirit guards for approval, he was grateful when they bade him follow. And so he did; upward, right through the cabin ceiling, he, the guards, and a killer who was no longer his enemy.

When Tara awoke, she was back at the cabin, in bed. Wil and Norma were standing over her, and Brandon was sitting at the foot of her bed. An RCMP vehicle was driving down the road in the distance, heading away from their cabin.

"Are you all right, Tara?" Norma asked. "You took a nasty bump."

She reached up and felt the bandage around her head. "I think so. Is everyone else all right?" she asked.

"Yes, Tara. Everyone's fine."

"What happened?"

Wil knelt at her side, opposite Norma. "You did it honey, you and that wonderful little boy of yours. The Amazing McKays saved the day!"

"Where's Ryan? What happened to the killer . . . the machine?"

"The killer is gone. You ducked at just the right moment, and I was lucky to get off a well-placed shot. The real Rick Silvey is recovering now in Vancouver. He's suffering from a little amnesia. Claims he can't remember the last few months of his life, but he should be okay. Anyway, when I opened the door of the cabin, you shoved Brandon out. As you tripped, the killer got off a shot of his own that just creased the top of your head. You're very lucky to be alive."

"She didn't trip," said Brandon, matter-of-factly. "Daddy pushed her."

"Daddy did what?" demanded Tara.

"He pushed you down so the bad man couldn't shoot you. I saw him!"

The room went silent. Finally, Wil muttered, "Amazing!"

"But, sweetie, Daddy's just a spirit. We can't even feel it when he touches us."

"He didn't touch," Brandon tried to explain. "He . . . pushed."

"Well, obviously he did something," Wil offered. "You're alive."

"Thank the Lord," Norma added.

Tara just stared at her little boy. Finally, she held her arms out to him, "Come here, little guy, and give Mommy a big hug."

As she snuggled her little one, Wil continued to bring her up to date. "I put a bullet through the circuit board on that machine, stopped it deader than a mackerel. The authorities are on their way here. They'll destroy it first thing tomorrow morning. But listen to this, Tara." Wil tapped Brandon's back. "Hey bucko, tell your Mom what your daddy did then."

"What did Daddy do, son?" Tara asked.

"He had a talk with the bad man's ghost, and then he took him up in the sky."

"He took the bad man away? Are you sure?" Tara questioned.

"Yes. Daddy and some other men took him to spirit jail. He won't hurt us any more."

"Are you sure?"

"Yeah, he told me!"

"What else did he tell you?"

"Um, he said he loves you and me a lot!" Brandon could not keep from smiling when he told her that.

"Honey, can you see Daddy now?" Tara asked cautiously.

"No. He's gone now. I can't see him any more."

Chapter 16
ONE THOUSAND, SIX HUNDRED FORTY-TWO

It was a lazy Saturday morning on a pleasant June day in Phoenix. Tara was asleep on the living room couch at her parent's home. She had risen early to help her dad with the lawn, hoping it would give her some relief from the stress and sorrow she had been feeling since the killer took Ryan away from her.

The brief celebrity status she and Wil enjoyed upon their return hadn't helped her fight off the depression. Wil had spared her the details while they were in hiding, but they all came out upon her return. In the four years they were gone, Tara's father and Wil's employees had struggled through hearings in over 40 different federal and state jurisdictions to clear the warrants that had been issued against her and the others. The hearings were complicated by the fact that those who cooperated in issuing the false warrants stood to be exposed if she was cleared.

They fought long and hard, and the last hearing was held just a week before the killer showed up at their cabin in British Columbia. After that, however, the news media was finally given a true account of Wil and Tara's part in the matter disorientation scandal. The reaction came the day they returned. The attention had been overwhelming at first, then gratifying. Tara had received many more than her obligatory fifteen minutes of fame. What pleased her most was the invitation of the university to return to her post-graduate studies, with the promise that a thesis on the resolution of the ecological crisis would guarantee her a doctorate.

Most of the furor was over now. But she hadn't been to church in two weeks, and she could no longer rid her mind of the thoughts that were pulling her down. She could not understand why God had taken Ryan from her, just because he left her for two minutes to save their son. Worst of all, she felt herself sinking into feelings of hatred and vengeance over the whole affair.

Her parents, given Tara's mood lately, had taken Brandon to the mall to buy him a new toy action figure. During their absence, Tara showered and plopped down on the sofa to read the newspaper. Within minutes she had fallen asleep.

After only twenty minutes had passed, however, she became restless, then started to toss and turn. Suddenly, she sat up, her eyes wide open. A persistent thought was nagging at her incessantly.

"One thousand, six hundred and forty-two," she muttered. "One thousand, six hundred and forty-two." She said it louder.

She had been dreaming, caught in a rerun of that dreadful day when the last remnant she had of Ryan was taken from her. He was trying to tell her something, something about the number she was repeating when she awoke. She strained to remember that day at the diner in Stone Creek. What were the words he used? The disoriented matter was returning, he said, atoms, molecules, plants . . .

"Bodies!" she shouted. If plants could re-form, why not bodies!

"One thousand, six hundred forty-two? Where did that come from? Ryan, are you there?" She stood and paced back and forth across the room. "Come on Tara, think!" she insisted. Then it came to her. "Days! That's it, one thousand, six hundred and forty-two days."

She started to count the days since Ryan's death. Confused, she retrieved a pencil and paper from the desk in the hall.

"Okay, let's see. Four years at 365 days, plus . . ." Furiously, she scribbled her calculations on the paper in front of her, then sat back and stared at the paper with a date scribbled on it. "Could it be?" she puzzled. "Oh, my . . ."

Stumbling over herself in haste, she threw on her hiking boots and grabbed her keys. As she rushed from the house, she snatched the cell phone her father had given her, and sprinted to the Jeep Cherokee. With a leap, she was in and had it started before the door could close. The car roared out of the drive, and she headed for the desert. On I-60, she fumbled with the cell phone to punch in a number.

"Hello?" a man's voice finally answered.

"Dad, I'm going to the desert. Don't ask me why, but I need you there!

"Tara, are you sure this is wise?"

"No. I'm not even sure I haven't gone crazy, but I have to follow this hunch."

"Tara, I don't know how to get there!"

"Wil knows. He's been there before. He'll know right where to go. Please hurry!"

"Okay, okay. But Tara, try to calm down and drive safely, don't do anything foolish! We'll be there as soon as we can."

"Thanks Dad." She hung up the phone and drove as fast as she could, praying as she went that she was right and that she could get there before it was too late.

After what seemed like an eternity, she parked her Jeep as close to The Hole as the desert trail would allow. Throwing open the door, she hit the ground at a full run, racing for the spot where she last saw Ryan alive. Beyond the ant colony she flew, heading up the rise and into her past. At the top, she stopped, flinging herself to her knees under the shade of a now thriving desert willow in full bloom. She struggled to catch her breath, stunned at what she saw in front of her.

The Hole was gone. In its place stood the old boulder, just as it had been so long ago. Strewn around it were the rotting carcasses and skeletons of desert animals in various stages of decomposition. To the right, she recognized the skeletal remains of what looked like a javelina. Was it the same one that disappeared in front of her eyes all those years ago? She gasped, her heart on fire.

Bodies, she thought, *dead* bodies all over the desert floor. If the matter was reorienting, like Ryan said it would, why are the animals dead? Why are the birds lying lifeless? Why hadn't the javelina revived so it could return to its desert home? All that was left were dead bodies, rotting in the sun. What good did it do for them to be reoriented after four and a half years?

She buried her face in her hands and started to cry.

"One thousand, six hundred and forty-two days," she shouted at the sky. "What good is it, Father? Ryan said that was the length of time it takes for the matter to re-orient to its old system, its old laws. Today is the one thousand, six hundred forty-second day since Ryan died! His dead body will come back today. I don't want a dead Ryan, Father!"

She was certain now that Ryan's body would return, but when it did, what good would it do? Would it be for no other purpose than to give her a body to bury? She couldn't bear it. Why had she come? So the Beast could triumph one last time? She slumped to the ground, sobbing in the clean white sand.

"Ryan," her voice struggled to whisper. "Oh Ryan. What will I do without you? I can't take it, God. How could you let this happen?"

Just as she felt she would sink into a hole from which she could not return, a memory flashed through her mind. It was of a hotel room in Dallas over four years ago, and of a prayer she had offered there. She forced herself up to her knees, closed her eyes and bowed her head.

"Father, are you there?" she asked, and the Spirit immediately whispered to her heart that He was. "I've learned to call you Father now. Thank you for that knowledge."

In the Spirit's warmth she felt an impression that her mind interpreted as, "You are welcome, my daughter." She hadn't felt such closeness to God since the day Ryan forwarded a message from Him in Washington. The scientist in her yearned to analyze the mechanism of communication, but the little child on her knees simply accepted it in humble faith and marveled at His nearness.

"Years ago," she continued, "you answered my prayer with such power and in a way I never expected. It boggles my mind whenever I think about it. I cannot tell you how grateful I am for that blessing, and for the wonderful man you sent me as a husband and the father of my baby." The Spirit's warmth seemed to grow in her heart.

"I should have learned something from that experience, Father, but it's been so hard. I should have been grateful for that time, however short, and remembered the message you gave me through him. I've had so many witnesses, and yet I'm filled now with anger and sorrow. I'm sorry. I'm so sorry. Please forgive me."

The Spirit washed through her like a cleansing flood, leaving her warm, with the words "you are forgiven" echoing through her soul. Startled, she took a breath and for a long moment basked in the wonder of God's forgiveness, weeping at the joy of purity that filled her heart. Gathering herself together, she eventually continued

"Oh thank you, Father," she whispered, hesitant about what she had to say next. "I have just one more thing I have to ask of you, and this one's going to be the toughest of all. I know, because it's for me. You've always known what was best for me. I need to trust you more.

Please help me to say, Thy will be done, and really mean it, Father. I've botched things up plenty, but I'm here now, where I felt I should be, and now I don't know why. If the reason is not what I had hoped, please help me to accept it. Help me to say, Thy will be done." She whispered it over and over. "Thy will be done. Thy will be done."

The Spirit continued to grow in her heart as she prayed, until it felt almost as though God was standing beside her, His hand on her head. The feeling left her certain of two things, two things she would never doubt again: First, that God lived, and second that He loved her more than she could possibly imagine!

As the experience subsided from the overwhelming feeling of God's presence to the warm glow of His love, another thought impinged clearly on her consciousness. Fish!

Fish? she thought. "Father, I don't understand."

She continued to kneel and listen, her eyes tightly closed. Suddenly, as though in an instant, it all became clear to her as pure intelligence flowed into her mind and heart, reviving memories long forgotten and displaying with crystal clarity their meaning.

She knew now what Ryan was trying to tell her at the diner in Stone Creek. He had been impressed with an article about the resurgence of fishing. She remembered the article as though she were reading it now. These were not all dead fish, like the animals that lay in her desert. Many were alive! She also recalled a study she had read some years ago about the extraordinary power of sharks to revive from death when water was run through their gills.

That was it! That was it, she thought. The bodies have to be revived as soon as they're reoriented! Her mind and heart were flooded with a feeling of positive assurance that this was the reason she had come.

Instantly, she felt, or heard, the impression, "Now, my daughter, open your eyes."

As she did, she became aware of a strange phenomenon taking place about twenty feet in front of her. Two human forms were starting to materialize. In less then a minute the first one was fully formed. But what Tara saw sent a wave of shock through her body that made her tremble with fear. It was the body of the killer!

Her fear only lasted seconds, however, as anger began to replace it. Blazing up into her heart, it pushed away the spirit she had felt. At the loss of the spirit, she gasped. Quickly she closed her eyes again.

"Father, I'm sorry. I have such anger in my heart toward this man. Let that depart from me now, I pray. Let me find a way to forgive him."

She paused, waiting, then rose. Walking carefully toward the body, she stopped at a safe distance to inspect it. The Spirit was close to her again as she was struck with a realization of how great this man's sufferings would be for the sins he had committed. She cringed and willed the vision away from her. Looking down now, she felt, for the first time, a deep compassion for the man she knew only as a heartless killer. Her mind was at peace as she formed the thought, *"Should he be revived?"* Immediately and firmly the impression came to her in the negative.

Satisfied, she turned to the other body that was forming in the sand. Watching expectantly, her fears and doubts resisted the joy her heart longed to embrace. Now fully formed, she could see it was . . .

"Ryan!" she shouted, running to his side.

He wasn't breathing. She felt for a pulse. His body was warm, as if only moments had passed since he died, but it had no heart beat. Tilting his head back, she placed her mouth over his and gave him two quick breaths as she had learned so long ago in a CPR class. Then she stopped, watching for a reaction. Nothing! Two more quick breaths.

"Please Father, help me!" she shouted, her voice echoing across the desert as precious minutes ticked by.

Ryan stood motionless behind Tara, his father at his side.

"Look at her Dad. Isn't she wonderful?"

"Yes she is, son. Whether you return or not, she's come through the refiner's fire, a pure and precious gem."

"But she followed the promptings, and here she is, fighting to bring me back. You understand now why I have to go, don't you?"

"Of course, son. It's just that you had to know the consequences. You've lived a good life, and because you held to the principles you learned, you're here. When you go back, you'll be mortal again. Free to do good, and free to make mistakes."

"Dad, when you told me I was called here to bring this chaos to an end, I thought it would be forever. I had no idea I'd have the chance to return to mortality."

"We can't always disclose everything, especially where there will be an opportunity to return. This was a very unusual assignment, son. A lot was at stake here, and without you in spirit form, it would have been impossible for you and Tara to accomplish what you did."

"But I can't tell you how happy I was when I learned the truth," Ryan continued. "Do you see my point? What's heaven for if you can't be happy there? When I learned I could go back, I realized I would never be happy if I didn't take the chance."

"I'm glad, son, and so proud of you."

"I'm going to miss this place, Dad . . . and you particularly."

"Well, not as much as you think."

"Am I going to forget?" Ryan asked, panic rising in his throat.

"No, no, but it won't seem as real to you when you return to mortality, and some things you will forget. Others you won't be allowed to remember. But all the time that you spent with Tara . . . and with Brandon, those years will seem almost like normal mortal memories to you."

"Will I remember you, Dad?"

"Yes, son . . . for the most part."

Ryan could see the love in his father's eyes as he looked at him and smiled. Tears began to form as he reached out and pulled Ryan toward him, giving him a strong and loving embrace. Overwhelmed by the feeling of his father's love, Ryan sobbed uncontrollably.

"Thank you Dad, thank you so much," he whispered after a moment. "Thanks for everything!" He stepped back and wiped his eyes, regaining his composure. "I'd better hurry."

"Yes. Without your spirit, your body will soon decompose as these others have. The window of opportunity is small. So go to her, son, and God be with you."

Stepping toward Tara, he hesitated and turned to look at his father, who nodded approvingly, then was gone.

"Dad, I have so much to learn!

His father's voice was as clear in his thoughts as when he was standing at his side. *"And I'll be waiting to teach you son."*

Ryan looked down at his body lying in the desert sun and swallowed hard. He knew what he was leaving behind, and he knew what difficulties lay ahead. He took one more look at Tara and closed his eyes.

Tara stopped to check for signs of life. It had been almost five minutes, but her faith was strong and she was determined. God had not brought her this far unless He wanted Ryan to live. But she was worried, she knew what could happen if he wasn't revived soon. Franticly, she hit him square in the chest, hoping once more to start his lifeless heart. Then she gave him five quick chest compressions, and another breath. She was getting dizzy, and almost fainted. How long could she go on out here alone? Forever, her heart shouted! Whatever it takes. But the rest of her body was staggering from the effort.

She gave one more guarded glance over at the lifeless form of the killer, then turned back, determined not to let Ryan suffer the same fate. What she saw made her jump, then burst into tears.

Ryan's eyes were open! He looked up at her, trying to smile.

She wiped at the tears streaming from her eyes. "Ryan!"

"Tara, you did it!"

"I can't believe it. Please tell me I'm not dreaming."

"You're not dreaming, Ant Woman. You followed the promptings and revived me," he whispered.

"Shhh, don't say another word. You look so weak."

"This is nothing. I was dead just a minute ago."

She laughed, then cried, then tried to brush the hair from his forehead. Remembering the other body, she asked, "Ryan, what about the killer?"

"He's gone, my darling, and won't be allowed to return. He'll never bother you again, I promise."

She smiled. "Oh Ryan, is it really you? Are you really alive?"

"Yes, yes." He could barely whisper. "But I'm a lot weaker than I expected to be."

He tried to reach up and touch her face, but he was too tired and his arm fell back to his side.

"No, no, stay still. You're too weak. Help is on the way."

"Tara, you can't imagine what it was like there, but it was nothing without you. I love you so much. I had to come back."

She looked up into the sky. "Thank you, Father! Thank you!" Looking back at Ryan, she said, "I can hardly believe it, but I do see the plan now with 'total clarity,' like you said. And I know that He lives, Ryan! I know it now like you know it. I know He loves me. Whenever I look at you, I'll always remember that, for the rest of eternity!"

He smiled weakly as she scooped his head into her arms and drew him close to her. Her heart pounded at the touch of his body as she wiped the newly formed beads of sweat from his forehead. She had yearned for so long to hold him, to feel him again. Leaning down to him, her eyes bathed his face in tears as she kissed his neck, his cheeks, then his lips.

Their kiss was interrupted by shouts in the distance coming closer. Her father and Wil would be there soon, she thought. How grateful she was for them.

The thought triggered a memory from their days at her uncle's cabin. Suddenly, she sat up and crossed her arms, giving him the best frown she could muster under the circumstances.

"Now I have a prompting for you, buster. You're alive again, so you have no more excuses. It's been way over a year, and you promised. You'll take me to the temple before this week is over if you have to do it in a hospital gurney! Do you understand?"

Chuckling softly, he responded with all the energy he could muster. "Yes dear!"

"Tara!" bellowed her dad, as he rushed headlong over the rise that hid them from anyone coming up the path to the boulder.

"Dad!" she shouted back.

As he approached her, his eyes grew like saucers. "Ryan?" he exclaimed.

"Yes Dad," Tara answered him, as Ryan managed a smile. "It's Ryan! He's here! He's back!"

Lonnie Johnson rushed to his side and knelt in the sand opposite Tara. "I can't believe this!" he said, reaching out tentatively to touch Ryan's arm. "How could it be? Are you all right, son?"

"Yes, it's me. Tara will explain later. I'm pretty good considering I've been dead for four and a half years."

Lonnie laughed awkwardly as Wil rushed up and over the rise.

"Good heavens!" he gasped as he approached the group. "Am I seeing things? Ryan, is that you?"

"Yeah, Wil," he rasped. "How's Norma?"

"Oh, she's great, but . . . my goodness," he stammered as he tried to take in the miracle that lay before him, "how are you?"

Lonnie interrupted, still snickering, "He says he's pretty good, considering he's been dead for four and a half years!"

Wil laughed, at the same time shaking his head in disbelief. "Well, for heaven's sake. Is there anything you guys do that won't amaze me?"

Lonnie bent down to examine Ryan. "What we can do to help?"

"Actually," Ryan managed. "I'm feeling better, but I don't think I'm going to walk out of here any time today. Did either of you two bring a spare gurney?"

"We'll get an ambulance," Wil offered.

"Oh yes. Right away," Lonnie said, pulling out his cell phone.

"You'll probably have to go back and guide them in here," Tara reminded Wil.

"Yeah, you're right." He turned to Mr. Johnson. "Lonnie."

Lonnie was talking to someone on the cell phone. Wil finally got his attention.

"We better meet them back at the trailhead."

"Oh yeah. Look," Lonnie said into the cell phone, "we'll meet you at Dutchmen's Trailhead. Okay?" He hung up and turned back to Wil. "Come on. Let's go back and lead them in. These two will want to be alone, until the ambulance gets here anyway."

Wil looked back at Tara and Ryan.

"We'll be fine," Tara said.

"I'm sure you will. See you shortly," Wil said as he turned to follow Lonnie. "I just can't believe it," Tara heard him say as he moved out of sight over the rise, "God must really love that girl!"

Turning back, she encircled Ryan in her embrace. "He does," she whispered in his ear. "He really does."

Gingerly, Ryan brought his arms up and wrapped them around her waist, holding her as tightly as he could. They lay there as Tara cried her thanksgivings to the God whom she once thought had abandoned her, and spilled her tears on His most recent gift, the man she loved.

"It *was* worth it, Ryan! You were right. It was all worth it!"

No matter what happened, she resolved calmly, her fear of the world was over. God lives! She knew that now, and she would never look for the Beast again.

Don't miss these other great books from,

CORNERSTONE
PUBLISHING & DISTRIBUTION, INC.
Ƨ
FAIR

Living Water: A Chronological Reading of the Four Gospels. Compiled by Daniel R. Hopkins.

Like the pieces of a puzzle fitted together, this harmony brings into one account every event in Christ's life. The story is told in sequence, using only the Gospels, the Standard Works and the Joseph Smith Translation. Don't miss the insights and inspiration that will come from reading the complete story of Christ this Christmas, told in this inspiring new arrangement. # 1005 Softcover $12.95

The Most Correct Book: Insights from a Book of Mormon Scholar. By John A. Tvedtnes.

What is "reformed Egyptian"? What do we know about Lehi in old Jerusalem? When did Christ visit the Nehites? Forty-seven insights on passages in the Book of Mormon answer these and other doctrinal and critical questions. Learn how Noah lit the ark with glowing stones, marvel at the similarity of the untranslated words to ancient Semitic words. Must reading for the new year. # 1002 Softcover $16.95

Restoring the Ancient Church: Joseph Smith & Early Christianity. By Barry R. Bickmore.

This book uses the records of early Christianity to show that Christians once understood the preexistence, temple ordinances, the true relationship between man and God, and many other teachings thought to be unique to Mormonism. Along with a clear explanation of the apostasy, this book shows when and why these teachings were lost. Carefully researched and clearly written! # 1001 Softcover $19.95.

Guess Who Wants to Have You for Lunch? A Missionary Guide to Anti-Mormon Tactics & Strategies. By Alan Denison & D.L. Barksdale.

This tremendously popular book takes the wraps off modern anti-Mormon "ministries" organized to lure away members and dissuade investigators. Be prepared for their methods and lies with this often humorous and always brilliant exposé. Includes advice on how to help those who have been disaffected, and a list of LDS resources. # 1004 Softcover $9.95.